THE TIGER SKIN

and Other Tales of the Uneasy
by Violet Hunt

THE TIGER SKIN

and Other Tales of the Uneasy
by Violet Hunt

Edited by
MELISSA EDMUNDSON

BRITISH LIBRARY

This collection first published in 2025 by
The British Library
96 Euston Road
London NW1 2DB
bl.uk

1 3 5 7 9 10 8 6 4 2

Tales of the Uneasy was first published in 1911 by William Heinemann, London.
The Tiger Skin novella was first published in 1924 by William Heinemann, London.

Cataloguing in Publication Data
A catalogue record for this publication is available from the British Library

ISBN 978 0 7123 5578 0
e-ISBN 978 0 7123 6884 1

Frontispiece illustration by Sandra Gómez.
Illustration on page 320: "Is the bones of the head of a man-tiger" from *Osteographia, or the Anatomy of the bones* by William Cheselden (London, 1733). From the British Library collection, shelfmark 458.g.1.
Cover design by Mauricio Villamayor with illustration by Sandra Gómez
Text design and typesetting by Tetragon, London
Printed in England by CPI Group (UK) Ltd, Croydon, CR0 4YY

FSC www.fsc.org MIX Paper | Supporting responsible forestry FSC® C013604

CONTENTS

INTRODUCTION

Violet Hunt's life spans two literary and social eras. She was born in the middle of the Victorian period, a time when many people subscribed to the belief that women were meant solely for the domestic space, and that their lives were defined by their relationships with men—as mothers, wives, sisters, and daughters. Yet she also grew up in a home that valued artistic expression and individual freedom. Hunt used this upbringing to her advantage as she explored—in both her personal life and her published writing—the new freedoms women demanded in the nineteenth century's final decades. This independent spirit that embodied the modern twentieth-century woman, however, was always at odds with the idealistic and "respectable" model of Victorian womanhood that loomed over her. The dichotomy, in turn, gave Hunt the subject matter for her fiction. Her protagonists often display the tensions Hunt herself felt as they try to free themselves from restrictive moral conventions. With these concerns, it is perhaps no wonder then that Hunt would eventually turn to the ghost story as a literary outlet that afforded even more opportunity to explore the thoughts and actions of people leading haunted, suffocating lives.*

Isabel Violet Hunt was born on 28 September 1862 in Durham, England. She was the eldest daughter of the painter Alfred William

* An earlier version of this introduction, focusing more closely on Hunt's biography, gender issues, and her New Woman writings, appeared in *The Latchkey: Journal of New Woman Studies*, vol. 11 (Summer 2022).

Hunt and the novelist Margaret Raine Hunt. Violet was privately educated prior to entering Notting Hill & Ealing High School, from which she graduated in 1877. Because of her father's connections to the Pre-Raphaelite Brotherhood, the Hunt household was frequented by many well-known artists of the day, including William Morris, William Michael and Dante Gabriel Rossetti, and John Ruskin. These influences led Violet Hunt to pursue her own artistic interests, including a period of study at the Kensington Art School from 1877–1879.* These artistic leanings were short-lived, however, as she decided to pursue a literary career instead.

Hunt found early success as an author and quickly made her name in London literary society. Her work appeared in prominent journals and magazines of the day, including *Black and White*, *The English Illustrated Magazine*, *Novel Magazine*, and *The Pall Mall Gazette*. She helped Ford Madox Ford manage *The English Review* in its early years and in 1921 co-founded PEN (an international association of writers originally standing for "Poets, Essayists, Novelists") with Catherine Amy Dawson Scott. A lifelong supporter of women's causes, Hunt was an active member of the Women Writers' Suffrage League and the Women's Social and Political Union. In her home at South Lodge, located in Kensington, London, Hunt gained a reputation as a literary hostess. From 1908–1918, she was romantically involved with the married Ford Madox Hueffer (later known as Ford Madox Ford), and often used the name "Mrs. Hueffer". This relationship ended badly and its aftereffects haunted Hunt for the remainder of her life.

* Barbara Belford, "Hunt, (Isabel) Violet (1862–1942), author and literary hostess", *Oxford Dictionary of National Biography*, 3 Jan. 2008.

Hunt's writing spanned a range of genres. She was a poet, novelist, short story writer, journalist, biographer, translator, and memoirist. Many of Hunt's novels revolve around feminist themes and feature "New Woman" characters. The aptly named Moderna, protagonist of Hunt's first novel, *The Maiden's Progress* (1894), rejects marriage for several years, wanting instead to experience life as an independent, single woman. *A Hard Woman* (1895) continues to develop the feminist themes Hunt had begun in *The Maiden's Progress*. The problems caused by restrictive societal expectations of women are central concerns in *Sooner or Later* (1904) and *The Celebrity at Home* (1904), each of which eschew traditional romantic plots in favour of more realistic depictions of women's often tenuous social standing as wives, lovers, and daughters within a male-dominated society. *White Rose of Weary Leaf* (1908), considered to be her best novel, fully develops the New Woman through its tragic heroine Amy Stephens.

Violet Hunt adopted the New Woman not only in her fiction but also in her own life. Recalling a meeting with the publisher William Heinemann in which she presented the manuscript of *White Rose of Weary Leaf*, Hunt recalls how she—and her book—must have shocked the prim and proper Heinemann. In a reminiscence included in a contemporary biography of the publisher, she describes herself as "the newest of New Women, on the staff of the *Pall Mall Gazette*, sometime dramatic critic, in the habit of dangling my chin over the barrier of the promenade at the Tivoli, alone, unchaperoned, two or three nights a week, armed with my *P.M.G.* Pass."*

* Frederic Whyte (ed.), *William Heinemann: A Memoir* (Doubleday, Doran and Company, 1929), p. 232. A "P.M.G. pass" is a press pass. The Tivoli Theatre of Varieties was a popular theatre and music hall located in West London.

Throughout her life, this flamboyant streak was always at odds with Hunt's desire to be respected, both socially and professionally. As an author and literary hostess, she associated with many well-known writers of the day but was also frequently judged by London society because of her bohemian lifestyle.

Reviews of Hunt's work were mixed, mainly because of its progressive subject matter and feminist themes that often clashed with conservative Victorian and Edwardian values. In its 25 April 1908 review of *White Rose of Weary Leaf*, the *Academy* noted the general "cleverness" of Hunt's writing, but had mixed feelings about the characters, particularly Amy Stephens, the New Woman protagonist.* May Sinclair begins her February 1922 essay on Hunt with a comment about this perceived quality in Hunt's fiction, noting that its repeated use by reviewers belied the genuine merits of her writing: "A writer who has once had the misfortune to be called 'clever' is damned for all the higher purposes of praise."† In her March 1917 review of Hunt's semi-autobiographical *Their Lives* (1916), Rebecca West described the book as "a work of art", recognising its uncompromising vision of human life. She declared that the book "gives a cold, white vision of reality that recalls Maupassant." For West, Hunt's emphasis on the troubled lives of two sisters was important to the overall thematic force of the narrative, stating, "It is an extremely unpleasant book. Most great books are."‡

* Review of *White Rose of Weary Leaf*, *The Academy*, vol. 74, 25 April 1908, pp. 716–17.

† May Sinclair, "The Novels of Violet Hunt", *The English Review*, vol. 34, February 1922, p. 106.

‡ Rebecca West, "The Art of Making Books", *The Daily News* [London], 2 March 1917, p. 4.

In addition to her novels, Violet Hunt was a gifted writer of supernatural fiction who had a lifelong interest in ghosts. Her mother translated Grimms' fairy tales and the noted folklorist Andrew Lang was a frequent visitor at the Hunt household.* Hunt remarked upon the prevalence of ghosts and folklore in her early years, saying: "Ghosts in our homes were taken for granted, and permitted to cross the border-line till they became rather common."† She recalled that her mother was often a spirit medium during private séances held at their home. This early interest eventually found its way into her fiction. Her collection *Tales of the Uneasy*, published in 1911, contains eight stories, plus the novella "The Tiger Skin", which was revised and republished in 1924.‡ A second collection, *More Tales of the Uneasy*, was published in 1925.

In the Preface to *More Tales of the Uneasy*, Hunt credits a conversation with Henry James which gave her the inspiration for the book's title. Hunt greatly admired James and the literary achievement of his novella *The Turn of the Screw* (1898), particularly its effect as a psychological ghost story. Her own psychological studies are reminiscent of James. In her Preface, Hunt comments on the appealing subtleties of what she calls "borderland ghosts", literary spirits that are "more interesting to me than out-and-out spectres."§ This liminality

* Barbara Belford, *Violet: The Story of the Irrepressible Violet Hunt and Her Circle of Lovers and Friends—Ford Madox Ford, H. G. Wells, Somerset Maugham, and Henry James* (Simon and Schuster, 1990), pp. 34–35, 48.

† Violet Hunt, "Preface", *More Tales of the Uneasy* (William Heinemann, 1925), p. xxii.

‡ This present edition includes the expanded 1924 version of *The Tiger Skin* (published by William Heinemann), which omits the hyphen in the title.

§ Hunt, "Preface", *More Tales of the Uneasy*, p. xxii.

is a defining quality of Hunt's supernatural fiction. In one of her best stories, "The Prayer", from *Tales of the Uneasy*, Alice Arne declares, "I think there are worse things than ghosts." This is chillingly true within the story, as the spiritual death of Edward Arne represents not only the tortured existence of a soulless man, but the death of love in a marriage, a very real occurrence that Hunt sets within the framework of a ghost story. Like Henry James, Hunt uses the supernatural sparingly. When it does enter the narrative, it is always a reflection of the choices living characters make as they struggle with regret, jealousy, and betrayal. In this way, the supernatural melds with the general mood of unease that defines both collections. This unease is always grounded in the real—the human element—rather than in the presence of ghosts. These stories are at their most disturbing when we read them as unflinching studies of human nature.

The Bookman praised *Tales of the Uneasy*, concluding that "Miss Hunt has once again proved that she knows as well as any living English writer how to write a short story."* May Sinclair, herself a specialist in supernatural stories, recognised Hunt's talent in the genre. She singles out "The Telegram", "The Prayer", "The Barometer", "The Coach", and "The Tiger-Skin" as works of imagination and the uncanny that approach "genius".† The stories in *Tales of the Uneasy* are indeed unique. Unlike other supernatural fiction of the time that tended to eschew in-depth explorations of unhappy relationships between women and men, Hunt uses this as a central theme in the collection. Many stories feature protagonists who experience some sort of emotional distress, and Hunt expertly utilises the supernatural

* Review of *Tales of the Uneasy*, *The Bookman*, May 1911, p. 97.

† Sinclair, "The Novels of Violet Hunt", p. 117.

and the macabre to reflect these characters' haunted lives. Yet, by ending her collection with "The Tiger-Skin", a story with no supernatural content, Hunt suggests that there can also be monsters in real life. The lack of ghosts makes this tale even more horrific as it confronts controversial ideas, such as censorship and child abuse, while simultaneously exposing the hypocrisy of social mores.

Violet Hunt died of pneumonia at her South Lodge home on 16 January 1942. She was buried with her parents in Brookwood Cemetery, in Brookwood, Surrey, England. Her obituary in *The Times* ended with the appraisal that her "path through life had not been easy, but she retained the affection of her friends, who knew that kindness of heart and feeling for the troubles of others lay behind her often acid speeches."* In the years following Hunt's death, her reputation as an innovative modern novelist was increasingly overlooked in favour of her role as organiser of the South Lodge salon and her love affairs with prominent authors of the day such as H. G. Wells and Somerset Maugham. With this predominant view, Violet Hunt seemed to exist only in relation to other people. Rather than "author" or "novelist", Hunt was labelled a "literary hostess". She became a conduit for other writers' genius, thereby diminishing her status as an accomplished author and social activist.

In many ways, Violet Hunt was both ahead of her time and pulled by the past. She was born in the Victorian era and internalised many of its values. At the same time, she was independent, intellectually curious, and embraced the emerging social freedom women experienced in the beginning decades of the twentieth century. Yet for all her modernity, Hunt was seemingly forever haunted by the

* "Miss Violet Hunt", *The Times*, 19 January 1942, p. 6.

spectre of Victorian "respectability" as her roles of literary hostess and mistress overshadowed her career as a professional writer. In her collections of uneasy tales, Hunt explored such moral complexities, creating stories that explore the cruelties and miseries humans inflict on one another. Hunt's literary ghosts are personal, but they are also universal.

MELISSA EDMUNDSON

MELISSA EDMUNDSON is a collector, scholar and editor specialising in strange and uneasy fiction—particularly by women writers of the Victorian and Edwardian periods. She has published several collections of classic short stories with Victorian Secrets and Handheld Press including *Women's Weird* and *Women's Weird 2* in 2019 and 2020.

A NOTE FROM THE PUBLISHER

The original short stories reprinted in the British Library Tales of the Weird series were written and published in a period ranging across the nineteenth and twentieth centuries. There are many elements of these stories which continue to entertain modern readers; however, in some cases there are also uses of language, instances of stereotyping and some attitudes expressed by narrators or characters which may not be endorsed by the publishing standards of today. We acknowledge therefore that some elements in the stories selected for reprinting may continue to make uncomfortable reading for some of our audience. With this series British Library Publishing aims to offer a new readership a chance to read some of the rare material of the British Library's collections in an affordable paperback format, to enjoy their merits and to look back into the worlds of the past two centuries as portrayed by their writers. It is not possible to separate these stories from the history of their writing and therefore the following stories are presented as they were originally published with minor edits only, made for consistency of style and sense. We welcome feedback from our readers, which can be sent to the following address:

British Library Publishing
The British Library
96 Euston Road
London, NW1 2DB
United Kingdom

THE TELEGRAM

Her mother was dead. Her life stood altered.

She would be no poorer, it was not that. She was an orphan, and all her mother had had came to her. That meant seventy thousand pounds, plate, linen and the freehold of a fine old house in Lower Seymour Street, that they had moved into a year before the old lady died.

Things were no more altered socially than they were altered pecuniarily, for the Damers' set naturally corresponded, as sets do, with their postal district, and Miss Alice Damer could therefore continue to command an entrance into the best circles. Only she realised that she must henceforth enjoy all these good things to the tune of a paid companion, having no poor and amenable relations handy whom she could draft into the household economy, and afterwards snub into a colourless, bare existence.

She was thirty-five, and her years did not weigh on her, except mentally. The first faint physical signs of the debacle were, so far, evident to herself alone, and then only in moods of unusual depression. She was still young enough to need a companion. Her pretty red-gold hair was as red as gold, as pretty as ever, her visits to her dentist as few, her eyes as deep, and her step as elastic, although she had given up dancing. She had made this sacrifice more from a sense of fitness, as a concession to the needs of the young girls coming up all round her, and who deserved their turn on the floor, than of social necessity. As a matter of fact, she had never been really fond of that over-energetic, disordering form of amusement. She loved the world and going up and down in it immensely, and her way of enjoying parties was to sit out if it was a dance, away from the music if it was a concert, and in the back of the box if it was a play. She was a flirt.

Not an outrageous, noisy, ill-bred flirt, but what is known as a quiet flirt, with many strong and efficient strings to her bow. Did one of them, being after all only catgut or mere man, snap occasionally—that is to say, get married out of the circle of her charm—Alice, in her quiet way, promptly renewed the string, and supplied herself with a new admirer, as good at fetching and carrying as the old. In her mind that was the chief use of admirers—to prevent one's *looking* neglected—of course one never really was!

She was a woman of many "affairs"; she liked living, not exactly in hot water, but in water at least warm, and was seldom seen talking to women, though she was quite nice to them, as intrusive but law-permitted aliens in the *pays du cœur*. None of her friends would have dared to ask her to a ladies' lunch, or any over-womaned party; a man had always to be "got for Alice," else she would have been hurt, and quite unable to play her part properly. She was unused to, unversed in her own sex.

On the other hand, she played fair and never took other women's men, or encouraged their husbands to play the pretty game with her. People said *that* for her, that she never made women unhappy, only men. She was never very sorry for a man's love-troubles, for she had a theory that a hopeless passion or two did a man no harm and that the more he proposed the merrier—for him. She never told any one how many offers she had refused. Men often did propose to her, and she refused them all, and boasted that she had never been engaged for even an hour, and that no man had ever kissed her. The bloom was not off Alice, unless so much mental coming and going in her courts had produced some such subtle effect.

"Why should I marry?" she used to say to Everard Jenkyns (good old Welsh family), when he importuned her to relax her rule in his favour, and even go so far as making the vast experiment of marriage with him as her partner. "There is no earthly hurry."

"No, but perhaps a heavenly one," he had inanely replied.

"I may never marry at all. Girls, economically, don't need to marry as they used to, and at any rate I am independent so far as money goes."

"So the way is clear for you to marry for love."

"I don't think I shall ever fall in love."

"Then take a man you like—and you like me?" Everard was not at that time sufficiently far gone in love to make him inattentive to, and unappreciative of the use and value of "cheek," in discussing such matters with his princess.

"Yes, I like you; but, as you know, I don't love you. And I'm so made that I must be quite sure in my own mind that I am absolutely, positively incapable of loving madly before I let myself go with any one, even you. Don't you see, in the interests of morality, one must be sure of oneself, or there might be catastrophe, with a strong nature like mine?"

"No," said Everard patiently and earnestly. "There would, I am sure, be no danger of that with you. Your husband might feel perfectly safe in your hands."

"Thanks. Why do you say that?"

"Because the power to flirt never implies the power to love, I am afraid."

"Well, Everard, you can't say that I flirt with you!" she exclaimed noisily.

"Oh, no. Your knowing that I am desperately, dully serious about you protects me a little, and you do pay me the doubtful compliment of taking no trouble to attract me. You honestly never put your best foot foremost with me, or pose like a heroine to your most humble valet."

"Yes," Alice agreed, laughing a little bitterly. "I promise you never to encourage you in any way. I would let you see me with my hair in curlers, if I wore them! Anything to convince you of the purity of my intentions. I simply will not have you say that I lead you on or encourage you."

"My God, Alice! I don't say it! I know well enough I am a d—d fool and have nothing whatever to go on."

"A fool to love me?"

"A fool because I am a lonely man and don't like being a lonely man, and yet this feeling of mine towards you will keep me so, so far as I can see. I don't suppose I shall ever marry. I know I shan't. That's what you've done, Alice, and I may just as well go away and make my will in your favour, for I shall never have any wife or child to leave my money to. I feel that it will be so."

"Really, my poor Everard"—she tried very hard not to look flattered—"this is most sad. I couldn't have believed there was such fidelity left in this wicked world, and to tell you the truth I don't believe it possible, even now. I'm really not vain enough—if I *am* cruel."

"Not so very vain, and not a bit cruel. I honestly believe if you thought you could get up any sort of feeling for me, you'd say so. You never will say it to me—but to some one else, I suppose. You are human like every one else. It's all rot about not being capable of loving; every woman is or is able to think she is, and that's enough in a great many cases. Oh, you'll find the man sooner or later, and I—well, I shall wish you every happiness and be godfather to the kids. Nice little flirt's kids, with pretty hair like yours. Now, I'd better go away to the Temple and make that will, as I've quite made up my mind to die a bachelor."

"Nonsense," said Alice sharply, more touched than she liked to own; "I won't even be friends with you if you go on like that. Leave things open. Not for me, of course. It must be quite understood that I don't accept any such sacrifice of your life as waiting for me would entail. Believe me, I know myself, and I know, somehow, deep down, that I shall never fall in love with you. That being the case, don't you think I should be really behaving rather badly if I allowed you to think that you could ever melt me by faithful service, and little things like that?"

"All right. Beggars don't choose. You shall have the faithful service all the same, and it shall not hope to melt you. Will that suit you?"

"We'll leave it at that, then," said Alice, permitting the young and promising barrister to kiss her hand, and devote his wits and energies and the rest of his life to her use. She could always find work for him.

He did it all as he had said. He was thus able to be "about the house." That was his retaining fee. Whether it was painful to him or not in his present state of mind to see so much of Alice Damer, it was a fact that he did have to meet her continually. She sent little business-like notes round to his chambers nearly every day—short, sensible, not encouraging notes. He made all the arrangements for their journeys and their parties and their entertaining of their friends. He saw her mother and herself off to the Continent every year when they went to do their cure, was attentive at the carriage door, bought the railway literature, and pumped up the air cushions. He could always be counted upon to be odd man at a dinner party, and if it was humanly possible, and sometimes when it was inhumanly impossible, threw over any other important engagement that he might have had—important to himself, be it understood. His clerk thought he led a "dog's life." What Everard thought was never recorded. What Alice thought was simply this, that Everard liked doing little things for her and was by temperament a born bachelor, although he still cultivated that touching delusion that he was lonely and wanted a companion. It was only that he wanted her, and seeing her this way, every day off and on, was really the pabulum his soul cried for; other and more full-blooded men would not have been content with so merely spiritual a sustenance. At any rate, he never showed any tendency to stray from the portal and outer courts of this austere temple of respectful worship. Alice had no cause for jealousy. Her victim never twisted or wriggled on the hook of her attraction, his ready smile on seeing her flourished as ever, only there was more "drawing" in it, as expressed by the hatchet lines of his mouth. In short, Everard grew thin.

His chest was rather narrow. He coughed often and tiresomely. Lung symptoms seemed to be developing themselves there. Alice, out of gracious regard for him, had suggested his accompanying her mother and herself to the Riviera one winter, instead of seeing them off and falling back into the fog of Charing Cross as usual. He had refused on the score of his pressing work, promising, however, to wear a respirator on the very bad days.

It was a pity he had not gone with them that time. For all that she was a flirt, and men were her material; Alice didn't know them at all. She met a man out at Cap Martin, a man Everard would have seen through at a glance. This common adventurer made love to her; he managed to engage the poor flirt's affections. There was nothing in it, no magnetism. He was a better flirt than she was, that was all, and while Alice had money, he had none.

She returned, and confided her woes. Everard had his work cut out for him. He interviewed this handsome predatory person, and succeeded in retrieving Alice's letters for her. It was a supreme bit of service, and Alice was truly grateful to him. The wretch went out of her life, leaving her in a rather deplorable condition of nerves and mind.

And Everard threw himself into the situation as no man who is not deeply attached to a woman unpicturesquely lovesick for another could have done. He visited her every day, and comforted and consoled her by allowing her to talk about it all. Alice's grief furnished the theme for many a dreary summer's afternoon, when Everard used to take her up the river to distract her mind. It was a trip she had always firmly refused to take with him in the old days on the score of propriety, an excuse that masked dread of boredom. Boredom was not in it now—it was acute tragedy. Poor Alice forgot all propriety when once she was towed well out into mid stream. There she gave way and allowed the echoes of Datchet and Laleham to echo with her sobs. For she had been awfully hard hit. Once, indeed, Everard remembered, but with no pleasurable sense of a lover's guerdon gained, she had leaned forward in the boat with the abandon of despair and kissed her patient confidant. It was the only woman's kiss Everard had ever received in his life, and it had tasted of salt tears! Still, it was a love symbol, the nearest Alice could do in the line he wished, or had wished, for perhaps he did not now desire her quite so urgently as he had done.

Everard had never been handsome at the best of times, but that summer season rang the final knell of his good looks. His crow's feet and his cheek and jaw lines were awful—Alice herself noticed them.

"I believe it is you, Everard, who are going to break down now!" she said to him once when it was all over, her misbegotten love buried fathoms deep, and she cared to look round her a little and notice what other people were doing.

The very violence of her passion had perhaps caused the flame to burn itself out in this young lady of the world, this parlour warrior, this heroine of a hundred ball-room fights. At any rate, her emotional crisis passed away, leaving her who was already hard a little harder than before to Everard's business precautions and his adroit playing of animated safety-valve to the deserted one. Alice, luckily for her, had not needed to confide in a member of her own sex.

Her zest for "the noble game" of flirtation had died down, too. She was less interested in men, and rather more interested in herself than she had been, and condescended to enjoy a party, even if she came away from it without the tendrils of a heart of sorts reaching after her. Her superficial bloom returned; she had never lost, only temporarily mislaid it. She was a fundamentally good-looking woman, with neat, regular features, a good figure and perfect constitution to fall back on. To Everard's satisfaction she now proved the validity of these fine assets of beauty.

But she had spoken a true word in jest. Everard Jenkyns went and had a bout of brain fever. He was popularly supposed to have broken down from overwork.

Alice Damer and her mother were most kind and solicitous, and as fussy about him as they could be without setting the public tongue a-wagging. Alice now worshipped on the altar of convention again, and would not have been seen up the river with Everard or near his rooms in Paper Buildings for anything. Her mother was old and unwieldy. So they "wrote." They were quite careful—but as it was, old friends opined that Miss Damer was going to settle down and take up with her old and tried suitor. When taxed with this by the ill-bred privileged she maintained boldly that there was nothing in it, that she and Mr. Jenkyns thoroughly understood each other. So they did. Everard was grateful without any expectation of favours to come, and thanked her prettily for grapes and books and things.

He recovered, and went about his own business as usual. Alice's business was not pressing just now, so the two rather lost sight of each other, Alice holding him in reserve for future extremity. She supposed, sometimes aloud, that he was "busy getting on" and making up for the time lost in his illness. There could be no woman in it?

"Rather a wreck—poor old Jenks!" his friends observed with affection, for he was a general favourite with men, and most unfairly persisted in attributing his state, not to the illness he had undergone, but to Alice Damer's fast-and-loose playing. She heard this, but tossed her head, confident in the good understanding that subsisted between her and her slave.

"I have never encouraged Everard. He knows I haven't," she declared to her mother.

"He says so. I think you have been quite horrid to him, Alice!" was the old lady's single solitary pronouncement on the situation. She said this lying on her bed during what was to prove her last illness. Alice was gentle and kind, but repressed all sentimental leanings on the part of the invalid, who had a mother's natural wish to see a vagrant-hearted daughter settled in love and marriage before she died.

"Mother, how often must I tell you that Everard—Mr. Jenkyns—and I understand each other?" she repeated coldly. She had never chosen to call Everard by his Christian name, though her mother, who was fond of him, always insisted on doing so, and Everard obviously liked it, and clung to this side entry into the intimacy of Alice's family. It did not matter. Alice and he, as before said, understood each other, and old ladies, every one knows, have a way of attaching themselves to young men, and selecting their daughters' suitors for them by the light of their own predilections.

And now, her dear, silly old mother was dead and buried, and the proud, sensible daughter sat all alone in the big Seymour Street drawing-room, with the three large windows that needed so much stuff for their curtains, and the beautiful Adams mantelpiece whose shelf Alice could hardly see over. The Damers had only been in the house a year; it was freehold, and Alice's. It was rather a large and dreary abode for one young woman to inhabit permanently, yet the young woman thought she meant to do so!

A companion, she sadly supposed, in that case must be procured sooner or later—later, preferably; if she could have her way, not at all!

Alice was nearly forty, though she looked younger. Why should she not use her age for all it was worth and establish herself on the easy footing of years of discretion? Nay, there would be complications there; her womanly instincts rebelled against the aspersion of "discretion" and the constant assertion of her maturity which would be involved in her adoption of that attitude. She would be asked to play chaperon herself, she would have to "dress old." No, she looked so young for her age, it would be ridiculous, when she could as easily carry the other theory through and pose as a breakable, compromisable commodity.

She must make up her mind to accept the duenna—she must get in a woman to quarrel with! It came very hard! She had been used to going about alone and receiving guests by herself in this house; for the last year Mrs. Damer had been unable to dine down or preside at her own table. She appeared beautifully capped and lappeted, to set the seal of chaperonage for a few minutes before dinner, and then prettily said good-night to her young guests when dinner was announced. Alice was quite equal to it, and always invited another woman, preferably married, to her charming dinners.

A companion would, by the conditions of her office, take part in every function, "quiet" dinners as well as noisy ones. It would be far worse than a husband, for a husband would at least leave the tea-hour free. All Alice's serious *tête-à-têtes* had been used to come off then, in the little room off the stairs, that was really part of the hall and in no way shut off, but so delightfully private. Little, soft, rosy cosy late teas had been Alice's great social weapon; all the more fetching were these free and easy interviews in that she wasn't in the least like an American, though she did see young men alone, with a mother stowed away somewhere in the upper fastnesses of the house.

This problem of the companion was associated with the first glimmering in Alice Damer's mind, of the possibility of a husband's suiting at this juncture. The notion of a companion precipitated him. He came in by the door of convenience.

A husband! Well, who was it wanted to marry her at that moment?

Men's names, long shelved, came into her mind, but not Everard's. Like the poor, she had him always with her. He was always available, but the others, unaccountably enough, did not rush into the arena of her requirements at once.

She must be growing old! Did people think her old? She had not noticed that they did, she could see no sign of "the coming of the crows' feet," of which this "backward turn of beaus' feet" was supposed to be ominous. For surely, a year ago, plenty of potential husbands lay ready to her hand?...

The signs of age, if there were any signs, were on the outside. Alice, internally, felt as fit as ever. She was still game for anything in the way of social folly, she could sit up as late as any one and dozed off happily the moment she got home and her head touched the pillow. She did not have to read in bed or play "patiences" to induce sleep. Her figure showed no fatal early inclination to "spread," she didn't know what it was to "sit over a fire," and she proudly refused to avoid lobster salad or anything else indigestible at supper...

Unless, indeed, the craving for marriage itself was a sign of age, a subtle token of the need for support, the birth of an instinct for clinging?

She rose and looked at herself in the old, unbecoming Empire mirror that Everard had got for her at a sale at Christie's once, for he was a connoisseur. No, very few lines, no look of fatigue, even in a bad glass! And as much colour in her hair, that poor Everard admired so, as ever there was!

Poor dear Everard!... No, not poor dear Everard. He had been growing rather slack lately, and forgot her flowers and fish and game now and then. He had been kind, of course, and considerate over her mother's death, had continually called to inquire, though the presence of authorised relations in the house had rendered his visits nugatory as far as she was concerned. Alice was formal about death. She had seen much of it. Still, she had liked to see his card in the hall, though unable to ask him to come in because of Aunts Polly and Gertrude. It had been an awful, unmentionable time, the sort of life that everybody must lead at times, when Death is in the house; but now it was over and the aunts had gone home, making her promise to give them a month at Taunton next week, when she had got things a little straight and done seeing lawyers. And that was over, too. Her nerves, that had been a little upset, though she had expected her mother's death, had righted themselves, too. She cried about her mother every day, but only once in the day, and she began to think she should like to see some one who wasn't "family." Why should she not begin with Everard? When the companion had come, or the husband, she would have very little opportunity for *tête-à-têtes* with him. Unless he was that husband? Well, we should see!...

She settled that it was to be to-morrow, a quite impromptu invitation. If it were ceremonious she could not have him alone, and she wanted him alone. She set about ordering a nice little dinner for him, consonant with his tastes, which unluckily she did not know. Everard had dined in Seymour Street before, but only on big formal occasions, never alone, so far as she remembered.

Everard replied in fairly good time. He did not say he was previously engaged—for he knew that she would never forgive him for not throwing the other people for her—but ill. At least, not ill, but with a very bad cold. As the dinner, she had said, was quite informal, might he ask her to postpone it a day or two until he had a little got the better of his cough, which would make him a rather tiresome guest, apart from the danger of chill, to which he found himself more liable than formerly. He would like to suggest Saturday night—his birthday?...

"What a funny old-maidish letter," was Alice's comment; "all about his cold and that! I never knew Everard notice a cold before? I suppose a man gets finicky, living so much alone. He's no exception to the rule. I'll have to wake him up a little."

His cool deferring of her invitation afforded him just that touch of masterful self-assertiveness Everard had always lacked in his dealings with this young woman. She now firmly made up her mind to marry him, that is, if he continued to carry things off so well. He would be better than a companion, and—there seemed to be nobody else!

At a quarter to eight on Saturday evening she was all ready, dressed in black and looking very handsome, on one side of the brightly burning fire, for there was a slight touch of frost in the air. Her senses were alert, she found herself actually listening for the sound of his hansom driving up to the door. Quite loverlike, she thought, with a little laugh, to herself! She remembered the last sentence in Everard's old-maidish letter, which she passed over on first reading. He had informed her that this was his birthday. She welcomed this as a touch of sentiment—the sentiment she had not in the old days been solicitous to cultivate in him, but had carelessly let die. She wished she could remember exactly how old he was to-day? If she had been able to allude to it it would have pleased him...

No use, she could not recapture the knowledge. She supposed he might be somewhere about forty? And he was late! How dared he be late, for her? Was there a fog perhaps?

She went to the window, parted the heavy curtains, and looked out. Rather misty—but not enough to prevent Everard from keeping time, if he had started early enough to dress! How rude if he hadn't?

She remained drumming on the pane with her long, slender fingers, looking down into the empty roadway.

She had not heard the door of the drawing-room open, but suddenly, before she had time to turn away from the window, Everard stood beside her with his handkerchief held up to his face, a familiar gesture of his for which she had often reproved him.

"How are you?" she asked him, rather frigidly. "What a draught you seem to have brought in with you!"

"May I shut the door?" Everard said, suiting his action to the words.

"Come to the fire, won't you? You are cold."

She spoke more cordially, but, in spite of her definite intention to propose herself to Everard that evening, the curious sense of physical alienation which she knew now had held them apart all these years, returned to her with tenfold vigour. Her instinct had been right. Physical leanings counted for something, and there was no real affinity between them. Alice shivered a little, for she was a sensible, business-like woman, and she firmly meant to override the absurd and awkward shrinking, and marry him. Her mind once made up, she never went back.

He was holding his thin, blue-veined hands to the blaze. His eyes seemed to avoid hers.

"Yes, that's right," she said. "I hope you have got a good appetite? I have ordered such a nice little dinner for you."

"How kind of you! But really, I eat very little except fish. My doctor has cut me down remorselessly."

"And do you attend to him? You never used."

"I have to attend to his orders. I am in rather a bad way, Alice. The base of one lung is quite solid... and the other is gone."

"Nonsense! I believe you're as right as I am, barring this little bit of a cold, that you'll soon get rid of. You haven't coughed once since you were in the room, do you know? I fancy that living alone as you do, you go and get ideas about yourself, and then rush out and call in a doctor who frightens you."

"May be," he said slowly. "Loneliness certainly doesn't improve one's perspective. And I haven't been inside any one else's house for a month."

"There now, what did I say? And what do you do, when you are at home? Sit over the fire and grizzle, and think of your sins—and mine, eh?"

"Not yours—much!" said he, with a chilling effect of partial forgiveness which benumbed Alice, whose fighting spirit was up in arms to bring him to her feet again.

The maid announced dinner, and Alice took his recalcitrant arm, which gave her the sense of being glued to his side. On the way downstairs she thought, "Poor dear, he will want civilising all over again!"

"You'll drink champagne?" she suggested, when they were both seated.

"No, water, please." He added, speaking to the maid, "Thanks, no soup!"

He allowed a helping of fish to be placed on his plate, but he did not eat a mouthful, that Alice could see.

The dreary dinner progressed. Alice Damer ate for two, and every now and then looked furtively at the man she had made.

It was her fault; she saw it now. This man had been her slave; she had been his inhuman master. She had laid him on the rack, she had starved his heart, for bread she had given him a stone. This was what their famous understanding had amounted to; the ruin of a man, a pale, thin, hectic mask, sitting opposite her, pretending to eat—the play of his thin wrists that manipulated his knife and fork drove her frantic—his sullen eyes refusing to meet hers, as in tones that only faintly represented the rich, soft, legal, measured voice she used to know, he responded gently but dully to all her conventional openings, and allowed the subjects she started so painstakingly to drop one by one. What would the servants think? Little pearly drops of dismay and effort broke out on her own white forehead; the effort she was making was too much for even her social fortitude. Yes, she knew she had behaved badly to him, but he might let her down more easily! Vexing of him! For what she had to do, must be done, in spite of difficulties.

The last course had been removed, two punctilious, slightly shocked maids had disappeared, and the couple were left alone over the walnuts and the wine.

She spoke to him quite crossly, in a voice she could hardly command. "Aren't you interested in *anything*, Everard?"

"Yes, dear, in some things—for instance in your calling me by my Christian name—for the first time," he replied quietly.

Alice felt uncomfortable. Such a direct thrust from this petrifaction suggested that he had seen through her, who hardly realised herself, and what she was doing.

"Oughtn't I?—I forgot."

"Oh, don't apologise, it doesn't matter... I wanted you to badly, once, do you remember? Strange, when it does come—one is more or less past caring—"

"Coffee?" she asked. "I make it myself now, as you see!"

"Yes, please."

She made it. She handed it. She even let her fingers graze his as she passed him the cup. It was literally the first time she had ever practised her own special art of flirtation in Everard's connection.

Then there fell a silence between them. The patent coffee machine ceased to bubble. Its duties were sped... Alice, sipping a restorative draught of the tonic liquid, broke the silence bravely. She felt that she owed it to him to take the initiative.

"I am feeling very lonely—now," she said softly.

"Poor child, you must be," he answered gravely.

"And I think I—I understand a little better how you must have felt all these years."

He lifted his fishy eyes for the first time to hers. "Yes, but I am used to it, now."

"But, Everard, it hasn't done you any good?"

"No, I daresay not."

"Everard, do you think—now—do you believe we—you and I, I mean, would have got on together?"

"How do you mean? In what relation?"

"I mean—in the usual relation—if I had wanted what you wanted?"

"Well, you know, I thought so, then."

"Not now?"

"No, not now. Did I not tell you that I had grown philosophical? Whatever is, is good."

"Oh, dear! Then you tell me that you think it is good, your living alone, with not a soul to talk to, or exchange an idea with, no one to look after you when you are ill, as you are now, but just to sit mooning over a dying fire—"

The ghost of a shrug was vouchsafed her. "Oh, I keep my fire up, and I mix my own grog and drink it, and warm my own slippers. It isn't so bad."

"Everard!" She rose to her feet and he imitated her, supposing that a move to the drawing-room was contemplated. "No, I am not going up yet, not till we have had this out. You do make it very difficult for me. It is as if you had lost the key—you will not understand *à demi-mot!*"

"Why should it be *à demi-mot?*" he repeated after her, catching, however, none of her fire. He sat down again and motioned her to do the same. Then he spoke, dully, but very clearly.

"Let us talk quietly, and not get excited over it. A man in my condition has no time for vagueness. I do understand, quite well, and I will show you that I do. You are willing to marry me now?"

"Yes," she cried breathlessly. "Yes, poor Everard! And you—you don't want me to any more?"

"I want nothing! Don't think of me. Let us consider only you. Now tell me, would this marriage be of any use to you?"

"Use to me to be married to you, Everard?" She started.

"Sorry, but I can only put it from the point of view of utility. My personal desires are dead."

"Ah, I killed them."

"Yes, my dear, you killed them. I can't pretend to any extravagant feelings of joy at what I suppose we must call your capitulation. You know, they give better terms to beleaguered fortresses the sooner they surrender? You, Alice, in your pride and impregnability left it too long. The wine got musty in the bottle, the cord got frayed and rotten. I am no good to you or anybody. My life is done. I thought all this out as I lay there—wrote some of it down even. I never thought

I should get a chance of telling it all to you in person. I could not rest. In my delirium—"

"Delirium! Oh, Everard, what nonsense!"

He put her exclamations aside. "Well, I have told it you now, and I shall rest in peace."

"If it's any consolation to you, you have had a good scold—a good go at me!" Alice cried angrily, adding with bitterness, "And plus the satisfaction of refusing me!"

"But not at all!" he said, turning surprised, lack-lustre eyes on her. "If you think a marriage with me would do you any earthly good, you shall have it. I ought to have made that clear—"

"I wanted to do good to *you!*" she wailed.

"Too late for that. I won't pretend, even to salve your conscience, Alice, that I care anything at all about it. Besides, your conscience has no need of salving. You were perfectly right not to marry me, in your heyday and mine, if you could not love me; you are very kind and perfectly in order to suggest it now, as a way of making me useful to you, as you have done in the past. I am at your service now, as ever. I am reserved to your use, as good as married to you already, though not you to me, and quite ready to go to church with you to-morrow, if you decide that we shall do so. I am your property... Only, my dear, it is a pity you tied me up in brown paper and left me on the shelf so long. Fatal delay! Unused, I deteriorated! You have had me warehoused so many years that now, when you choose to untie me and take me down, you find that you have to make allowance for depreciation of stock. I think I wrote that to you—or said it!... How it did amuse Mrs. Clarkson!"

"Who's Mrs. Clarkson?" she asked through her tears.

He did not answer, but rose, and took her in his arms. Pale flickers of posthumous triumph lighted up his kind, lined face. Weakly victorious, he enfolded her, and she shrunk and shivered out of his embrace.

"What is it, dear?"

"Nothing, oh, nothing! Only, I don't believe I *can* marry you, Everard, after all!"

He did not ask her why, and she could hardly have told him that the momentary contact had affirmed the sense of physical aversion she had always thought she felt for him. Now she was sure. Oh, what was she to do?...

She stood timorously away from him, as it were freed from the clasp of a corpse. How could she tell him that? And then she reflected consolingly that according to his own words marriage meant so little to him now, that she need perhaps never kiss him when they were married.

Her colour returned a little as she formulated this evasion... Many a conscientious woman has forced herself before now to marry a wreck, to pay conscience money.

There was a good fire burning, she motioned him to one of two leather-covered chairs drawn up on opposite sides of the fireplace. "It's warm here. We won't go upstairs. I am really getting rather frightened about you, Everard. I was incredulous at first, but I do believe now, that you *have* been ill."

"Yes, I have been very ill."

"But why come out? Why didn't you send an excuse—ask me to come to you?"

"Would you have come? Well, as a matter of fact, a telegram was sent you. Mrs. Clarkson *said* she had sent it."

"Mrs. Clarkson—your landlady—your bedmaker? Oh, dear, how unkind you must have thought me!"

"No, I don't know that I thought anything about it. I said she might send it, and then it passed out of my mind entirely. Everything did go clean out all at once, somehow... it's a most unusual sensation—very like death, I should think."

"Everard, I believe you ought to be in bed now, you ought not to be here—pleasant as it is. Go home, and I'll come and nurse you to-morrow. I can safely do that. I am—engaged to you!" She spoke with mouth awry, putting the greatest constraint upon herself.

He smiled. "Awfully kind of you, dear, but I've got a nurse already. Mrs. Clarkson is a nurse."

"Everard! you're dreaming! Do you mean a white-capped creature, with starched cuffs? How could you be here if that were so?"

"I don't know, but I *am* here, you see. Mrs. Clarkson certainly did send you a wire to say I couldn't come. She asked you to come to me, I believe, though I forbade her. As I told you"—he sighed—"I forgot it all..."

"But then why have you come, and why haven't I got the wire?"

"Wrongly addressed, I fancy. I was too ill to speak much. She looked the address up in my book and I have only your old one there."

"It shows how I've neglected you."

"But it's as well you didn't come. The nurse is excellent. These hired people do best because they have no feelings, whether it's merely putting on a poultice, or finally laying you out—"

"Oh, don't, Everard!"

He rose. He looked preoccupied.

"It's after midnight. Do you realise how late we have been talking, right into the night? The daylight will surprise us in a minute!... Oh, dear me! I must be off." He rose, and stood, wavering like a windblown taper. "Good-night, dear Alice, I shan't forget you have kissed me—once in your life. Oh, no, twice; once on the river—that day, the twelfth of July. I loved you—I wish you had loved me too!"

"I did—I do," she averred, her lips chattering.

"Too late!" said he, taking a woollen comforter out of his pocket.

"Everard, I don't think you are fit to go home alone. Let me send some one with you. Or stay here, the servants are not gone to bed, and there's a spare room, slept in only last night. Aunt Polly—"

"And your reputation?"

"I'll risk that," she said. "I've behaved too badly to you not to make you some amends."

"But it's all nonsense. I am all right. Strength has been given me—"

"How funnily you talk! Well, since you *will* be foolhardy and go back to your nurse—is she pretty? You know I don't believe in her. You are thinking of your landlady, who's been mothering you a little, as she should." She put out her hand and rang the bell. "A hansom, please, for Mr. Jenkyns."

"You shouldn't have done that," he said. "I meant to walk."

"Well, you aren't going to be allowed to walk! You must take no risk. Have a good night's rest, and be well enough to marry me to-morrow—by special licence." She looked up in his face with terror-stricken audacity. How could she do it!

"Would you really?" He was out in the hall by now, and the maid was whistling for a cab. "Well, we'll see!"

"I'll come to you at eleven in Paper Buildings. I know the way. I've been there once."

"Dear Alice, how unmaidenly you are grown all of a sudden! I like it, though. It is some compensation—"

"But will you really marry me if I come?"

"If I can," he answered gravely.

The hansom had come rattling up. She gave a twist to the comforter. "Keep it well over your mouth..."

"I will kiss your hand first."

She controlled herself. His touch was pain to her. She wailed, as the hall door closed—

"Oh, I don't love him! He is dead. I have killed him! I'll marry him, that is my vow!"

The strayed telegram was brought her next morning on the tray with her tea. It had been as Everard had surmised, wrongly addressed to the old house. It ran—

"Mr. Jenkyns unable to go to you to-night. Ill. Come if prefer."

"She must have been in a rare fright when she wrote that, whoever she is!" thought Alice, who could not bring herself to believe in the presence of a nurse in 82 Paper Buildings.

Her exaltation of last night had left her. Everard was such a wreck, poor dear! Every bit of charm, and he never had much, had departed and left him sear, dry, stupid and unsympathetic. But she meant to marry him, and repair her sins, and be able to live without a companion. Even an invalid husband was better than a hired solacium. She would go and see him this morning, but of course they could not really be married at once, out of hand, like that. In a week or so, after a few preparations had been made and when he had been nursed up and made to look a little less ghastly. She could not allow a ghost to lead her to the altar. Then they would go off somewhere warm for the honeymoon, to the Riviera or Egypt, and Everard would revive under the combined influences of sun and agreeable society, and love—that is, if he was still capable of feeling the kindly glow of a delayed, but at last gratified passion.

Perhaps he was not quite so dead after all; perhaps in time she would find herself able to submit to his kisses without a politely suppressed shudder? Though she could easily account for that symptom of hers. Starved physically and mentally, as he seemed to be, what wonder that all the magnetism had gone from him? Alice, none other, would nurse him back to life, make a charming, attentive, affectionate husband of him, one whose kisses she would get not to mind so much.

She drove down to the Temple and dismissed her carriage at the gate on the Embankment, and walked up, quite unnecessarily, for Everard's rooms in Paper Buildings had a road in front where a carriage might stand. But she did not mind walking. It was a lovely morning. The famous fountain in the court was playing merrily, and suggested springing hopes of all sorts—and possibilities of revival. She walked along to Everard's rooms with a light step, laughing a little to herself at the thought that she was going to earn for him the reputation of being "a dog." She did not suppose many young ladies sought out the dry student lawyer in his rooms! His landlady, or laundress, whichever it was, would be shocked, and a good thing too. His character was altogether too immaculate, and a picturesque smudge or so would improve it in the eyes of men. Alice had all the sweet, headlong depravity of mind of the excessively innocent. Using her tortoiseshell pince-nez, she read the name of Everard Jenkyns printed on the wall on the right-hand side of the open door of number eighty-two, and plunging into the dimness, began to ascend. She met a man on the first landing who looked like a doctor. He seemed in a hurry to get to his hansom, which she had observed standing there. He merely peered in her face and passed on before she could ask him if he was the doctor, and if so, how Mr. Jenkyns was?

She went on ascending till she found the right door, knocked, and stood there, breathless...

A foolish fear assailed her as she waited. She found herself dreading the first sight of Everard as he would appear on opening the door to her; she remembered with annoyance the poor, lank, gawky face, which always made her think, as she used to tell her mother, of a boy's compendious clasp-knife, with all the blades open! He would smile, of course, and look pleased to see her; it was a strong step for haughty Alice Damer, whom he had sighed for so long, to visit a man in his rooms at half-past eleven and ask him to marry her!

He was a long time coming!... She rang again, more firmly...

The door was opened, by a nurse. Everard had not been raving, then! He was probably in bed?... She formally muttered his name.

The nurse seemed to have been expecting her. Murmuring, "You would like to see him, Ma'am?" she led the way into the sitting-room, out of which the bedroom obviously opened. The door was ajar. The nurse did not stop...

"But not in there!" Alice stammered.

A strong note of disapprobation pierced in the woman's voice as she turned round sharply—

"Why not? He's dead. You're not going to faint?"

"Oh, no," said the poor girl, striving to adjust herself to these new and unexpected circumstances. Like a proud, plucky automaton she entered the bedroom, and looked on the form that was faintly outlined under the sheet, so thin Everard had grown. She had good nerves, and could always bear shocks well. But an immense, searching pity, a world of value for the dead man, combined with self-depreciation, filled her, and she wept silently. Her noble calmness and self-restraint won the admiration of the nurse, who had been condemning the heartless creature wholesale for having left her sweetheart to die alone as she had done.

"What was it, Nurse?" she asked.

"Double pneumonia. Collapse. I telegraphed to you, Miss—you are Miss Damer, I believe? He objected, but when once he became unable to speak, I took it upon myself. I thought you would want to be here."

"Of course. But I have only just got it."

The nurse accepted the *amende*. She could not realise that Alice was struggling to form a comment on the apparent inconsistency of a man sick unto death being able to dine with her, hoping at the same time that dates would be proved not to fit and all be normally explained. She stammered something vague as the nurse laid down the covering sheet, and disclosed the still face, looking, however, no more emaciated than Alice had seen it in life and no longer ago than last night.

Alice was painfully aware of the tacit suggestion on the woman's part that she should bend down and kiss that waxen mask, and recoiled, though the nurse had said no word.

"Oh, I can't kiss anybody dead... It's awful of me, Nurse, but I can't!"

"Some can't!" said the nurse resignedly. And this girl was the poor gentleman's fiancée, so she had understood?...

She was a little pacified when Alice unfastened the bunch of lilies of the valley that she was wearing, and laid them on the dead man's breast. Then she turned away and dried her eyes. She was a beautiful creature, the nurse thought, and was conscious that the faulty young lady was slowly acquiring her sympathies.

"When did he die? When was it?"

"We don't know exactly, Miss. In these cases—But he last spoke about seven."

"What made you think of sending to me?"

"Because, Miss, for days before, when he was wandering worst, he talked about you. We gathered, the doctor and I, that he was more or less engaged to you, Miss, but that you was rather too fond of putting him off. Said it had been going on for years, and that he was fairly worn out. So he was, poor man; he hadn't an ounce of flesh on his bones to spare—"

"Yes, but—" the girl exclaimed impatiently, "I want to get at the facts. He died, you say, this morning at seven o'clock?"

"Spoke last at seven o'clock last night, Miss, I said. Died some time in the night, or, may be, directly after he did speak. At least, part of him may have died, as ignorant people seem to think. He was hardly breathing at a little before eight, but the last spark may have held on longer."

"I suppose you know, Nurse, that he dined with me last night, at a quarter-past eight," said the girl stonily, looking away from the nurse's apathetic face, which changed at once, sympathetically;—

"Miss, you're upset! You took it so calm at first. Have some brandy. You have had a shock. One understands—"

"He dined with me," Alice repeated obstinately.

The nurse stared at her, and shrugged her shoulders. Poor girl! She was evidently one of the outwardly quiet ones, who smother the symptoms of disturbance, only to feel the shock more keenly. People take these things in such a variety of ways. The idea of the dinner party had got fixed in her mind by the shock; she was unable now to let go the idea of Everard's keeping his engagement with her. She had received the telegram all right, of course, there could be no doubt of it, and some domestic reason had prevented her from responding to the summons. Or, possibly, that same backwardness and want of interest which had affected the smooth course of the engagement had been at work. She hadn't cared for him much, though she had been persuaded into giving her word...

In an even tone, calculated to restore the shattered nerves of the shaken girl, the nurse remarked—

"Mr. Jenkyns' sister-in-law, the one that lives in France, will be here presently, to see about the funeral arrangements. He wanted you to have all his old china and books, Miss, he used to say so, and doubtless that will be done..."

But Alice Damer had gone resolutely across to the bed from which the two, in the course of conversation, had unconsciously deviated.

She dexterously turned down the sheet, and stooping, performed the rite of love, the little act of devotion which she had refused him just before. What was she saying? Mrs. Clarkson observed closely what she considered one of the curiosities of mental stress.

"I kissed him last night, when he came to me... So you see, whether I liked it or not, I did kiss a dead man! And it's no use minding now, is it?"

She kissed him repeatedly, with a pale semblance of passion.

The nurse took her arm gently and led her away from the bed, and she submitted to be placed in a chair.

"Miss, now you've done that, you'll feel better. I should go home if I were you. Take that hansom outside. It's the one you came in, perhaps—and you haven't paid him?"

Alice signified a negative to this, helplessly, but allowed the nurse to pin her veil on for her. It hid her tear-stained face a little. Then the good woman led her downstairs and out on to the pavement. Sure enough, there was a hansom waiting there, and the nurse hailed the driver.

Gruffly, he turned round, and stared at them.

"And I say," he appeared to be remarking, "and I say, who's going to pay me my fare?"

"Why, the lady will, of course. Get in, Miss, I'll hold your dress away from the wheel."

But the cabman was not satisfied, nor did he address himself to the task of resuming his drooping reins. He seemed to have had a shock too.

"No, I didn't mean her. Who's going to pay me three bob for last night and for waiting 'ere?..."

"That's no affair of ours," replied the nurse cheerfully. "You must take the lady—where to, shall I say, Miss?"

Alice, crouching inside, mumbled the address of her home.

The cabman swore.

"No, I'm damned! You get out. I ain't a-going near that blasted house again for nobody! Took a fare from there last night, I did, and drove him here, and here I may stop till Domesday, I suppose, before I sees a shilling of his money! 'Tain't right!..."

He was obviously drunk, but not dangerous, so the nurse thought.

"Come, come!" she expostulated.

Alice, frightened, prepared to get out.

"Oh, what's the matter?" she moaned.

"Matter! Matter's this. I drove him here right enough, and pulls up where he told me—and my gentleman doesn't get out, seems as if he was a-going to make a night of it in my cab. Drunk, I says to myself, and I opens the trap, meaning to take my fare and clear him out, but Lord bless me—why, there wasn't no one there!"

"He'd got out, of course," said Mrs. Clarkson, "while you weren't looking."

"'Bilked,' says I. And, thinks I, I'll just come and wait here till I sees my gentleman come down those stairs again."

"You'll never see him come downstairs again," said the nurse, with a flash of inspiration, "except in his coffin! Come, get on! Take the lady where she wants to go."

She thought of it all—afterwards... but then nurses see such queer things! She had taken the cabman's number.

THE OPERATION

"Yes, I think that might hang a day longer. I can finish up the mince for my lunch, and you must do something with the turkey legs for dinner. Let me see—and there's fish to-day. And then—well, suppose you make a savoury?"

"Master don't care for savouries, Ma'am!"

"A sweet, then. I don't care. And that's all, I think?"

Mrs. Joe Mardell, in her neat morning shirt, coquettishly finished with a man-like tie, and the severity of her attire much modified by the bows and loops of waved hair that crowned her head, turned and was about to leave the dark basement of the little house in Kirriemuir Street, West Kensington, when a door in the upper regions banged.

"There, he's off, and I wanted a cheque!" Mrs. Mardell observed with mild irritation. She glanced at the kitchen clock with a degree of confidence she did not place in the elegant time-keeper, cased in jewels, that hung on the front of her shirt. "Why, it's only half-past ten?"

"Master's early gone this morning," said the cook. "Gladys took his breakfast up only ten minutes ago." She paused, then summoning her courage; she asked—

"Ma'am, are people usually buried on Christmas Day?"

"Why, you silly woman, it depends on what day they die. Who's been dying?"

"I'll swear," said the woman eagerly, "that I saw a corpse being carried down the steps of number thirteen just over the street opposite nearly a week ago, and I reckon it back Christmas Day!... It's been worrying me ever since. Yes, I saw the mourners and hearse and feathers and all—done quite proper. I was looking out of the front staircase window—"

"Neglecting your work, Vance? Serves you right. You saw Whiteley's sale cart, perhaps? You were looking sideways through the red panes, and glass, you know, refracts oddly... Who lives at number thirteen?"

"Oddly enough, Ma'am, I don't know, though I mostly could tell you the names of everybody in the street. I might ask one of the tradespeople—should I?"

"Yes, do if you like. Brr!" She shivered affectedly, strong in the pride of her health and good looks. "It seems a cold time to choose to be put into the ground! One would sooner be cremated, this weather!"

Holding up her crisp befrilled skirts, the second wife of Joseph Mardell, the popular comic actor, who was just now drawing crowds to his Christmas extravaganza at the "Quality," made her way up from the dark basement to the abodes of light above. Noiselessly, she let fall behind her that swing door at the top of the staircase which effectively divided the world of society from its service, and exchanged stone and oil-cloth for soft carpets and silken curtains. It was a very pretty little house—*her* house. She admitted Joe into it. Her husband-lover, Joe. She had managed to keep him her lover. All wives should. She glanced, as she passed by, at the hat-stand in the hall. Joe had stupidly gone without his fur coat, though it was freezing. Or was it that it needed a stitch? How careless of Gladys! He had left his big umbrella too, for there it bulged in the rack, beside her own delicate silver-topped one. Careless Joe, willing enough to ignore the mere physical claims of the self he morally bowed to! Moreover, he forced every one else to do so likewise. He must have his own way, and brooked no check where his mental desires were concerned. It was perhaps the secret of his sway over men—and women.

She thought of him, Joseph Mardell, the greatly-sought-after, and hers, with complacent affection, glancing up consciously at the branch of mistletoe which was entwined with the square glass lamp that hung over the front door. Joe had passionately kissed her under the mystic bough, a week ago, for luck, on the first night of the successful piece. And luck had come, and seemingly remained with them. The booking was splendid. And they were rehearsing a more serious play that was to follow the Christmas jollity. Joe was so busy he didn't know where to turn for a spare five minutes. She did not complain, for if things went on like this they would be able to move out of West Kensington, where you couldn't get a smart parlour-maid to stop with you. Gladys and her finger-nails was a sore trial.

She entered the dining-room, and her eyes sought the sideboard. Ah, Joe had had some sense after all, and had remembered to refresh the inner man before leaving, as the violated Tantalus betokened. He lay in bed late. He rarely breakfasted, and never with her. She rose at eight—on principle; she could not afford to keep actors' hours and ruin her complexion.

She stood pensively by the small piece of Sheraton furniture before she opened a drawer and took out of it what she had come to seek. Last night's oranges and apples beamed there on a pretty dish. Joe's cigarette boxes, flung about, needed tidying up. The presentation silver bowl given to Joe by his fellow-actors on the occasion of his first marriage, shone in the centre with dignified lustre. They had chosen something quite different to present to him as a memento of his second venture. That was in her room now. The bowl had a dwarf fern in it now, but sometimes it ran over with punch, or was packed with roses. Another use was contemplated for it; if Joe and she were to have a baby, which, sadly enough, did not seem likely, the bowl would be used for the christening.

Mrs. Mardell took a pretty little checked duster out of a drawer, and went upstairs to her drawing-room on the first floor. She carefully picked up an iridescent bead off the carpet, the spoil of the dress she had worn last night, and placed it on an ash-tray. She then proceeded to rub up the several minute objects on her silver-table, wishing heartily that she could afford to have them lacquered, and thus dispense with her daily task. So occupied, she looked wholly pretty and half domestic, a little soubrettish, like those neat-aproned maids who flutter early about a stage-scene and usher in and lay the tables for tragedy.

There was no harm in Florence Mardell. She was a smart, novel-reading, Sandown and Ranelagh going woman, easily dressed, easily amused, a little detached, perhaps, in her interests, and careless of the more serious issues of life, but quite willing to simulate and assume social crazes as they came up. She played a good game of Bridge. She glanced at the deep Reviews as well as the *Windsor* and *Pearson's,* and improved her mind on the slightest opportunity. You could always get her for a subscription lecture of sorts, and she quite approved of Female Suffrage, without, however, actively concerning herself in its propaganda. She never "fagged." She was always beautifully dressed in a severish, strapped, mock-manly style, and could wear successfully the very largest hats when they came in.

She had been the widow of an officer, and had lived at Wimbledon in a big dull house standing in its own grounds. She had first set eyes on Joe Mardell playing a strong "Macheath" in *The Beggar's Opera,* to the most ineffective "Polly Peachum" of Julia Fitzgerald. Miss Fitzgerald was his wife; had she but known it, it might have made a difference, but very likely it would not have. Then and there she had fallen in love with the actor across the footlights, impulsively, violently, madly, and she had not rested, being of an acquisitive, pugnacious, predatory habit of mind, until she had persuaded a journalistic friend of hers and his to bring about an introduction. With her effective crown of real golden hair, waved and curled *in extremis,* her clean, fresh suburbanity, she had fascinated "Macheath." He was known to be weak, *volage,* and full of moods. Florence was, on the contrary, strong and pertinacious, she had taken him in a mood, and let her love profit by it. With fond remorselessness she had driven him to drive his wife to divorce him. All this she had compassed in her own calm detached way, as if unconscious of the larger issues she was stirring—another woman's happiness, a man's honour, and an actor's art, for Joe was a genius, and recognised to be one, in spite of, some people said because of, his strange limitations. A little man, almost a dwarf, he could play the burly Falstaff and the courtly Biron; he could write articles in the Reviews; he could hold supper-tables in a roar. Julia Mardell's happiness had been sacrificed, for she adored, and was known to adore, her husband. To oblige him she had condescended to make use of some of the more complicated and recondite cogs of the machinery of the English law of divorce, and had tamely surrendered, without humiliating him, one of the most fascinating men of the day to another woman. Yet Julia was quite as good-looking as Florence, if in a different style. She was the full-souled, full-breasted, large-eyed Junoesque female type, and only undertook the playing of a minx like Polly Peachum to suit Joe. Such a majestic walk as hers, such dark swimming eyes were of no avail to the actress who aspired to play one of the wayward mistresses of the highwayman. It was the measure of Julia's love and her power of self-abnegation. Joe was prepared to take the whole play on his own shoulders, only he must have a sympathetic woman to act with. He did find Julia sympathetic in those days when he loved her, and before the pretty widow from Wimbledon had leaned out of her box and shaken her golden locks at him. Then one day the two women met. Matters were arranged. Joe, susceptible, weak, hustled and busy, succumbed... Lawyers acted for him. Julia was compliant: Florence "keen." Joe worked on and was divorced while rehearsing a new play. He himself never knew how it all happened!

There was a large signed photograph of Julia in Joe's study now, standing unframed, concave and dusty on the mantelpiece; Joe had not dared, or cared, to give it a more polite or permanent abiding-place. Indeed, Florence had had some thoughts of removing it from its even so humble position; her friends wondered how she could possibly bear to have it there for Joe to see every day! But she was capricious. One never knew how she would take things. It was their expressed opinion which perhaps induced her to let it stay, curled up and drooping slavishly as time went on, and the dust and heat of the fire brought its proud head low.

Florence bore Julia no grudge, she should think not, indeed! Julia had been very good about it, had made no difficulties, but on the contrary, had smoothed and made easy the path of divorce for the man she loved.

That is, if she really did care for Joe. She had been so terribly callous in her interviews; so full of zeal to give him his freedom. It was hardly human, so the woman who had profited by her action thought, and certainly not very womanly. Florence could not imagine herself allowing a cold business-like lawyer to dictate her a letter bidding Joe come back to her herewith; a summons intended, of course, for ultimate publication. It disgusted Florence, this horrible business of sueing for restitution of conjugal rights! Julia's formal petition was refused by Joe in another cold letter, equally intended for publication. Florence had actually read the two inhuman missives printed together in the daily paper. Divorce had followed in due course.

"Oh, you tamely died!" Yes, little frivolous Florence, who had never read Tennyson, would have taken the advice of the Egyptian and would have "clung to Fulvia's waist, and thrust the dagger through her side." She was a true woman, like Cleopatra, and knew that the elemental passions, once raised, must have full mastery. A man all to oneself or nothing! That was her philosophy.

The feelings of the man in question? The state of his affections? No matter! Florence did not see herself considering them, or taking any deadly sex insult lying down. She considered that Julia's poor-spiritedness did really verge on meanness. She had accepted money from Joe—an allowance to enable her to leave the stage. Report said that she had grown stout. Report said that she had taken to drink. Lies probably, so generous Florence said. Nobody in Florence's world knew anything about Julia excepting Miss Walton, who had introduced them. And though the two women had continued their intimacy, it was with the tacit agreement that the name of Julia should not be mentioned between them. There were plenty of other subjects to talk about. Miss Walton was, like everybody else, more than half in love with Joe... Funny how they all were! Rather nice—for Joe's wife, since Joe did not bother with any of them...

Mrs. Mardell, after having polished the silver diligently, turned her attention to the room. She ordered the chairs, according to some abstruse social system of her own, and flicked her duster about feebly here and there. She did not feel very "fit." Rather queer, on the contrary! All-overish! She could not have told you what it was, but she was mysteriously conscious of something excessive—something outrageous, like severe pain in wait for her. She seemed to apprehend its nearness instinctively, as a patient seated in the dentist's chair watches the eminent practitioner's feet moving and is aware in all his sensitive enamel of the imminent grinding of the file that has been set going.

Perhaps it was the long-continued strain of the cold that was affecting her. The frost had lasted since before Christmas, and had been very severe...

She paused. The little clock on the mantelpiece tinkled half-past eleven. Supposing she were to give herself a slight moral fillip—go upstairs and try on her new dress, and see how it fitted, after having been "back" twice. She was sure in this way to obtain a sensation, pleasurable or otherwise.

She mounted another flight, feeling every step to be an effort. She lit the gas-stove in her room, and dismissed the dilatory housemaid, whom she found on her knees examining the pattern of the carpet. Then she dragged a tall cheval glass into position, having due regards to unbecoming cross-lights, and undressed. Her white, handsome shoulders appeared; she looked ten times prettier than she had done in the severe morning shirt and tie, and she knew it. She stood for a few minutes before the mirror, complacently admiring herself and in no hurry to don the heavily-trimmed corsage that awaited her verdict. It lay beside her, half in and half out of the flowered cardboard box, interleaved with tissue-paper, and with intersecting lines of tape winding it into its cage. Her eyes rested on it with feminine appreciation of the elaborate building of the silk lining, with its white bone cases crossing and recrossing the back of it, and the high collar which was to fit in under the very lobe of the ear. Still she deferred the pleasing moment of assumption, standing still and preening herself; soft lappets of Valenciennes lace flowering out as a frame to the pink skin...

Suddenly, taken by surprise, without a cry or a moan, she cowered and was bent, bent nearly double. Agonising pangs shot through the framework of her body. Her eyes were glassed over with tears, and through them she stared out on the world, bewildered, peering to see from which point the next arrow of dolour would fall!

It came again, without fail it came again, this time no stabbing thrust, but a sword, driving, delving laboriously through her vitals in a lingering, painstaking manner. She was by now prepared and well frightened, and she groaned aloud. Her breasts rose and came together, as in some strange health exercise, under the laces and ribbons...

My God! Was it—? Was the silver bowl downstairs going to be used at last?

No, it could not be. The thought was dismissed as soon as formed. A chill on the liver? The extreme cold... What a fool she was to prance about like a peacock in front of a glass for half-an-hour half dressed! What else could she expect? That silly stove gave no heat...

She gathered to her a dressing-gown that lay near and sat still, cowering. A long pause! She could not think. But she received no physical intimation of the recurrence of her agony.

Five minutes later she boldly rose, defying it, and, tore the new dress out of its rustling ward without stopping to untie the tapes that controlled it. With a screech of tissue-paper it yielded itself into her hands, and she put it on.

Then she laughed. The pain was forgotten. She wriggled about happily.

"Yes, it still catches me... just there! They must have it back. I'll go to Madam about it, on—let me see?—Tuesday..."

Taking the precaution of putting her arms properly into the warm dressing-jacket this time, she wrapped the dress up again, tied the white tapes across it, put the lid on firmly, and with the little stylograph Joe had given her, methodically scored out her own name from the label, thus substituting that of the dressmaker printed all over the box.

The exertion, slight as it was, roused again the smouldering fire of pain. She sat down helplessly on her bed, giving herself up to it. Her eyes were like those of a dumb animal in the death anguish, as she stared across at her reflection of her already distorted features in the glass. Rolling to and fro, she grasped and relaxed alternately the fronts of her peignoir, knotted feverishly in her palm.

"What the *divil* is it?" she murmured. "I feel as if my life was going!"

She did not think of calling any one—Vance or Gladys the impotent housemaid; no one could help her. She was but a poor human passage-way for these relentless throes that passed Juggernaut-like through her shrinking body. It was like a garden roller, when it was not like many scythes set on one axle turning, twisting inside her. What had she ever done to suffer so? No child of Joe's could be so cruel and tear its mother thus!... Nay, she had not conceived, unless it was some monstrous impious growth that was rending her, and would not soften or relax till it killed her... She really thought she was going to die!...

Presently, when all was quiet again in the tortured battleground of her body, she rose and pushed her hand through her bows of waved hair and flung it back hideously and crossed the room. Apologetically almost, for fear of provoking a recurrence of the horror, she dragged herself downstairs, and to the swing door at the head of the kitchen stairs. She now felt the need of a confidante. She must tell some one. The housemaid was too young. Vance was fairly motherly. Pushing open the door, she sat down on the top step, with her peignoir gathered round her, and stretching out her legs allowed them to hang over into the dark abyss of Vance's domain.

By the time she felt able to raise her voice and call Vance she had decided not to confide in her. The cook would immediately "think things," and she wanted no fuss. It was not "that" either, she only wished it was... For then there would at least be some compensation in baby fingers to smooth pain away.

In response to her weak summons the cook appeared at the foot of the stairs. Even in the dim penumbra of a London basement, a person unpreoccupied by her own symptoms would have realised at once that Vance was discomposed—agitated in some unusual way. Her cap was hanging by one hairpin, her floury arms were nervously rubbed one against the other. But Mrs. Mardell noticed nothing in other people to-day. She addressed Vance slowly and deliberately.

"Vance, please I want you to make me a nice cup of tea—at once. I shall not be able to eat any lunch. I think I'll wait till six, and have something with Mr. Mardell."

"Ain't you feeling well, Ma'am?" asked the cook spiritlessly.

"No, not very—a little all-overish. It will be nothing, only I don't feel like eating a solid meal."

"Nor I can't say I feel like cooking it!" Vance observed bitterly. "I'm that upset! I've been across and asked."

"Asked what?" inquired Mrs. Mardell wearily.

"About the funeral that I saw with my own eyes leaving that house on Christmas Day... It's not natural, I said, to go getting buried on Christmas Day—"

Mrs. Mardell interposed impatiently. "You don't mean to say you went and asked at the house if they'd had any one die there? Really, Vance—"

"It's no good saying that now, Ma'am; I had to know. And it's only a Nursing Home, not a private house, so I've done no harm. And"—the woman's voice grew low and hoarse—"nobody ain't died there—not yet—that's all!"

She put her apron to her face.

"Good gracious, Vance!" Mrs. Mardell cried. "Tell me more about it!"

"Ma'am, they've only got one patient there—a lady. She was going on all right, but she had a relapse this morning, just about half-past eleven, their cook said it was. She had an operation three weeks ago, and no good, and it's got to be done all over again this afternoon at two o'clock, and they can't tell as it will be successful, this time."

"Well, my good woman, don't you worry. Let's hope that the lady will get over it. People do, you know, or there would be an end of nursing homes. I really feel so poorly myself that I can't get up much sympathy with other people's aches and pains. Be quick and get the kettle on, or is it boiling already?"

"Yes, Ma'am, you shall have it in a minute. Ma'am, you may not believe me, but I seen a proper funeral, and the hearse waiting, and the corpse carried out and down those steps... and the bearers with crape on their hats and so attentive, and one of them was no bigger than Master... I thought of Master the moment I saw him... And she was a big woman, for she took a big coffin..."

"You are settling that it's the woman who's lying ill there now who has got to die, I see. What's her name?"

"I asked, but the girl didn't know it, only that she was an actress."

Mrs. Mardell gathered in her legs decisively.

"Come now, Vance, don't stand there gossiping and unhinging yourself with fancies; get me my cup of tea. I shall be all right, I expect, when once I have had something warm. Bring it to my room. I shall lie down a bit, I think."

She rose to her feet, closed the swing door, dismissing Vance and her dreary soothsaying vision, and passed upstairs. Her day was spoilt. The pain did not seem to be going to recur, luckily, but the deadly feeling of uneasiness which had succeeded it certainly increased. Her legs were weak and could hardly carry her. People who have seen an apparition are said to feel just so. But as she reflected it was Vance, not she, who had seen the ghost!

She paused half-way up the stairs to look out of the window on the first landing, whence Vance declared she had watched the lugubrious tableau. Mrs. Mardell had never gone in for knowing her neighbours, it was wiser not, or else she would have been aware of the industry that was carried on at number thirteen, a red-brick sham artistic villa, just like her own house—like every other house in the street. She could only make it out by pressing her face against the window, and then she only saw it aslant, and red, through the vicious stained glass that occupied that particular pane. Eight steps led up to the front door of it, as eight steps led up to hers. Surely it was awkward for the incoming patients—many of them, presumably, too ill to walk? She wondered what sort of cases they took there. It would depend...

Julia, she had heard, had grown very fat—at thirty... That indicated something abnormal, in a youngish woman!... Something that had to be removed, generally... She laughed... She wondered why she laughed...

"Your tea, Ma'am!" said Vance suddenly at her elbow. "I thought I would bring it up to you myself."

Mrs. Mardell was a little ashamed that Vance should discover her staring out of the window at the scene of her absurd cock-and-bull story. She turned and coldly bade the cook precede her to her bedroom with the tea. Vance accepted the rebuff meekly. She looked cowed and thoroughly upset, and as if no merely domestic trifle could affect her now, broken to tragic issues as she had been.

The tea, as Mrs. Mardell had expected, revived her, and enabled her to lay a nice little plan for a quiet afternoon indoors. She proposed to telephone for Miss Walton to come and sit with her for a bit. She needed something or somebody to pick her up. Of course there was Charlie Bligh, a nice boy whom both she and Joe liked; she might telephone him to come and take her out to dine, as he often did... But no, she wasn't looking Carlton form; it wouldn't be fair to Charlie to ask him to take out anything that wasn't gay and smart. Besides, it would be rather mean to leave Joe to eat his dinner all alone when she had not even said good-morning to him. She had often left him for dinner, of course, and he had never thought of objecting, verbally at least—but just now that he was so busy and overworked she felt sure that he would like her, sitting beside him at his dinner, even though she could eat nothing. She saw herself delicately invalidish, in her soft draperies, picking at some grapes... She felt mysteriously drawn to Joe, dear Joe, who was working for her now, who never attempted to control her social movements, who took what she gave him and was always as ready to flirt with her as if he were not married to her! She had managed Joe well! No, she wouldn't leave Joe to-night, but get Miss Walton, who would surely stay with her till Joe returned about half-past five, as usual.

Miss Walton, over the telephone, signified her willingness to come and have a good chat. Mrs. Mardell made up her mind to take things easy. She was really unwell, she had eaten nothing since breakfast, she felt empty, shaken, swelled and sore. She could not have got her exquisitely adjusted corsets on if she had tried, or endured the pressure of them round her body. A tea gown was clearly indicated. She assumed one, and a little lace cap that went well with it. Sighing deeply, she lay down on the rose-coloured chintz sofa in the drawing-room, shaded by a soft standard lamp, breathing timorously, existing furtively, unnoticed. She hoped it would pass her by, this brooding eagle of pain waiting to tear her.

She had brought her jewel-case downstairs with her and idly toyed with her trinkets. There were three trays, lined with velvet. They twinkled with precious stones. She took every piece in order and examined them slowly, seriously. All the while, her fingers seemed to know that down at the bottom of the box lay their real objective, a thin, crumpled, tousled letter folded small and turning up at the corners. Florence Mardell had received it a few days after her marriage, and although it was only a letter from a woman, had forborne to show it to her husband.

The letter was not actually malicious or even disagreeable, but it had dismayed her, and shocked her. She had kept it in case Julia should ever choose to lay aside her extraordinary tolerance and become human again. She read it over now to remind her of what it contained. Indeed she had intended to do so when she fetched the box. The by-play with the jewellery was only a blind—self-deceiving, a sop to her superficial consciousness.

> *"Now it is all over, my strivings have not been in vain, and Joe passes from me to you must not mind my writing to you, Florence. I think that, on the whole, you will prefer to know what I feel, and that the woman you have supplanted is not your enemy. Joe loves you, and as the woman Joe loves, you cannot be abhorrent to me. Convention forbids me to be your personal friend, your feeling possibly, and perhaps my own, for I am but a woman after all, and the open wound that was left in my life when Joe was torn from my side would be chafed and kept raw by the sight of him merged now in your life. Yes, it is better so. I cannot, will not, see him either—though Joe is not conventional...*
>
> *"Joe is nothing that is not splendid. I did, I do love him so passionately, that I cannot hate you, Florence, as you see. You are the fair new temple in which he worships the spirit of Beauty and Love and Life. The law has clanged the door to, none may dare to interrupt the Litany he prays there, on his knees. God bless you.*

"But oh, my dear, keep him there. Never undress the altar. No more shifting for Joe, if we women can help it. He is a great man—he must be treated like a great man. These upheavals are bad for him, from every point of view. So be practical as well as passionate, and condescend to learn from me, who failed, how not to lose him. Only approximately can you learn, for the wind of art blows its children where it listeth. You know what an artist he is, and all artists are nothing but divine children. But, Florence, on your life, don't treat him as one. Don't let yourself 'mother' him as I did and be mad enough to sink the mistress in the sister, the friend even. That was my fatal mistake, I abstracted my sexual self till I became at last the caterer for his mere physical welfare, the confidante of his passing flirtations. Oh, the bitterness of those smothered confessions, those despairing returns of him, broken, marred and dispirited, to the one who surely loved him! Do this, my dear, as I did, and then one day he'll come to you, as he came to me, and put his head on your knee and ask you to divorce him. So you're both ruined in your several ways. He cannot go through it a second time.

"Now listen. You must. I know. I would have you always a little inaccessible, puzzling, capricious even. I would ask you to dare to appear selfish, if you can manage it. Preserve your delicate tangibility, punish any slight infringements of your rules, close your door to him at nights when he has been naughty or careless. What it will cost you! But it is the right way.

"You have an enormous pull by not acting with him, believe me! One gets so common, so cheap to a man, when he is used to knocking one about all over the stage, as Katherine, say, or insulting one as Nancy. Stay away from the theatre and accept as many dinners without him as you can. Although there isn't the very slightest

chance of his losing you, don't let him feel as convinced of that as you are yourself. You see what I mean, don't you, Florence? I heard you were very clever, as well as a little frivolous.

"I have thought all this out, in many sleepless nights, for your benefit and his. Yes, it is Joe that I am thinking of, and shall think of till I die. And so of you, too.

"Oh, don't for goodness' sake be offended by this letter, or take a dislike to me, for whether you like it or no, you will never be quite free of me, any more. Thought, strong thought, does permeate matter and finds itself able to overthrow its mere material resistance. I have proved it, no matter how. I won't weary you with attempted explanation. I should not fancy you were psychic. But be sure that there will be a little of me in all your relations with Joe, I shall have a word in your ménage and you must not let the thought of it make you uncomfortable. Do you suppose I could have let him go so easily, if I had not this power to console me? Take it, as the slight penalty of kidnapping a man out of the ward of a devoted woman. You see how it is, he comes away, she offers no material or spirited opposition, but he brings inevitably some of her atmosphere along with him. Joe never actually ceased to love me; he only began to love you. I never misconducted myself—funny phrase!—so I am still his true and faithful wife, bone of his bone, flesh of his flesh, and where he is, henceforth, in some sort, I am. It cannot be helped.

"It is a good thing that I am not vindictive and that I don't hate you, since our relation must necessarily be so close. I assure you that it will not inconvenience you, annoy you, or trouble you at all, at least not until the bands of the spirit are loosed in one of these great, bare, soul-stripped, unaccounted-for moments of life, that come to all of us sometimes. Then, you know, one can't tell, or

> *foresee... The spiritual bonds and relationships assert themselves and enforce attention... I can't quite promise to shield you, then, to free you from the circle of the charm... But are you so frivolous, Florence? Won't it interest you—awe you—soothe you?*
>
> *"Ah, don't fear me, don't hate me—bid your flesh comply with me... I am only the ghost of a wife—a power of love that can't circumscribe itself, even though it would. There is a physical lien between us, undoubtedly. I won't drag it if I can help!... I'll try to control—I don't know what I am writing—something writes for me. But trust me. Julia."*

"What a cat!" said Mrs. Mardell.

She folded up the letter again and laid it at the bottom of the box. It was almost actionable, she thought, a threatening letter. Or else the letter of a mad spiritualist—utter sentimental, impossible rot. What would Charlie Bligh, or any other daylight person think of it?

Strangely enough, she had more or less taken Julia's advice! It was sensible, and thus she supposed germane to her own character. She had not "mothered" Joe, what woman in her senses would? She needed no deserted, defeated schemer to hang about her, in the spirit, to tell her that! She knew men as Julia with all her preachments had evidently never known them, and the result of her wise treatment of Joe was that he was devoted to her, extraordinarily so, for a busy man. Of course he worked hard, too hard, harder than he had done in Julia's time. It had happened so, success had brought its own tension and high pressure. He was not, as Julia and her friends might like to suggest, trying to drown the memory of her in a round of forced activities. He was only taking fortune at the flood and making dramatic hay while the sun of critics favour shone. Not for a moment did he regret the step he had taken, his was an essentially light nature, he never brooded, and he detested heroics. The writer of that letter, with its tedious mixture of sentimentality and preoccupation with material cares, must have bored Joe to death, in the days when she had him all to herself and could claim consecutive opportunity for worrying him. And now, of course, a masterpiece of supreme tactlessness, like all failures, she turned critic and took on herself to give good advice.

Florence Mardell laughed. The reading of the letter had acted as even a better fillip than the trying on of the dress, and had nearly made her angry.

"I suppose"—she tossed her little gold crowned head—"that it is very good of her to give me the straight tip, and volunteer to overlook my ménage, generally, like a sort of superior lady housekeeper! I am not so bad at it myself, thank you?" She worked herself up to a sneer. "Much obliged to Julia, I'm sure, for haunting me, especially as she appears willing to confine herself merely to bothering the sensible mistress of the house, and doesn't go frightening the servants and making them give up their places. Vance wouldn't stop a minute—"

Her brow furrowed a little as she remembered the white, frightened face of Vance that morning.

"It's a fairly cool thing, though," her thought resumed, "for one woman to tell another, flat, that she considers herself part of her because she happens to have adored her husband and does still, I suppose. Man and wife—no, wife and wife—are one flesh... Ha! Ha!..."

It was two o'clock, her face changed. Arrowy tinglings, growlings as of a chained monster inside her slender frame, punctuated her words. The pain had come again...

When Miss Walton came in she would ask her to ring up a doctor. She could not have dragged herself to the instrument now.

*

The front door bell rang. She heard Miss Walton's cheery voice making inquiries about Mrs. Mardell's health as she shook the balled snow out of her boots on to the hall mat, and plumped her umbrella into the rack. Mrs. Mardell sat still, physically incapable of rising, though she had had but a short bout of pain this time.

She had made up her mind to question Miss Walton about Julia. Julia's affairs seemed for the moment essentially her concern. She felt no malevolence towards her in spite of the re-reading of the letter. Miss Walton, the confidante, had never been allowed to see that letter. She should see it now, if she was good and satisfactorily confidential?

"Well, dear, how are you?" Miss Walton had come in, her work-a-day nose reddened with exposure, and her hands thickened with chilblains. "I suppose you are feeling the continuous cold, like the rest of us. And you know, you little minx, that you look best in a tea gown."

"Do I look well?"

"Well, a bit bleached, perhaps, and your eyes rather funny and starey, as if you'd been seeing ghosts?"

"Vance has, she says."

"A ghost in West Kensington! Nonsense!"

"It was a mock funeral, Vance says," Mrs. Mardell remarked in an even voice. "Coming out of a house in this street on Christmas Day, when there was nobody died in it, as they told her." She looked closely at Miss Walton's face. "Do you know any one at number thirteen? An actress, Vance says—"

"Bless her. Christmas pudding, I should say. No, I don't know a soul in this street besides yourself—"

Mrs. Mardell, with a sigh of relief, leant back again.

"But, I say, Florence, you do look dicky," Miss Walton continued. "What have you been doing with yourself?"

"Perhaps you'll say it is Christmas pudding with me too," replied Mrs. Mardell, laughing feebly. "But I don't know—somehow, I've had a horrid day. I seem to have got a sudden attack of lumbago, or sciatica or something."

"It doesn't sound likely, at your age."

"No, does it? But it's pains right through me at intervals all through the day. I had a fearful bout, just before you came. I daresay it's nothing—"

"Rheumatism, probably," said the other. "Nothing so absurdly painful when it gets hold of one. Here's tea—nice hot tea. It will do you good."

"I've had two goes already."

"Oh, have a third! Nothing like tea for us women! Here, let me pour it out. Your poor little hands are trembling."

"No, I'll manage. Sugar? I forget if you take it? And lots of milk?... Alice, how long is it since you saw Julia?"

Mrs. Mardell was surprised at the coolness of Miss Walton's reception of the seldom pronounced name. She might have reflected that the other woman had no particular reason to be shy of it, for she had been Florence's and Julia's confidante during the stormy times of the divorce and had managed to be loyal and friendly to both. She now replied offhandedly to Mrs. Mardell's question—

"Not for six months. Lost sight of the poor dear, rather."

"And when you last saw her, how did she look?"

"Handsome, but rather too fat. I can't say I much liked the look of that, for she's still quite young. I always fancy it means morbid growths, and that kind of thing. Poor old Juley! One never even sees her name in the bills now, does one?"

"Retired on the allowance Joe makes her, I suppose," said Florence Mardell bitterly. "I can't think how she could bring herself to take his money?"

"Only that she's poor, of course."

"How poor?"

"One can't tell," replied Alice Walton, "with people like Julia. She's Irish. She's the kind of woman who pays a man from Douglas's to come and wave her hair, and dry it on towels that you can't see for the holes! You understand. She's the sweetest, cleverest, untidiest soul alive! She took a flat in Paris with a friend, and the state of that flat, I'm told, after a week of Julia, beat even the *femme de ménage* they got in to do for them! They never dressed or ate, but lay about all day in peignoirs and smoked cigarettes. They got in a hypnotist to talk to them about Joe, I believe. Julia makes no secret of her devotion to Joe, as I suppose you are aware?... Now, Florence, keep your feet up—there's a good girl! You look ghastly."

"Yes, I know. So she's still mad on Joe? Tell me more about her. She isn't a woman of much taste, I fancy—can't dress a bit?"

"No, but a generous creature, full of impulses and never a mean one among them. I do admire her character, I confess."

"So do I," said Florence Mardell. "And so did Joe, I believe."

"Does. He can't help seeing her qualities, and being flattered by her immense devotion to him. Though, of course, he's used to it—he can't help being faskynating! He's such a sprite and yet so strong. Julia was as big again as he was, pretty nearly. He admired her awfully, as little men do always admire big women."

"I'm not very big, yet Joe admires me."

"Oh—I know he does and long may he continue. He may, for Julia, that's one thing, she's strictly 'hands off,' I know. She's never made the slightest attempt to get him ever to go and see her."

"He wouldn't go if she did."

"I shouldn't be too sure of that," said Miss Walton, carried, by love of her subject, beyond the limits of tactfulness. "And what would it matter? Joe was truly fond of her till you came along, you little witch! And she's never done anything to set him against her or hurt his self-love. That's what a man minds. I don't see how he could have refused her a thing like that, nor could you. No, give her credit for her generosity, I believe he proposed it and that she refused to see him, steadily. Nobody in theatrical circles thought for one moment you'd keep him against her. The betting was all that, if she had tried, she'd have got him back in a month."

"No, not if she'd tried, she wouldn't," said Florence Mardell earnestly. "She loved him too much!"

Her lips sketched a grimace as she spoke; her hand moved to her side and her eyes filled with tears.

"What is it, dear? The pain again?"

"I was afraid of it—my body was, I mean. But it luckily doesn't seem to mean business, this time. And I don't believe I could feel any more,—I don't seem to have any organs left. It's the peace of emptiness—exhaustion! Do, dear, let me go on talking and thrashing out things. What I meant when I said that Julia loved him too much, was this, that it is a mistake to love so openly and make such a noise about it. Men don't value affection that's cried from the house tops. It just disgusts them. Love at breakfast, love at luncheon, love all day; it's sure to pall. Love shouldn't be mixed up with daily bread-getting.

It should be a speciality, not a sort of smoking mixture, advertised on every passing omnibus."

"Go on, child, you interest me. Why, you yourself simply adore Joe!"

A faun-like, tormenting expression Miss Walton had never seen there, came over Florence Mardell's face, as, in the weak exhausted voice of a privileged invalid, she proceeded—

"I adore Joe as smart women permit themselves to adore the thing they value and mean to keep. I believe I prize Joe, not for what he is, though I'm aware he's a genius, but for what he means to me—light and kisses and frocks and champagne. There isn't so much of that as there would be if Julia and her allowance didn't stop the way! I love Joe because he's the fount of life to me, because I feel good when he is in the room, and dull when he is out of it. I happen to know that I shouldn't feel that about him if he came to me ill and hipped and unsuccessful. Sounds mean, but it's true. I perfectly enjoy the placards telling me that he can make a cat laugh, and critics saying he is like what Garrick used to be. An 'abridgement'—what is it? I am quite cross with him when the notices are poor, and I don't in the least long, then, to take his head on my shoulder and comfort him. It's he who has to comfort me."

"Julia had a rather different theory!"

"Yes, and Julia lost him and I got him. She called him her boy and her baby! He even told me so, saying how nice it was of her. Quite sincere! He thought so, I daresay. I knew better, as if any man liked to be made to feel small! She'd have handed the moon down to him if she'd had it in her power, and when he cried for such a little easy thing as a divorce, of course she gave it him. A fool, I call her."

"I don't know about that," the friend replied, combatively. "Greater love hath no woman, than she lay down her marriage lines for her husband."

"Well, I love him, but I couldn't have done that! I should simply have had to stick to him just the same. And then—if he had thrown me over, nothing would ever have induced me to take money from him!"

"But if you were extravagant and nearly starving?"

"I'd have found a man to support me and buy me frills!"

"Then you couldn't have loved him, to degrade the thing he had once set store by."

"If Joe had left me, anything could have become of me for all I cared!... I see what you are driving at, Alice, you think I can't feel love as Julia does, because I haven't got beetle brows meeting over my forehead and a big contralto chest to sigh with. My way with Joe, whether I do it from self-control or inclination, comes out best. A man like Joe needs a lot of spoiling, but not from the woman he cares for. I let outsiders do it for me. I don't cosset him, or make a point of being home every afternoon from my calls at an unearthly hour to dine with him. If a boy offers me a dinner, I accept and Joe gives me my taxi fare, and looks me over, and sees that my dress, for the other man, mind you, is all right. Nor do I wait up for him when he comes back, I just see supper's laid out all right and the fire kept up and go to bed. I don't make him look ridiculous by fetching him at the theatre, as some actors' wives do. Julia, I hear, used to take parts that didn't suit her, so as to ensure her being on the spot with him, every night. I never know where he is and I don't go getting his pals to play detective and tell me. I may be conceited, but I do flatter myself, that wherever Joe is, he is thinking of me, and of how soon he can get back to me."

"I think you are perfectly right," Miss Walton replied rather sardonically. "It's the best view to take of marriage, and for a woman married to a popular actor, the only one. Do you happen to know where Joe is, now?"

"Yes, I happen to be able to tell you. He is at the theatre, rehearsing the new play. They must be through by now, though! He'll be here in a minute. I haven't seen him since yesterday. We dine together at six o'clock!"

"And it's half-past five now. Well, I must be off. Good-bye, old girl, and I wouldn't neglect those pains if I were you. I expect it's only rheumatism, but as a general rule internal pains should not be ignored. You look rather flushed—"

"I must go and put on some powder before Joe comes. Good-bye. Tell Gladys to come and clear away the tea as you go out."

Mrs. Mardell was left alone, with two imperfectly drained teacups and some broken crumbs of cake on a Japanese tray. The spirit lamp under the kettle had gone out—she missed its cheerful flame. She was hemmed in, her knees were imprisoned by the flaps of the tea-table so that she could not lie back... She felt disinclined to move and go upstairs for that dust of powder that was to impress Joe... Everything was a bother... she felt very stupid, but she had no more pain, thank God!...

So she sat on, waiting for the maid to clear away the tea things and set her free, bolt upright in her hostess corner of the flower-begarlanded sofa, with the pink-shaded lamp behind her, convenient for reading, only she did not want to read. Her head drooped, till her face was in shadow. Her eyes were fixed on a Liberty cosy corner that adequately filled an ugly bare place in the room but that no one ever sat in—and then and there she had a vision.

It seemed to her that her sight pierced through the faint scaffolding of white wood pillars that bore up the inane piece of furniture. She had a view of a cold, bare room distempered in pale green, and nearly empty of furniture, excepting for a bed and an arm-chair. Presently, she distinguished a table made of slabs of glass, covered with bits of shining steel and physic bottles. She smelt a strong odour of ether. Then sundry persons surged into her field of vision, though they had been there all the time; two white-capped nurses, bending solicitously over a bed where a third person lay with long black hair spread over the pillow. A woman, who was speaking so faintly that Florence felt rather than heard what she said.

"You are sure you have sent for him?" the image seemed to say urgently. "Nurse! Nurse! It's the 'Quality Theatre'!"

"Yes, Madam, we have telephoned through—'Quality Theatre.' It would have been as well—! Can you not give us your husband's home address, Madam?"

"I don't know it," the patient replied wearily. "But he will be at the theatre. He is always at the theatre. It's his life now. He'll come... he'll come!"

"Surely, Madam—"

The nurse turned away to speak to a colleague who had apparently only recently left the room and now returned. Florence then saw the features of the woman on the bed, features never seen by her except across the footlights, charged with bright white and rose. They were grey and unrecognisable now, yet Florence knew whose they were.

She heard the conversation of the two whispering women the while.

"She's sinking fast," said the elder nurse.

"She'll last till he comes, I think," replied the younger. "He's just telephoned through that he's on his way here!"

With her words the whole house and its ramifications were now revealed to Florence Mardell—as it were the open front of a doll's house. She saw the steps leading up to the door—there were eight of them—the hall, the staircase and the room where the patient lay, at one and the same time. She heard a jingling of bells and the prod of a swift hansom suddenly pulled up at the behest of the urgently waved umbrella of a man within—her husband. She saw him leap out and dash up the steps to the door that was flung open as soon as he touched the bell. She missed no single stage of his progress upstairs to Julia's room. The nurse opened the door of it, admitted him, and passed out herself. Florence recognised Joe's familiar gesture—the overcoat hastily flung off and thrown aside, disclosing the dapper little ordinary man, with the long lock of hair, that was his mark of genius, lifting on his forehead as usual, as he impetuously advanced towards the bed. She realised the weak complaisance that stood for paradisaical joy on the face of the woman lying there, whose light of life was too nearly extinguished to permit of a finer demonstration. But the actor's face was a marvel. This expression, evoked for the beloved dying woman only, was of such a tragic madness as no mime could ever hope to originate or imitate. Florence had never seen that look on his face, and sharp knowledge shot through her that even if she in her turn lay dying she would not see it then. A sob shook, but did not interrupt her steady absorption in the sight spread before her.

Her hungry eyes watched the discreet nurse left in charge retire to the mantelpiece and thoughtfully examine her sleeve links, as the lover, with passionate solicitude and a cunning born of intimate usage, sat down and laying his arms round his mistress's neck, raised her a little, so as to gain her ear for the last whispers of love.

As a ghost to earth returned, the second wife apprehended the dreadful sense of the words those two exchanged together. Joe spoke with no sense of renewal, but as if Julia and he had parted but a few hours, or it may be days, ago. Florence could not resent, but she suffered the first pangs of a lifelong sorrow as she listened to Julia's faint sighs of content, her weak rejoinders to Joe's protestations of undying fidelity, his vows that turned to old, wise, baby talk, and the promises she wrung from him so easily...

The nurse still fumbled with her sleeve links, blinded by unusual tears.

"You will see me buried?" Julia exacted, her hands twisting in Joe's hair, playing with the long lock... "You will make all the arrangements for me, Joe, won't you? I want *you*—I want you to manage it!..."

Vance was right. Joe was the puny ghost mourner... And Florence looked on eagerly again.

"It shall be our wedding... our remarriage!" He soothed her. "We meet again—to part no more... you and I, Julia, my Julia..."

What did he mean to do when Julia died, as die she must? It was very near now. Florence listened and looked, their voices seemed fainter, more furtive; the scene in the bedchamber was growing evanescent, ragged, as if there were rents in the film. She sometimes feared, so eager was she to see the whole of her own tragedy, that she was beginning to distinguish the wooden lines of the supports of the cosy corner that framed and crossed her view. She realised that Julia's hour was approaching and that the vision would fade with its instigator. The doctor had come in and the other nurse. She could detect on all three faces the professional discouragement painted there by their foreknowledge of the event. They would look cheerful, normal again, after what must be, was over. But Joe's face surely could never be set in comic lines again, those muscles, so deeply inured to tragedy, might never relax or unbend...

She knew it when Julia died, though at the precise moment no one spoke, no one moved in the room for a while. Julia died, where she listed, where Joe would have her—in his arms. The shape of Julia would never go out of them. There would never be room there any more for Florence, whom he had not loved!...

She raised her head with a jerk. The pink cushions and hangings of the Liberty cosy corner filled up the lines of the woodwork again. The pillars framed triviality as usual.

She was sitting in her own drawing-room, and Gladys the stupid maid, was there—just come in to take away the tea things.

Mrs. Mardell spoke.

"Dinner will be late to-night."

"Yes, Ma'am, I see it's just gone half-past six now."

"Your master is kept... He has things to see to..."

Gladys, eager to show she understood, interrupted. "Yes, Ma'am, Vance will keep dinner back."

She folded up the table and set her mistress free. Mrs. Mardell had no more pain and knew she would not have any more, but she sat on in her place until seven, the hour at which her husband usually left for the theatre during this piece, in which his part entailed a somewhat lengthy and careful make up...

She heard the twist of the latch key in the door below, and for the first time in her life, shrank from meeting the eyes of the man she adored with a new and passionate love. But it was the lover of Julia who would come in to her and say something kind, as usual. Kind—merely kind was all he had ever been, in all these years of her blindness. She put out her hands as if to push him from her, and her lips almost framed the words, "Stay, oh, stay away!"

No use, no use! Her observation, tensely quickened, told her that he paused in the hall, for there was an abrupt cessation of all movement. He was hesitating?... Then he made up his mind to the disagreeable duty. So Florence read the gesture. His sturdy dutiful footsteps could be heard ascending... a wild whiff of ether seemed to precede him!...

Her eyes dropped uncontrollably, as he touched and turned the handle of the door gently... It was done. He was in the room.

How did he look? She must know. She raised her sad eyes, and contemplated the dwarf-actor standing there on the threshold of the pretty cheap drawing-room, oppressing, appalling her with his overpowering dignity. His hair was disordered, and clung, matted, to his damp forehead; the long lock fell over it in the style of one of the good-natured roysterers he excelled in portraying. But his face had the make-up of a clown; the dark features stood out in a mask of putty-coloured whiteness, all but the lips, which had no red. Those eyes which had just looked on death, stared down on her, not unkindly, but unseeing...

She spoke at last, to break the awful spell which was winding itself round and round her, more than for any other reason.

"Julia is dead," she said.

"I know." He took a step forward into the room, and made a cold gesture of menace. She recoiled—then rose and faced him.

"She died in my arms. I loved her."

He turned away. It was as if he had laid a book aside and a leaf had been folded down. He muttered, with a semblance of forced preoccupation with the business of life—

"I just looked in to tell you that I am going straight back to the theatre."

"Without any dinner?" she shrieked. Then, more calmly—

"Well, you will have something to eat when you come home, won't you? What time will that be?"

It was the first time in her life she had asked such a question, and his answer to it, delivered over his shoulder as he went downstairs, cut her to the heart.

"Perhaps never!"

Scant consolation! She knew that he did not mean to kill himself—at least not yet, for he had promised to make the arrangements for and attend Julia's funeral.

THE MEMOIR

Did women in Society ever "speak" to other women, when a man dear to them both was concerned?

Had such an outrageous course ever been pursued since the days when Chriemhild "spoke" to Gudrun in the midst of the Rhine stream?

Little Lady Greenwell pondered this, time after time, day after day, as she sat dressed in her ineffectual Paris best, alone, in crowds, in sunlight gardens, lamp-lit ball-rooms, unlit boudoirs arranged for cosy gossiping teas. She never talked gossip, but she listened to it. A great deal of it covertly was about herself, or rather about her husband. That was one of the reasons why she felt that she ought to speak—speak kindly, seriously, effectively.

She fully meant to tell Cynthia what it was her duty to tell her, but she could not make up her mind to take the first plunge into unconventionality.

So, she sat about through a whole season, watching Sir Hilary's social triumphs—she herself never triumphed—and arranged her speech, carefully composing it beforehand, rehearsing it, canvassing the relative claims of diplomacy and frankness, fulness and brevity, emotion or matter of fact. What arguments should she use, and which let go? Which, having regard to the character of Cynthia Chenies, would be likely to affect that volatile lady most? Should she plead her own years the more, her own looks the less? Should she take high moral grounds?

Should she put forward the young widow's personal expediency? It all depended on what form of admonishment Cynthia would take best.

Lady Greenwell was honest enough to admit to herself that she proposed to lecture Cynthia as much for her own good, as Cynthia's. Truly, she felt that it would be a difficult thing to keep self out of it, or as much in the background as possible.

"Just you let my man alone!"

That was what Kate of Wapping would have said to Peg of Limehouse, and no more ado, but could Lady Greenwell of Highfields, Hungerford, and 50, Carlton House Terrace so bluntly declare herself to the Honourable Mrs. Chenies of Portland Place? Did well-bred women do these things? It seemed at once so absurdly simple, just as you might ask some one to take his foot off your dress and no offence, and at the same time so appallingly impossible a thing to do. Women in Society were not supposed to show when they were annoyed, ask for explanations, or to "act straight."

How they suffered in consequence of these absurd fetishes of conduct they set up, women alone knew. Moreover, such a subject, even if it were fairly and squarely discussed between two exceptional women, would represent the merely primitive appeal of the one to the other's generosity, and generosity, though permissible in Wapping or Limehouse is not the "thing" in Mayfair or Portland Place.

Yet some women were really and truly generous at heart—Cynthia was, she was sure. Had it not been for the presence between them of this male bone of contention, Sir Hilary, Lady Greenwell would have been quite fond of Cynthia Chenies. She did not dislike her even now, when Cynthia was making her so uncomfortable, and she admired her sincerely, her frocks and her style. Hilary, did, and she could not help following suit in this as in all else.

And, naturally, Cynthia could not help liking Hilary and his open attentions. Who could help liking Hilary and complying with him when he chose to flirt, and he always did choose? He was a born flirt, and he was eight years younger than his wife. Wives, who were burdened with odious supernumerary years, must, of course, give their man a little rope, and Mabel Greenwell gave hers a good deal.

Hilary Greenwell was a traveller, who came home and wrote books about it. He danced and dashed through a season, and then packed up and went to risk his life on some inaccessible mountain or other. Of course, when he came back, brown as a berry, and with sheaves of notes and measurements, he was the rage, and women simply "clawed him" for their parties, and adored him for their boudoirs.

Cynthia Chenies was no exception to the rule. Though a widow, she was little more than a girl, and looked a mere child. At the parties she gave in her big house, so Hilary would say, you always expected to see the dolls set up, and find pips in the orange juice soup, and have to mumble the "pretend" biscuit joint. Childlike, she knew no measure in her appreciation of the handsome traveller returned, and people were saying now that she was making a fool of herself, and that Lady Greenwell didn't like it.

They were wrong there, Lady Greenwell wasn't jealous at all. She was sure of Hilary, and would not have insulted him by display of vulgar jealousy. The effect of the scandal on her only amounted to discomfort. Great discomfort she might say, and even annoyance, and a few wet pillowed nights, loyally concealed from Hilary. She was neither young nor beautiful: it behoved her to be clever. She could, she knew, keep his love, though she was unable to restrain those loose tendrils of his fancy which waved airily to and fro, catching here and there temporarily on the fair upstanding flowers that bloomed every year in the great parterre of London's garden of seasonal delights. Hilary loved her and her only. She must do nothing foolish.

Whatever she felt, whatever she said to Cynthia Chenies, must be a secret for Sir Hilary, a matter between Cynthia and herself. Some women—fools!—thought little Lady Greenwell—would have rushed at once to their husband with an appeal or a command, to "put a stop to it at once," thus definitely estranging the coveted man without affecting the issue in the desired way. No, it rested with her and her alone, to convince Cynthia of the awkwardness of the situation created by Cynthia's careless compliance with the fancies of the irresponsible Hilary, a situation merely irksome to his wife, but positively injurious to his wife's friend. Great interests on either hand were not concerned. No one's heart was in it.

Punctuality was Lady Greenwell's virtue—consequently her husband's too. She sat on the sofa at the Creswicks', fan in hand, handkerchief in lap. The man who was going to take her in stood over her chair, uttering the usual commonplaces, when the door opened to admit one single, smiling lady—Cynthia Chenies, late as usual, wearing the cluster of flowers she always wore, and that every one attributed to Sir Hilary's devotion. Lady Greenwell happened to know that Mrs. Chenies ordered them at the florist's for herself. But how could she tell people that!

She saw, what, of course, other people saw, Cynthia's careless delicately possessive glance at Sir Hilary, a glance that effectually singled him out, as it were, from a group of like patterned men, clustered about the fireplace. So stupid of Cynthia! Nothing else, of course. Lady Greenwell knew, as well as if she had been told, that Betty Creswick would send the two in together. Suppose she spoke to Betty Creswick, and asked her not to join the tacit conspiracy that prevails in well-regulated, pleasure-loving society, to give the woman, whenever it is possible, to the man she is supposed to want? Never! She would die sooner! For Society would resent such an anti-social proposal and protect its own joys and convenience.

It must go on although it was making her miserable. Would this wretched season never come to an end? Not that she need expect to find any intermission of her troubles even then! For there would come visits, "country-housing" up and down the length and breadth of England and Scotland, the three would be asked constantly to meet each other. She had been so nice to Cynthia, that people all thought that Lady Greenwell had accepted it. There would be no rest for her till the late autumn, when Sir Hilary had agreed to go with a party of men on an expedition to locate a continent somewhere. He would be away for four months.

As a loving wife she ought to have dreaded this approaching separation; she was shocked to realise that in her heart of hearts, she was looking forward to it. She would not see the light of his countenance, but then, neither would the other! Jealousy makes sad dogs-in-the-manger of us all. And she would have the delight of his frequent letters. That is, unless he wrote to Cynthia too?

If only she had had a child! Cynthia had one, Cynthia, a widow, with no husband now to bind faster to her side therewith! What a pity it all was!

Dinner was announced. Sir Hilary gave Cynthia his arm, with a certain look... proud... protecting... sheepish rather... Yes, she *must* speak.

She placed her hand lightly on the sleeve of she knew not whom, and followed Hilary and Cynthia into the dining-room. She was miserable, she was sure that Hilary, had he but known how unhappy she was making herself, would have tried at once to alter his line of conduct. And he would have failed! Of that, too, she was sure. Man can do nothing in this line, of himself alone, save by the grace of the woman who is leading him astray. It was settled; she must speak to Cynthia!

Cynthia Chenies, who was not lacking in perception, realised at once the meaning of the innocently diplomatic, intensely special glance which Lady Greenwell, placed exactly opposite, fixed upon her, as soon as everybody was seated.

"Mabel Greenwell means to speak to me!"

She could harbour no other thought, from the fish onward. She was a nervous, lazy woman, and the fear of a "woman's row" was intensely repugnant to her. She hated fuss about men, and bad form, and unconventionality of any kind. Her affair with Sir Hilary, whatever it might mean to her, was openly, at least, quite within the bounds of her world's convention, and she deeply resented any attempt on Lady Greenwell's part to draw it out of its limbo of self-chosen vagueness.

To herself, she was willing to admit that she loved Sir Hilary very well, nay, desperately. She was less willing to admit that she suffered over this illicit attachment, and yet did suffer a good deal, for she was a good woman, and Lady Greenwell a healthy woman, so the chances were she would never get him honestly.

She knew Sir Hilary loved her, was fond of Mabel, and respected them both. That being the case, he would not do either of them a wrong for the whole world.

There it was! What an *impasse!* Three scrupulously honourable people caught in a net! No issue but death, and she could not contemplate even Mabel's death with equanimity. Mabel had been very kind to her, and she and Mabel would have been the greatest friends if Sir Hilary had not stood between them.

Though she pitied Mabel for her age, her plainness, she could not help feeling a little angry with Mabel for having presumed to marry Sir Hilary; she should not have allowed Hilary to persuade her that she was a suitable wife for him. Hilary was so plausible. Once, however, having committed the initial error, Mabel should not have hoped to keep him, except by courtesy.

She knew Sir Hilary well enough not to feel obliged to talk to him, so she plodded imperturbably through the menu, eating a good deal to justify her taciturnity. "Oh, I am so hungry," she said once or twice, "I have been down to Brighton to-day to see the boy!"

Sir Hilary never worried. He quietly looked after her, gave her her own way now as ever. She was heedless, he safeguarded her reputation as well as he could. He never wrote to her when he was away; she would have forgotten to destroy his letters. He called on her not too often; he dined with her now and then, generally with his wife. There was no need to compromise her by overt acts of this sort. The mad, bad, sympathetic world was kind enough to cater for the indulgence of their affection; in all the ragôuts of society were they skilfully combined, and discreet opportunities of meeting served up to them daily, with the result that every one was happy and amused, except Lady Greenwell, who had been born and bred in the country and never could acquire London's cynical tone.

Once or twice, however, before this evening, Cynthia had suspected some such strata of unsuspected bourgeois feeling in

Mabel. She almost wished Betty Creswick would not be so kind to Hilary and herself, and a little kinder to Mabel. She sometimes even avoided dull parties where she knew he was going. Not so Sir Hilary, he had no scruples of this kind. He adored her, he told her so—"and as there's nothing wrong about it all, why shouldn't we see as much of each other as people will let us?"

"Ah, but other people—"—an ellipsis for Mabel, whom it pleased her to mention to him as little as possible. But he understood, in his breezy, butterfly way.

"Mabel is all right. Mabel's a good sort, and understands me. She isn't such a fool as to trouble about gossip."

He never said more. It was tacitly assumed between them that Mabel was awfully fond of him and all that, but "demonstrations would simply bore her, you know." Meanwhile, he loved Cynthia with every fibre of his being—all save the domestic ones, it was understood—she was his Egeria, his goddess, his good angel, the woman he thought of last thing at night and the first thing on waking, in the jungle, on the veldt, on the frozen Himalayan slope. He was hers—hers only. No one else cared, not even Mabel, who had "settled down."

Cynthia Chenies hardly realised it, but this passion had come to be her life. She breathed and dressed but for Hilary. She was a cold woman, and content with its platonic manifestations, but she technically regretted the immense waste exemplified in the position of the lover, tied for all his days to two women, neither of whom was or could be everything to him.

She caught Mabel's eye now and again full of timid reticences and prudent punctilios, but expressing over and above all others, the simple emotion that betrayeth itself in speech.

"I must speak, or burst!" the poor woman fancied Mabel saying, and shivered over her chocolate *mousse.*

The moment came. Sir Hilary left soon after dinner to attend an Ethnological Society's meeting, and Lady Greenwell timidly offered to motor Mrs. Chenies home. For some fateful reason or other, that lady's brougham was not forthcoming.

"It is frightfully out of your way, Mabel!" argued the trapped fly.

Gently, but firmly, the spider informed her that a mere difference of a mile and a quarter did not in the least constitute out-of-the-wayness, and the hostess settled it by her vague encouragements.

"So nice of you to chaperon each other like that!"

Mrs. Chenies hardly grasped the significance of Lady Creswick's remark until the knees of Lady Greenwell and herself were safely stowed under the same bearskin rug.

"I wanted to speak to you, Cynthia," began Lady Greenwell honestly, without preface or pretence.

"Did you?" replied the other, shrinking as far away from her companion as she could into the corner of the motor. Then, collecting herself, she said, "You can, you know."

"It is a little difficult for me—but then—I must remember it is for your good, Cynthia."

"Oh, for my good!" exclaimed Mrs. Chenies, stung by the familiar, too familiar exordium. "You must remember I am not a mere girl—I am a widow."

"That is just it," continued Lady Greenwell, delighted. "A young and"—with a gulp—"pretty widow."

"Oh, don't mention it," the other begged her flippantly.

Though her tone grated on and disturbed Lady Greenwell, that lady continued, almost apologetically—

"That is the right way to take it, dear, not seriously! Just a little hint, you know—laugh about it as much as you like when I am done, but listen to me for a minute...! Could you not contrive, dear, to see a little less of Hilary—my husband?"

"I know he's your husband, Mabel, well enough!" Mrs. Chenies jerked out crossly. "And I don't see so much of him as all that!"

"Oh, I know, dear, I know all about your friendship—your intimacy... it's nothing at all, nothing at all... only you see people will talk."

"Yes, bother them!"

"We mustn't pay too much attention to gossip, of course, but we owe it to—ourselves, to take some notice of what is said. You may want to marry again?"

"Never!"

"Oh, don't say that!" pleaded the other pitifully. "You are sure to—so young and pretty. But don't you think, that meantime, that people should couple your name and Hilary's is prejudicial—rather to you? Of course, I know—"

"What?"

"That there is nothing at all serious between you—nothing at all, Hilary"—she blurted out the indecent fact—"Hilary is devoted to me, and always has been, he has never swerved for the fraction of an instant. Besides, he would not—"

"Would not what?"

"Oh, Cynthia, you do make it so difficult! You seem so stony... You aren't offended?"

"No, of course not, I only wanted to know what it was Hilary wouldn't do?"

Her careless use of the beloved's name hurt Lady Greenwell a good deal. She drew herself up—

—"Would not allow himself to make love to another woman during his wife's lifetime. You may as well take that for granted. Only—he is younger than I, and heedless, and you are most attractive, while I am a plain woman, well-dressed. And the world thinks, of course, the usual thing! Oh! Cynthia, help me! And it would not matter, of course, if it were not for you and your reputation, though I can't deny that it makes me very uncomfortable to hear him lightly spoken of."

"What do you want me to do about it?"

"I said what. See less of him. See him only at my house."

"Will you give him your orders, then, not to call at mine?"

"Dear Cynthia, how could I do that? What do you think of me?"

"I think you are like all women—want to get some one else to pull the chestnuts out of the fire for you. Why should I do your dirty work? And it would not do either, I couldn't forbid him my house without creating remark, and doing exactly what you don't want done—getting him talked about. Nor can I go and tell Betty Creswick not to send us in to dinner together—"

"Of course you can't tell her, but there are methods—"

"And I refuse to employ them, and let all the world think I am doing it because I have a guilty conscience or because you have been making a scene. You don't want that surely?"

"No." She shuddered. "Then it has been no use my speaking, practically? And, Cynthia, you can have no idea what it has cost me!"

"I am truly sorry, but, indeed, dear, this sort of carriage lecture never does any good. You can't have straight talks to women. No woman can employ another woman to help keep her husband for her—it really isn't done."

"Keep my husband! But have I not been telling you, Cynthia, all this time, that if I thought for one moment that my husband had been unfaithful to me in word, or thought, or deed, I would not have spoken to anybody at all about it, I would just have died! It is precisely because I do believe in him—"

"Then it makes it quite simple—go on believing in him. You may," replied the other woman, drily, as the carriage stopped at the door of her own house. "Good-night, Mabel! Thank you for the lift."

"And are you cross, Cynthia? Believe me, I meant well."

"You meant well by yourself, eh, dear? Just realise that you were speaking for yourself—"

"Oh, Cynthia, you *are* cruel."

"Yes, but honest. Think it over. Let it all be as if it hadn't been. Shall I kiss you?" She paused, with a light foot on the step.

"Yes, please. You know I am really fond of you, Cynthia, but you seem to have beaten me."

"Oh, no!" asseverated Mrs. Chenies, "only convinced you that these sort of things can't be done."

They kissed.

"I had doubts about the wisdom of it at the time," murmured Lady Greenwell. "I thought you might say it was tactless. Hilary says I have no tact."

"Never mind, you are sure he loves you, and that's better than tact—that's everything!"

Mrs. Chenies was shaking out her skirts on the pavement, pulling out her latch key...

"So that's all right. There's an end of it—"

"Yes, and come to dinner to-morrow night, will you?"

"Yes, dear. Good-night!"

Two hands met and clasped over the window-bar of the carriage. Lady Greenwell watched her friend in, and whirled away. Mrs. Chenies rushed impulsively upstairs to her room, and threw herself on her bed in an agony of weeping. They were tears both for herself and Mabel.

It was a year later. Mrs. Chenies in modified mourning—for she had made herself as black as she dared—rang for admittance at the door of Greenwell House. The very house seemed in mourning. It used to be furnished exotically, with variegated hangings and things Hilary had brought back from abroad. Cynthia shivered. She had been sent for. Why? Why did Mabel Greenwell want to see her? The cords of their friendship had been sensibly loosened. It was perhaps as well. They mourned in their separate corners—of London.

She was ushered into the presence of a little woman whose deep official weeds seemed almost to obliterate her slight frame and make her fade into the surrounding blackness. She rushed at and clung to her handsome visitor, and kissed her mournfully and deliberately on both cheeks.

"Dear, dear Cynthia, how good of you to come to me!"

"Dearest Mabel, how good of you to be willing to see me!"

"Oh, I wanted you—somehow—so much! I believe, when all is said and done, Cynthia, I am fonder of you than I am of any one!"

Mrs. Chenies winced and suffered herself to be kissed again on both cheeks. She looked extremely handsome in her glowing purples and blues. The widow's inexpressive eyes were merely dimmed and bleared by her tears, those of Cynthia Chenies shone, and she was not so silly as to redden the lids by dabbing them with a handkerchief, as Lady Greenwell did.

"He was so fond of you, Cynthia! He has left you to me as a sort of legacy. We often spoke of you." Cynthia started. It had surely been a tacit convention between herself and the dead Hilary, that—

"Yes, I ventured at last to tell him about that talk I had with you once, and he took it just as you did. He laughed at me and said that I had no right to worry you with that sort of thing and that you were perfectly justified in being 'short' with me, as you were, Cynthia, you know. He thought it very nice of you to forgive me and go on seeing us as usual."

"Yes, yes, but I saw very little of him alone after that."

"He went away so soon after, didn't he? That was perhaps a good thing—it gave one time—"

"I don't think you had any need to tell him."

"Oh, my dear, what could it matter? There was such perfect confidence between us, and I preferred that a trifling incident like that should not be allowed to interfere with it. Surely you don't mind?"

"Not now!" replied Cynthia Chenies, with an effort. "And I suppose you had a perfect right to do as you liked about it."

"That's all right then. And Hilary said—dear thing!—when he left me to go on that wretched expedition that killed him, that I was to be as nice to you as I could, and see as much of you as you would allow me to do, and so I have, and so I mean to."

"Don't, don't cry so, dear!"

"Oh, do let me cry—it helps me! And how can I help it, when I think of the dearest husband ever woman had, lost to me, gone—gone—killed, out there alone, among horrid savages... Why, Cynthia, you are crying too!"

"I can't help it either," said the other savagely, disdaining to wipe her tears away.

"Cynthia, you were fond of him, too—now don't say you were not!"

"I was."

Lady Greenwell rose. She looked taller. She looked grim.

"And that is the reason I thought—I made up my mind that you were the proper person to consult about this..."

"This?" asked the other, following the direction of those sad sunken eyes.

"Yes! It was his last wish, Cynthia!" Lady Greenwell pointed to a large bulging packet lying, with a magnificent despatch box, close to her elbow, and continued, in her thin, nervous, passionate voice—

"You know, when he got ill over there—it came on so gradually—he never ceased writing to me till the very last—he got his secretary to send home the MS. of his new book to me. He wanted me to see to the publication of it. I was to edit it, if he never came back to do it himself—and I was to ask you to be co-editress."

"Good God!"

"Oh, don't be frightened, dear, there is nothing to do, it is all done. I did it, only, as he said you were to see it, before it came out, I could not but prepare to carry out his dear wishes. And now I must tell you, as he is gone, I should like to call it *Memorials of a Noble Soul*, something like that, and add some of his letters to me. I have them all here, in this despatch box, I never destroyed a single line of dear darling Hilary's—"

"They will make a most interesting book!" murmured Mrs. Chenies, looking away.

"Yes, won't they, only, of course," Lady Greenwell breathed softly, with a watery smile of triumph, "they will want some editing. They are too intimate, too personal for the ear of the general public. It could not be otherwise. But, still, I don't think the public should lose because he was in love with his wife, do you?"

"No, certainly not."

"There is a great deal in them of purely general interest, of course, but it still wants weeding of lover's phrases and endearments and so on. So I thought the best plan would be for me to read them all aloud to you, and consult you as to what is to be left in, or struck out."

Cynthia Chenies groaned aloud. Lady Greenwell smiled. She had gained confidence.

"Cynthia, dear, how like you! You were always afraid of hard work, and there is nothing—nothing bores you so much as listening. Hilary noticed that. 'These brilliant women!' he used to say."

"Let's have the letters," ejaculated Mrs. Chenies bluffly. She adjusted a cushion or two behind her shoulders. "I have learnt how to listen lately. Let's have tea first."

"Certainly!" Lady Greenwell rang the bell. Tea was brought. The hostess dispensed it. Then, with many a reminiscent pause, and sob and dab of the handkerchief, Lady Greenwell opened the despatch box, and produced letters tied up in blue, Hilary's favourite colour. It was the colour of Cynthia's eyes. She fidgeted in her place, and Lady Greenwell offered her another cushion—"because this will all take time."

"I'll read the first that comes," the widow of Hilary declared, when they had both settled down. "I am not afraid of your knowing, Cynthia, how fond he was of me. This one begins—he generally begins so—*'Dear little woman'*—we can leave that out if you like?"

"You can't. It shows character," observed Mrs. Chenies sombrely. "Go on."

Thus encouraged, Lady Greenwell read, shyly at first, but with gathering confidence, as the map of her husband's affection unrolled itself under her faltering tongue. She read faster. The session was going to last interminably, the letters were good, but long!

"Very vivid! Most interesting!" Mrs. Chenies remarked now and again, drumming with her foot, and with her face turned away.

"It is really rather too intimate!" Lady Greenwell blurted out. "Listen to this—*'Darling, my darling.'* I can scarcely bear to read it. *'All night I lie and toss on my uncomfortable rugs, and think—think of you, darling, and your soft breast!'*"

"You might put 'cheek' there, instead of 'breast,' if you liked?" interposed the co-editress hastily. Lady Greenwell looked up.

"Very well." She used a little pencil at her girdle. Then she resumed—

"*'And I realise how the thought of one sweet woman at home, can be at once the joy and the torture of the traveller. For I don't know if it is most sweet or most bitter, this remembrance of happier hours in altered circumstances. It is joy, but then, sometimes the agony of separation is too keen to be...'* Oh, that he should feel it so! I'll go on, Cynthia, if you don't feel too much bored. *'I stretch out my hands, I look for you, for your warm kind arms—'*"

"You certainly will have to strike all those rhapsodies out," Mrs. Chenies remarked coldly. "He must have been very ill then. Are the letters all like that? If so, they won't make a book of very general interest."

"Ah!" Lady Greenwell exclaimed. She was tossing over the letters feverishly. "They seem to have got mixed! This is one of the English series—written from the Creswicks' place. That must have been sent the summer before he went, for that's the only time he ever went to Betty Creswick's alone. It was the very week I spoke to you, Cynthia."

"I wish you would not keep on bringing that in," interposed Cynthia Chenies irritably, "you were quite right, and I was quite wrong, I see that well enough, now. Go on. We are both dining out to-night, I suppose?"

"Not I," said Lady Greenwell haughtily. "I shall never dine out again." She read on a little to herself. "He didn't like being there without me a bit," she murmured. "In fact, he loathed it."

"Why didn't you go with him, then?" asked Mrs. Chenies, though she knew well enough. She had been one of the Creswick party, and the letter explaining Mabel's reasons for defection had been read aloud to her. But Lady Greenwell couldn't know that.

"Oh, I got a bad chill at the very last moment, and had to wire I couldn't go. Cynthia, shall I read this letter?"

"Of course. It's part of his life, I suppose."

"'*My own little brown bird,*'" read Lady Greenwell softly, "'*I was so grieved to leave you, tucked up in bed, a darkened room and with only a hired nurse to hold your little hot hand. Here I may say I am not enjoying myself a bit, and yet we are a very gay party and everything jolly. But I can't get any fun out of it without you to talk it over with me, after we've gone to bed at four in the morning. Dear little woman, why did you make me go alone? The Creswick ménage is a bit noisy for your quiet sober husband. One gets a little tired of the society of brilliant women—they flash and coruscate—and finally weary. I can't help thinking of a certain still small brown bird at home sitting on the bough, and waiting for me.*' Oh,

Cynthia, I do believe, here is something actually about you—he mentions you by name—"

"I'm the brilliant woman that wearies, am I not? Well, let us hear what he says about me."

"Shall I? I've read them all a hundred times, but I don't quite remember, so if it annoys you, mind, it is your own fault. Here goes! *'The Cynthia of the Minute is really a little overpowering. She seems quite to enjoy saying risque things and compromising herself...'* I really don't think I ought to read this to you, Cynthia?"

"Read it or I shall snatch it out of your hands."

"Well, you are sure you won't mind? *'Poor little Cynthia, she is astonishingly indiscreet, but she means no harm. She is a dear, nice, ordinary simple woman, pretending to be a sad rake, but as good as gold, really—'"*

"As good as gold, really!"

"Well, isn't that nice for him to say that! Poor dear boy, he always did go straight to the heart of the matter, didn't he? He was, as a matter of fact, awfully fond of you, and this just shows it. He knew you through and through—though. What's the matter?"

"Give me some hot water to drink," gasped Mrs. Chenies. "Is—this your revenge, Mabel?"

"Dear Cynthia, aren't you well? You do use such odd stagey words. Revenge! I am your friend and always will be. My husband wanted us to be friends."

"Well, then, do let us keep friends," said Mrs. Chenies, drinking her scalding hot water hastily and rising. "I must go. An early dinner for the theatre... Tommy Vavasor..."

"But what about the letters? I have only read two."

"Of course, you must leave that out about me," said Cynthia, speaking very fast and knotting her fur round her neck as if she wanted to throttle herself, "and all personalities about people still living. And you must not print names. But, as for the rest, I should give the letters in their entirety. Go ahead, that's my advice to you. You can hurt none, and your collaborator gives you *carte blanche*."

She escaped. She preserved no memory of the passage from Lady Greenwell's dull drawing-room to the gaslit street outside. She bitterly resented the dead man's view of her innocent attempts at disillusioning him, on the only occasion they had met previously to his departure and after his wife's lecture, and she would have given her best jewel to discover whether Mabel's quite thorough revenge had been carefully planned or not?

She married young Lord Vavasor within the year, and contrived, without exciting any suspicion, never again to be alone in the same room with the widowed Lady Greenwell again. But she longed as she had never longed for anything else, to hear of Lady Greenwell's remarriage.

THE PRAYER

I

"It is but giving over of a game,
That must be lost."—PHILASTER.

"Come, Mrs. Arne—come, my dear, you must not give way like this! You can't stand it—you really can't! Let Miss Kate take you away—now do!" urged the nurse, with her most motherly of intonations.

"Yes, Alice, Mrs. Joyce is right. Come away—do come away—you are only making yourself ill. It is all over; you can do nothing! Oh, oh, do come away!" implored Mrs. Arne's sister, shivering with excitement and nervousness.

A few moments ago Dr. Graham had relinquished his hold on the pulse of Edward Arne with the hopeless movement of the eyebrows that meant—the end.

The nurse had made the little gesture of resignation that was possibly a matter of form with her. The young sister-in-law had hidden her face in her hands. The wife had screamed a scream that had turned them all hot and cold—and flung herself on the bed over her dead husband. There she lay; her cries were terrible, her sobs shook her whole body.

The three gazed at her pityingly, not knowing what to do next. The nurse, folding her hands, looked towards the doctor for directions, and the doctor drummed with his fingers on the bed-post. The young girl timidly stroked the shoulder that heaved and writhed under her touch.

"Go away! Go away!" her sister reiterated continually, in a voice hoarse with fatigue and passion.

"Leave her alone, Miss Kate," whispered the nurse at last; "she will work it off best herself, perhaps."

She turned down the lamp, as if to draw a veil over the scene. Mrs. Arne raised herself on her elbow, showing a face stained with tears and purple with emotion.

"What! Not gone?" she said harshly. "Go away, Kate, go away! It is my house. I don't want you, I want no one—I want to speak to my husband. Will you go away—all of you. Give me an hour, half-an-hour—five minutes!"

She stretched out her arms imploringly to the doctor.

"Well..." said he, almost to himself.

He signed to the two women to withdraw, and followed them out into the passage. "Go and get something to eat," he said peremptorily, "while you can. We shall have trouble with her presently. I'll wait in the dressing-room."

He glanced at the twisting figure on the bed, shrugged his shoulders, and passed into the adjoining room, without, however, closing the door of communication. Sitting down in an arm-chair drawn up to the fire, he stretched himself and closed his eyes. The professional aspects of the case of Edward Arne rose up before him in all its interesting forms of complication...

It was just this professional attitude that Mrs. Arne unconsciously resented both in the doctor and in the nurse. Through all their kindness she had realised and resented their scientific interest in her husband, for to them he had been no more than a curious and complicated case; and now that the blow had fallen, she regarded them both in the light of executioners. Her one desire, expressed with all the shameless sincerity of blind and thoughtless misery, was to be free of their hateful presence and alone—alone with her dead!

She was weary of the doctor's subdued manly tones—of the nurse's commonplace motherliness, too habitually adapted to the needs of all to be appreciated by the individual—of the childish consolation of the young sister, who had never loved, never been married, did not know what sorrow was! Their expressions of sympathy struck her like blows, the touch of their hands on her body, as they tried to raise her, stung her in every nerve.

With a sigh of relief she buried her head in the pillow, pressed her body more closely against that of her husband, and lay motionless.

Her sobs ceased.

The lamp went out with a gurgle. The fire leaped up, and died. She raised her head and stared about her helplessly, then sinking down again she put her lips to the ear of the dead man.

"Edward—dear Edward!" she whispered, "why have you left me? Darling, why have you left me? I can't stay behind—you know I can't. I am too young to be left. It is only a year since you married me. I never thought it was only for a year. 'Till death us do part!' Yes, I know that's in it, but nobody ever thinks of that! I never thought of living without you! I meant to die with you...

"No—no—I can't die—I must not—till my baby is born. You will never see it. Don't you want to see it? Don't you? Oh, Edward, speak! Say something, darling, one word—one little word! Edward! Edward! are you there? Answer me for God's sake, answer me!

"Darling, I am so tired of waiting. Oh, think, dearest. There is so little time. They only gave me half-an-hour. In half-an-hour they will come and take you away from me—take you where I can't come to you—with all my love I can't come to you! I know the place—I saw it once. A great lonely place full of graves, and little stunted trees dripping with dirty London rain... and gas-lamps flaring all round... but quite, quite dark where the grave is... a long grey stone just like the rest. How could you stay there?—all alone—all alone—without me?

"Do you remember, Edward, what we once said—that whichever of us died first should come back to watch over the other, in the spirit? I promised you, and you promised me. What children we were! Death is not what we thought. It comforted us to say that then.

"Now, it's nothing—nothing—worse than nothing! I don't want your spirit—I can't see it—or feel it—I want you, you, your eyes that looked at me, your mouth that kissed me—"

She raised his arms and clasped them round her neck, and lay there very still, murmuring, "Oh, hold me, hold me! Love me if you can. Am I hateful? This is me! These are your arms..."

The doctor in the next room moved in his chair. The noise awoke her from her dream of contentment, and she unwound the dead arm from her neck, and, holding it up by the wrist, considered it ruefully.

"Yes, I can put it round me, but I have to hold it there. It is quite cold—it doesn't care. Ah, my dear, you don't care! You are dead. I kiss you, but you don't kiss me. Edward! Edward! Oh, for heaven's sake kiss me once. Just once!

"No, no, that won't do—that's not enough! that's nothing! worse than nothing! I want you back, you, all you... What shall I do?... I often pray... Oh, if there be a God in heaven, and if He ever answered a prayer, let Him answer mine—my only prayer. I'll never ask another—and give you back to me! As you were—as I loved you—as I adored you! He must listen. He must! My God, my God, he's mine—he's my husband, he's my lover—give him back to me!"

—"Left alone for half-an-hour or more with the corpse! It's not right!"

The muttered expression of the nurse's revolted sense of professional decency came from the head of the staircase, where she had been waiting for the last few minutes. The doctor joined her.

"Hush, Mrs. Joyce! I'll go to her now."

The door creaked on its hinges as he gently pushed it open and went in.

"What's that? What's that?" screamed Mrs. Arne. "Doctor! Doctor! Don't touch me! Either I am dead or he is alive!"

"Do you want to kill yourself, Mrs. Arne?" said Dr. Graham, with calculated sternness, coming forward; "come away!"

"Not dead! Not dead!" she murmured.

"He is dead, I assure you. Dead and cold an hour ago! Feel!" He took hold of her, as she lay face downwards, and in so doing he touched the dead man's cheek—it was not cold! Instinctively his finger sought a pulse.

"Stop! Wait!" he cried in his intense excitement. "My dear Mrs. Arne, control yourself!"

But Mrs. Arne had fainted, and fallen heavily off the bed on the other side. Her sister, hastily summoned, attended to her, while the man they had all given over for dead was, with faint gasps and sighs and reluctant moans, pulled, as it were, hustled and dragged back over the threshold of life.

II

"Why do you always wear black, Alice?" asked Esther Graham. "You are not in mourning that I know of."

She was Dr. Graham's only daughter and Mrs. Arne's only friend. She sat with Mrs. Arne in the dreary drawing-room of the house in Chelsea. She had come to tea. She was the only person who ever did come to tea there.

She was brusque, kind, and blunt, and had a talent for making inappropriate remarks. Six years ago Mrs. Arne had been a widow for an hour! Her husband had succumbed to an apparently mortal illness, and for the space of an hour had lain dead. When suddenly and inexplicably he had revived from his trance, the shock, combined with six weeks' nursing, had nearly killed his wife. All this Esther had heard from her father. She herself had only come to know Mrs. Arne after her child was born, and all the tragic circumstances of her husband's illness put aside, and it was hoped forgotten. And when her idle question received no answer from the pale absent woman who sat opposite, with listless lack-lustre eyes fixed on the green and blue flames dancing in the fire, she hoped it had passed unnoticed. She waited for five minutes for Mrs. Arne to resume the conversation; then her natural impatience got the better of her.

"Do say something, Alice!" she implored.

"Esther, I beg your pardon!" said Mrs. Arne. "I was thinking."

"What were you thinking of?"

"I don't know."

"No, of course you don't. People who sit and stare into the fire never do think, really. They are only brooding and making themselves ill, and that is what you are doing. You mope, you take no interest in anything, you never go out—I am sure you have not been out of doors to-day?"

"No—yes—I believe not. It is so cold."

"You are sure to feel the cold if you sit in the house all day, and sure to get ill! Just look at yourself!"

Mrs. Arne rose and looked at herself in the Italian mirror over the chimney-piece. It reflected faithfully enough her even pallor, her dark hair and eyes, the sweeping length of her eyelashes, the sharp curves of her nostrils, and the delicate arch of her eyebrows, that formed a thin sharp black line, so clear as to seem almost unnatural.

"Yes, I do look ill," she said with conviction.

"No wonder. You choose to bury yourself alive."

"Sometimes I do feel as if I lived in a grave. I look up at the ceiling and fancy it is my coffin-lid."

"Don't please talk like that!" expostulated Miss Graham, pointing to Mrs. Arne's little girl. "If only for Dolly's sake, I think you should not give way to such morbid fancies. It isn't good for her to see you like this always."

"Oh, Esther," the other exclaimed, stung into something like vivacity, "don't reproach me! I hope I am a good mother to my child!"

"Yes, dear, you are a model mother—and model wife too. Father says the way you look after your husband is something wonderful, but don't you think for your own sake you might try to be a little gayer? You encourage these moods, don't you? What is it? Is it the house?"

She glanced around her—at the high ceiling, at the heavy damask portieres, the tall cabinets of china, the dim oak panelling—it reminded her of a neglected museum. Her eye travelled into the farthest corners, where the faint filmy dusk was already gathering, lit only by the bewildering cross-lights of the glass panels of cabinet doors—to the tall narrow windows—then back again to the woman in her mourning dress, cowering by the fire. She said sharply—

"You should go out more."

"I do not like to—leave my husband."

"Oh, I know that he is delicate and all that, but still, does he never permit you to leave him? Does he never go out by himself?"

"Not often!"

"And you have no pets! It is very odd of you. I simply can't imagine a house without animals!"

"We did have a dog once," answered Mrs. Arne plaintively, "but it howled so we had to give it away. It would not go near Edward... But please don't imagine that I am dull! I have my child." She laid her hand on the flaxen head at her knee.

Miss Graham rose, frowning.

"Ah, you are too bad!" she exclaimed. "You are like a widow exactly, with one child, stroking its orphan head and saying, 'Poor fatherless darling.'"

Voices were heard outside. Miss Graham stopped talking quite suddenly, and sought her veil and gloves on the mantelpiece.

"You need not go, Esther," said Mrs. Arne. "It is only my husband."

"Oh, but it is getting late," said the other, crumpling up her gloves in her muff, and shuffling her feet nervously.

"Come!" said her hostess, with a bitter smile, "put your gloves on properly—if you must go—but it is quite early still."

"Please don't go, Miss Graham," put in the child.

"I must. Go and meet your papa, like a good girl."

"I don't want to."

"You mustn't talk like that, Dolly," said the doctor's daughter absently, still looking towards the door. Mrs. Arne rose and fastened the clasps of the big fur-cloak for her friend. The wife's white, sad, oppressed face came very close to the girl's cheerful one, as she murmured in a low voice—

"You don't like my husband, Esther? I can't help noticing it. Why don't you?"

"Nonsense!" retorted the other, with the emphasis of one who is repelling an overtrue accusation. "I do, only—"

"Only what?"

"Well, dear, it is foolish of me, of course, but I am—a little afraid of him."

"Afraid of Edward!" said his wife slowly. "Why should you be?"

"Well, dear—you see—I—I suppose women can't help being a little afraid of their friends' husbands—they can spoil their friendships with their wives in a moment, if they choose to disapprove of them. I really must go! Good-bye, child; give me a kiss! Don't ring, Alice. Please don't! I can open the door for myself—"

"Why should you?" said Mrs. Arne. "Edward is in the hall; I heard him speaking to Foster."

"No; he has gone into his study. Good-bye, you apathetic creature!" She gave Mrs. Arne a brief kiss and dashed out of the room. The voices outside had ceased, and she had reasonable hopes of reaching the door without being intercepted by Mrs. Arne's husband. But he met her on the stairs. Mrs. Arne, listening intently from her seat by the fire, heard her exchange a few shy sentences with him, the sound of which died away as they went downstairs together. A few moments after, Edward Arne came into the room and dropped into the chair just vacated by his wife's visitor.

He crossed his legs and said nothing. Neither did she.

His nearness had the effect of making the woman look at once several years older. Where she was pale he was well-coloured; the network of little filmy wrinkles that, on a close inspection, covered her face, had no parallel on his smooth skin. He was handsome; soft, well-groomed flakes of auburn hair lay over his forehead, and his steely blue eyes shone equably, a contrast to the sombre fire of hers, and the masses of dark crinkly hair that shaded her brow. The deep lines of permanent discontent furrowed that brow as she sat with her chin propped on her hands, and her elbows resting on her knees. Neither spoke. When the hands of the clock over Mrs. Arne's head pointed to seven, the white-aproned figure of the nurse appeared in the doorway, and the little girl rose and kissed her mother very tenderly.

Mrs. Arne's forehead contracted. Looking uneasily at her husband, she said to the child tentatively, yet boldly, as one grasps a nettle, "Say good-night to your father!"

The child obeyed, saying, "Good-night" indifferently in her father's direction.

"Kiss him!"

"No, please—please not."

Her mother looked down on her curiously, sadly...

"You are a naughty, spoilt child!" she said, but without conviction. "Excuse her, Edward."

He did not seem to have heard.

"Well, if you don't care—" said his wife bitterly.

"Come, child!" She caught the little girl by the hand and left the room.

At the door she half turned and looked fixedly at her husband. It was a strange ambiguous gaze; in it passion and dislike were strangely combined. Then she shivered and closed the door softly after her.

The man in the arm-chair sat with no perceptible change of attitude, his unspeculative eyes fixed on the fire, his hands clasped idly in front of him. The pose was obviously habitual. The servant brought lights and closed the shutters, drew the curtains, and made up the fire noisily, without, however, eliciting any reproof from his master.

Edward Arne was an ideal master, as far as Foster was concerned. He kept cases of cigars, but never smoked them, although the supply had often to be renewed. He did not care what he ate or drank, although he kept as good a cellar as most gentlemen—Foster knew that. He never interfered, he counted for nothing, he gave no trouble. Foster had no intention of ever leaving such an easy place. True, his master was not cordial; he very seldom addressed him or seemed to know whether he was there, but then neither did he grumble if the fire in the study was allowed to go out, or interfere with Foster's liberty in any way. He had a better place of it than Annette, Mrs. Arne's maid, who would be called up in the middle of the night to bathe her mistress's forehead with eau-de-Cologne, or made to brush her long hair for hours together to soothe her. Naturally enough Foster and Annette compared notes as to their respective situations, and drew unflattering parallels between this capricious wife and model husband.

III

Miss Graham was not a demonstrative woman. On her return home she somewhat startled her father, as he sat by his study table, deeply interested in his diagnosis book, by the sudden violence of her embrace.

"Why this excitement?" he asked, smiling and turning round. He was a young-looking man for his age; his thin wiry figure and clear colour belied the evidence on his hair, tinged with grey, and the tired wrinkles that gave value to the acuteness and brilliancy of the eyes they surrounded.

"I don't know!" she replied, "only you are so nice and alive somehow. I always feel like this when I come back from seeing the Arnes."

"Then don't go to see the Arnes."

"I'm so fond of her, father, and she will never come here to me, as you know. Or else nothing would induce me to enter her tomb of a house, and talk to that walking funeral of a husband of hers. I managed to get away to-day without having to shake hands with him. I always try to avoid it. But, father, I do wish you would go and see Alice."

"Is she ill?"

"Well, not exactly ill, I suppose, but her eyes make me quite uncomfortable, and she says such odd things! I don't know if it is you or the clergyman she wants, but she is all wrong somehow! She never goes out except to church; she never pays a call, or has any one to call on her! Nobody ever asks the Arnes to dinner, and I'm sure I don't blame them—the sight of that man at one's table would spoil any party—and they never entertain. She is always alone. Day after day I go in and find her sitting over the fire, with that same brooding expression. I shouldn't be surprised in the least if she were to go mad some day. Father, what is it? What is the tragedy of the house? There is one I am convinced. And yet, though I have been the intimate friend of that woman for years, I know no more about her than the man in the street."

"She keeps her skeleton safe in the cupboard," said Dr. Graham. "I respect her for that. And please don't talk nonsense about tragedies. Alice Arne is only morbid—the malady of the age. And she is a very religious woman."

"I wonder if she complains of her odious husband to Mr. Bligh. She is always going to his services."

"Odious?"

"Yes, odious!" Miss Graham shuddered. "I cannot stand him! I cannot bear the touch of his cold froggy hands, and the sight of his fishy eyes! That inane smile of his simply makes me shrivel up. Father, honestly, do you like him yourself?"

"My dear, I hardly know him! It is his wife I have known ever since she was a child, and I a boy at college. Her father was my tutor. I never knew her husband till six years ago, when she called me in to attend him in a very serious illness. I suppose she never speaks of it? No? A very odd affair. For the life of me I cannot tell how he managed to recover. You needn't tell people, for it affects my reputation, but I didn't save him! Indeed I have never been able to account for it. The man was given over for dead!"

"He might as well be dead for all the good he is," said Esther scornfully. "I have never heard him say more than a couple of sentences in my life."

"Yet he was an exceedingly brilliant young man; one of the best men of his year at Oxford—a good deal run after—poor Alice was wild to marry him!"

"In love with that spiritless creature? He is like a house with some one dead in it, and all the blinds down!"

"Come, Esther, don't be morbid—not to say silly! You are very hard on the poor man! What's wrong with him? He is the ordinary, commonplace, cold-blooded specimen of humanity, a little stupid, a little selfish,—people who have gone through a serious illness like that are apt to be—but on the whole, a good husband, a good father, a good citizen—"

"Yes, and his wife is afraid of him, and his child hates him!" exclaimed Esther.

"Nonsense!" said Dr. Graham sharply. "The child is spoilt. Only children are apt to be—and the mother wants a change or a tonic of some kind. I'll go and talk to her when I have time. Go along and dress. Have you forgotten that George Graham is coming to dinner?"

After she had gone the doctor made a note on the corner of his blotting-pad, "Mem.: to go and see Mrs. Arne," and dismissed the subject of the memorandum entirely from his mind.

George Graham was the doctor's nephew, a tall, weedy, cumbrous young man, full of fads and fallacies, with a gentle manner that somehow inspired confidence. He was several years younger than Esther, who loved to listen to his semi-scientific, semi-romantic stories of things met with in the course of his profession. "Oh, I come across very queer things!" he would say mysteriously. "There's a queer little widow—!"

"Tell me about your little widow?" asked Esther that day after dinner, when, her father having gone back to his study, she and her cousin sat together as usual.

He laughed.

"You like to hear of my professional experiences? Well, she certainly interested me," he said thoughtfully. "She is an odd psychological study in her way. I wish I could come across her again."

"Where did you come across her, and what is her name?"

"I don't know her name, I don't want to; she is not a personage to me, only a case. I hardly know her face even. I have never seen it except in the twilight. But I gathered that she lived somewhere in Chelsea, for she came out on to the Embankment with only a kind of lacy thing over her head; she can't live far off, I fancy."

Esther became instantly attentive. "Go on," she said.

"It was three weeks ago," said George Graham. "I was coming along the Embankment about ten o'clock. I walked through that little grove, you know, just between Cheyne Walk and the river, and I heard in there some one sobbing very bitterly. I looked and saw a woman sitting on a seat, with her head in her hands, crying. I was most awfully sorry, of course, and I thought I could perhaps do something for her, get her a glass of water, or salts, or something. I took her for a woman of the people—it was quite dark, you know. So I asked her very politely if I could do anything for her, and then I noticed her hands—they were quite white and covered with diamonds."

"You were sorry you spoke, I suppose," said Esther.

"She raised her head and said—I believe she laughed—'Are you going to tell me to move on?'"

"She thought you were a policeman?"

"Probably—if she thought at all—but she was in a semi-dazed condition. I told her to wait till I came back, and dashed round the corner to the chemist's and bought a bottle of salts. She thanked me, and made a little effort to rise and go away. She seemed very weak. I told her I was a medical man, I started in and talked to her."

"And she to you?"

"Yes, quite straight. Don't you know that women always treat a doctor as if he were one step removed from their father confessor—not human—not in the same category as themselves? It is not complimentary to one as a man, but one hears a good deal one would not otherwise hear. She ended by telling me all about herself—in a veiled way, of course. It soothed her—relieved her—she seemed not to have had an outlet for years!"

"To a mere stranger!"

"To a doctor. And she did not know what she was saying half the time. She was hysterical, of course. Heavens! what nonsense she talked! She spoke of herself as a person somehow haunted, cursed by some malign fate, a victim of some fearful spiritual catastrophe, don't you know? I let her run on. She was convinced of the reality of a sort of 'doom' that she had fancied had befallen her. It was quite pathetic. Then it got rather chilly—she shivered—I suggested her going in. She shrank back; she said, 'If you only knew what a relief it is, how much less miserable I am out here! I can breathe; I can live—it is my only glimpse of the world that is alive—I live in a grave—oh, let me stay!' She seemed positively afraid to go home."

"Perhaps some one bullied her at home."

"I suppose so, but then—she had no husband. He died, she told me, years ago. She had adored him, she said—"

"Is she pretty?"

"Pretty! Well, I hardly noticed. Let me see! Oh, yes, I suppose she was pretty—no, now I think of it, she would be too worn and faded to be what you call pretty."

Esther smiled.

"Well, we sat there together for quite an hour, then the clock of Chelsea church struck eleven, and she got up and said

'Good-bye,' holding out her hand quite naturally, as if our meeting and conversation had been nothing out of the common. There was a sound like a dead leaf trailing across the walk and she was gone."

"Didn't you ask if you should see her again?"

"That would have been a mean advantage to take."

"You might have offered to see her home."

"I saw she did not mean me to."

"She was a lady, you say," pondered Esther. "How was she dressed?"

"Oh, all right, like a lady—in black—mourning, I suppose. She has dark crinkly hair, and her eyebrows are very thin and arched—I noticed that in the dusk."

"Does this photograph remind you of her?" asked Esther suddenly, taking him to the mantelpiece.

"Rather!"

"Alice! Oh, it couldn't be—she is not a widow, her husband is alive—has your friend any children?"

"Yes, one, she mentioned it."

"How old?"

"Six years old, I think she said. She talks of the 'responsibility of bringing up an orphan.'"

"George, what time is it?" Esther asked suddenly.

"About nine o'clock."

"Would you mind coming out with me?"

"I should like it. Where shall we go?"

"To St. Adhelm's! It is close by here. There is a special late service to-night, and Mrs. Arne is sure to be there."

"Oh, Esther—curiosity!"

"No, not mere curiosity. Don't you see if it is my Mrs. Arne who talked to you like this, it is very serious? I have thought her ill for a long time; but as ill as that!—"

At St. Adhelm's Church, Esther Graham pointed out a woman who was kneeling beside a pillar in an attitude of intense devotion and abandonment. She rose from her knees, and turned her rapt face up towards the pulpit whence the Reverend Ralph Bligh was holding his impassioned discourse. George Graham touched his cousin on the shoulder, and motioned to her to leave her place on the outermost rank of worshippers.

"That is the woman!" said he.

IV

"Mem.: to go and see Mrs. Arne." The doctor came across this note in his blotting-pad one day six weeks later. His daughter was out of town. He had heard nothing of the Arnes since her departure. He had promised to go and see her. He was a little conscience-stricken. Yet another week elapsed before he found time to call upon the daughter of his old tutor.

At the corner of Tite Street he met Mrs. Arne's husband, and stopped. A doctor's professional kindliness of manner is, or ought to be, independent of his personal likings and dislikings, and there was a pleasant cordiality about his greeting which should have provoked a corresponding fervour on the part of Edward Arne.

"How are you, Arne?" Graham said. "I was on my way to call on your wife."

"Ah—yes!" said Edward Arne, with the ascending inflection of polite acquiescence. A ray of blue from his eyes, rested transitorily on the doctor's face, and in that short moment the latter noted its intolerable vacuity, and for the first time in his life felt a sharp pang of sympathy for the wife of such a husband.

"I suppose you are off to your club?—er—good-bye!" he wound up abruptly. With the best will in the world he somehow found it almost impossible to carry on a conversation with Edward Arne, who raised his hand to his hat-brim in token of salutation, smiled sweetly, and walked on.

"He really is extraordinarily good-looking," reflected the doctor, as he watched him down the street and safely over the crossing with a certain degree of solicitude for which he could not exactly account. "And yet one feels one's vitality ebbing out at the finger-ends as one talks to him. I shall begin to believe in Esther's absurd fancies about him soon. Ah, there's the little girl!" he exclaimed, as he turned into Cheyne Walk and caught sight of her with her nurse, making violent demonstrations to attract his attention. "She is alive, at any rate. How is your mother, Dolly?" he asked.

"Quite well, thank you," was the child's reply. She added, "She's crying. She sent me away because I looked at her. So I did. Her cheeks are quite red."

"Run away—run away and play!" said the doctor nervously. He ascended the steps of the house, and rang the bell very gently and neatly.

"Not at—" began Foster, with the intonation of polite falsehood, but stopped on seeing the doctor, who, with his daughter, was a privileged person. "Mrs. Arne will see you, Sir."

"Mrs. Arne is not alone?" he said interrogatively.

"Yes, Sir, quite alone. I have just taken tea in."

Dr. Graham's doubts were prompted by the low murmur as of a voice, or voices, which came to him through the open door of the room at the head of the stairs. He paused and listened while Foster stood by, merely remarking, "Mrs. Arne do talk to herself sometimes, Sir."

It was Mrs. Arne's voice—the doctor recognised it now. It was not the voice of a sane or healthy woman. He at once mentally removed his visit from the category of a morning call, and prepared for a semi-professional inquiry.

"Don't announce me," he said to Foster, and quietly entered the back drawing-room, which was separated by a heavy tapestry portiere from the room where Mrs. Arne sat, with an open book on the table before her, from which she had been apparently reading aloud. Her hands were now clasped tightly over her face, and when, presently, she removed them and began feverishly to turn page after page of her book, the crimson of her cheeks was seamed with white where her fingers had impressed themselves.

The doctor wondered if she saw him, for though her eyes were fixed in his direction, there was no apprehension in them. She went on reading, and it was the text, mingled with passionate interjection and fragmentary utterances, of the Burial Service that met his ears.

"'For as in Adam all die!' All die! It says all! For he must reign... The last enemy that shall be destroyed is Death. What shall they do if the dead rise not at all!... I die daily...! Daily! No, no, better get it over... dead and buried... out of sight, out of mind... under a stone. Dead men don't come back... Go on! Get it over. I want to hear the earth rattle on the coffin, and then I shall know it is done. 'Flesh and blood cannot inherit!' Oh, what did I do? What have I done?

Why did I wish it so fervently? Why did I pray for it so earnestly? God gave me my wish—"

"Alice! Alice!" groaned the doctor.

She looked up. "'When this corruptible shall have put on incorruption—' 'Dust to dust, ashes to ashes, earth to earth—' Yes, that is it. 'After death, though worms destroy this body—'"

She flung the book aside and sobbed.

"That is what I was afraid of. My God! My God! Down there—in the dark—for ever and ever and ever! I could not bear to think of it! My Edward! And so I interfered... and prayed... and prayed till... Oh! I am punished. Flesh and blood could not inherit! I kept him there—I would not let him go... I kept him... I prayed... I denied him Christian burial... Oh, how could I know..."

"Good heavens, Alice!" said Graham, coming sensibly forward, "what does this mean? I have heard of schoolgirls going through the marriage service by themselves, but the burial service—"

He laid down his hat and went on severely, "What have you to do with such things? Your child is flourishing—your husband alive and here—"

"And who kept him here?" interrupted Alice Arne fiercely, accepting the fact of his appearance without comment.

"You did," he answered quickly, "with your care and tenderness. I believe the warmth of your body, as you lay beside him for that half-hour, maintained the vital heat during that extraordinary suspension of the heart's action, which made us all give him up for dead. You were his best doctor, and brought him back to us."

"Yes, it was I—it was I—you need not tell me it was I!"

"Come, be thankful!" he said cheerfully. "Put that book away, and give me some tea, I'm very cold."

"Oh, Dr. Graham, how thoughtless of me!" said Mrs. Arne, rallying at the slight imputation on her politeness he had purposely made. She tottered to the bell and rang it before he could anticipate her.

"Another cup," she said quite calmly to Foster, who answered it. Then she sat down quivering all over with the suddenness of the constraint put upon her.

"Yes, sit down and tell me all about it," said Dr. Graham good-humouredly, at the same time observing her with the closeness he gave to difficult cases.

"There is nothing to tell," she said simply, shaking her head, and futilely altering the position of the tea-cups on the tray. "It all happened years ago. Nothing can be done now. Will you have sugar?"

He drank his tea and made conversation. He talked to her of some Dante lectures she was attending; of some details connected with her child's Kindergarten classes. These subjects did not interest her. There was a subject she wished to discuss, he could see that a question trembled on her tongue, and tried to lead up to it.

She introduced it herself, quite quietly, over a second cup. "Sugar, Dr. Graham? I forget. Dr. Graham, tell me, do you believe that prayers—wicked unreasonable prayers—are granted?"

He helped himself to another slice of bread and butter before answering.

"Well," he said slowly, "it seems hard to believe that every fool who has a voice to pray with, and a brain where to conceive idiotic requests with, should be permitted to interfere with the economy of the universe. As a rule, if people were long-sighted enough to see the result of their petitions, I fancy very few of us would venture to interfere."

Mrs. Arne groaned.

She was a good Churchwoman, Graham knew, and he did not wish to sap her faith in any way, so he said no more, but inwardly wondered if a too rigid interpretation of some of the religious dogmas of the Vicar of St. Adhelm's, her spiritual adviser, was not the clue to her distress. Then she put another question—

"Eh! What?" he said. "Do I believe in ghosts? I will believe you if you will tell me you have seen one."

"You know, Doctor," she went on, "I was always afraid of ghosts—of spirits—things unseen. I couldn't ever read about them. I could not bear the idea of some one in the room with me that I could not see. There was a text that always frightened me that hung up in my room: 'Thou, God, seest me!' It frightened me when I was a child, whether I had been doing wrong or not. But now," shuddering, "I think there are worse things than ghosts."

"Well, now, what sort of things?" he asked good-humouredly. "Astral bodies—?"

She leaned forward and laid her hot hand on his.

"Oh, Doctor, tell me, if a spirit—without the body we know it by—is terrible, what of a body"—her voice sank to a whisper, "a body—senseless—lonely—stranded on this earth—without a spirit?"

She was watching his face anxiously. He was divided between a morbid inclination to laugh and the feeling of intense discomfort provoked by this wretched scene. He longed to give the conversation a more cheerful turn, yet did not wish to offend her by changing it too abruptly.

"I have heard of people not being able to keep body and soul together," he replied at last, "but I am not aware that practically such a division of forces has ever been achieved. And if we could only accept the theory of the de-spiritualised body, what a number of antipathetic people now wandering about in the world it would account for!"

The piteous gaze of her eyes seemed to seek to ward off the blow of his misplaced jocularity. He left his seat and sat down on the couch beside her.

"Poor child! poor girl! you are ill, you are overexcited. What is it? Tell me," he asked her as tenderly as the father she had lost in early life might have done. Her head sank on his shoulder.

"Are you unhappy?" he asked her gently.

"Yes!"

"You are too much alone. Get your mother or your sister to come and stay with you."

"They won't come," she wailed. "They say the house is like a grave. Edward has made himself a study in the basement. It's an impossible room—but he has moved all his things in, and I can't—I won't go to him there..."

"You're wrong. For it's only a fad," said Graham, "he'll tire of it. And you must see more people somehow. It's a pity my daughter is away. Had you any visitors to-day?"

"Not a soul has crossed the threshold for eighteen days."

"We must change all that," said the doctor vaguely. "Meantime you must cheer up. Why, you have no need to think of ghosts and graves—no need to be melancholy—you have your husband and your child—"

"I have my child—yes."

The doctor took hold of Mrs. Arne by the shoulder, and held her a little away from him. He thought he had found the cause of her trouble—a more commonplace one than he had supposed.

"I have known you, Alice, since you were a child," he said gravely. "Answer me! You love your husband, don't you?"

"Yes." It was as if she were answering futile prefatory questions in the witness-box. Yet he saw by the intense excitement in her eyes that he had come to the point she feared, and yet desired to bring forward.

"And he loves you?"

She was silent.

"Well, then, if you love each other, what more can you want? Why do you say you have only your child in that absurd way?"

She was still silent, and he gave her a little shake.

"Tell me, have you and he had any difference lately? Is there any—coldness—any—temporary estrangement between you?"

He was hardly prepared for the burst of foolish laughter that proceeded from the demure Mrs. Arne as she rose and confronted him, all the blood in her body seeming for the moment to rush to her usually pale cheeks.

"Coldness! Temporary estrangement! If that were all! Oh, is every one blind but me? There is all the world between us!—all the difference between this world and the next!"

She sat down again beside the doctor and whispered in his ear, and her words were like a breath of hot wind from some Gehenna of the soul.

"Oh, Doctor, I have borne it for six years, and I must speak. No other woman could bear what I have borne, and yet be alive! And I loved him so; you don't know how I loved him! That was it—that was my crime—"

"Crime?" repeated the doctor.

"Yes, crime! It was impious, don't you see? But I have been punished. Oh, Doctor, you don't know what my life is! Listen! Listen! I must tell you. To live with a— At first before I guessed when I used to put my arms round him, and he merely submitted—and then it dawned on me what I was kissing! It is enough to turn a living woman into stone—for I am living, though sometimes I forget it. Yes, I am a live woman, though I live in a grave. Think what it is!—to wonder every night if you will be alive in the morning, to lie down every night in an open grave—to smell death in every corner—every room—to breathe death—to touch it..."

The portiere in front of the door shook, a hoopstick parted it, a round white clad bundle supported on a pair of mottled red legs peeped in, pushing a hoop in front of her. The child made no noise. Mrs. Arne seemed to have heard her, however. She slewed round violently as she sat on the sofa beside Dr. Graham, leaving her hot hands clasped in his.

"You ask Dolly," she exclaimed. "She knows it, too—she feels it."

"No, no, Alice, this won't do!" the doctor adjured her very low. Then he raised his voice and ordered the child from the room. He had managed to lift Mrs. Arne's feet and laid her full length on the sofa by the time the maid reappeared. She had fainted.

He pulled down her eyelids and satisfied himself as to certain facts he had up till now dimly apprehended. When Mrs. Arne's maid returned, he gave her mistress over to her care and proceeded to Edward Arne's new study in the basement.

"Morphia!" he muttered to himself, as he stumbled and faltered through gaslit passages, where furtive servants eyed him and scuttled to their burrows.

"What is he burying himself down here for?" he thought. "Is it to get out of her way? They *are* a nervous pair of them!"

*

Arne was sunk in a large arm-chair drawn up before the fire. There was no other light, except a faint reflection from the gas-lamp in the road, striking down past the iron bars of the window that was sunk below the level of the street. The room was comfortless and empty, there was little furniture in it except a large bookcase at Arne's right hand and a table with a Tantalus on it standing some way off. There was a faded portrait in pastel of Alice Arne over the mantelpiece, and beside it, a poor pendant, a pen and ink sketch of the master of the house. They were quite discrepant, in size and medium, but they appeared to look at each other with the stolid attentiveness of newly married people.

"Seedy, Arne?" Graham said.

"Rather, to-day. Poke the fire for me, will you?"

"I've known you quite seven years," said the doctor cheerfully, "so I presume I can do that... There, now!... And I'll presume further— What have we got here?"

He took a small bottle smartly out of Edward Arne's fingers and raised his eyebrows. Edward Arne had rendered it up agreeably; he did not seem upset or annoyed.

"Morphia. It isn't a habit. I only got hold of the stuff yesterday—found it about the house. Alice was very jumpy all day, and communicated her nerves to me, I suppose. I've none as a rule, but do you know, Graham, I seem to be getting them—feel things a good deal more than I did, and want to talk about them."

"What, are you growing a soul?" said the doctor carelessly, lighting a cigarette.

"Heaven forbid!" Arne answered equably. "I've done very well without it all these years. But I'm fond of old Alice, you know, in my own way. When I was a young man, I was quite different. I took things hardly and got excited about them. Yes, excited. I was wild about Alice, wild! Yes, by Jove! though she has forgotten all about it."

"Not that, but still it's natural she should long for some little demonstration of affection now and then... and she'd be awfully distressed if she saw you fooling with that bottle of morphia! You know, Arne, after that narrow squeak you had of it five years ago, Alice and I have a good right to consider that your life belongs to us!"

Edward Arne settled in his chair and replied, rather fretfully—

"All very well, but you didn't manage to do the job thoroughly. You didn't turn me out lively enough to please Alice. She's annoyed because when I take her in my arms, I don't hold her tight enough. I'm too quiet, too languid!... Hang it all, Graham, I believe she'd like me to stand for Parliament!... Why can't she let me just go along my own way? Surely a man who's come through an illness like mine can be let off parlour tricks? All this worry—it culminated the other day when I said I wanted to colonise a room down here, and did, with a spurt that took it out of me horribly,—all this worry, I say, seeing her upset and so on, keeps me low, and so I feel as if I wanted to take drugs to soothe me."

"Soothe!" said Graham. "This stuff is more than soothing if you take enough of it. I'll send you something more like what you want, and I'll take this away, by your leave."

"I really can't argue!" replied Arne... "If you see Alice, tell her you find me fairly comfortable and don't put her off this room. I really like it best. She can come and see me here, I keep a good fire, tell her... I feel as if I wanted to sleep..." he added brusquely.

"You have been indulging already," said Graham softly. Arne had begun to doze off. His cushion had sagged down, the doctor stooped to rearrange it, carelessly laying the little phial for the moment in a crease of the rug covering the man's knees.

Mrs. Arne in her mourning dress was crossing the hall as he came to the top of the basement steps and pushed open the swing door. She was giving some orders to Foster, the butler, who disappeared as the doctor advanced.

"You're about again," he said, "good girl!"

"Too silly of me," she said, "to be hysterical! After all these years! One should be able to keep one's own counsel. But it is over now, I promise I will never speak of it again."

"We frightened poor Dolly dreadfully. I had to order her out like a regiment of soldiers."

"Yes, I know. I'm going to her now."

On his suggestion that she should look in on her husband first she looked askance.

"Down there!"

"Yes, that's his fancy. Let him be. He is a good deal depressed about himself and you. He notices a great deal more than you think. He isn't quite as apathetic as you describe him to be... Come here!" He led her into the unlit dining-room a little way. "You expect too much, my dear. You do really! You make too many demands on the vitality you saved."

"What did one save him for?" she asked fiercely. She continued more quietly, "I know. I am going to be different."

"Not you," said Graham fondly. He was very partial to Alice Arne in spite of her silliness. "You'll worry about Edward till the end of the chapter. I know you. And"—he turned her round by the shoulder so that she fronted the light in the hall—"you elusive thing, let me have a good look at you... Hum! Your eyes, they're a bit starey..."

He let her go again with a sigh of impotence. Something must be done... soon... he must think... He got hold of his coat and began to get into it...

Mrs. Arne smiled, buttoned a button for him and then opened the front door, like a good hostess, a very little way. With a quick flirt of his hat he was gone, and she heard the clap of his brougham door and the order "Home."

"Been saying good-bye to that thief Graham?" said her husband gently, when she entered his room, her pale eyes staring a little, her thin hand busy at the front of her dress...

"Thief? Why? One moment! Where's your switch?"

She found it and turned on a blaze of light from which her husband seemed to shrink.

"Well, he carried off my drops. Afraid of my poisoning myself, I suppose?"

"Or acquiring the morphia habit," said his wife in a dull level voice, "as I have."

She paused. He made no comment. Then, picking up the little phial Dr. Graham had left in the crease of the rug, she spoke—

"You are the thief, Edward, as it happens, this is mine."

"Is it? I found it knocking about: I didn't know it was yours. Well, will you give me some?"

"I will, if you like."

"Well, dear, decide. You know I am in your hands and Graham's. He was rubbing that into me to-day."

"Poor lamb!" she said derisively; "I'd not allow my doctor, or my wife either, to dictate to me whether I should put an end to myself, or not."

"Ah, but you've got a spirit, you see!" Arne yawned. "However, let me have a go at the stuff and then you put it on top of a wardrobe or a shelf, where I shall know it is, but never reach out to get it, I promise you."

"No, you wouldn't reach out a hand to keep yourself alive, let alone kill yourself," said she. "That is you all over, Edward."

"And don't you see that is why I did die," he said, with earnestness unexpected by her. "And then, unfortunately, you and Graham bustled up and wouldn't let Nature take its course... I rather wish you hadn't been so officious."

"And let you stay dead," said she carelessly. "But at the time I cared for you so much that I should have had to kill myself, or commit suttee like a Bengali widow. Ah, well!"

She reached out for a glass half-full of water that stood on the low ledge of a bookcase close by the arm of his chair... "Will this glass do? What's in it? Only water? How much morphia shall I give you? An over dose?"

"I don't care if you do, and that's a fact."

"It was a joke, Edward," she said piteously.

"No joke to me. This fag end of life I've clawed hold of, doesn't interest me. And I'm bound to be interested in what I'm doing or I'm no good. I'm no earthly good now. I don't enjoy life, I've nothing to enjoy it with—in here"—he struck his breast. "It's like a dull party one goes to by accident. All I want to do is to get into a cab and go home."

His wife stood over him with the half-full glass in one hand and the little bottle in the other. Her eyes dilated... her chest heaved...

"Edward!" she breathed. "Was it all so useless?"

"Was what useless? Yes, as I was telling you, I go as one in a dream—a bad, bad dream, like the dreams I used to have when I overworked at college. I was brilliant, Alice, brilliant, do you hear? At some cost, I expect! Now I hate people—my fellow creatures. I've left them. They come and go, jostling me, and pushing me, on the pavements as I go along, avoiding them. Do you know where they should be, really, in relation to me?"

He rose a little in his seat—she stepped nervously aside, made as if to put down the bottle and the glass she was holding, then thought better of it and continued to extend them mechanically.

"They should be over my head. I've already left them and their petty nonsense of living. They mean nothing to me, no more than if they were ghosts walking. Or perhaps it's I who am a ghost to them?... You don't understand it. It's because I suppose you have no imagination. You just know what you want and do your best to get it. You blurt out your blessed petition to your Deity and the idea that you're irrelevant never enters your head, soft, persistent, High Church thing that you are!..."

Alice Arne smiled, and balanced the objects she was holding. He motioned her to pour out the liquid from one to the other, but she took no heed; she was listening with all her ears. It was the nearest approach to the language of compliment, to anything in the way of loverlike personalities that she had heard fall from his lips since his illness. He went on, becoming as it were lukewarm to his subject—

"But the worst of it is that once break the cord that links you to humanity—it can't be mended. Man doesn't live by bread alone... or lives to disappoint you. What am I to you, without my own poor personality?... Don't stare so, Alice! I haven't talked so much or so intimately for ages, have I? Let me try and have it out... Are you in any sort of hurry?"

"No, Edward."

"Pour that stuff out and have done... Well, Alice, it's a queer feeling, I tell you. One goes about with one's looks on the ground, like a man who eyes the bed he is going to lie down in, and longs for. Alice, the crust of the earth seems a barrier between me and my own place. I want to scratch the boardings with my nails and shriek something like this: 'Let me get down to you all, there where I belong!' It's a horrible sensation, like a vampire reversed!..."

"Is that why you insisted on having this room in the basement?" she asked breathlessly.

"Yes, I can't bear being upstairs, somehow. Here, with these barred windows and stone-cold floors... I can see the people's feet walking above there in the street... one has some sort of illusion..."

"Oh!" She shivered and her eyes travelled like those of a caged creature round the bare room and fluttered when they rested on the sombre windows imperiously barred. She dropped her gaze to the stone flags that showed beyond the oasis of Turkey carpet on which Arne's chair stood... Then to the door, the door that she had closed on entering. It had heavy bolts, but they were not drawn against her, though by the look of her eyes it seemed she half imagined they were...

She made a step forward and moved her hands slightly. She looked down on them and what they held... then changed the relative positions of the two objects and held the bottle over the glass...

"Yes, come along!" her husband said. "Are you going to be all day giving it me?"

With a jerk, she poured the liquid out into a glass and handed it to him. She looked away—towards the door...

"Ah, your way of escape!" said he, following her eyes. Then he drank, painstakingly.

The empty bottle fell out of her hands. She wrung them, murmuring—

"Oh, if I had only known!"

"Known what? That I should go near to cursing you for bringing me back?"

He fixed his cold eyes on her, as the liquid passed slowly over his tongue...

"—Or that you would end by taking back the gift you gave?"

THE COACH

It was a lonely part of the country, far north, where the summer nights are pale and light and scant of shade. This summer night there was no moon, and yet it was not dark. For hours the flat, deprecating earth had lain prone under a storm of wind and rain. Its patient surface was drenched, blanched, smitten into blindness. The tumbled waters of the Firth splashed on the edges of the plain, their wild commotion dwarfed by the noise of the wind-driven showers, whose gloomy drops tapped the waters into sullen acquiescence. Half a mile inland the road to the north was laid. Clear and straight it ran, with never a house or homestead to break it, viscous with clay here, shining with quartz there, uncompromising, exact, like the lists of old, dressed for a tourney. Its sides were bare, scantily garnished with grass. This was nearly a hedgeless country. In places the undeviating line of it passed through a little coppice or clump of gnarled, ill-conditioned, nameless trees. They seemed to lean forward vindictively on either side, snapping their horny fingers at each other, waving their cantankerous branches as the gusts took them, broke them, and whirled the fragments of their ruin far away and out of ken, like a flapping, unruly kite which a child has allowed to pass beyond his control. The broad white surface of the road was not suffered to be blotted for a single moment. Nothing could rest for the play of the intriguing air-currents, surging backwards and forwards, blind, stupid and swelled with pride, till they had got completely out of hand and defied the archers of the middle sky. They staggered hither and thither like ineffectual giants; they buffeted all impartially; they instigated the hapless branches at their mercy to wild lashings of each other, to useless accesses of the spirit of self-destruction. Bending slavishly under the heavy gusts, each shabby blade of grass by the roadside rose again and was on the *qui vive* after the rustling tyrant had passed.

It was then, in the succeeding moments of comparative peace, when the directors of the passionate aerial revolt had managed to call their panting rabble off for the time, that great perpendicular sheets of rain, like stage films slung evenly from heavenly temples, descended and began moving continuously sideways, like a wall, across the level track. A sheet of whole water, blotting out the tangled borders of herbage that grew sparsely round the heaps of stones with which the margin was set at intervals, placed there ready for breaking. When the slab of rain had moved on again, the broad road, shining out sturdily with its embedded quartz and milky kneaded clay, lay clear once more. Calm, ordered and tranquil in the midst of tumult and discord, it pursued its appointed course, edging off from its evenly bevelled sides the noisy moorland streams, that had come jostling each other in their haste to reach it, only to be relegated, noisily complaining, to the swollen, unrecognisable gutter.

At a certain point on the line of way, a tall, spare, respectable-looking man in a well-fitting grey frock coat stood waiting. The rain ran down the back of his coat collar, and dripped off the rim of his tall hat. His attitude suggested some weary foredone clerk waiting at the corner of the city street for the omnibus that was to carry him home to his slippered comfort and sober pipe of peace. He wore no muffler, but then it was summer—St. John's Eve. He leaned on an ivory-headed ebony stick of which he seemed fond, and peered, not very eagerly, along the road, which now lay in dazzling rain-washed clarity under the struggling moon. There was a lull in the storm. He had no luggage, no umbrella, yet his grey coat looked neat, and his hat shiny.

Far in the distance, from the south, a black clumsy object appeared, labouring slowly along. It was a coach, of heavy and antique pattern. As soon as he had sighted it, the passenger's faint interest seemed diminished. With a bored air of fulfilment, he dropped his eyes and looked down disapprovingly at the clayey mud at his feet, although, indeed, the sticky substance did not appear to have marred the exquisite polish of his shoes. His palm settled composedly on the ivory knob of his trusty stick, as though it were the hand of an old friend.

With all the signs of difficult going, but no noise of straining or grinding, the coach at last drew up in front of the expectant passenger. He looked up quietly, and recognised it as the vehicle wherein it was appointed that he should travel in this unsuitable weather for a stage or two, maybe. All was correct, the coachman, grave, business-like, headless as of usage, the horses long-tailed, black, conventional...

The door opened noiselessly, and the step was let down. The passenger shook his head as he delicately put his foot on to it, and observed for the benefit, doubtless, of the person or persons inside—

"I see old Joe on the box in his official trim. Rather unnecessary, all this ceremony, I venture to think! A few yokels and old women to impress, if indeed, any one not positively obliged is abroad on a night like this! For form's sake, I suppose!"

He took his seat next the window. There were four occupants of the coach beside himself. They all nodded formally, but not unkindly. He returned their salutations with old-fashioned courtesy, though unacquainted seemingly with any of them.

Sitting next to him was a woman evidently of fashion. Her heavy and valuable furs were negligently cast on one side, to show a plastron covered with jewels. She wore at least two enamelled and jewel-encrusted watches pinned to her bosom as a mark for thieves to covet. It was foolish of her. So at least thought the man in the grey frock coat. Her yellow wig was much awry. Her eyes were weak, strained, and fearful, and she aided their vision with a diamond-beset pince-nez. Now and again she glanced over her left shoulder as if in some alarm, and at such times she always grasped her gold-net reticule feverishly. She was obviously a rich woman in the world, a first-class train-de-luxe passenger.

The woman opposite her belonged as unmistakably to the people. She was hard-featured, worn with a life of sordid toil and calculation, but withal stout and motherly, a figure to inspire the fullest confidence. She wore a black bonnet with strings, and black silk gloves heavily darned. Round her sunken white collar, a golden gleam of watch-chain was now and then discernible.

At the other end of the coach, squeezed up into the corner where the vacillating light of the lamp hung from the roof least penetrated, a neat, sharp-featured man nestled and hid. His forehead retreated, and his bowler hat was set unnecessarily far back, lending him an air of folly and congenital weakness which his long, cold, clever nose could not dissipate. He was white as old enamel.

But the man whom the gentleman in the frock coat took to among his casual fellow-travellers was the one sitting directly opposite him, a rough, hearty creature, who alone of all the taciturn coachful seemed disposed to enter into a casual conversation, which might go some way to enliven the dreariness entailed by this somewhat old-fashioned mode of travelling. Gay talk might help to drown the dashing of the waters of the Firth lying close on the right hand of the section of road they were even now traversing, and the ugly roar of the wind and rain against the windows. This—by comparison—cheerful fellow was dressed like a working man, in a shabby suit of corduroys. He wore no collar, but a twisted red cotton handkerchief was wound tightly round his thick squat neck. His little mean eyes, swinish, but twinkling good-humouredly, stared enviously at the neat gentleman's stiff collar and the delicate grey tones of his suiting. Crossing and uncrossing his creasy legs, in the unusual effort of an attempt at conviviality, the man in corduroys addressed the man in the frock coat awkwardly enough, but still civilly.

"Well, mate! They've chosen a rare rough night to shift us on! Orders from headquarters, I suppose? I've been here nigh on a year and never set eyes on my boss!"

"We used to call him God the Father," said the elder man slowly... "But whoever it is that orders our ways here, there is no earthly sense in questioning His arrangements, we can only fall in with them. As you admit, you are fairly new, and perhaps you do not as yet conceive fully of the silent impelling force that sways us. It is the same in the world we have left, only that there we were only concerned with the titles and standing of our 'boss,' as you call Him, and obeyed His laws not a whit. I must say I consider this particular system of soul transference that we have to submit to, very unsettling and productive of restlessness among us—a mere survival and tiresome superstition, to my mind. It has one merit; one sees something of the under world, travelling about as we do, and meeting chance, perhaps kindred spirits on the road. One realises, too, that Hades is not quite as grey, shall I say, as it is painted! But perhaps," he added, with a slight touch of class hauteur, "you do not quite follow me?"

"Oh yes, Master, I do," eagerly replied the fellow-traveller to whom he chose to address his monologue. "Since I've been dead, I have learned the meaning of many things. I turn up my nose at nothing these days. I always neglected my schooling, but now I tell you I try to make up for lost time. From a rough sort of fellow that I was, with not an idea in my head beyond my beer and my prog, I have come to take my part in the whole of knowledge. It was all mine before, so to speak, but I didn't trouble to put my hand out for it. Didn't care, didn't listen to Miss that taught me, or to Parson, either. He had some good ideas too, as I've come to know, though Vice isn't Vice exactly with us here, now, in a manner of speaking. If God Almighty made us, why did He make us, even in parts, bad? That's what I want to know, and I'll know that when I've been dead a bit longer. Why did He give me rotten teeth so that I couldn't chew properly and didn't care for my food and liked drink better? It's dirt and digestion makes drinking and devilry, I say."

The smart woman interrupted him with a kind of languid eagerness, exclaiming—

"I must say I agree with you. Since the pestle fell on my shoulder in that lonely villa at Monte, I have realised what the dreadful gambling fever may lead to. It had made those two who treated me so ill, quite inhumane. They had become wild beasts. I ought never to have accepted their treacherous invitation to luncheon, never tempted them with my outrageous display of jewels! And look here, I was tarred with the same stick, I gambled too—"

She rummaged in her reticule and fished out a ticket for the rooms at Monte Carlo.

"I always call that the ticket for my execution. Though my executioners were rather unnecessarily brutal. They will attain unto this place more easily than I did. Hardly any pain. The hand of the law is gentle, compared with the methods of—"

The man in the grey frock coat raised his finger warningly. "No names, I beg. One of our conventions…!"

"Have a drop?" said the calm motherly woman to the excited fine lady. "Your wound is recent, isn't it? Yours was a very severe case! A bloody murder, I call it, if ever there was one, and clumsy at that! And you only passive, which is always so much harder, they say! I can't tell, for I was what you may call an active party. They don't seem to mind mixing, they that look after us here! They lump us all together—travelling, at any rate! Though when I think of what I was actually turned off for well—the way I look at it, what I did was a positive benefit to Society, and some sections of Society knew it, too, and would have liked to preserve my life."

"But what, Madam, if I may ask, was your little difficulty?"

"It is called, I believe, Baby Farming," she replied offhandedly, receiving her flask back from the smart woman and stowing it away in a capacious pocket. As she spoke, a shudder like a transitory ripple on a rain-swept stream passed over her hearers, with the exception of the thin man in the far corner, who preserved his serenity. Raising his sunken chin, he observed the last speaker with some slight show of interest.

The man in grey apologised.

"Excuse us, Madam. A remnant of old-world squeamishness, uncontrollable by us for the moment. Though perhaps, if you will, you might a little dissipate our preconceived notions of your profession, by explaining clearly your point of view."

"Delighted, I'm sure," she answered. "Funny, though, how seriously you all take it, even here! The feeling against my profession seems absurdly strong below as well as above. I was hooted as I left the court, I recollect. It annoyed me then considerably. I thought that those that hooted had more need to be grateful to me if all was known and paid for. I saved their pockets for them and their lovely honour too. They knew they owed all that to me. For the rest, they did not care. They went on, bless 'em, raising up seed for me to mow down as soon as its head came above ground, and welcome! Sly dogs, no thanks from them! But those shivering, shrinking women that came to me, some of them hardly out of their teens, some of them so delicate they had no right to have a baby at all!—Ah, if only I hadn't let myself take their money it would have been a work of pure philanthropy. But I had to live, then! Now that that tax has been taken off, one has time to think it out all round. But Lord!—Society, to cry shame on me for it! They might as well hang any other useful public servant, like dustmen, rat-catchers, and such-like ridders of pests. Good old Herod, that I used to hear about at school, knew what he was doing when he cleared off all those useless Innocents! He was the first baby farmer, I guess."

"You take large ground, Madam," said the man in the frock coat, a trifle huffily.

"And I have the right," said she, her large determined chin emerging from its rolls of fat in her eagerness. "You men ought to know it, and you do well enough, when you're honest. I was only the 'scapegoat, and took on me the little sins of the race. It's an easy job enough, what I did, but there's few have the stomach for it, even then. You couldn't call it dirty work either. You just stand by and leave 'em alone—to girn and bleat and squinny and die."

"No blood, eh?" the man in the corner said suddenly. "I like blood."

"What a fine night it has turned!" said the man in the grey frock coat, raising the sash and putting his head out of the window... "Something rather uncanny, eh, about that man?" he remarked under his breath, half to himself, half to the man in brown corduroys.

"Take your head in," said the latter, almost affectionately, "or you'll be catching cold, and you've a nasty scar on your neck that I could see as you leaned forward, and which you oughtn't to go getting the cold into."

"Oh, that!" said the other complacently, sitting down again, but averting his gaze carefully from the man in the corner, for whom he seemed to feel a repulsion as marked as was his preference for his cheerful *vis-à-vis*. "That! That's actually the scar of the blow that killed me. A fearful gash! He was a powerful man that dealt it. He got me, of course, from behind. I never even saw him. I was drafted off here at once, his hand had been so sure." He felt nervously in his pockets. "I have a foulard somewhere, but I am apt to mislay it."

"You should do like me, have a good strong handkercher and knot it round your neck firm. I've got a mark of sorts on my neck too, but it isn't an open wound—never was," the bluff man sniggered. "It is sheer vanity with me, but I don't care to have it seen. It goes well all round, mine does—done by a rope, eh!"

He paused and nodded slyly. "For killing a toff. Nice old gentleman he seemed, too, but I hadn't much time to look at him. Had to get to work—"

He was rudely interrupted by a screech from the baby farmer.

"Lord!" she cried, "do I see another conveyance coming on this lonely road? I do 'ope so. I'm one for seeing plenty of people. I always like a crowd, and I must tell you, this sort of humdrum jogging along was beginning to get on my nerves."

They all jerked themselves round, and peered through the glass panes behind them. The taciturn man alone reserved his attention.

Sure enough, a dark object, plainly outlined in the strong moonlight which now lit up the heavens, where heavy masses of cloud had until now obscured its effulgence, was plainly visible. It blotted the ribbon of white that lay in front of them... Nearer and nearer it came. All heads were at the windows of the coach... Now it was seen to be a high-hung dog-cart, of the most modern pattern, drawn by a smart little mettled pony, and containing two slight young girls... The one that drove held the ribbons in hands that were covered with white dog-skin gloves, and which looked immense in the pallid moonshine.

"What an excitement!" said the stout woman. "We shall pass them. Some member of one of the country families about here, I suppose."

"I hope—for all things considering, I'm not a bloodthirsty man," the man in corduroys muttered anxiously under his breath, "that we're not a-going to give them a shock! Bound to, when we meet them plumb like this! 'Orses can't abide the sight of us, mostly, no more than they could those nasty motors when they first came in. And we're worse than motors—they seem to smell us out at once for what we are!"

"If you do really think that pony is likely to swerve," said the man in the grey suit, anxiously, "would it be of any use our asking old Diggory to drive more slowly and humour them?"

"Couldn't go no slower than we are!" replied the man in corduroys. "Besides, it's not the pace that kills! I'll bet you that pony's all of a sweat already!"

The dog-cart approached. The faces of the two young women were discernible. They were white—blanched with fear, or it may have been the effect of the strong moonlight. There was no doubt that they were disturbed, and that the girl who was driving fully realised the necessity of controlling the horse, whose nostrils were quivering, and on whose sides foam was already appearing in white swathes...

"It won't pass us!" said the man in the corner, speaking suddenly. He rubbed his hands slowly one over the other. "There will be blood!"

"For goodness' sake stop gloating like that!" said the stout woman. "It turns my stomach to hear you. Wherever can you have come from, I wonder? 'Tisn't manners... I say, can't we hail them?" she inquired of the man in grey. "All give them one big shout?"

"They wouldn't be able to hear us," he replied, shaking his head sadly. "You must not forget that we are ghosts. We are not really here."

"Ay, and that's what the beasts know!" cried the man in corduroys. He jumped about. "That 'oss won't be able to stand it. The kid'll not be able to hold him in..."

"They're on us!" screamed the smart woman. "Oh, my God! Do we have to sit still and see it?" She covered her eyes with her hand.

"Yes, Missus, I reckon you have, and what's more, run away after like any shoffer that's killed his man and left him lying in the roadside. Old Diggory's got his orders."

The snorting of the pony was now audible. The coachful of ghosts distinctly saw the lather of foam dropping from its jaws. They were able, some of them, to realise the agonised tension of one girl's hands, pulling for all she was worth, and the scared sideways twist of her forcedly inactive companion. Alone the face of the yellow carriage-lamp glared, immovable...

Then it flew down, and was extinguished. There was a crash, a convulsion—and the great road to the north lay clear again.

The Coach of Death rolled on remorselessly past a black heap that filled the ditch on one side. It lay quite still, after that almost human leap and heave...

The smart woman fainted, or appeared to do so. The baby farmer sat silent.

"It's iniquitous!" exclaimed the man in grey, turning round from the window—his eyes wet, "to leave them behind like that without a word of inquiry, when it's our conveyance has done all the mischief!"

He groaned and fidgeted...

The man in corduroys tried to soothe him. "We ain't to blame, Sir, don't you think it!" he repeated. "As you said before to the lady, we aren't really here!"

"That is little consolation to a man of honour," the old man said sadly. "Still, as you say, we are but tools—"

He devoted himself to the smart woman, who revived a little under his civil ministrations.

"After all," she said, "aren't we somehow or other all in the same boat? I shouldn't be surprised if those two nice girls didn't join us at the next stage. If they do, we'll make them tell us how they felt, when they first saw the coachful of ghosts coming down on them. They're certainly dead, for they were both pitched into the ditch with the cart and horse on top of them. Did anybody see what became of the horse? No... Well, we must settle down to dulness again, I am afraid, or, suppose, to while away the time we all started to tell each other the story of how we came to be here? A lively tale might cheer us all up, after the accident."

"Agreed, Madam, heartily for my part," said the man in grey, "though my own story is very humdrum, and not in the least amusing. You want, of course, an account of the particular accident that sent me here. Very well! But, ladies first! Will not you begin, Madam?"

She tossed her head, with an affected air.

"My story, perhaps," she insinuated with modesty, "might not be very new to you. It was in all the papers so recently."

"That will not affect me," he answered, "for if, as I presume, it was a murder case, I never read them."

"I read yours then, Missus, I expect," said the man in corduroys. "I generally get the wife to read them out to me—anything spicy."

"And yet the people that did it are not hanged yet, if, indeed, they ever are, poor souls! I am quite anxious," said the smart woman, "to see how it goes. If the pair are really sent here, I suppose I shall be running up against them some night or other, on one of these transference parties. It will be very interesting. But"—she leaned across to the baby farmer—"could we not persuade you to give us some of your—nursery experiences, Madam?"

"There's not much story about the drowning of a litter of squalling puppies or whining kittens," said that lady shortly, "we want something livelier—more personal, if I may say so. From a remark that gentleman in the corner let drop a while ago, I fancy his reminiscences would be quite worth hearing, as good as a shilling shocker."

"My story," replied the individual thus pointedly addressed, "is impossible, frankly impossible."

"Indecent, do you mean?" The smart woman's eyes shone. "Oh, let us have it. You can veil it, can't you?"

"Have you ever heard of mental degenerates?" he asked her compassionately. "I was one. I was called mad—a simple way of expressing it. I was a chemist. I dissected neatly enough, too, like a regular butcher. They did quite right to exterminate me."

His head dropped. He seemed disinclined to say more. Still the smart woman persisted.

"But the details—?"

"Are purely medical, Ma'am. Not without a physiological interest, I may say. Interesting to men of science, pathologically. The"—he named a daily paper much in vogue at that time, "made a good deal of the strong sense of artistry—of contrast—the morbid warp inherent in the executants—"

His head sank again on his chest.

"I do believe," said the baby farmer, nudging the smart woman, "that we shall find he's the man who killed his sweetheart and then carefully tied her poor inside all into true lover's knots with sky-blue ribbon. Artist, indeed! They're quite common colours—blue and red—"

"Disgusting!" The delicate lady from Monte Carlo shuddered, and turning coldly away, joined in the petition proffered by the other ghosts to the breezy man in corduroys, to relate his experiences.

"Oh, I'll tell you how I came to join you and welcome!" he said, rolling his huge neck about in its setting of red cotton. "Well, to begin with, I was drunk. Equally, of course, I was hard up. My missus—she's married again, by the way, blast her!—was always nagging me to do something for her and the kids. I did. Nation's taking care of them now, along of what I did. Work, she meant, but that was only by the way. I did choose to take on a job, though, on a rich man's estate, building some kind of Folly, lots of glass and that, working away day and night by naphtha flares, you know. He was one of those men, you know the sort, that has more money than a man can properly spend, and feels quite sick about it, and says so, in interviews and so on, in the papers a working man reads. That's the mischief. He was always giving away chunks of money to charities and libraries and that sort of useless lumber, but none of it ever seemed to come the way of those that were in real need of it. They said the money had got on his nerves, and would not let him sleep o' nights, and that he was afraid by day and went about with a loaded stick and I don't know what all. And he was looked after by detectives, at one time, so the papers said—again the papers, putting things in people's heads, as it's their way. So one blessed evening I was very low—funds and all, and my missus and the kids hollering and complaining as they always do when luck's bad. Lord bless them, they never thought as they were 'citing their man to murder. Women never do think. And going out with their snivelling in my ears, I passed the station where he landed every evening after his day in town, and I happened to see him come out of the train and send away his motor that was a-waiting for him all regular, and start out to walk 'ome alone by a short cut across a little plantation there was, very thick and dark, just the place for a murder. Well—I told you I was half drunk—I raced home and got something to do it with—a meat chopper—to be particular—"

The old man opposite put his hand nervously to the back of his neck.

"Ay, Mister, it takes you just there, does it? You look a regular bundle of nerves, you do. Well, as I was saying, I went round by a short cut that I happened to know of, and got in front of him and hid in the hedge. Ten mortal minutes I waited for my man to come by. Lord, how my hand did tremble! I'd have knocked off for two pence. I was as nervous as a cat, but all the same, it didn't prevent me from striking out for wife and children with a will when my chance came. I caught him behind with my chopper, and he fell like a log. Never lifted a hand to defend himself—hadn't got any grit. Ladies, I don't suppose I hurt him much, for he never even cried out when I struck or groaned when it was done. Then I looked him over, turned out his pockets and collared his watch and season ticket and seals and money. Money—hah!—I had been fairly done over that. Would you believe it of a rich fellow like him, he hadn't got more than the change of a sovereign on him."

"Shame!" ejaculated the taciturn man in the corner.

"I admit it was hard on you," the man in grey observed kindly. "Very hard, for I believe the retribution came all too quickly. You foolishly left your chopper about to identify you, and were apprehended at once by our excellent rural police. Yet the law is so dilatory that you lay in gaol a whole year before you were free to join your victim here?"

"Right you are, mate. Yes, I swung for it, sure enough. Short and sweet it was once I stood on the drop, but it still makes my poor old throat ache to think of it."

He wriggled and twisted his neck in its ruddy cincture...

"Now, governor, I'm done, and if you've no objection we'd all like to hear how you came by that ugly gash of yours? It wasn't no rope did that. Common or garden murder, I'll be bound."

"Certainly, my man, it was a murder—a murder most *apropos*. The circumstances were peculiar. I have often longed to get the ear of the jury who tried a man for relieving me of my light purse and intolerably heavy life, and tell them—the whole hard-working, conscientious twelve of them, trying their best to bring in an honest verdict and avenge my wrongs—my own proper feelings, surely no negligible factor in the case! They could not guess, these ignorant living men, whose eyes had not yet been opened by death to a due sense of the proportions of things—that I bore the poor creature no malice, but instead was actually grateful for his skilful surgery that had severed the life-cord that bored me, so neatly and completely."

"It isn't every one would take it like that!" remarked the smart woman. "Yet that is, more or less, how I feel about these things myself. Only in my case it is impossible to speak of skilful surgery! I was disgracefully cut up. I couldn't possibly have worn a low dress again!"

"Have you ever heard?" said the man in grey thoughtfully, "of the Greek story of the Gold of Rhampsinitos, and the inviolable cellar he built to store it in? According to the modern system, my gold was hoarded in my brain, where fat assets and sordid securities bred and bred all day long. The laws that govern wealth are hard. You must give it, devise it, you must not allow it to be taken. But for my part I would have welcomed the two sons of the master builder who broke into the Greek King's Treasure House. In the strong-room of my brain it lodged. With one careless calculation, one stroke of a pen, I could make money breed money there to madden me. I was lonely, too. I had no wife to divide my responsibilities. She might even have enjoyed them. But I dared approach no woman in the way of love—I did not choose to be loved for my cheque-signing powers. I was not loved at all. I was hated. Unrighteous things were done in my name, by the greedy husbandmen of my load of money. Then I was told that I went in danger of my life, and I condescended to take care of that—for a time—only for a time!

"One dark winter evening—I forget what had happened during the day, what fresh instance of turpitude or greed had come before me—I was so revolted that I kicked away all the puling safeguards by which my agents guarded their best asset of all, and gave the rein to my instinct. I disregarded precautions of every sort—with the exception of my faithful loaded stick, and the carrying of that had come to be a mere matter of habit with me—and I walked home from the station alone and unattended, up to my big house and good dinner which I hoped—nay, I almost knew—that I should not be alive to eat: And indeed, as luck would have it, on that night of all nights the trap was set for me. The appointed death-dealer was waiting—he took me on at once. I got my desire—kind, speedy, merciful, violent death. I never even saw the face of my deliverer."

"By George!" softly swore the man in corduroys. "This beats all. Are you sure you aren't kidding us?"

"No indeed, that is exactly how I felt about it, and if I had known of knowledge, as I knew of instinct, what was going to happen, I would have thought to realise some of my wealth before setting out to walk through that wood, and made it more worth the honest fellow's while. But as you are aware, a millionaire does not carry portable gold about with him, and my cheque-book which I had on me would, of course, be of no use to him. Alas, all the poor devil got for his pains was exactly nineteen shillings and eleven pence. I had changed a sovereign at the book-stall to buy a paper, and out of habit, had waited for the change."

The man in corduroys was by this time in a considerable state of excitement. He had rent the red handkerchief fiercely from his neck, and now made as if to tear it across his knee...

"Why, governor!" he exclaimed passionately, "do you mean to say it was through you that I got this here"—he put both hands behind his head and interlocked them, "in return for giving you that there cut at the back of your neck? Well, how things do come about, to be sure!"

"Gently, gently! my man," the elder soothed him. "Don't be so melodramatic about a very ordinary coincidence. See, the ladies are quite upset. It doesn't do to allow oneself to get excited here—it's not in the rules. If I had made the little discovery you have done, I don't think—no, I really don't think I would have made it public. This undue exhibition of emotion of yours strikes me as belonging to the vulgar world we have all left. But since you have allowed it to come out, and every one is now aware of the peculiar relation in which we stand to each other, you must let me tender you my best thanks, as to a most skilful and firm operator, and believe me to be truly grateful to you for your services in the past."

"Quite the old school!" said the smart woman.

"I must say, Sir,—I consider you the real gentleman," said the baby farmer.

"I am a gentleman."

"And a fairly accommodating one!" said the roughman, wiping his brow where, however, no sweat was. "It isn't every man as would give thanks for being scragged!"

"Every man isn't a millionaire," said his victim calmly.

The smart woman, leaning forward, tapped the old gentleman amiably with her jewelled pince-nez.

"But we belong to the same world, I perceive," she said, "and I am quite able to understand your refined feeling. It is as I said in my own case. Indeed if those two good people, who shall be nameless, had only dealt with me a little more gently, I don't know that I should not forgive them absolutely. I shall at any rate be perfectly civil when I do meet them—only perhaps a little distant. But that Monte Carlo existence I was leading when they interrupted it, was really becoming intolerable! No one who hasn't done it, thoroughly can realise what it is. Glare, noise, glitter, fever—that heartless, blue, laughing sea they talk of in the railway advertisements—"

The baby farmer, left out in this elegant discussion, obviously took no pleasure in it, but staring straight before her, muttered sulkily—

"Cote d'Azur and Pentonville! There's some little difference, isn't there, between one life and the other? Yet I enjoyed my life, I did, and as for gratitude, I can't say as I see all those blessed infants a-coming up to me, and slobbering me for what I did for 'em. I may meet them, but they'll not notice me. It isn't in human nature. Their mothers' thanks was all I got, and they thanked me beforehand in hard cash for what I was a-going to do. Lord, what's a ricketty baby more or less? I say, we're slowing up! Going to stop perhaps, and a good thing too!"

"Yes," said the man in the grey frock coat, still enouncing his curt sentences to the unheeding listeners, "I am able to cordially thank the man who rid me with one clean scientific blow of my wretched life and all its tedious accessories. A skilled workman is worthy of his hire."

"Mercy!" muttered the baby farmer. "Is he never going to stop? If it was for nothing else, he ought to have got scragged for being a bore!"

But being fully wound up, though in the excitement of arriving at the depôt no one was attending, the man in grey continued, "Suicide I had thought of, but abhorred, though on my soul I had nearly come to that, and then it was merely a question of courage—you spoke truly, Sir. Mine was a thin, pusillanimous nature, as you said. You came by, a kind Samaritan, and sacrificed your own good life freely to rid me of my wretched one. I think I told you that when you were being tried, I followed urgently all the details of the trial, and made interest with the authorities here to allow me to appear to the judge in his sleep, say, and instil into his mind some inkling of the true state of my feelings towards you. I do not know, however, if you would have thanked me, for life may have been no sweeter to you than it was to me—you spoke of an uncongenial helpmate, I think? Still one never knows. I might have been the means of procuring you some good years yet, in the full exercise of your undeniable vigour and remarkable decision of character. But it was apparently not to be. You followed me here, after a long interval of waiting, and now we have met, face to face. The introduction on that dark night was worth nothing. I like your face. We shall probably never meet again—their ways are dark and devious here, so I am the more glad of this opportunity of opening my mind to you on a delicate subject, perhaps, but one that has always been very near my heart. By the way"—he lifted his stick with its shining ivory crown into view. "Did you notice this? You read the papers, you said, and they told you it was heavily weighted and that I carried it always as a precaution. Well, on that eventful night for both of us—perhaps you were too hurried to notice?—but I never used it. Accept it now, will you not, as a memento?... I think, from sundry truly unearthly bumpings, that we seem to have come at last to our journey's end...

I am right, the coachman has got down from his perch and taken his head under his arm... We part. Mesdames, I salute you. Again, Sir—" He addressed himself more particularly to the shamefaced man in corduroys—"Farewell. Very pleased to have met you!"

One by one, the passengers faded away into the distance. The polite old man paused in the semblance of an inn yard where the coach had drawn up. A pale proud woman's face, shining up by the step, had touched him. She was an intending passenger, and she was alone. She wore white dog-skin gloves, but no hat. Unusual, he fancied, in a woman of her class. On looking closer, he saw that she had a hat, but that it hung disregarded over her shoulder by an elastic, and was much battered and destroyed. He decided to speak to her.

"You are the lady we killed, I think?" he asked gently.

She acknowledged with a bow that it was so.

"We could none of us do anything," he apologised, "or I hope you will believe—"

"Certainly, Sir, it was no fault of yours, or indeed of the company's, I am sure. The accident was inevitable!" so she assured him, smiling faintly. He looked at her kindly. There was blood on the hair, he was able to convince himself... "But Rory—our pony—never can pass things, at the best of times, and the look of your conveyance was certainly rather unusual. And at that time of night we rarely meet anything at all on the Great North Road. We choose that time on purpose, my sister and I—we had been staying away for a week with friends, and we were going home. When we saw you coming, Lucy said, half in jest—she is older than I—'Suppose that thing in front were the Coach of Death the foolish country people talk about? They say it travels this way once a year, with its cargo of souls, on St. John's Eve.' I bade her not be superstitious, but I confess I thought the vehicle looked odd myself, and I did wonder how Rory would stand it. When it came nearer I saw distinctly that the coachman was headless, and I laughingly told my sister so. She bade me not disturb her, for death coach or live coach, she meant to do her best to get Rory past it. She failed—"

The man in grey looked nervously around. He was alone with the young lady in the dull inn yard. The headless coachman was preparing to ascend to the box seat again...

"Where is your sister now?" he inquired.

"She lies at the bottom of the ditch. Rory has galloped home. She fell on her head, but she is alive still. When they find her in the morning, she will be dead, I know that. For now I know all things. I am at peace... you need have no care for me..."

"Let me at least put you into the coach," he begged. "And you will prefer the corner seat?"...

She took it; he went on—

"It looks, however, as if you were going to have all the accommodation to yourself, for this stage at all events."

He raised his hat; she bowed.

"I am grieved that I cannot have the pleasure—that I cannot offer to accompany you, but I have my marching orders..."

He raised his hat again... The coach moved on out of the yard. Soon it was lost in the mists... The summer dawn was just breaking.

THE BLUE BONNET

"... a little spark in a blue bonnet who fought like the devil at Preston."—BOSWELL.

The tourists peered past the grey stone pillars of the gateway into the courtyard, paved with round cobbles, grass-grown in between. The low sculptured doorway gave admittance to the old manor house that had so fascinated the lady of the party from the first moment she had cast eyes on it.

"Oh, this is a bit of the real thing!" she had exclaimed fervently, when, five miles out of Richmond, the road had ceased to follow the course of the Swale, mantled all the way with heavy oak and hazel copses. They seemed to hang like hairy beards from the beetle-browed face of the cliffs that shelter the east bank of the river. "The very real thing!" she had continued, as the wagonette turned out into the open moorland, and their town-bleached cheeks were bathed at once in the pure sullen airs that roamed over it, softened and suffused with the tears of an April storm gone by. "This is the real Yorkshire moor I've read of, bare and empty, with not a single dwelling to be seen. Yes, there's one!"

For as their conveyance dived down into the scarp of a hill, she sighted beyond the now familiar river which wound again into view, directly crossing their path, and the low bridge of quite modern construction which spanned it, the square mass of a house commanding the river bank. It seemed to stand, bulldog like, on the slight acclivity, posing as guardian of the ford at that place, which was certainly all that had served for crossing a hundred years ago. So her instructive companion remarked to the eager lady. She grew more and more enthusiastic.

"John, I can't possibly pass it! I couldn't reconcile it with my historical conscience to go by without an attempt to see it. It's like a grey-haired woman standing stranded on the edge of the world, an old Ariadne of a house, waiting for ever by the side of the flood... Ask the driver what they call it?"

"Wallburn Old Hall," said the stolid Yorkshireman, flicking a fly off his horse's ear.

Three blind hopeless windows which had been closed up for the tax looked over the old garden garth. The eyes of the persons looking thence could have swept the stream and the narrow neck which formed the ford. The stone flagged courtyard of the house was enclosed by buildings on all sides but one. On the west, looking towards the river, was a ruined battlement on which a man might still walk and survey the country round for miles. But it was now insecure, the inner rubble exposed. Clumps of wild mustard and garlic sprang from every cranny and crevice and made a yellow blaze that lit up the grey substance of the pile. The lady unable to contain herself longer, requested the driver to pull up and let them have a look. Her companion took out a guide-book and read aloud, as they sat in the break in the streaming sunshine.

"Wallburn Old Hall... fortified manor house... dismantled..."

"I should think it was!"

"*Et pour cause. The* old Cause of all! Listen! Family of Daunet. There's the shield on the door, evidently—see all that *répoussé* work?—only we can't read it from here."

"The book says: 'The ancient family of Daunet, who beareth sable guiltie, argent and a canton ermine...' Yes, Guy Daunet's tomb is in the church at Redmire—remember it?—His feet are cased in brass-toed sollerets. Above his lady's head are three shields of arms. She appears to have been a Conyers. Well, they seem to be pretty well extinct now. The last Daunet was out and killed in the fifteen. There were Daunets in the Great Rebellion, Daunets in the Gunpowder Plot—in the Rising in the North—"

"Poor romantic dears!"

"Yes, that's the plague of lost causes. They swayed the emotions so forcibly and through the emotions the very lives of the old families—those that had any good in them. One imagines them, up to the very latest day, having an indistinct glimmering of their own original *raison d'être*, that is, lands given in exchange for service... Their modern representatives have lost even the glimmering. Well, oughtn't we to be driving on?"

"Oh, no. After what you've been making out, I must have a try to see over it. I want to make out that blurred shield over the door. Gules argent and canton ermine, was it? They can but refuse us."

The young couple alighted, under mute protest from the driver, and entered the courtyard, the lady bold, the man nervous, deprecating. They received forthwith a Teniers-like vision of an interior. Farm-hands were sitting round a wooden table, placed in the oak-panelled greasy blackness of a low raftered hall. All looked up, and ceased pulling at their mugs. A frowsy young girl of eighteen, wiping her mouth, came forward.

"Could we see over?" The glint of a silver coin in the lady's hand pleasingly accentuated her request.

A voice came from the interior as the girl stood hesitating and shy.

"Mind, hinny, thou'st not take the lady anywhere it isn't safe. Keep out of the room the captain's leg came through. And mind, the stairway beyont isn't much to crack on."

The girl thus admonished, turned and led the enthusiastic pair in and up the rich darkness of the stair.

"That's the best part of it her mother told her to leave out!" whispered the lady. "That about the captain's leg. It sounds most exciting. Ask her—or I will." The girl, questioned, replied over her shoulder.

"It's a tale, ma'am. A long while back it were—ages and ages. They do say a man's leg came through the floor, and he's always called the capting. The boards is rotten just there, and was then. That whole end o' the house is fair gone to powder. My grandfeyther used for to say that a man's leg made it coming through. But it was long before his time, and he were a very old man. The ceilings of that part of the house is that powdery, would you believe it, that we can always scrape the plaster and get a bit for baby."

"How funny and utilitarian! And is it haunted?"

"Grandfeyther always said 'twas."

"Who by?"

"They do say a poor man went clean daft there—came home and found every one lying dead about the place."

"But what had they died of? Plague?"

"The smit? Naw. Grandfeyther allus said 'twor a tragedy, same as they has in the papers now-a-days."

"Where is your grandfather now?"

She jerked her finger over towards the north.

"Churchyard. But he knew all about this place. His feyther before him was ostler about the inn at Redmire—you'll pass it on your way to Bolton. He always said there was a hiding hole here, and mor'n that, a secret way, but teacher says that's all nonsense and we mustn't waste our time looking for it, besides it isn't safe. We shut oop this part, and just pack into the other, where it's still pretty good, and at Michaelmas we've all got to go out and Lord Scrope is going to pull the old place down."

"Shame!"

"Oh, I dunno. It's fair rotten."

"Are you sure you can't take us into the rotten part—just for once before it all goes?"

"That I cannot. The worst room is the one the man's leg came through—they call it the Lady Christina's room. And it's there Grandfeyther says the priest's hole was."

"It was generally out of the principal room in the house," said the man. "They wanted him under their own hand and to be able to feed him at night. Come along, Mary, you really can't see it."

"I suppose not." She sighed. "But I do somehow seem to see Christina—the Lady Christina. I suppose her spirit is about? Why 'Lady'? The Daunets had no title."

"These people always dignify ghosts and raise them to the peerage. Let's see if we can't make up a story for her. Christina Daunet and her lover—was he the man who went mad or the priest she hid?"

They were descending the stairs. Their cicerone broke in suddenly.

"Nay, that weren't the way. The real heir was troth-plight to the Lady Christina, and he was drowned one day here in the ford, here under her very eyes."

"Another touch!" said her companion eagerly. "So legend grows. Let us go and sit out on the hill, here and look towards the ford, and

I'll try to reconstruct her story for you. I'm not a novelist for nothing. This is how the man went mad when he came home."

There was no priest. The lover was that "little spark in a blue bonnet that fought at Preston" Boswell speaks of. I've always wanted to connect him up with a story. Miss Christina Daunet—not Lady—was tall and pale, and a fine girl, so long as she had enough to eat, and nothing to brood on. But her adolescence and greatest need of nourishment happened to coincide with Jacobite times of stress, when loyal subjects starved in order that the Stuarts might come by their own. The females of her family were used—even hardened to the more domestic consequences of the males' unfaltering loyalty. When the fuss was about priests, Christina's own grandmother had successfully concealed one in the hiding-place in her room—that very room that we were not permitted to investigate, looking towards the ford and the road to Richmond. To-day her own mother lay there, eighty, bedridden, daft and doited.

These two women were the widow and daughter of the last Daunet of the direct line. Since the great Guy of the canton ermine, the race had continually dwindled. So many of them had been strangled, so many hanged and drawn and quartered, a half-dozen desiccated heads belonging to the strain had rotted on Temple Bar. Cold steel and a touch of poison had been responsible for some others, and thus the foolish, forlorn race had been cleared off to make room for persons of finer judgment and less realistic ideals. Acts of attainder, recusant fines, had impoverished their estates, and mulcted them of their goods, till of all the broad lands, castles and noble manor houses that had bred and sheltered and maintained Daunets for the King's service, only the austere, embattled farmhouse on the

Richmondshire moors remained, and therein the two women that alone bore the fine fighting name slowly pined and withered away.

They had not enough to eat. Yet their appetites were no larger than feminine appetites are reputed to be. Sir Christopher Daunet, Christina's father, was killed at Sheriffmuir when his little daughter was a year old, and her mother, grown doited with the shock, lived on to give very little trouble, and represent no great charge on the family finances. She lay always in her big room in the south-west wing. Her heavy four-post bed, too mighty and perhaps too rotten to be moved, remained firm in its old place on the safer part of the flooring; the tester was hung by heavy rings to the ceiling. Her daughter, ministering to her slight wants, had learned to walk warily round the bed.

Christina Daunet was loyal—as women are loyal. She realised very fairly that this task of the reinstatement of the Stuart dynasty on the throne of England had been set by Providence on her and hers, incidentally carrying with it the doom of extermination set on the race. Their blind inherent loyalty clustered as it must, round the losing side which sucked in, naturally, these people who always went where their advantage was not—and the losing side had drawn in her father, her uncle, even the man she loved.

She loved her cousin, Charles Daunet of Scanwood. Scanwood House lay three miles hence on the Richmond Road. Charles was the only son of her father's only sister. Christina and this young man were early troth-plighted—they were about to wed—but the Stuarts came first. It was the Cause that intervened and forbade the innocent banns. Charles Daunet allowed the just impediment and went out as a matter of course. He was more eager for the day of the stranger's crowning than for the morn that should usher in his wedding with Christina whom he knew and loved. He had left her too easily. Folk in the neighbourhood said he was slack. Christina herself admitted that Charles was more of a fighter than a lover. But the Stuarts called! What was a Daunet to do?

She cried sometimes and mourned over her baulked betrothal with her only confidant, a certain Luke Daunet. Her father had had a son, but he was not her mother's child. Luke lived with them—his mother had been innkeeper's daughter over at Redmire, a good girl enough till Sir Christopher Daunet came her way. He lived so near, at Wallburn, and he was not the man to leave so fair a flower ungathered.

Madam Daunet was not a hard woman. She undertook the child's maintenance when its mother died and Sir Christopher fell at Sheriffmuir. Luke grew up. He was not "all there," but he was an honest, kindly, gentle fellow, and for the two lonely women he did a man's work about the place. There was not much to do. There was not a beast left in the stable, except a wall-eyed, knock-kneed pony that Luke rode into Redmire or Marske now and then to buy necessaries. They could afford no other servant. The white-handed proud Christina tended her mother, cooked, and did the inside work of the house. It was all one. When the Prince should come into his own, Christina would do so likewise.

Of that she had doubts sometimes, especially when the wind whistled over the moor, and the stream ran heavy and turbid below the garden, so that the ford was ill to cross. The Prince's final triumphing then seemed surer than her own. Charles had been away now a long while. He had not been assiduous about her for many months before his departure to join the Prince. He had sent her no message first or last. She had even heard of another lady...

For rumours flew. The news of the brief Stuart apotheosis at Edinburgh, tidings of the Prince's meteoric Court at Holyrood, had filtered down to Redmire, and the bar of the inn there. Preston fight, too, was mentioned. She thought, but was not sure, that Charles had been noticed there. Now the Prince was marching south... had marched...

On that day of December, mild and calm and presageless as it seemed, Christina was ill at ease, peevish, apprehensive. She went about the houseplace and courtyard with her ears pricked to the free roving wind that might have brushed her Charles's bonnet in passing, as he marched south with his troops? Or, weary of this fairy listening, she would droop her eyes, till they rested dreaming on the waterway below the dip of the hill where Wallburn Hall stood. Then she would raise them slowly to look a little higher on the level where the turrets of Scanwood were just visible nestling in their encompassing woods. Scanwood was a fine place, and would it be hers some day?

Puzzled, like a fox that is hunted, she snuffed the air and could not tell which way danger, or perhaps bliss, might come. Had the Prince's army passed them on its way south? For indeed the last news Luke had brought had been that the Stuart heir was marching on his own capital, with his victorious rabble of Highlanders. King George was quaking. Would not Charles, if this were so, have to pass by Scanwood to see to his domestic concerns? Her mother babbled for ever of drums; the old woman would have it that she heard them...

"They've gone by, my dear, they've gone by. Oh, the bonny lads!... The Prince has gone into England, never to leave it again, dearie. Listen to the old doited woman, for she speaks truth. Rub-a-dub!... Rub-a-dub!..."

"Whisht, whisht, mother!" Christina now and again murmured softly but not imperatively, as she stood by the window and herself with her slight long fingers performed the manœuvre known as drumming on the pane. Yes, her heart lifted; he had passed, at a point perhaps miles away, too far for him to get leave to call in and see his sweetheart. She must have patience. One day soon she would be looking out of this very window and she would see Charles on his fine horse crossing the ford at the old place, coming to her, with a light heart, and all his troubles and hers behind him, cast aside, healed, over and done with. She could discern the very spot now where the bottom was nearest and the water shallowest, even exposed at times in drought. The waters flowed glumly over it now, there had been much rain to swell them. Sometimes, to the excited girl, who stood there, her nerves wrought by the faint vocal rub-a-dubbing that came from the bed behind her, it seemed that the water gathered itself up into shapes—shapes of horses and men. The little waves seemed to rise obediently under the harsh wind, and form themselves into the semblance of uncanny humanity. They massed themselves and menaced, yes, she came to fancy that one figure rose again and again from the sullen flow to shake a quivering fist at her. She stared the silly vision down. Soon the water ran by as usual, huddling, lumping itself into small ridges under the wind, but nothing so tall as a man.

She turned to receive and divert the mother's peevish voice. The old woman had ceased to imitate the drums; she was now convinced in her senile way they had passed. She talked strange nonsense, used strange names. "Bound for the South, they are... The Bridge... Swarkstone! Swarkstone."

"Where's that, mother?"

"Bad luck! Bad luck! The Bridge… No further… Swarkstone. No further. Back! Back! I'm cold, Christina. I'm cold…"

"The day's changing and you feel it," said Christina sadly, altering the position of the coverings. It was all she could do.

"Nay, 'tis the smit of death I've got, Christina! I know it."

"Oh, mother, not now, just when we are going to be so happy." But her heart did not back her words. "Look here, I'll have Luke go to Redmire at once and get you some of Betty Candlish's cordial. She promised me some for you the moment I wanted it, and you seemed low as you do to-day. We won't let you die just yet."

"Ay, but can you keep me?" said the voice from the bed gently. "It's that I've got and no mistake. I've felt it all day… Come back and kiss me, Christina. You're a good girl—a very good girl… The Bridge at Swarkstone—I saw him there—the Prince… Remember that, Christina."

"Yes, mother, I will, though I never heard of such a place in my life!" cajoled the girl as she went downstairs to seek the half-witted Luke and confide her errand to him.

He sat, as usual, on the oak settle, swallowed up in the glooms of the chimney corner. She roused him up, and told him what she wanted. She helped him to saddle the pony and watched him potter slowly up the hill towards Bolton. Then she re-entered the house and cut up, on the corner of the big seamed oaken table, some vegetables which she had fetched from an outhouse. Into a pot on the fire she threw the sliced turnips and carrots. There was not much fire to hang over, but her forehead got hot, her cheeks flushed, and her hair escaped a little from its binding.

Presently, having put the mess to one side on the hob, she walked slowly out into the courtyard to get air, of which she suddenly felt a violent need. She languidly ascended the few broken steps that led up to the old battlement. At that time one could still walk along it without having one's attention too much distracted by the necessity of picking one's way among the rubble. She strolled backwards and forwards, enjoying the fresh moorland air that caressed her reddened cheeks and blew her pale yellow hair away in an easterly direction.

Holding her hand to her forehead instinctively to restrain it, though there was no one to be seen for miles, she scanned the country to the south. Her blue eyes roved over the low rolling hills that let her see a very long way. But not as far as that bridge at Swarkstone, six miles south of Derby, where the lines of her fate had been converging for several days past, and were now radiating away from thence in ragged streaks and strands of fugitive soldiers and brutal complacent pursuers.

She was overcome with a sudden trepidation, a rush of feeling that somehow impelled her to get back to the room where her mother lay, and see for herself how the helpless woman was getting on. But she sat down on the parapet, which at the point where she was still stood firm at the side of the battlement next the road. Overcome by a sudden faintness, she hid her face in her hands. She had eaten very little to-day. Her back was to the road, and her eyes, should she uncover them, would have rested on the empty grass-grown courtyard.

It was not empty. A noise like a dead leaf twisting startled her. Luke come back on foot, without the pony! She had pressed her knuckles into her eyes until her eyes had grown hazy and suffused, and it was a second or two before she saw there was actually a man in the courtyard below her. A man, not Luke...

His bonnet, faded by sun and wind and rain, had once been blue. She heard his breath that came quickly, and, very drily, scenting a beggar and a demand for alms, she asked him his business.

He raised his drooping head.

"Charles!"

"Christina, quick! Who else is here? Can you harbour me?"

"What? What?"

"I come from Derby—the rout at Derby. We got six miles beyond and turned back... I am pursued. Quick, can you hide me, will you? They will search my house at Scanwood, they are there now..."

Christina was not looking at him. She had half turned when he spoke of Scanwood, and her eyes pried into the bosky mazes lying between... The fugitive thought that the brusque movement had its occasion in a natural change in her sentiments towards himself. He deserved no better, he had practically deserted her, he had never written—a woman scorned!... Yet in his urgent necessity he must needs appeal to her again...

"Christina, an answer, I beg of you! Shall I go further for a shelter?"

"Take off that cap—reach it up to me here. Now go in to the chimney corner—you know it—sit down—at ease. Not another word."

While speaking she had taken the blue cap and flung it down into the chapel garth on the other side of the wall. The cluster of "ramps" and fronds of wild garlic parted and opened to receive it and came together again. Meantime such was the power of insistence in her voice that the fugitive obeyed her as he would obey the military word of command. Heavily walking over the stones of the courtyard, he took his place on the settle in the chimney nook and crossed his legs negligently. He could still see Christina standing on the battlement looking down towards the ford. She stood first on one leg and then on the other; she agitated her body strangely, she made signs. Then faint sounds, voices, the clink of bridles, came to his ears from the direction in which she looked. His pursuers most likely, for the noise came from Scanwood. He stretched his legs, stiff from two nights' exposure, further out in an attitude of ease as she had bidden him. He did not know what Christina meant to do. She was revengeful—then she would give him up? She meant perhaps to save him? Well, his life belonged to her. He waited.

Five minutes ago Christina had seen his enemies taking the ford, a well-found troop of horse, and a stoutish personable man riding at their head. Charles Daunet, from the ingle nook, could not see them but he could see his Christina make a trumpet of her white hands and hear her bawl—yes, bawl—to them over the battlement—

"Good gentlemen, hear me. Will you please to take some refreshment? I cannot allow you to go by me, for it is lonely here at Wallburn Hall."

"Is that what you call it?" said a clear voice. "Wheel, men."

Charles Daunet saw the speaker ride into the little courtyard at the head of his troop, and dismount. He was a fine florid man of forty or so. He wore a high fixed cap with upon it the White Horse of Hanover; his gaiters were white and at his saddle he carried a dead turkey. Christina had descended from the battlement, and had gone to the horse's head. The man spoke breezily.

"Captain Butler at your service, Mistress. We will eat a crust with you, the more so because we come to search you in the King's name."

"Do you say so?" Christina replied, setting the tone of the interview in a way that made Charles Daunet shiver. "Come you then in, in the King's name. George or James, 'tis all the same to me, a woman. It's long enough since a man came this way. I was wearying for the sight of one."

The Captain laughed heartily.

"Business, first, Miss, if you please. We have a warrant to take a certain Colonel Charles Daunet of Scanwood, who fought for the Pretender at Preston and gave us honest ones a dance of it."

Christina looked faintly bored.

"My cousin of Scanwood! Is he not at home?"

"We have spent two hours ferreting for him there, and the housekeeper bade us come here. She said he was a good friend of yours."

"She is chary of her information," said the girl composedly. "I was more than friend, I was once sweethearts with him, for my sins. But I have no care for the fellow now." She tossed her head. "Come in, come in, you and your men, as many as the roof will shelter. The wine cask is low, but we will do what we can. I am alone here—nearly."

"My men—some of them—must search the house."

"Ay, let them search closely! I was always one for formality. But see they take heed of the flooring of the upper rooms, which is indifferent and might let one of them through, especially if he be a fine man like yourself, Captain!" She giggled. "Shall I go along with them, and indicate the places where the maggots cling and the mouse gnaws, and all is gone to fine powder?"

"No, they must shift as best they can, and you shall stay here and talk with me. Our man should be here, without your knowledge, perhaps, since you say you and he have fallen out?"

"We fell out," said Christina carelessly, "when he chose to leave me to go and fight for a man I had never seen and didn't care for. He should have stayed here and taken care of his own."

"I am with you, Mistress. Little as he is, though, he fought us like the devil at Preston. His blue bonnet was everywhere, and he fairly swinged our poor fellows! The Duke is wild to have him strung up. Well, men, off with you! Thoroughly, mind. Every corner! Is there a cursed hiding hole here?"

"Yes, in my mother's room," said the hostess languidly. "She lies there bedridden. Speak her fair and gently, and she will instruct you to find the way in. On the left-hand side of the fireplace—a bolt shaped like a beetle. Only it's iron, and if Charles is there—so much the worse for him."

"You've got a spirit—nasty at that. Well, let's in. 'Tis hot, and your liquor comes not amiss."

Christina led the way under the low-browed doorway to the kitchen, where Charles Daunet was sitting. She made straight for the corner where he was, and lifting up a wooden flap of the settle, rummaged for a bottle of spirits. Aloud she said—

"Get thy great foot out of the way, Luke, wilt 'a!"

"Ay, who's that?" asked Captain Butler, apprehending the sullen inmate of the chimney corner for the first time.

"That! That's a poor foolish cousin of mine," she replied, rising from her knees with the bottle, a little flushed with stooping...

"You seem full of cousins—"

"Yes, but this one's on the wrong side of the blanket. He's not over quick, but he'll answer a civil question, no doubt. Now then!" She took Charles Daunet roughly by the wounded shoulder, and he winced. "Look up, speak to the captain, can't you?"

"What's your name?" asked that personage humorously, entering into the spirit of the thing, but he got no answer. Christina shrugged her shoulders.

"Truth, he's got no name, by the rights of it. Or if he has, it's the same as mine. Luke Daunet, at your service. Drat you, Luke, why don't you stand up and speak for yourself?"

Still the man on the settle did not move.

"He's taken that way sometimes, Captain. A fit of the sullens. As obstinate as a mule, and you can't get a word out of him; and another day he'll rattle away fit to deave you. Poor sort of company for a girl like me! We just have to give him house room and a bite and a sup now and then for kinship's sake."

She poured out a glass of mead and the captain took up the glass and raised it to his lips.

"A kiss before I drink!"

He put his hand on her shrinking shoulder. The kiss lit on her ear. The man in the corner looked up sharply.

"Be quiet, Luke. Don't you see I never gave it?" she said, as if to a froward jealous baby.

"It isn't to his taste, eh?" said Butler. "Ha! Ha!"

"Never you mind his tantrums, Captain. We never take any notice, mother and I." She filled his glass again. He sat down near the end of the table. She made shift to sweep the fragments of vegetables away with the carroty knife, but the captain raised his hand.

"Let be!" he said… "Come and sit here, if this surly fellow will permit it. I shall like to watch his face." He put his burly arm out, and, not before she knew what she was doing, proud Christina Daunet was sitting on a trooper's knee and playing with his beard.

There was a sound of feet and much stamping overhead. Presently, with a sharp ugly crash of splintering timber, the booted leg of one of Butler's men came through the ceiling and dangled helplessly. Christina jumped off the captain's knee and burst out laughing.

"There! I told you 'twould happen."

"Bravo, Tim Jobling! I'd know his leg in a hundred. Gad, I can hear him squealing like a pig up there!"

"'Tis in my mother's room!" exclaimed Christina suddenly. "'Twill frighten her to death."

"You shan't go till they come down. They'll be here directly. Look you, it's all right now. Tim Jobling has gotten back his leg. They have him by the shoulders, and hoist him up so. He's still swearing, though I can't hear. You shall hear me roast him."

Christina did not sit on his knee again, but leaped away with a coquettish grimace as the members of the search party came downstairs. Sheepishly came Tim Jobling at the tail of the group, minded to avoid Butler's merriment.

"Found naught, Cap'n, except one doited old woman in bed."

"My mother!" interposed Christina proudly.

"Ay, Walters, keep a civil tongue in your head, it can do you no harm. Did you put your blade thro' the bed?"

"We did, ay, and the old body sat up, and talked gibberish. She frightened poor Tim so that he stepped back sharp and through the flooring."

"His leg came out just there," said Butler, pointing to the comminuted fracture of laths and planks that sagged down from the ceiling. "Well, Tim, you're no worse and you've given me and my young lady here very good amusement. Your leg wagged like a mouse's tail in the trap. My word!... Well, well, there's meetings and there's partings, Mistress... We'll have to be jogging away. Our man's still to seek. What's this place Redmire?" He spoke to Christina, taking her by the chin.

"It's a lost sort of place, three miles away from here. Marske's a deal more likely. Yet why should I be helping you to catch the poor escaped fellow? You'll hang him, I'll warrant, and though he's despised me, I don't wish him that much harm. I was never fond of telling the hunt which way the fox had gone."

"Do you say so?" He looked judicial, and stroked his beard. After a pause—"Still, I'll just have the correct name of that last place you mentioned... You've no call to be careful for Charles Scanwood, he's given you the go-by, you say. A man merits a rope for neglecting a pretty wench, over and above being punished for the hell he gave us all at Preston. That blue bonnet of his was like the clout of the devil himself. Well, well, adieu. Thank you for your mead, and if ever I'm this way again—"

"Go, since go you will," said she, "I shall see or speak to no man but you here this side of Lady Day. So, Captain, farewell. Grant me a favour?"

"Ask it."

"My cousin, here—"

"Sulky-face! Ay."

"He's got business for me in Marske. The ford's swollen. We have no horse. Let him ride behind one of your men so far? You're going to Marske to look for Scanwood?"

"Certainly, Miss, we'll oblige you. Tim Jobling shall take him behind. Come, men, saddle. We must be off."

"Give me a letter—so that the next company passes this way don't trouble me," she said.

He scribbled something in a pocket-book, and tore it out. She took it.

"Another glass before you go?"

"I'll not say no to that. Here's to King George! Will you toast him?"

She drank it down.

"Just a good excuse to get a drink," she said.

"Right. Women have no call to meddle with politics. And your cousin?"

"You can try him. But I fear he's stubborn. These sullen fits last for days. Here, Luke, drink to please me and the kind captain."

She held the cup to his mouth and whispered, *"Return here as soon as may be."*

Aloud she sneered, "Look you, the great baby! He is suffering me to spill the good liquor. His lips are close shut—"

"Waste no more time on the lout that will not drink when a lady begs him," the captain said. He wiped his lips. "Well, good-bye, then... You were so glad to see me, you'll not refuse me a kiss at parting?"

"What are you thinking of, Captain Butler?" she minced affectedly. "And before your men, too."

"Be hanged to my men! They're busy getting off. You're the prettiest picking I've seen since I left my barracks at Hounslow and I cannot leave it unkissed!"

He forced her lips. The man in the chimney corner stirred.

"Touches him nearly," said Butler, whose eyes shone... "I could do with another, given freely. Maybe, if we were alone—"

She shook her head.

"No good, eh? Your promise, Madam, was finer than your performance. But I'm a gentleman. Come, my lob-lie-by-the-fire, stump up!"

The man in the ingle nook, with one reproachful glance at Christina, rose. He tottered a little, and appeared dazed. Captain Butler, in sudden haste to be gone, clapped him on the back.

"Come, my little fellow, don't keep us waiting. We're bound to catch our gallows-bird before dark!"

The haggard eyes of the fugitive were fixed now on Christina, and now on the stained kitchen knife that lay on the table.

"It's the money," she said hastily. "I was forgetting."

Opening a shabby little leather bag that hung at her girdle, she produced a silver coin.

"Here, take it, Luke. For all that Betty Candlish would have given us credit. There goes! Don't drop it, ye daft goneril! And, mind, you'll have to come back by the bridge up Marske way, for these kind gentlemen won't be coming back, I fancy. It's saving him a matter of two miles, Captain, thanking you kindly, and my mother pining for her drops."

The troopers in the yard were all mounted now, their bridles clinking, their horses pawing. Christina, standing by Captain Butler's stirrup, bickering with him gaily to the last, watched her lover out of the corner of her eye, as he doggedly passed out, and hoisted himself up behind the man called Tim. He seemed woefully stiff. Christina supposed him to have a hurt somewhere, or was it merely the result of two nights' exposure? If it was the former, she promised herself a month's delicious nursing. Yet not a look did he cast in her direction as he rode away, uncovered, leaving one of Luke's old caps, which she had reached down from a nail for him, on the table beside the kitchen knife and the carrot scrapings.

She saw it when she went in again. His negligence of any head covering must have looked odd and indifferent, but then his sullen and cross demeanour had tallied exactly with her account of him. She was proud of the part she had played.

Yet the first thing she did when the sounds had died away was to catch up a rough cloth, not over clean, that lay there, and rub her lips with it till the blood came.

Then she sat down for a little while with her head buried in the self-same cloth, crouching low in shame, remembering bitterly the indignities to which she had submitted in order to secure her false lover's safety.

Half an hour she sat like this. Then the old clock in the corner struck wheezily. It was three o'clock in the afternoon.

She remembered her mother. She ought to go and see and comfort the old woman. Perhaps the rough troopers had frightened her. Heavy-footed, hating herself, loving Charles, she ascended the crazy stairs.

The troopers had frightened her mother indeed. She was dead!...

The daughter, dry-eyed, left alone with death, did what was necessary. She washed the body of her beloved, and dressed it, and laid her arms across her breast with a little sprig of marjoram out of her garden between the fingers, and covered up the cracked dim looking-glass with a fair white cloth. She went downstairs and procured a plateful of salt, which she laid on the dead woman's chest to fend off the evil spirits. She drew down the blinds of the windows that looked out over the garden on to the ford, and sat down near the horribly yawning hole in the flooring to await Luke—or Charles. Neither of them might come for a good hour or more. She did not know which would be the first. Charles might not come for days, but when he did he would be of good comfort, and grateful to her for saving his life at the expense though it were of half an hour's desperate but not irremediable degradation. It was nothing to her, considering the result, perhaps as little to him, and yet more than once during the ordeal she had fancied he was on the point of interposing and forbidding, at the risk of his life, the desecration of the lips that were his, and his only. He might not, perhaps, be willing to kiss her... No matter, she would dress his wound, and shelter him and be a mother, not a mistress, to him a while. He had not slept in a bed, nurse-tended by kind white hands, since Preston fight... He would kiss the hands sometimes?... So she dreamed...

About five o'clock she heard the thud of a horse's hoofs, trotting briskly towards her from the ford. Charles had been in luck, and had somehow or other managed to get hold of a horse?...

She ran down, leaping, in her haste to go the nearest way, over the gaping chasm that shelved in like the hangman's drop, in the middle of the floor.

"My beloved!"

A man stood, sheepish, in the house place. It was Captain Butler.

"You!" she stammered, and reeled.

"Yes, 'tis I, poor fool, come back to know more of you and your wiles, my beauty. For that you are; and may be, now that I've given my men the slip for an hour, you'll let me have that kiss?"

Christina was holding on to the high back of the settle.

"Ay, there's no doubt about it, you're a gay piece, and no one could call you kissing shy. I like it. But that poor lad who sat there—he couldn't stomach so much freedom, I fancy. You made his poor heart ache, and lost him his wits, now, wasn't it?... Well, well, he's the best judge of his own feelings, may be he's as well out of this troublesome world..."

"What do you mean, Captain?"

"Only that that cousin of yours slipped off from behind Tim Jobling crossing the ford, and was washed away almost before we in the front knew what was happening. It's my belief he did it on purpose."

"Drowned! Charles!"

"Is that his silly name? I thought you mentioned some other. He said something to Tim, I believe, before he let go—"

"What was it?"

"Oh, if you care to hear! He said that he found the woman he loved was no better than a harlot, and he didn't care for his life any more since 'twas so. He just slipped off behind—"

"And didn't any one lift a finger to help him?" she wailed.

"Couldn't, I tell you, he was a deal too quick for Tim, seeing as he did it o' purpose. No, Miss, make no bones about it, his death lies at your door."

She tottered, and he held out a clumsy hand.

"Come, put it all behind you. Why should a fine girl like you sorrow for a half-witted yokel like that? You broke his heart, but what right had he to cast those bleary eyes of his on you? You are for a better than he. Come now—be pleasant! You didn't use to look bashful. One would think it was a different woman I've come back to. You're handsome enough, though, in all conscience, even with that face of thunder on you. Will you or won't you, Mistress Daunet? Will you come to me—my pretty?"

He took a pull at the stoup of liquor that was where he had put it down, and held out his arms.

Still the woman stood, dazed, dumbfounded, her ordinarily quick brain acting slowly. She began to realise, by a series of successive shocks, that there was no one left to be helped or saved by diplomacy. She kept her distance, still eyeing the dark wet knife on the table... She spoke at last, sombre, taciturn...

"My mother lies dead upstairs."

"Does she so? Well, 'twas her time to die, wasn't it? We'll bury her decently. Come."

He sat there, glorying in his work, his legs well apart, smiling fatuously, waiting for the fair sulky girl to forget her immediate griefs and fall on his neck for solace and comfort.

"Dawdling! Playing the maiden, eh? You'll come in the end. What if your mother is dead? Eighty, I think she was? Trooper Tim gave her a fright. Finished her off..." He was slightly drunk. "I've left my men at Scanwood. I fancy its master is likely to seek the old earths after all... Come, still thinking on your mother? Devil, don't I tell you she was old and ripe for death? We'll give her Christian burial, and do all things in order..."

He fumbled in his pockets. And Christina's hand made a quick outward movement.

"And will you bury me decently too?" said she, advancing at last. With the dignity of a queen she sat down on the knee of the amorous captain, who fancied the hour of surrender had come. Indeed, he had some small excuse for thinking so, for with a gesture of abandonment she flung one long arm round his neck.

"Ay, but don't strangle me!" he whispered, his chin buried in her bare neck. Christina's other hand was busy at his coat lapel.

She found the place, just over the collar bone—she had no science but she just happened on it,—and drove the long kitchen knife in straight. Its work was not done then. With an effort she drew the knife out and used it again. Captain Butler, before he fell off the chair, saw her eyes glazing, and for one moment held a dead woman in his arms.

"And that, I think, was the way it was," said the romancer to his patient listener, as they sat together on the bare hillside sloping to the Bridge on the other side of the ruined battlement, and let their hands run through the cool straggling grasses that clothed its sad bleakness a little. He raised his hand, that had been fumbling negligently in the ground beside him.

"Look here! A daffodil! This must have been poor Christina Daunet's garden!"

THE WITNESS

I

I was sitting over my fire in my hut in Penanga Creek, Wyoming, when the idea came to me—weakly, dreamily, at first, but later on strongly and vividly, that I must go home. It was, as I confusedly made it, seven years since I left Europe. I felt the thing that had driven me forth less keenly, and I realised that in seven years things must have quieted down a bit. Sally, too, being of a cheerful, easy-going make, would have forgotten what had happened on that one night, since in the nature of the case there could have been no discovery, no scandal.

No one could have known anything about it, no one had witnessed her act except Roger, my dog, who now lay so quietly, numb with advancing age, between my feet in front of the fire. Roger had been only a year old on that short summer night, a clumsy, flopping puppy that followed me unsteadily, swaggering from side to side, down the garden path of the old haunted manor house where Sally James lived. It was flagged with broad white stones, and the gate of it opened straight on to the road that led to Durham, to Darlington, and to the other ends of the earth, where I am now.

I ran away, like a coward, and yet not a coward, for I loved Sally James and I knew too much. I turned at the gate, and I gazed back at the windows of the house with their close-drawn blinds. I thought they looked like eyelids let down over anxious dreams. I saw the one window in the oldest part of the house where Sally, half dressed, was peeping through the blind, annoyed, yet uncomplaining at my departure. She knew men; she thought I was just going to put my head under the pump, and freshen my aching brain and my eyes that had looked on so much since they closed in sleep the night before. Then after a walk over the common, with my dog at my heels, I should return to her, stay with her through the long years to come, and profit by her crime. She had rid me of a nuisance. She did not realise—how could she, being hard Sally James?—that I could not bear the thought of seeing her face again. She was so careless of other people's feelings that she knew less of what I felt than the silly young dog who slunk at my heels—or the pert robin that perched on the cheek of the gate-post. The robin, with its head on one side, seemed to stare at me and leer horribly as I closed the gate behind me, and went out into the world for ever. I never meant to see Sally again, I never meant to write or receive a letter; I never meant to look at a newspaper again; I never meant to know if she were tried for murder or not. I only knew that I did not mean to chance having to bear evidence against her.

There was very little likelihood of that. Mrs. James, the bouncing, jolly widow and my secret love, had saved money left her by her late husband and had managed to buy the freehold of Dewlap Hall, an old manor house that had seen better days. It had been one of the homes of the Conyers family, but it was now little more than a forlorn, dejected farmhouse, standing alone in a couple of acres about three miles out of Durham. It looked even a better place than it was. Once you were inside you saw that its ruin was only a question of time. It was slowly crumbling, festering, powdering away. Half the rooms were unsafe, the walls of the others were shored up, partitioned off, reduced to a fourth of their original size. One floor was taken bodily away—I have been told, to lay the ghost. The sharp, jagged rafters sagged downwards from the sides. The floor of this room was cobbled, it had lancet windows: people said it was the old chapel. Sally used the place as a wash-house; it opened out of her kitchen, which was the old and only hall of the first house. That, Mr. Wilson the vicar had told us, was built in the time of Edward II. Of course the house was haunted. A grey lady. Sally's bedroom, above, must have been taken off the whole top of the hall, the floor was very bad, and though originally it must have been a handsome-sized, airy and pleasant room in spite of its low ceiling, the late owner had mistrusted the eastern portion of it so much that he had walled it off with boards and some concrete, calmly reducing the best bedroom to a cell about ten feet square.

It was big enough for two people, for Sally and me, drunk with love. I believe Sally and I would have made love if we had been fastened in a barrel studded with nails, and rolled down to the sea. But not room enough for three.

On that night, Sally and I, absorbed in each other, had not heard the heavy drunkard's footfall of my wife on the creaking steps of the staircase that led up from the house place below, and the sound of the door of the room where we were, being slowly pushed open. The heavy bolt that should by rights have gone across it, was lying on the wicker chair by the bed. Sally, in her wild confidence in the impossibility of molestation in this lonely part of the country, had omitted to run it into the thole holes on either side of the lintels, as usual. When you did that you made the chamber into a real castle of strength, but she had forgotten all but me.

And poor mad Mary, my wife, stood like the ghost of Dewlap Hall, and watched us. Sally, half dazed, may have thought that she *was* the ghost...

Anyway, she struck out with the heavy iron bar that lay ready to her hand. She was strong. Hardly another woman could have wielded it. My dog Roger looked up from where he slept, crouched on my coat at the foot of the bed on Sally's packing-box...

The iron bar was immensely weighty, my poor old wife fell like a log. Roger turned up his eyes... I said, "Down, Roger!" and Roger lay down. Though a mere puppy, he was well trained.

Sally dropped the bar, with a loud clang on the floor. There was nobody below to hear it. It lay there, till seeing my eyes fixed on it, she picked it up easily and replaced it on the chair without even looking at it. But there was no blood or even hairs on it, I could have told her, for I had got hold of Mary by that time, and felt her, and I was perfectly sure that she had been stunned—killed outright. So far as I could see, the skin was not even broken. Her clumsy straw hat was of course smashed, battered in, and her very thick black hair lay like a mat over the crown of her head.

Sally asked me if she were dead, and I answered, yes, stone dead. Sally shrugged her shoulders, as who should say, It's fate. Then without blinking, she put a petticoat on over her nightgown, and drew the strings of it tightly round her waist till I should have thought they would have cut her, but I expect she didn't feel much at that particular moment. At least, I didn't. I kept my eyes on her all the time; I thought it might prevent me from going mad. And Sally was sure to know what to do. It was her murder...

It was a very warm night, and getting on for two o'clock, I should have thought, but no light pierced through the pieces of red gingham that Sally had hung up and gathered into a curtain for the window.

I watched Sally. She came up to me and took hold of Mary's feet, and then dropped them again after I had taken the corpse by the shoulders. She stood a moment, a bit mazed, then she thought of the bar and went to it where it lay on the chair by the bedside. She lifted it, and examined its iron surface...

"Give it to me," I said. I stupidly thought of burning it.

"Nonsense!" Sally said, quite sharply, wiping it on her nightgown and replacing it on the chair. "Let it stay there where it always lies. Old Betty is used to the sight of it."

She was wise. She returned to me and my burden. She took hold of Mary's feet again, and didn't drop them this time, but tied a towel round her ankles, thus binding them firmly together. Then, both of us breathing heavily, we got the body down the stairs. I went first. I could not see Mary's face, but I saw Sally's, and her lips were red, and tightly primmed. Roger, clumsily trying to pass us and our burden on the narrow flight of steps, got under our feet and nearly threw us down, and she unclosed her lips to swear at him. If she had not spoken, I believe I should have dropped.

We laid Mary on the stone-flagged kitchen floor, while Sally fumbled with the latch of the wash-house. There was a door out of that into the back yard, and thence into a little orchard, and out of that into the wood which stretched away towards Finchale Priory at the back of the house to the north. It was conveniently full of old abandoned pit shafts. I knew that well enough. But it was not until we gained the door of the wash-house that it occurred to me what Sally meant to do, and had meant to do from the moment we first lifted Mary to bring her downstairs.

There was a little more light now, but still it was not light enough to see, and I hoped it would not be until we got into the shelter of the woods. Sally held the feet, as before. She swung a lantern by a string from her teeth, she had refused to let me carry it. Sally had not much faith in me at the best of times, and now when so much depended on it, I could see that she meant to see to everything herself. Roger followed us; he was very humble and submissive since Sally had spoken to him so roughly.

She swore again, but not at him, for he kept out of her way. It was when the long brambles caught the hem of her nightgown that hung below the petticoat. Her eyes flashed a little now and then in the light of the swinging lantern...

"I can hardly walk, I've got the bloody hem of my shift so wet," she said, roughly.

"Can you manage?" I asked, speaking very faint. She had said "bloody"!

"Yes. Good thing it's dew, not blood, after all!" she reassured me. "Don't talk. I've no breath for talking. My word! I sweat, and no mistake!"

I didn't want to talk. I was thinking of Mary, slung between us, dead as dead. And the last time I saw her she was dead drunk in the streets of Cardiff, reeling about, carrying on her trade. There was no need, that was the shame and disgrace. I was earning good wages at Neath as a colliery man, and gave her her fair share. But she had always taken too much and never been respectable, not even when I married her. They say those two things go together, and luckily there were no children. As soon as I found out what she was up to, I left her, deserted her, people would say, and drifted to Durham. That was full two years ago.

How did she find out that I had come to Durham, and was working at the Elvet pit? I never wrote to her once. How did she know I was living with Sally James in her house three miles out of Durham? How had she tracked me? I could not tell, then, and I don't know now!

I was wondering, wondering, and the undergrowth grew thick and the nut boughs lashed my cheek in the dark. I stumbled a little as we got along with *that* between us, and I forgot to keep step with Sally, and she swore at me for an awkward fool that was giving her, a weak woman, all the work to do.

We came at last to the old pit shaft Sally and I knew of, for it had been one of our trysting places in her husband's lifetime. Most of these disused shafts are walled round with brick, but this one wasn't, for some reason or other. It was carelessly staked round with wattle, waiting to be done properly, I suppose. A drunken man could easily fall in and no one be any the wiser. For a pit shaft is so deep that you can see the stars in the daylight.

Mary must have walked all the way from Cardiff. It was the first time I felt sorry for her. I had been till then so angry with her for coming ferreting and spying, that if you had asked me, I should have said I was glad she had got her deserts. But I could not help seeing the worn soles of her shoes as we heaved her over the edge of the hole, and they were fairly walked through. I felt sorry for her then.

Mary was gone, without sticking or any awkwardness, and Sally breathed hard. She put out her hand and fondled Roger.

"Good dog!" she said. "He never barked. He won't tell tales of us, will he, pet?"

Roger licked her hand, as an answer to her question. He was even at that age a wonderfully bright, intelligent dog.

Then Sally stooped, and tried to pick the long bramble trail out of the hem of her nightgown. It resisted—it was hopelessly entangled.

"Stand on it," she said, "while I walk on a bit. One can always get rid of followers that way."

She alluded to the old superstition that a girl who attracts the wild wood tendrils will always have plenty of sweethearts. Her white feet were quite bare... I never knew a hardier woman than Sally. She looked down into the shaft once, though of course there was nothing to see, it was too dark and deep down; then she turned round sharp and decided...

"We had best get back to bed now," she said cheerfully. "There's a good piece of night left, and I'm sure we both need a rest."

I caught her up in my arms, and carried her home, it was only a little bit of a way, no distance at all, though coming out it had seemed so terribly long. She liked being carried. Once she put up her mouth and kissed me.

I took her in and set her down in the middle of the house place. She tottered a little, like a china ornament when you have been shifting it. She turned to go upstairs again. I could not manage it.

"Sally," I said, "I think I'll go and get a wash."

"Do," she said, "and you can draw yourself some cider. There's plenty in the barrel in the corner there."

I watched her ascend the stairs, rather heavily. Then I whistled my dog. The door of the house stood open, the dawn was just breaking. I latched it carefully behind me, and went away down the garden path. I looked back once—only once. Then I took my resolve definitely. I have never seen her since.

*

I secured a passage out West, and we sailed, my poor dog and I, the very next day. And in my panic I have never looked at a paper from that day to this. I don't know whether there was an inquiry or not, or whether any suspicion fell on Sally; I should say not, she is too clever. Of one thing I am quite sure; the body was never found. They never are when they are lost like that. I have an idea too that my wife Mary was never even missed in Cardiff—who cares when prostitutes die or disappear? If, as was probable, no one had chanced to see her approach Dewlap Hall in the early hours of the morning, then there was absolutely no witness of Sally's crime except myself and my dog Roger.

Yet, the thought that plagued me all through that night passes through my mind, and worries me still. I had deserted Mary—I had not seen nor communicated with her or any of my old friends in and near Cardiff—I am a Welshman—for three years!

So how did she know where to find me? Did she settle to visit all the great mining centres in turn? And did she draw Durham early in the game, and when she got to Durham, how did she get wind of my living at Dewlap with Sally James?

My thoughts, for the last seven years, have not been pleasant, but they are all the company I have had. I have worked hard here, I have even had a bit of luck and been able to lay by a little, but I have hardly spoken to a single soul. The last man who spent a night in my cabin was a taciturn Japanese who had less conversation than even Roger.

It is killing me. That is why two nights ago I took up my pen and wrote to Sally. *Mrs. James, Dewlap Hall, near Durham, England*. I must see her again. And to-day I have managed somehow or other to mail the letter. Now I wait.

*

I waited a good month. Then there came an answer, an answer I had ridden in for to Blizzardville every other day all through the time, speaking to no one except the clerk at the window of the post office—an uncommon dull and slow dog he was.

She wrote—

> "You wretch! What a surprise to hear from you! Have you returned to your senses? I congratulate you. Your letter seems to mean that you have, and I don't mind saying how glad I am! Oh! George, how could you walk off like that, and I lying there expecting you to come back after you had had a wash and a drink to buck you up. Men always feel these things so much more than women, at the time. As for me, you'd be surprised to hear it, but sometimes at nights I feel as much remorse as you would have me. Only then when the good daylight comes in at the pane I feel so different, one would not believe it was the same woman. Morning thoughts always are more cheerful. You see, I can't forgive her for coming to dig me and you out in our happiness. She had nothing more to do with you. She drank, she sold herself, she got what she deserved, even if it was *me* that gave it to her. I saw it all as I lifted that great bar. She came meddling, and like all meddlesome fools, she got what for. If you had considered it yourself for one moment you never would have left me like that. But now you have thought it over, and you've thought better of it, and you are coming back to me! Come, only come! All is serene, as I daresay you know. Nobody bothered. William Dysart fooled about me a little when you left the field free, but I treated him with a high hand and I am shot of him except

> for a lowering look he gives me over the top of his pew, in Church on Sunday. They say he is my enemy, but even he can't see to the bottom of a pit shaft, and there's no evidence. I am respected in the place, and I can marry any one I please, and when I please. Shan't it be you, George? Aren't you and I bound by the memory of that night and what I did to get you? Come. Your own wicked, level-headed Sally.
>
> "P.S.—I suppose the dog Roger, who was a puppy then, has died a natural death? Poor old dear! I was jealous of that dog, I always felt you liked him nearly as well as you liked me. Peace be to his bones."

Roger looked up at me, as I looked down his way when I came to that last piece all about him. I believe I read it aloud softly. I am in the habit of talking to Roger. He knows perfectly well what one says to him. I stroked him. "Dead? Not a bit of it, old dog!" I said. "We are all alive and kicking, aren't we? Very well preserved, eyes a little bleary perhaps, not many teeth in our head, but those sound, and that's half the battle."

Roger fawned on me. He is a quiet, taciturn creature, like his master, and I verily believe the sound of his own voice has got to scare him almost as much as mine does me.

"You'll come to England with me, old dog, won't you? You and me'll never be parted; she must take us both for better or worse, eh?"

Roger's tail wagged. He said nothing, but of course he understood.

I could not have left him, even if I had wanted to, to die alone in a strange country. Besides, he knows all about me. He saw it all. I can still see him looking pensively down into the pit shaft, after...

He is my only confidant, for of course I never let on to any one, I could never risk giving Sally away. But a dog! Yes, I am glad he knows.

I could not get ready to leave for about a week, and before I started I got another letter from Sally. It must have been written not much more than a day after the first letter, and there seemed no particular reason why she should ever have written it. It was rather incoherent. The thought of our meeting again must have troubled her, must have a little turned her head. She mixed up all sorts of things in her letter, and mentioned Roger again three or four times, in connection with William Dysart, who she seems to fancy has got his knife into her. A despised lover, but still—I began to fear that the sight of my dog would distress her, remind her of that awful night, when suddenly and without thought or premeditation she up and did a sin for me!

What was I to do? It was but woman's nonsense at the best, and I could not leave my faithful beast to pine and starve because of a woman's whim! I consoled myself with the reflection that a hard, sensible woman such as Sally had proved herself to be, would not allow any mere fancy to affect her for long. She would force herself to get over it, and ignore it as she had the other. I settled it the way I wanted to and took Roger with me.

I made one tiresome discovery on the way home. I was pretty deaf, and could hear very ill unless the speaker addressed himself especially to me, and general conversation not at all. This saddened me. Even a slight deafness makes a man such a nuisance, and I thought it might put Sally off, or even set her wilful mightiness against me. Sally was never very patient at the best of times. You see I thought of everything in relation to her. Her crime, and her heartlessness and want of feeling with regard to it, seemed not to affect my appreciation of her in any way. Indeed, I admired her devil-may-carishness because it was on the whole the most decent way for her to behave. I should have hated her to whine and snivel...

I walked out from Durham one fine Sunday morning in May, Roger trotting at my heels. I had asked no questions about Sally and her circumstances. I knew from her letter that she was well, and moreover I experienced some difficulty in framing questions, or indeed in getting into conversation at all. I do not believe I spoke more than two consecutive sentences all the way back, and those I mumbled in my beard, for all the world as if I were tongue-tied. No one bothered about me, I expect I was singularly unattractive, and for the most part I was left severely alone. I had lost all convivial habits, I did not care to see or hear anything. I never looked at a paper, my one idea was to see Sally again.

Roger was not so unsociable. Indeed, my trouble with him was that he was the reverse. He seemed to be continually getting into conversations, and eventually into fights, with other dogs. One dog, a sandy, weedy terrier, lame of one leg, that we met as soon as we got out at Durham station, he seemed, after having fought handsomely with, to take a great fancy to, and the wretched lame cur chose to follow us all the way out to Dewlap Hall. It was disturbing, and I should have preferred to have kept my faithful dog entirely to myself at a moment like this. I was going to meet the woman I loved again after all these years. And only Roger knew what had been.

It was Sunday morning, and I heard bells ringing at the different churches all the way out. Sally was standing in the clear morning light, at the low door of her house close to the monthly rose-bush which stood as high as she did. There was but one rose on it. She wore a pink cotton dress. She had grown a little stouter. She held her hand straight across her forehead, against the sun which came into her eyes, and made her frown—or was it the sight of me? For indeed, her black eyebrows were cruelly drawn down as Roger and I and Roger's friend came up the flagged path. But all she said was, as she took her hand away from her face and laid it in mine—

"Come in."

She pulled me inside, and shut the door in Roger's face. He set up a whine.

"Poor Roger!" I said in spite of myself, and my wish not to annoy her. "Don't you remember him?"

"Yes, but why did you bring the wretched creature here? I thought he was dead. I understood you to say so..."

She stood there, quaking, quivering with anger. I had never seen Sally so unmanned...

"Never mind the dog, Sally,—kiss me."

She kissed me, then she said thoughtfully—

"Perhaps, on the whole I had better have him in?"

She opened the door, and drove away the stranger dog. Roger she seized, hauling him in by the collar. She then carefully bolted the door with one hand, sticking to Roger with the other.

"Have you got a chain?"

"What for, Sally?"

"To chain him up. I can't have him loose. He's been talking to that mongrel of Dysart's—I know the malicious beast—and when dogs get talking together—now—"

"Talking! My dear Sally!"

"Oh, you know what I mean. It was William Dysart who directed Mary here that night, or rather morning. He's longing to get his knife into me—or you."

"But was there an inquiry? I didn't read any of the papers, I was so afraid of what I might see there... you understand?"

She looked at me narrowly. Then she tossed her head.

"Silly fellow, there was nothing to make you uneasy. There was not a word of gossip. No one knew. There was one woman less on the streets of Cardiff, that's all."

"But you said William Dysart directed her here?"

"Yes, that came out, in a roundabout way, but he didn't know who she was, or that she didn't just come here and go straight back again where she came from. If only you had taken my hint?"

"What hint?"

"About Roger."

"You do puzzle me, Sally... You only said you supposed he was dead. Well, he isn't, that's all, and mighty glad I am of it. And he isn't used to being tied up, and I'm not going to put upon the old dog now."

"I can't help it. He doesn't go free in my house! We must talk it over. Meantime..."

She left me abruptly—Sally never dawdled, not even over a murder. Trailing Roger helplessly by the collar, she went into the wash-house next door. I followed her grumbling a little, but still quite her humble slave. She made his collar more secure and then tied him to the copper. Then she reached up to a high shelf, and gave him a handsome plateful of bones and a pat on the head that had more of monition than of kindness in it. Roger looked up at me. He seemed to understand the situation better than I did. "Keep in with her, don't irritate her!" he seemed to say. He shivered and seemed cold.

"Tell him to be a good dog and behave himself," she said to me, "and he shall be loosed to-morrow, if I can feel quite sure of him... Things are changed a bit, George, since you were here, and it is easy to see you have not kept pace with them. We must brush you up, and bring you up to date..."

She was very nervous. I followed her out of the wash-house, closing the door behind me, as she bade me, over her shoulder. In the living-room, she turned and faced me.

She was a very beautiful woman, was Sally James. Her white teeth showed keen, as her short upper lip was drawn up from them. It made her look fine, but a bit cruel. She was not a very big woman, but stately, majestic even, at times, though she was only a farmer's widow and daughter. Just now, as she stood there, her arms at her sides, her broad breast, covered with pink print, was like a queen's. She was holding herself in readiness for my first embrace, and I longed for it too, and yet—I distrusted her... She was without principle, a figure of shifting sand. She would always do exactly as she liked, and at the moment when she liked... And she hated my dog.

I invented excuses for her...

"It is all association," I thought, as I hung back. "She is not so heartless as she seems. The dog was in the room when it happened, and by the shaft when we heaved Her over. He reminds her... She has some feeling..."

My distrust turned all at once to tenderness, and I sat down on the settle and took her in my arms. She was very soft and yielding, and she sat meekly on my knee and kissed me passionately again and again. Then I kissed her back just the same. The tall clock ticked as it did on The Night... only louder...

There did not seem to be a soul about. I asked Sally if she had no servant to help her.

"I've a woman—old Betty—do you remember her?—comes to help me all the week through, but she stays away on Sundays. The farm hands sleep nearly a quarter of a mile away. You'll stop to-night, George?"

I said I would. In my heart I wondered if her room was still the same, and if I could stand it!

II

A movement in the room awoke me. I opened my eyes slowly, and in the grey light I put out my hand and missed Sally. She had left my side.

I put some clothes on and went down the little steep single stairs, lit only by one dirty, cobwebby window. The scanty twilight, for that was all it was as yet, slid in and on to the white lintels, cracked and seamed with age—I never liked the dawn, when people die. The moon was paling quietly in the sky. The morning star still lingered there. At the corner where the stairs turned sharply, I looked down at my feet and remembered the job we had to get Mary past it! Drops of sweat broke out on my forehead just as they had done then. That and the dawn! I was very nervous. It was nearly the same as that other night.

Sally was not in the house place. I stood—turning on my heels—and wondered where she was. I made no doubt that she was walking in her sleep—that seeing me had brought back all the sensations of that dreadful night, and that she was repeating them. Perhaps she had remembered the light on the lintel, the turn of the stair too?... What I feared was that she had gone wandering along the same dreary path through the wood, as far as the shaft. And then, when she got there, suppose her remorse was too much for her and she were mad enough to throw herself over!... Such things have happened—I had seen *The Bells* and *Macbeth.* Sally was rather like Lady Macbeth, and Lady Macbeth, strong-minded as she was, rued her deed, and walked in her sleep, and rubbed her hands. Sally had no blood to think about—only dew on the hem of her nightgown that time... You couldn't tell blood from dew at night...

I heard a click—something like the sound made by one earthenware pan rubbing against another, in the wash-house... I had maligned Sally in my thoughts. She had merely gone downstairs to feed Roger! The last remark she had made on going to bed was that he looked weakly, and on his last legs, and should by rights be put away before he suffered pain. Dogs die so hard, she had said. I opened the door that led into the old stone-paved chapel Sally used as a wash-house, and stood the beer-casks in.

Sally, in her plain nightgown, was standing there barefoot on the cobbled stones. She looked a bit cranky. Her black hair hung partly down her back, and in elf locks, that were curls overnight, in her eyes. She had a great quantity of hair, and out of vanity she never took it all down when she went to bed, but half arranged it with pins and coloured ribbons. Her arm was raised to a high shelf whence she had taken Roger's provender earlier in the day. The movement made the fronts of her nightgown gape, and show her breast.

She started when I came in, and dropped her arm guiltily.

"Go away, go away!" she screamed, and put her hand behind her back. "Go away, and let me finish the job!"

"What job, in Heaven's name," I cried, "at this hour of night? We saw to the dog—no need to feed him again!"

"Feed him, you idiot!... Poison him, more likely—anything to get him out of the way!"

I went up to her and laid my hand on her arm.

"I do believe the sight of Roger, who saw you murder Mary, has put you clean out of your wits, Sally, my dear."

"And what about you and your wits, bringing the beast here—!"

She rushed at poor Roger, who squatted at the extreme length of his cord, staring at her calmly, boldly, as if inviting her to stick him with the knife she brandished. He was never like any other dog. He did not plunge or bark. I saved him, I took the knife out of her hand, and flung it into a meal-tub close by.

"Fool, fool!" she yelled, but I put my hand over her mouth, and forced her back on the tub, so that she sat on the knife. I was so sure she was going mad that it made me calm and strong, and I tried to soothe her and speak gently to her, as one does to an invalid.

"What do you want to kill my poor old dog for, Sally?"

"I must. I must. He's dangerous."

"Dangerous without a sound tooth in his head?"

"He has a tongue in his head—"

She looked at me narrowly, dragging down the outside corners of her eyelids like a bulldog. Then she pulled the fronts of her nightdress to, and tried to speak reasonably. She succeeded more or less, but it was a great effort to her.

"Don't you know what has happened here while you have been away sulking at the other end of the world?"

I said nothing on purpose, so as not to put her back up. She stood staring at me, waiting for me to say something. I was so long, she began to shake in the cold... And Sally never could keep quiet for long. Her temper broke out and she shouted at me.

"Don't look so stupid, George!... God, it sends me mad!"

"Dear, try and tell me quietly." I sat down on an empty barrel. "Come here. Sit on my knee—"

She waved me away. She moistened her lips. "Don't treat me like a child or a madwoman, George. It is serious, sober earnest. I am telling you facts—not lies. The police—damn them!—have got a new weapon, and they use it for all it is worth..."

She wrung her hands and walked up and down.

"Oh, to think that all this time we have made pets of these wretched animals, and trusted them—I had a pet dog once—I put it away because it watched me, though I wasn't doing anything wrong. Yes, we used to let them go about with us, and see all we did, and listen to all we said! Who minded talking secrets with an animal in the room, or doing anything one liked in a whole farmyard of beasts—then? We didn't know that dog of yours was lying at the foot of the bed when Mary was done for: I never even thought of him! We actually let him go with us to the edge of the shaft and see us throw her in! God, what fools we were!"

"But what can a dog do, you silly darling?"

"He can get us hanged! Get us both hanged! Why, your beast there—the very moment he got into England he must have learnt his power; he must have blabbed our whole story, and to that animal of Dysart's, too, the very last person—!"

I tried to soothe her.

"Sally, my dear, it's awfully cold here! You're shivering. Do let us get back to bed!"

I said that, but indeed I was getting to be afraid of her, in bed or out of it.

She took no notice of me, but went on—

"You never looked at a paper, you tell me, and yet they were full of it two years ago—the wonderful new discovery. Since then I've never known a moment's peace. My life has been hell. You may thank your stars you were out of it and had left me to bear the whole brunt of it."

"For goodness' sake explain!" I said crossly.

She came quite close to me and whispered, "The police! It's a new dodge of the police. I hate 'em and their filthy methods! They get hold of animals—dogs preferred, because they're more intelligent—and shut them down there in cellars, behind locked doors, and then they torture them, rack them... George, can you bear the idea of Roger tortured, racked,—kept without water for a week! Oh, if you had heard, as I have, scores of times, only I've run away and said nothing because of my guilty conscience—if you'd heard the pitiful howls and whines at the back of the police station there, and knew that some poor helpless beast was being made to betray and give evidence—"

"But I don't see how a dog, or any animal indeed, could let on to what it knew even if it tried," I said, as grave as a judge, to pacify her.

"Oh, that's a mere matter of detail. The police have got a code—they manage to communicate with the beasts. They count the barks—"

"Ha! ha!" I laughed.

"Don't dare to laugh, you ignorant fool. Have you never heard of those spiritualist affairs? The spirits rap, and the medium tells you what they are saying. Well, the dog barks—it comes to the same thing—"

She sighed deeply and seemed relieved. It was now quite day. Her candle flared. She was waiting for me to speak. I was thinking of what would be the most soothing thing to say… It would not come. I was at my wits' end. The only thing I could think of was to get her back to bed and send for a doctor.

I moved slightly in my indecision. She caught my hand. Hers was very hot.

"George, what are you going to do? I've explained clearly, haven't I?"

"Quite." I had now fixed on a plan of action.

"And now, Sally darling," I said softly, "just you get back to bed, and I'll settle Roger, and then I'll bring you a nice cup of tea."

That plan failed. She screamed, and beat the air with her hands.

"Settle him? Not you. It takes a man to do that—or a woman like me! No, I know you. You want me to go quietly, while you untie the dog, and let him go free to get us hanged—me, at any rate. I murdered Mary—you only looked on. And your dog. What'll *you* get? I shall swing for it. He's sure to have told Dysart's dog, and the police'll get wind of it—Dysart'll take care of that. He's only waiting—has been these ten years. And then they can howk Mary up—what's left of her—and the damned dog'll tell them who put her there."

"Do you suppose Roger would betray us?" I said, humouring her. She was crying now, violently, against my heart.

"But, George—under torture—there is no knowing what he might do. Is there, Roger?"

She left me, contemptuously, and bending down a little, spoke to Roger as if he were a human being. That gave me a turn, and I felt very queer. She seemed so sure of herself, and her tale. Roger appeared to listen. He barked three times... then four times... then more. I lost count. But Sally didn't, apparently. She wiped her eyes on the sleeve of her nightgown, tossed her head back and cried triumphantly—

"There, he says I had better warn you! He can't be quite sure—he's not so young as he was—his power of endurance is weakened! That's what he says, as well as he can—to me who understand him... Did you notice," she continued, "how Dysart's dog limps? Well, that's because—every one knows it, though it's supposed to be a secret—the police examined him—tormented, I call it—a year ago, in connection with a case of arson. Dysart's ricks were set on fire—" she chuckled.

"Who was accused?"

"Me."

"And did you—"

"That's not the point. But Dysart's dog was got to admit that he had seen one of my men loitering about at an awkward time—the time when it happened, in fact. The police couldn't make anything of his evidence—it was too scanty, luckily; but all the same, he's gone lame ever since. I hate the police as I hate sin... Brutes they are!... Roger, good dog, tell me how did you learn the code in this short time?"

Roger barked gently, a little chain of barks.

"From Dysart's dog, he says. It's quite simple. Well, George, look here—no, I'm not cold when I'm interested—I'll go on getting it from Roger, and perhaps I'll be able to convince you that for his own sake, Roger had better be put out of the way. He wishes it..."

"I *am* convinced," I said. I was convinced that she was off her head on this particular point, and that a good rest would set her right. I put my arm round her, and tried to kiss her and lead her away. But she pushed me off.

"Go and sit over there. Don't worry me. I want all my wits about me now, and once you see the danger—if you love me you won't set the life of an old toothless, worn-out dog against mine, for that's what it comes to."

"I do love you, Sally... Now, Roger, stand and deliver. Answer the lady."

There is no good fighting hallucinations, it is best to humour them. Any doctor would have agreed with me that it was useless to argue with a woman so terribly excited as Sally was. There she stood, barefooted on the stone floor, in the light circle that the candle made, waving her arms and casting shadows of awful length and shape. The black jagged ends of the rafters of the broken flooring over her head framed her in spikes, as they sagged and drooped towards the middle of the room where she was. Nice home-coming for a man after all those years!... I wished, then—how I wished!—I had stayed in Wyoming with my faithful Roger, and only seen Sally as I remembered her, plucky, resolute and sensible, instead of the all-to-pieces madwoman remorse had made of her.

But she was determined to go through with the mad farce. She stooped, tossed back her hair and fixed Roger with her eyes. He met them as dogs do without flinching or turning away. Poor dear old Roger was so faithful and so old, I did wish she would leave him alone. But no—

"Roger," she said solemnly, "did Dysart's dog warn you of the state of things here, and of what might happen to you?"

A lot of little orderly barks answered her. Though Roger always did bark when you spoke to him in a certain domineering tone, it was fairly horrible.

Sally turned to me, and her voice was lifted with pride.

"He says yes, that he is fully informed. Moreover, Dysart's dog has told him that his master has had suspicions of you ever since a certain tramp woman he met on the Witton-Gilbert road was so keen on finding her way to you. William Dysart told her she would probably find you in bed with me, blast and curse him! I am glad I burnt five of his ricks!"

"Come, come, Sally, does my dog really say all that?" I mocked her.

"He says that and a lot more. That Dysart went straight to the police this morning after seeing you and your dog walk across the market-place—now, then!"

"Damn it all, that's where Roger picked up the cur first," I called out, for I own this struck me. And the dog's manner was disquieting. All this was exciting and very bad for him. He shivered and whined very low.

"Roger, Roger, old man!" I caressed him and talked to him as if he was human and sensible, as indeed he was, but only as dogs—the best of them—are. "Don't take on so! What is it? What's the matter?"

"He'll tell you fast enough," Sally said, grinning. She went up to him, too, and passed her hands over his back. "Come, tell us all about it, good dog."

I couldn't bear to see her lay her Judas hand on him. I shouted, "Don't you touch my dog, you—" I couldn't find a word bad enough for her—not even one of the worst; all my love for her had gone, melted away.

"All right!" she answered carelessly, desisting.

So we both stood at an equal distance from Roger, who barked incessantly for about five minutes. I thought I noticed gaps between the groups of barks, as it were, but even now I cannot be quite sure. Sally had got me into the same state as the dog, we were both beside ourselves—fairly bewitched, I think.

Now Sally translated, in a level voice. Her quiet was more awful than her bluster.

"He says, 'Master, save me from the torture. I am old, I have not many months to live. Shoot me first. I may not be able to stop myself from betraying you—and her. Shoot me, in mercy! Shoot me!'"

"Is that so, Roger?" I asked him. The spell wrought on me so that I began to believe it. "Do you want me to kill you?"

He barked—yes, he barked horribly.

Then I turned on Sally, and she held up her head and looked me with insolence in the face, and the dog began to plunge and strain on the cord, barking furiously all the time.

"You devil," I yelled, "you are taking me in! This is all a plan got up to make me put away my faithful old dog!"

"Look at your dog!" she said, calmly. "He has more sense than you. Do you know what he is trying to do? He's trying to commit suicide—he says it's his only chance, if you won't shoot him. You coward! Afraid to put him out of his misery and help him to get out of the way before he's forced to betray you! Go and get your gun! Kill him, man—or let me."

I came out of my maze just in time. I saw Sally whip the knife out from under her and go for Roger with it. The dog had nearly succeeded in strangling himself—he had come to make gurgling noises in his throat... But I was all there, now...

"Don't you do it, old dog!" I up and shouted. "I'll settle her, as she settled Mary!"

And that is why I am sitting here in Durham gaol waiting to be hanged, and a good riddance too. I don't care to live... Poor Roger did manage to commit suicide. He knew.

THE BAROMETER

There existed a few years ago, in the Yorkshire wolds, a state of affairs in which the barometer was more consulted than the Bible, and the only barometer in the district hung in the hall of the Vicarage and belonged to the parson, who scanned it daily and out of its abstruse lettering gave no hope to his pining household. The relentless needle stood ever at "set fair," and the terrible drought, which had already lasted for six whole weeks, continued. The dreary sheet of sky overhead stretched in its pitiless blueness over the baked brown earth that lay beneath, parched and cracked and yawning for rain. In between the rift set apart for their habitation, walked sad human beings, sighing and complaining, full of vague physical uneasiness and sense of stress of longing.

The Church and Vicarage of Barmoor, and the few cottages to which it ministered, made the only break in the wilderness of moorland that stretched away for miles to Pickering on the one side and Danby Moor on the other. Three trees grew near the Vicarage: the boughs of one hung over the roof of the lean-to, and made a landmark over the moor. In the early spring they had been fine bunches of verdure. Now their tattered and disconsolate foliage hung motionless, shrinking day by day into the brown semblance of what were once green leaves. A little beck ran at the bottom of the parson's garden, but it was now all but dry. Everything was dried and wasted, except the heather which sprouted and thickened and browned under the desolating shine of the pitiless sun, while the air above it quivered with refraction.

"The air is dancing!" cried the parson's boys, lying in the thick tufts and looking towards the low ridges that bounded their moor to the north. Later on it grew so hot that the very sun was veiled in mist, and the air did not dance any more, but stood still with weariness, so the children said, again. A lighted candle, held in the kitchen garden, flared straight up, like a pillar.

The children tried it—they tried everything—everything permissible under the strict system of Vicarage discipline—to amuse themselves, in these days, when their elders were too tired and cross to undertake to keep them happy. They wandered about together, their arms heavily linked round each other's shoulders, dragging their feet along the cinder paths in an irritating unison. They stood now, in their baggy little home-made clothes, on the path that led down the kitchen garden, bordered with feeble flowers. It was only bordered; the middle patch of ground was, perforce, devoted to useful vegetable cultivation. The living of Barmoor was not a rich living, and the Rev. Matthew Cooper, its incumbent, stood very low in position, birth, and education.

His gardener, who was also the sexton, was digging the potatoes for early dinner. He grunted while he dug, and his back was turned to the children, who watched, with a kind of fascination born of ennui, the turn of the fork and the roll of the loose mould, and the horny hand that came down every now and then and gathered up the harvest of his toil and flung it into a basket. Saunders was careless, and let several potatoes roll back into the furrow, out of the eight or so that each turn of the fork should yield.

"Oh, Saunders, look, ye've missed one!" piped the youngest child.

"Happen I have, Master John," replied the old man. "It's ower hot to be fashed!"

The child sighed.

"Won't it really rain soon, Saunders dear?" he asked wearily. He had heard so much lately of this wonderful rain that was to heal all ills and make the world a pleasant place again. Childlike, he had forgotten what rain was like, and how he hated it, since it kept him indoors, and spoiled his play.

"Happen it may, happen it mayn't!" muttered the old servant sulkily. With a sudden access of spite, he added, "Didn't the master pray for it i' church last Sunda'? But some folks has no influence with the Almighty. A'm sayin' that the Lord ought to do it for His ain sake—the bonny garden's fair perished for the want of a little kindly moisture."

"I think it will rain soon!" said the youngest child again gravely. In his blue eyes was something of the rapt look of a visionary.

"Well, it doesna' look much like it," grumbled the old fellow, pointing up with his fork to the sky that hung above, a wall of greyness, and coming very close to earth, somehow. "What for suld it rain, think'st tha'?"

"Because it must in the end," replied the child sturdily. "It wants to rain so badly. It is like me, when I want to cry and can't. Oh, Saunders, there's another potato you've left. What a lot you miss!"

"Gan awa'! Gan awa'," said Saunders impatiently, "and let me get done. Gan awa' an tew Hannah!"

He shook his pitchfork at them with playful savagery, and they turned away.

"Listen, Willie," said the child called John, confidentially taking his brother's arm, and leading him towards the kitchen, a low, one-storied outhouse attached to the house, overshadowed by the biggest of the elm trees. "Listen, Willie; I think the sky is like a great wall, very thick, and yet very brittle. There's all sorts of queer things going on the other side of it, that we can't see."

"Tell us," said the elder boy, dimly interested.

"There's great bulls roaring, and sparks flying, like in Hobbie Noble's forge, and a noise—such a noise! If there comes a hole in the wall; we shall see it." His eyes dilated; he squeezed his less poetical minded brother's hand.

"Hout!" said the listener, "I don't care for that story much. Let us go in, and bide with Hannah a bit."

The Vicarage rooms were damp and insufficiently lighted, but the Vicarage kitchen was bright and pleasant. Hannah's lime and marl floor was freshly washed, her copper vessels as bright as the mirror in Mrs. Cooper's best bedroom; but in spite of all these signs of previous activity the girl herself was sitting in a limp and weary attitude, her knees apart, and a great bowl of peas between them, which she was "podding" for dinner. Her eyes were heavy; her big lump of flaxen hair hung on one side of her head; her clumsy red hands moved among the pods lazily and inattentively. "Deary me—a deary me!" she murmured to herself at short intervals.

"Now, bairns!" She roused herself as the two slunk in. "I've not time for none of you. Gan awa' and play, there's good childer!"

"Don't be cross, Hannah!" said the eldest timidly. "We've only comed in for a sup of milk."

"The milk is all gone sour," she replied shortly. "Ye mun just content yersel's wi' a drink of water from the pump. Now be off with you!"

She gave the thin, inoffensive house-cat a hoist with her foot, and settled down to her peas again.

The pump in the garden had gone dry long since and Hannah knew it. The water they used in the household—that all the village used—came from one place, the well at the bottom of the village, which had luckily continued its functions in spite of the drought.

The children, as Hannah knew well enough, did not really want anything to drink, they wanted nothing but the antidote of human conversation to the restlessness and uneasiness that they shared with Hannah and Saunders, and what their father was apt to call "the lower animals." The house-dog was as restless as they, and would neither play with them nor stay quiet in his kennel. The hens fluttered brusquely in the hen-house, and the feverish rushing of wings that went on there made it an unpleasant abiding-place for the children. They sometimes amused themselves by going in to hunt for eggs, but they left them alone to-day, and wandered on to the open study window, where the Reverend Matthew Cooper, in hot, black clothes, was working at his sermon for next Sunday, putting his hand up to his head every now and again.

The two little boys were always somewhat in awe of their stern father, and all they dared do now was to stand and watch him, until the intermittent scraping of their feet on the walk in front of the window roused him from his meditations. He looked up; his brow was pained.

"Well, my laddies, what do you want?" He spoke kindly enough, but his voice dragged with fatigue and oppression.

"Father," asked the eldest child, "Father, tell us; why don't they send rain when you pray for it?"

"You had better go and ask your mother," said the Vicar, with the sort of grim humour in which he usually dealt. He was by nature a hard, cold, God-fearing, painstaking, undeveloped man, conscious of having a wife who managed him. "What about your lessons? Willie, I gave you a chapter to write out. Go and do some work if you can't play."

"But we've got a headache, Father."

"So have I—splitting. Run away now, and let me go on with my sermon. I haven't even chosen my text yet... '*Who doeth great things and unsearchable... Behold, He withholdeth the waters and they dry up... He bindeth the waters in His thick clouds, and the cloud is not rent under them... He destroyeth the perfect and the wicked... If the scourge slay suddenly, He will laugh at the trial of the innocent!*'"

The children left him, in desperation, and, going down to the bottom of the garden, took off their socks and sat with their feet in the diminished brook. The dog would not come with them, but snapped and growled at John when he tried to make overtures to it. Hannah, who came to look for them to fetch them to early dinner, could not find them, though they were only under the shade of the big rowan-bush near the brook-head. But she did not trouble herself to look very far, she herself could not have told you what ailed her.

"I cannot find them, mistress," she said to their mother sitting, carving-knife in one hand and fork in the other, before the family joint, which Hannah had set before her, previous to going in search of the truants.

"Oh, very well! if they don't choose to come in to their meals!"

Mrs. Cooper helped her husband to a plateful, and sent it in to him to his study, which he had intimated he was too busy to leave.

She ate a small portion herself—not much—it was too hot to be hungry. She was a hard woman, and the absence of her two little sons did not affect her appetite in the least.

The kind-hearted maid gave them what she called "a bite and a sup" later on, when they came and put their apprehensive heads round the door cheek. She did not scold them. The youngest boy looked very pale and white, and avoided her eyes.

"Poor bairn!" she said, "he wants setting up with the sea air."

The two children lay down after they had eaten, and slept on a heap of sacking, very clean and dry, near the woodstack. Their little bedroom was over the kitchen, and easy of access, but very dreary in the daytime because of the huge tree that overshadowed it. Hannah did not think of sending them up there, but flung a sack over their bare legs as they lay, and did not disturb them.

As the afternoon wore on to evening the hush became oppressive. Not a breath, not a sound of birds twittering, of fowls fluttering. Only the far-away moo of a discontented cow in an outhouse somewhere in the hills sounded like a faint trumpet call, and emphasised the stillness. The sky seemed nearer than ever now, and oppressively near, and all-encompassing.

As Hannah crossed the yard, just before supper, to throw a pail of scrapings into the pig-trough, she heard a noise. It was not Hodgson's cow... It might have been the grinding of one of Miller Farsyde's flour wagons on the quartz that sprinkled the road up there beyond the brow—half-a-mile away. She did not know what it was—a very faint rumble. She thought no more of it, but as she crossed the courtyard on her way back something dropped on to the back of her hand which she could have sworn was a rain-drop...!

The thought passed. Her country mind again was a blank. She gave the boys a shake as she passed in. "Come now, wake up! 'Tis supper time!"

The youngest boy stirred and frowned.

"Is it come?" he said—"the hole in the wall?"

"Whatten hole? Whatten wall? Whatten rubbish is the child talking about?" she said carelessly, brushing the loose straws off his jacket with strong sideway pats, and leading him in to the dining-room where supper was spread. Willie, the elder and more prosaic of the two, manifested some interest in the items of the meal. It was beans and bacon and porridge, too solid fare for such a day as this had been. The Vicar had finished his sermon, and was sitting in his place, as pale as his white tie, but otherwise placable enough. The eldest child went round to his own high chair in silence, but the youngest crossed the room to his mother's side and pulled her by the sleeve.

"What ails ye, laddie?" she asked not unkindly.

"Will you give me a kiss, Mammy?" he asked shamefacedly and in a low voice, lest his brother should hear, and taunt him for being a "mammy pet."

"What nonsense!" Mrs. Cooper said, with all the helpless shyness of a hard woman. She stooped down and kissed her little appealing son, nevertheless. "Now, sit down, and eat your supper quietly. Well, Mr. Cooper, how have ye got on with your sermon?"

"Badly!" replied her husband. "I seem to have such a weight on my brain—an oppression! It is quite dreadful. It is so bad, it really can't last—something must happen. Eat your supper, John, and don't stare."

For the youngest child's eyes were constantly fixed on his father, and little questions seemed to be trembling on his lips. He said nothing until supper was over, when he begged his mother to read to them, in which request he was seconded by his elder brother.

She got the big family Bible and reverently flirted the pages...

"Read about the Israelites and the Plagues of Egypt," suggested Willie.

"Very well," the mother said equably. Her day's work was done, she had time now, and was willing to please the children in their own way.

"'*And Moses stretched forth his rod towards the heaven, and the Lord sent thunder and hail—*'"

"I wish He would," murmured the Vicar.

"'*And the fire ran along the ground, and the Lord rained hail upon the land of Egypt...*'"

She was going on in her monotonous, uneducated voice, when the youngest child suddenly screamed and hid his face in the cushions of the sofa.

"Whisht, whisht!" she called out, by way of soothing him. "Why, you silly body, haven't ye heard it all before?"

The child continued to sob.

His face remained hidden. Sternly his parent ignored his hysterical outburst.

"How old were the children of Israel?" asked Willie, by way of distracting the attention of his elders from this bad conduct on his brother's part, which would assuredly end in both being sent off to bed. Crying was never allowed. "Were they as old as me, or only as old as John?"

Mrs. Cooper now gave her mind to the destruction of this erroneous impression under which her children had been labouring, and when it was done she raised her voice, and called "Hannah!"

to the maid, who was to be heard moving heavily about in the passage.

John raised his tear-stained face from the sofa, a wild terror in his eyes. Willie clasped his hands together, and together they pleaded with an unaccountable vehemence...

"Oh, no, no, Mother; please, Mother—we don't want to go to bed. We can't! We can't!" both wailed.

"And what for no?" asked the mother, raising her strongly marked black eyebrows. "Why not to bed, to-night, same as other nights?"

"Because—because—oh, Mother! because we want another story. We want Abram and Isaac," pleaded William. It was only an excuse, and the mother knew it.

"One story is quite enough for one evening," she answered severely; "and John did not behave particularly well over that; I won't hear any fond nonsense. Now you just trot along both of you! You are both as cross and sleepy as you can be. Bed's the safest place for you!"

Her rough soothing was of no value. The children's faces, as Hannah came in, were blanched with terror. John ran up to the kindly servant-maid, and hid his face in the folds of her linsey gown.

"I want to speak to you," he sobbed.

"Noo, what then, ma honey?" said Hannah good-humouredly, stooping, till her smooth head touched his touzled one. "Well!"—as she raised her head—"did ye ever hear the like? What sets ye asking that? Mistress, he wants to know if they mayn't creep in aside of father and mother to-night?"

"Please let us, Mother," they murmured, almost inaudibly.

"I never heard anything so fond!" exclaimed Mrs. Cooper, laughing grimly. "Be off with ye both quietly, now, and let me hear no more nonsense."

"We did once, Mother!"

"Once! Yes! when they were mending the roof of your bedroom; but the roof's safe and sound over your heads now, at any rate. Why," she laughed, "why, when I give ye a nice big bed to yourselves, should I go and cram my own and the master's with two tiresome children, to kick me black and blue before morning? What are ye afeared of, I say?"

But they would own to nothing, and averted their eyes. A little underswell of sobbing, whimpering breaths testified to their distress.

"What's come to the bairns, I wonder?" She was puzzled, through her thick mental hide of unsympathy. "They're as fractious! It's this unked weather sets us all out of our wits."

"It *must* break," said her husband, "there's no sense in it. We may have rain to-morrow. I forgot to look at the glass as I passed in to-night. There may be a change soon, nay, there must be... Come here, children, and say your prayers, and let's have no more crying."

They all at once realised the hopelessness of it all, and came meekly to his knee, Hannah folded her hands and looked on approvingly at the two flaxen heads, as in their innocent, pretty, piping voices they begged blessings on their hardened elders, and murmured deep contrition for the sins they had not yet committed. They wound up as usual with the prayer—

"'*Lighten our darkness, we beseech Thee, O Lord, and by Thy great mercy defend us from all perils and dangers of this night; for the love of Thine only Son, our Saviour Jesus Christ. Amen.*'"

Sadly they rose and kissed their parents, who had so carelessly crossed them in their strong instinctive desire, and murmured inaudible good-nights. Then Hannah, taking a little submissive hand of each, led them out of the room.

They went past the weather-glass in the hall, whose strongly marked signs and signals of change they were too young, and Hannah too ignorant, to understand, and walked round by half roofless passages to the kitchen. Then Hannah, laughingly propelling "mischief in front of her," inducted them up the shaky wooden staircase that led into the large room where they always slept, brooded over by the enormous over-arching elm-tree. Its branches tapped the little skylight pane when it was windy, but now they hung still like a drooping banner in a calm.

"I do believe it's that ugly, girt tree they're feared of!" Hannah thought to herself.

During the passage towards their sleeping place they said nothing, but the fingers of the younger child closed and unclosed round the maid's stout thumb, and the touch struck her as very cold.

"I'd let you both creep in aside o' me," she said, "only I'm that fleyed o' the mistress! She'd find us out, as sure as my name is Hannah Cawthorne."

She set down the candle on the chest in the long, low, empty loft-room. The chest and the bed were almost the only articles of furniture in it. The wooden rafters that supported the roof made fanciful bars and arches over the white dimity quilt. The bed was large, clean and comfortless.

When the two children had undressed and lain down, Hannah Cawthorne, of a gloomy North Country turn of mind that ran continually on omens and predestinations, could not help thinking how like two corpses laid out they looked, lying so straight, their little bodies outlined under the quilt, their eyes wide open and staring at the roof. It made her uncomfortable.

"There's nought to be afeared on," she thought, trying to bring comfort to herself merely, for the children were still, submissive and past all repining now. "It's as safe as a church, but all the same... Now shut your eyes," she said aloud, "there's good lads, and say 'Gentle Jesus' till ye feel the sleep coming on ye. Oh, ye'll sleep fine, trust me. Shall I leave ye the light?"

This was a wild stretch of authority. She might have lost her place over it. She was relieved when they shook their heads and declined it.

"See here," she went on, producing an apple from her pocket. "See here, ye can munch this atween ye."

She laid it down on the coverlet, but no little hand came forth to take it.

"Poor bairns, they're sad-like... Eh, she's a hard woman, is the mistress! If they were mine, shouldn't I like them to nestle in aside o' me! This room is fair lonesome. Naebody could hear them if they were to skrike out..."

"What are ye looking at, my honey?" she asked John curiously, for the child's eyes remained obstinately fixed on the roof, as if he saw something there.

"He's looking at the hole in the wall," volunteered the eldest boy at last. "He's shiverin'."

"Hap him up in your arms, ma bonny bairn, that'll soon warm him... Now I must be going, lads... Good-night to ye both..."

Hesitating, reluctant, she took up her candle and made a start for the door.

"I don't half like leaving them," she murmured, as she stole out casting a last look at the two children, lying clasped, according to her recommendation, in each other's arms. Their faces were hidden in each other's necks, their sad apprehensive eyes were closed, obediently summoning sleep.

Gently snecking the door, she blundered down the rickety staircase, and made her way back into the other, safer part of the house. Ignorant, she passed by the mysterious oracle hanging in the hall, unable to read or understand the plain meaning which its hands now bore.

"Eh, but she's a right hard woman, is the mistress, and master follows her in all things. *He'd* have let the poor childer come in aside him, when they begged and prayed fit to turn a heart of stone..."

She did not toss on her hard pallet, but lay stupefied in the heavy slumber that was the meed of her arduous existence. Upstairs, in the best bedroom, the Reverend Matthew Cooper slept off his headache. His wife did not drowse, but lay by her husband's side, straight and still as she had laid down, congratulating herself on the great healing storm that was even now breaking over the Vicarage, gloating over its promise of recomfiture and peace... It thundered and lightened for two hours.

When morning dawned the great drought was over, and the air was refreshed.

Hannah, the maid, rose and went about her duties with a light heart, and presently, having started the kitchen fire, called the parson and his wife to resume theirs.

When it was time, she pulled her dirty kitchen apron aside, put the kettle where it could not for the moment boil over, and went to call the parson's children.

She went up the crooked stair and opened the door gently, "not to waken them sudden." The first thing she saw, before she screamed, was the wide, jagged hole on the rafters above the bed where they still lay in each other's arms. The lightning that, guided by the tree which hung over the roof, had passed through to the innocent children and dealt them their unearned and undeserved death, had not divided them. They were quiet and unchanged in appearance except for some little blue marks like shot in the forehead of the one and the breast of the other.

THE TIGER SKIN

"'Tis but a little piece of childhood thrown away."

JOHN FORD.

She wandered about the wards at the Infants' Hospital, a privileged person, tolerated but ignored, looked on askance by the properly caparisoned, certificated, trained nurses. She was not a nurse; she was not even a probationer, except by courtesy: she was the daughter of the distinguished Founder, Dr. Emeric Favarger. She spent a great deal of her time there lounging about, asking queer absurd questions of the impatient nurses and the polite visiting doctors, getting into the way generally as only privileged persons can do. She was no good; she could not even amuse a baby or keep it quiet until expert assistance should arrive. She came often to the Hospital, it was understood, because she liked it, because the grey-green walls and absence of decoration was soothing to her, and the rows of white cots, to the number of thirty, each with its frontal brass denoting the name and style of its godparent and pecuniary backer that lined the sides of the room satisfied her sense of proprietorship. For her own name, Adelaide Favarger, figured over one bed, and she was used to take up its chance, ofttimes varied, puling occupant every now and again, or would linger, casting her longing liquid glances at somebody's baby as it lay there in peace and comfort with a few of the creases of ill-nurture and ill-usage smoothed out and eased by proper care and the bands of merciful sleep.

She was twenty-five years of age, unmarried, motherless, the doctor's only daughter. He was grown old and excessively rich, and long since had found himself able to retire from the activities of the profession. He still had his room in the Hospital, lectured there twice a week and saw foreign doctors, departmental authorities, philanthropic cranks and persons interested in this new and expensive departure of baby culture which he had inaugurated at his own expense, hoping that his example would inspire and lead to eugenical cultivation of the uncounted progeny of the struggling, uninstructed masses.

At home, in the immense, wool-gathering house he rented in Portland Place, so large and rambling that his daughter and he, both weedy, unfleshly specimens of the humanity in which they were so deeply interested, were lost, overshadowed and swallowed up. He had a room in the basement called his study, the door of which was kept always closed. Behind this rampart he was understood to be engaged in original and sometimes dangerous experiments. He entered it never from the house above, but by a door that gave on the mews at the back. As people said, anything—all sorts of things—might be going on in that house and never be heard of; vivisection being quite the most harmless practice hinted at. It was known that Dr. Favarger bred and kept there animals—any amount of cats; he wrote and commented on the habits of these creatures in the monthlies. He was a clever fascinating old man who might have been asked out to dinner every night in the year, had he chosen to let himself figure in the list of society's possible guests. But that he had always refused to do and his daughter, more or less unwillingly perhaps, shared his self-imposed ostracism. She was not the kind of girl whom hostesses made much of or asked at a moment's notice to fill up a gap at their dinner tables. She had no cordiality, no *entrain*, no "go." She was handsome but not pretty; curiously attractive but not obviously charming; the living image of her father, whose aquiline, sardonic nose she had inherited, as well as the passionate, regretful eyes wherewith her mother, frighted, oppressed to death, it was said, had dowered her.

But no restraint was put upon her own exercise of hospitality in Portland Place. She might ask anyone and everyone she liked to dinner, and she constantly availed herself of the privilege. Her dinner-parties were singular and interesting. Her father's sinister but suave personality was an asset. For one reason or another the proportion of male guests who put their knees under the old mahogany dining-table and drank her father's old port was far in excess of the female, but "Miss Adelaide" did not object to this disproportion. She was as strange and interesting as he was. Still, sly, silent, with an air of biding her time, at eighteen; by the time she was twenty-five the mature reserve of passion in her eyes was, while attractive, terrifying; she seemed, in her fierce, exotic, tigerish dresses, to glow in her dark setting, a meagre, pallid Circe who drew to her with rich cates and wine the ready-made beasts of the world, and shook no deterrent wand at them. These were Miss Favarger's famous evenings—smoke of cigars, fume of liqueurs, conversations reeking of indecency under the guise of scientific discussion. Her father, the cynical heartless old man, nothing loth, led the talk, holding forth from sheer love of airing views and theories quite over the heads of the audience of ill-educated, inferior, second-rate men that his daughter almost nightly provided for him. And for her days, they were spent between one of the three big yellow satin sofas that almost furnished the drawing-room of Portland Place, reading excessive and highly spiced novels, or on foot, ambling round the wards of the Hospital that stood for the expression of both her's and her father's theories of life. She had no sense of humour but much tolerance, and listened patiently to the cruel old man telling her friends that his daughter was far and away the only maleficent microbe in the establishment—that miracle of asepticism. Though he gibed at her and her friends before her face, he allowed her to do exactly as she liked, gave her plenty of pocket-money to carry out her whims so long as he was not invited to have an opinion about them, and with no consideration for her youth and the life she would have to live when he was gone, fared, stately and contemptuous, towards the grave of known finality that awaited him. He had done his best for the world in the inauguration of a higher ideal of infant-feeding and early physical culture and, for his daughter, he had fulfilled his duties towards her mind and body as he conceived of them. He had given her the best of educations. She had been to a school by the sea as a child; as a girl she had gone up to College. She herself had insisted on being highly trained and educated up to the zenith of her powers and, at sixteen, had all her views for her future cut and dried. Concentrating herself with feverish intentness on her goal of efficiency she had managed to do well at Oxford, though her friends said that the effort had cost her dear, and that she had been screwed up to the required pitch by her vanity. The girls of her year who had come out below her in Honours used to laugh when they met afterwards in the street, this crank who had forced herself to outstrip them, and noted her peering, as her habit was, under the hoods of perambulators on her way to lectures on Eugenics and Baby Culture. They had heard all about her fixed determination to marry and worthily contribute to the World Force.

At Somerville Hall she had made no secret of her intention to bear an eugenical child or two, first having selected its father carefully. But who was going to select her who had no charm, for her own sex or the other? Oh yes, she talked of nothing else at tea-parties and walks, and bored them so that, at leaving, she had made no harvest of life-friends. They tossed their learned young heads and quite expected some day to hear of Adelaide Favarger, in spite of her big talk, as the feeble, hang-dog mother, if a mother at all, of one puny infant by the usual self-selecting father who would just have got hold of her for her money. That is, if any man came forward, and this, in spite of her wealth, they were inclined to doubt. She wasn't a girl who appealed to the men that marry. They felt that, and they were right.

For, looking at Adelaide Favarger with the instinctive cunning of the male that makes, in the long-run, so surely for what Adelaide herself called the "World Purpose," men were likely enough to pass her by as sexually ineligible for motherhood. Though Miss Favarger would be rich and able to afford a proper establishment, she evidenced no aptitude for housekeeping or for satisfying a husband's standard of comfort and pleasure. She could do pretty much as she liked now, and there was the dreary, ill-managed, ill-cleaned house in Portland Place, with its unprobed corners and high ceilings, its flights of stone stairs glimpsed in passing, that seemed to drop you into unplumbed depths of basement and scullery-dom. Though the hall and dining-room were full of valuable mahogany furniture, its dull unpolished surfaces reflected nothing. The drawing-room was handsomely upholstered throughout with rich, heavy damask covering the sofas and chairs. Curtains of the same material masked such scanty light as filtered in through the tall windows that no housemaid could or did reach up to clean, and soared out of sight into the dusty cornices. They were mostly kept drawn, and the chance hand of the visitor, essaying to draw them further apart, shook out a musty flavour that nipped the nostrils and compelled him to desist.

Adelaide's dinners were ill-cooked and depressing. The service was scrambling or non-existent. Adelaide kept jumping up and down herself to fetch things. But the cigars were prime and the wine, Dr. Favarger's own province, excellent. He himself would have none of it. As soon as the sweets were put on it was the old doctor's custom to stuff his creased napkin into the middle of his plate and to rise and leave the room without good-byes to the guests or comment from Adelaide. It was always the same. He did not, as a rule, appear again: he appeared to dislike the kind of men that his daughter invited, yet he exercised no sort of control over her visiting list.

These men he despised were quite sorry to see him go; he was witty, cynical and fascinating. Adelaide was proud of him.

She observed that there was one of her men whom he did not altogether dislike for, although he would not sit out the dinner even for Wald Ensor, the first time that this young man dined in Portland Place, her father stayed until the coffee and cigars were put on. Perhaps it was because he had himself introduced his daughter to the young fellow at the Children's Hospital. Ensor had come in to inquire after a child which he had himself been instrumental in bringing in the day before. It was dying of malnutrition. Its slum mother, stupid, underfed and wretched but not vile, could not nourish it properly, even if she would...

The image of the tall, handsome young man holding the perishing child in his arms had never left Adelaide; she had fallen in love with Wald Ensor and, with Adelaide, to fall in love was to ask to dinner.

Ensor came. He was a great success with both Adelaide and her father, because he was so different from Adelaide's other young men, and especially from the second-rate Chelsea artist whom she had asked to make a fourth, and whom, between the first and second course, she already condemned as a survival of her old days of bad taste. Regarding Ensor, she began to think she preferred gentlemen even when not clever. His manner was perfection. He was shyish, greyish, content and self-contained, talked respectfully to her father about his Hospital and his cats, and prettily to herself about the subjects in which a young lady should be interested. Adelaide was not interested, but she instinctively forbore to disabuse him.

The dinner went on to the satisfaction of all but the fourth guest. Miss Favarger was too young, too reckless, too unversed in feminine strategy to conceal the trend of her feelings and, directing as she did all her conversation and her glances towards Ensor, she seriously alienated the liking of her whilom friend, ally and limner, Mr. Wallace Marks, R.I.B.

He bided his time, however, and what time Dr. Favarger presided over his own table, listened to the conversation in a frankly bored manner, which contrasted with Wald Ensor's polite attention to the talk which he only half approved as coming from the lips of this savage, irresponsible old savant, the indifferent but natural guardian of a young girl's morals and mentality.

"There is something," the old man was saying, "something to be said for the woman who systematically ill-treats her child."

Adelaide protested conventionally. "Nothing!" she said.

"My daughter," her father said spitefully, without looking in his daughter's direction, "wishes to impress you with the fact of her well-known love for infants. She does not, however, really care for them in the least and, I may say, has never considered this matter scientifically in her life, although she is always hanging round the Hospital and hindering my young assistants. If she had a child of her own she'd neglect it. Cruelty masked by philanthropy!" He pointed dramatically at his daughter sitting glowering and silent at the other end of the table. "Look for it, it's there!" His fine nose appeared cold, sharp and ferrety. He did not smile, and Ensor shuddered...

Adelaide made a conventional wry face. She was used to and did not really mind being teased by her extraordinary parent. Mr. Marks had heard this kind of thing scores of times, but Ensor was sorry for her, disproportionately so. The old man continued:

"Yes, believe me who have no illusions on the subject that, on the lines I have been mentioning to you, Ensor"—Ensor almost leapt at the direct addressing of him; what had he to do with child-murder?—"even child-murder is excusable, obeying as it does an almost forgotten and laid-away animal instinct, as of a cat, say, who by some circumstances or other has been disturbed or distressed before parturition and rendered hysterical—"

"Good Lord! An hysterical cat!" ejaculated the bounder, less shocked than bored.

Dr. Favarger, taking no notice of him, continued his sentence—"will tear, break the backs, eat or otherwise destroy the litter that she knows herself to be unable to feed or attend to. So do wretched servant girls, faced in their hour of trial with the problem of the disposal of illegitimate offspring, quite correctly reserve to themselves the right of destroying what their instinct tells them they will not, in future, be able to protect and nourish."

"No, father!" Adelaide suddenly protested, and her tone was sincere. "Father, think of it! The tender, young life, the helpless weakling, bone of one's bone, flesh of one's flesh... Motherhood is so sacred. It should, of course, be subsidised by the State. Illegitimacy especially. A capitation fee for every child. The State to grant a mother the wherewithal to nourish herself properly, and maternal feeling would do the rest."

Dr. Favarger smiled, a smile without kindness in it. She had that too, as well as his nose.

"What you sloppily call maternal feeling, Adelaide, is variable and overrated. It may come with the milk. But, at the crucial moment of birth, neither maid nor mistress would have any of these fine feelings. The woman has suffered physically; she is exhausted and therefore irresponsible. Instinct, maternal enough, though not, Adelaide, in your ridiculous sense, dominates her. For if she disobeys her instinctive wisdom, does not take prompt and necessary action, but makes an attempt to salve the 'tender, hapless infant'"—he sneered—"she may have to watch it through her care surviving, possibly, as a hopeless idiot—"

"Of course," he continued, "I except cases of mere speculative, money-grabbing cruelty such as baby-farming. If a woman kills or ill-treats the child of another, no natural, economical, physiological instinct can possibly come into play since it is not her own child—not even that exceedingly natural motive whose investigation has been neglected—Mother's Vanity!"

"Mother's Vanity," said Adelaide, stressing the second word.

"Yes, an important factor in these matters, but in most cases it is not necessary to plead it, for Nature's broad back may easily take the blame. But when a woman of our own class, maybe, is brought before the magistrate and fined or imprisoned because she has taken a broom to the ugly duckling or, by systematic bullying or ill-treatment, brought a weakly, ungracious, ill-begotten brat to the point of extinction, she might plead Mother's Vanity and contend that she is only doing what every other animal does when her young are not up to sample and seem degenerate to her keener sense. My cat, Phillippa, for instance—"

Adelaide sneered conventionally. The bounder fidgeted. Ensor preserved his attitude of somewhat strained attention.

"—had a fine litter of four, the other day. I found one of them, to my uninstructed eye as healthy as the others, lying on the cold stone floor for three successive mornings before it died. Phillippa had thrown it out of the box. She had refused to feed it—she had just weeded it out. Why? It was unfit to live, and if you study these trials that come up every now and then and read carefully the descriptions of the victims given by the officers of the S.P.C.C., you'll see that in most cases these brutalised, neglected children are slow, unprepossessing, unpleasant and revolting in their habits. They work up, through, the first few years of their infancy, unpetted, neglected, ill-treated; they can be marked down as certain to develop all the successive stages of degeneracy. They are obviously better dead. Did ever any pretty, healthy, fetching child, like the child in 'Bubbles,' appear in court on such a plea? And that's where Mother's Vanity comes in!"

Adelaide, whom this conversation had ceased to please or interest, rose. The bounder heaved a sigh of relief. Ensor, though he had been interested, even a little charmed by the old man's manner and directness, could not help deploring that the conversation had not post-dated the young girl's formal departure to her own domain.

Old Dr. Favarger left the room with her. He said to her in the hall, before he hobbled away to his own study and sleeping apartment on the ground floor: "You have picked up a gentleman for once."

She walked on as if he had not spoken. She always made a point of not answering her father when he was rude to her, and his approval of Ensor, though not unpleasing, was absolutely immaterial to her. She loved him; she meant to have him—whether through the door of marriage or no. It was not all one to her; she hoped for a mate in the scheme of things, but for him, somehow she would do without legal sanctions...

She went upstairs to the drawing-room to await the two men, and flung herself down on one of the great yellow sofas with the black cushions. She was too nervous even to smoke. She was convinced, not perhaps for the first time, that she had found the eugenical father at last.

Wald Ensor, the gentleman according to Dr. Favarger's acceptance, left sitting after an atrocious dinner with a man who fulfilled none of the doctor's conditions, felt extremely uncomfortable. His annoyance grew as his messmate started a familiar conversation. A wretched artist from Chelsea, self-styled modern, with white hair and a dyed moustache, to whom the host and young hostess had hardly vouchsafed a word all through dinner! The old man had been presumably annoyed by the Cockney accent. He had talked, although she neither answered nor listened, psychology with Adelaide; his pert, under-bred voice had broken all the while through Dr. Favarger's cultivated tones. Now the father and daughter were gone this creature actually ventured to psycho-analyse his young hostess, and Ensor did not know how to stop him, though he made various efforts to do so, fidgeting about on his Spanish leather-covered chair in vain...

"Nice girl, very!" the wretch went on. "With a face like an old master—one of those Primitives, don't you know! Lots of drawing about. Pity she's so morbid!"

Wald Ensor made a piteous gesture of denegation.

"Oh yes, she is. Talks of nothing but eugenics and so on. Thinks of nothing but the other thing... It's only a mask with these blessed women, you know, all that rot about child-bearing being subsidised by the State. She is an erotomaniac—that's what she is—sits about on sofas, livery-yellow for choice, and begs men to love her! They do that fast enough, she is very good fun—but they don't marry her. No, sir! Do you know the great Gertrude? Do you know the reason they put up with her—she is the cook—and why the dinners here are so confoundedly bad?"

"No, I don't," Ensor answered fiercely. He didn't think he could stand it any longer; he wanted to throw his glass in the fellow's face. He rose stiffly...

The other man, nothing abashed although their conversation had lasted barely five minutes, rose too, saying amiably, "So! Let's join our fair hostess."

He continued as they passed out, "Cook's no artist, but can't be parted with, see? Mutual aid society. She's up to games of her own, is the fair Gertrude. They found a baby she had just had in a dressing-table drawer, so Adelaide told me. While she was sitting. Time for confidences, eh? I paint; she talks. Keeps her face alive! Seen my pic. of her in 'The New'? Not bad, though I say it as shouldn't. I've caught the subterranean devil of her..."

They had got upstairs by this time. The artist opened the drawing-room door and disclosed Adelaide sitting, as suggested, but not voluptuously. Her head was resting stiffly on the black satin cushion. There was room for one beside her, and Marks slipped into the place.

Miss Favarger looked put out—it was not what she had intended. She seemed helpless, and Ensor, with a spasm of jealous disgust, took an early opportunity of making his adieux and left them.

He never dined in that house again. He could not bring himself to risk meeting men of that stamp...

Yet he pitied her. He admired her. Her great, fixed, discontented eyes haunted him. He felt as if a white, plaining lady's hand was stretched to him from out of the weltering sea of bounderism. Miss Favarger, a lady, could not *really* like that sort of man? No, for if anything, she seemed rather to like *him*!...

After this she wrote continually, begging him to accept her hospitality in some form or other. She varied the form of her invitations, and he still refused steadily to come to her house. She ingeniously assumed that it was because her father insisted on plain fare and high thinking, and suggested that, if he could not stand her cook, he might take her out to dinner at some "foreign place—some low pot-house," as she phrased it. No, indeed, he laughed to himself. He knew that, if he were to succumb to her blandishments, he would certainly take her somewhere decent; he did not choose to pander to her taste for Bohemianism; he would save her from herself or her friends!

He conceived some such plan as this after the refusal of each fresh invitation, and quite fancied the idea of rescuing this really nice girl from second-rate people, taking her to respectable restaurants and showing her how a decent man would behave to a girl who did him the honour of dining with him alone. The girl was motherless; her father did not pretend to look after her. She had a fine character, was generous and large in her ideas, she gave freely and was kind and tolerant to her own sex and would never, he was sure, go back on anyone. The disreputable cook now—he was sure, in keeping her on, Miss Favarger was undertaking a work of charity! She had obviously had what is called a "misfortune" in her class; she had possibly gone through a tragedy—a dead child. Adelaide was not the sort of person who would turn a human being out of doors in any circumstances whatever, especially a woman in the condition in which her servant found herself. Preoccupied, indifferent, perhaps indolent, she made no excuses for her unusual tolerance, and even condescended to discuss the details of it with such worms as Ensor's fellow-guest of a few weeks ago. Merely an error of taste, the result of her unmothered, unchaperoned state. She was, at bottom, a really well-bred woman. Ensor, a rover, a man who had knocked about the world, had yet preserved his vast shyness and a modicum of innocence, thought he saw clearly that it was the time and the place which were out of joint with Adelaide. Her morals were mediaeval, with no present parallel except perhaps one which should be found in the *milieu* of the South Sea Islands.

Thus he came to invite her to dine with him at Prince's; she had tea with him on the slopes in Kensington Gardens; they walked together in Hyde Park on Sundays. The handsome girl protesting vehemently that she hated dressing up and posing as one of the smart set, created quite an impression of that kind. In vain Ensor assured her that, to mingle casually with that select denomination at Church Parade, was not to be within a hundred miles of being "of" it; that to dine at Kettner's with a man alone was sufficiently unconventional. Adelaide continued to protest, to beg him to take her to his flat and to discuss sex questions in a loud voice over restaurant tables. She called it eugenics. Ensor, now stung by sex to a certain degree, had become self-conscious and did not enjoy these discussions. The more he came to admire Adelaide the less he liked them. This oddly handsome young woman, sitting there, her elbows on the table, her hands propping her hard chin, her burning eyes fixed on the shy man opposite to her who was trying to quieten her and make her eat her dinner, made both conspicuous. Her chosen topic, ventilated in rather a loud voice, caused him to seem more British than usual, and ever so little ridiculous. He could stand any amount of talk of this kind from platforms or on the stage, with the footlights between him and the exponents of the New Feeling, the New World Movement, the New Morality she spoke of so fluently. But here, among the shaded red lights with discreet foreign waiters gliding about, the chance *commensals* treated willy-nilly to subjects usually relegated to classrooms outraged his simple sensitiveness and ordinary canons of decency. The only thing that at all saved the situation was the girl's astonishing absence of self-consciousness; she talked like a boy—some clever, morbid lad just home from College; her sedulous use of slang helped the impression. Yet all the while her eyes belied her and, occasionally, her voice. Now and then an outrageous note of sex-bitterness pierced through her level, lazy accents and brought their talk home with a rush from the distances of impersonality. It was when Adelaide Favarger's eyes, ceasing to appear eager or piercing, became sombre and heavy; it was when her sharp, grating voice grew mellow and trailing that Ensor feared and admired her most, and such moments were growing more and more frequent. He stuck to it, however, and the dinner went on; he was not one to throw the queer, graceless, disconcerting woman over.

Had he not been the most retiring, most modest of men, he would have realised that the girl was head over ears in love with him. He would have disliked—he would have refused to realise it, for then he would be forced, in some way, to formulate his own feeling for her, and that was a queer mixture of sensual pity and revolted admiration. There were times when he thought he fully grasped what she wanted of him, and so glad of her assumption that his refusal to dine with her in Portland Place represented merely a protest against the inefficiency of her cook. This silly, worn-out theory which now, at all times and all seasons, was put before him as an explanation of his continual snubbing of her, was a convenience to him since it effectually masked his reluctance to be the father of her so-called eugenical child.

Wald Ensor, like her other men friends, always saw Adelaide home after their evenings together. Unlike the others he always left her on the step as soon as the door answered to her key, and the dark hall of her father's house swallowed her up. No Bianca Capello complications for him! She used to say, sometimes, what would she do if Gertrude by accident forgot she was out and put up the lock, but, as a rule, her "good-nights" were a miracle of sour brevity and conciseness.

One night, in July, they had been to the Exhibition together, and had sat late listening to the band playing *Tristan*. The outdoor performance was but a pale and vapid reflection of the heat and passion of the Opera House, but, their nostrils choked in the dust-fumed lower air, sitting side by side in the still, shadow-flecked radiance, they found it affecting. Adelaide had talked less than usual. The summer skies that year were light and clear of clouds. And when rather late, satiate of emotion, tired physically with pacing the horny gravelled walks, they returned to Portland Place, the wide paved street seemed to sleep lonely under a Norwegian midnight. Something like an etiolated sunlight shone on its raddled stones, and the stern house-fronts standing a long way back. There were some trees in the garden next to Adelaide's house which hung over the steps on one side, and made a sort of shade. There was a big party higher up in the street, and some cabs stood waiting in the middle of the roadway, a file of blunt, indistinguished shapes whence the figure of a man now and then disengaged itself, did something to a vehicle, and was absorbed again. Adelaide had insisted on Ensor dismissing the taxi which had brought them from Shepherd's Bush at Oxford Circus. Together they walked across the broad, stony expanse. The young girl held her exiguous skirts tightly round her thin, distinctly well-shaped legs. She knew they were fine; she knew she had a beautiful figure...

When they had attained the broad, flat step in front of her door, she turned a little sideways to scan her companion who stood waiting for her to effect her entry, and bid her a formal and friendly good-bye as usual. He was not looking at her, but dreamily back across the street they had just traversed. He was still a little bemused by *Tristan*, his head full of the remembrance of seductively appealing, adroitly moving harmonies—

"Come in and have a drink!" Adelaide said carelessly, over her shoulder. Her voice was rough and throaty.

The demand startled him; he had thought to have cured her of all that. This request was out of order, and he did not reply.

She faced him but did not meet his eyes.

"Why won't you?" she asked peevishly. "Even if you won't dine? What have I done? Why am I doomed—cursed...?"

"My dear Miss Favarger!"

"Miss Favarger be blowed!" she said, speaking—and looking—like a schoolgirl. She caught the lapel of his coat and fumbled at it.

"For God's sake," she said, "don't insult me so! Come in, just for a moment."

Wald Ensor came back to his rooms in Ebury Street some time in the early, piping dawn, and found a cablegram lying in his letter-box which told him of the sudden death of a distant but beloved relation out in California, a man in whose business he had a concern. A day or two later he had arranged his affairs and sailed for the other side. He had found time before he left to forward a bulky package to Miss Favarger containing the skin of a tiger which he had shot himself under striking and romantic circumstances, and of which he had often spoken to Adelaide, but had never allowed her to see, since it was a settled thing that she never came to his rooms. But it "went with" her, somehow, he had thought, and she had looked flattered when he told her so at their last meeting.

He had now a very friendly feeling towards her; she seemed to him on a whole, since their mutual experience, to be a saner, worthier member of the community than before.

He did not fancy, when he stepped carelessly off this hemisphere, that he was leaving Europe for so long a time. But it was so. He married out in California. He conceived this marriage to have been accomplished from motives of pity—an idea of giving a woman, much buffeted by fortune, a home, but, as a matter of fact, Adelaide had awakened the zest of the feminine in a man who had imagined himself to be a confirmed bachelor. His attempts at civicism were not blessed in the usual way for, after they had been married five years, his wife died in giving birth to a child, which died. Then he drifted, cured of this casual impetus towards a settled life. He did not carry on his cousin's affairs with success. He started several other adventures in the world of business, all of which failed, for he had not what is called *la main heureuse.* With an orange grove that did not pay and a moderate income, sensibly diminished by the paying of mortgages on a property about which he was still hopeful and would not let go, he returned to Europe, deciding to lie low until matters in Florida should have righted themselves. He was too proud to take his place in society and go out while his only dress suit was shiny at the knees. He avoided London. He did, however, call once at Portland Place, found new inmates established there, and was told that old Dr. Favarger was dead and Miss Favarger gone, no one knew where, and taken the cook with her.

It was in Yorkshire, on a market day in Beverley, that he met Adelaide again.

At first sight she seemed very little altered, only he had always imagined she was taller. She was walking with her old staccato step that suggested some congenital weakness—a slightly stiffened spine—on the rough cobblestones of the market square, about and among the pens and square docks of prisoned, lowing cows and calves and indifferent, sullen bulls. She was not alone. Her companion was a beautiful girl of about fifteen, a whole head taller than herself. Perhaps that was why he thought her shrunken? There was about her and her clothes a slightly countrified air; she was dressed in a style very different from that aggravated, rather meretricious one in which the old Adelaide had been wont to make her points and striven to enhance her own rather peculiar charm.

The two were leaning their elbows on the well-worn wooden rail of a square which enclosed the unruly stock and were watching with great interest the movements of a handsome animal which had, as nearly as possible, succeeded in wrenching his neck free of the headstall. His discontented, inflamed eyes, his stubby, determined shoulder, his dull, passionate intentness on freedom seemed to fascinate one of the women...

"Nice beast, isn't he, Phyllis?" she murmured.

"Yes, but he'll get his head out in about a minute," the child said nervously.

The elder woman, appearing to find enjoyment in the spectacle of her timidity, said, "He'll have the whole place cleared in no time then!"

Her hand stole towards the frayed rope that bound the steer: "We'll stay and see the racket, shall we?"

The child pleaded, "No, don't undo it, Addie! Oh, I do believe you're going to! Please let's go home. Mary must be tired and cold, waiting in the car all this time!"

"Mary be damned!" Adelaide said. "Who cares for Mary?"

"But I'm tired, and cold too, if that's anything!"

"You are? Well, come along then. Mustn't kill you."

Laughing complacently she turned and faced Wald Ensor. The long, last look of farewell with which she had enveloped the splendid, fierce and restless animal had not left her humid eyes...

Quickly she recognised him and righted herself. She put, with the full suggestion of her town manner, the pince-nez that hung round her neck by a chain of antique workmanship up to her eyes, asking in a thin, hard voice:

"Is that you?"

Then she hesitated. She raised her arm as if to ward off a blow, and her collection of parcels, tied all together, fell to the ground and, the string breaking, rolled in all directions. The tall child bent down to pick them up. Ensor was about to forestall her, but a gesture from Adelaide seemed to him to be intended to prevent and forbid him doing so. There was an awkward pause... Then Adelaide, indicating with her pince-nez the stooping figure of her young companion, and looking carefully away, pronounced quickly, in the style of a formal introduction:

"Wald! My daughter, Phyllis." She murmured, as if it were an afterthought, under her breath, "What do you think of her?"

"How do you do?" Wald Ensor said, with equal formality, when the child, her cheeks reddened with stooping, resumed an upright position. She took no notice of his salutation, nor did she hold out her hand. She was not very well brought up. She appeared concerned because one of the parcels was missing, and wondered aloud if it had rolled into the stall under the feet of the bull...

"Never mind," said Adelaide fondly. There was pride in her voice. None of the lowing cows, untethered but morally anchored to the posts to which their calves were firmly bound, their mother love taken into consideration by the cunning butcher, who relied on it more surely than any rope that was ever spun of hemp, showed more maternal solicitude. Ensor was touched at once, as she meant him to be.

So the restless, theory-ridden Adelaide was happy and settled at last, her hopes satisfied, her eugenical requirements fairly well carried out through this girl, with her bucolic graces, her obviously sterling health, a maternal product of great value. She had golden hair, blue eyes, and a complexion of roses and again roses. There were hardly any lilies in her composition and, although she was lovely at fifteen, chances were she would be raddled at twenty-five. Ensor noticed that the bare hand clutching the wooden rail was not like her mother's, but large and clumsy. She probably had feet to correspond. The dark, bushy eyebrows which struck a note of savagery in the simple, placidly sensuous countenance suggested at least one coarse male progenitor. He surmised that Miss Favarger had, in effect, succeeded in capturing a thoroughly healthy mate—had married a prize-fighter, perhaps—her ambition in the old days—something rustic, fair and saxon.

Adelaide released her under-lip which she had drawn in and bitten till it bled, as her habit was, and spoke quickly with an awkward cordiality that reminded Ensor of the first time she had invited him to dinner in Portland Place. There was the same uncertain, deprecating, almost offensively peremptory manner as of one continually expecting to be refused.

"Where are you staying, Wald? At The Antelope? Here on business? Well, you can do it all from High Walls—we'll motor you in every day. Let's go and get your things out of the hotel. The car's there, as it happens—waiting for us."

"Thank you, I hardly think I—" so Ensor was saying at intervals, and continued to say. He felt annoyed, hustled, overborne by this aggressive, overweening personality with which he had again come into contact. Miss Favarger's love of domineering—he didn't know what her new name was—had once been modified by a touching physical unfitness, but she had grown out of the delicacy of the young girl and was now—well!—a woman to count with.

He thought of all this as he walked behind her and Phyllis through the thronging market-place. They threaded the fusty, interested groups collected round this or that shrewd Cheap Jack extolling yards of tawdry lace, coarse netting warranted never to tear, rough crockery warranted never to break, and Ensor could hardly hear Adelaide's voice through the clatter of hoofs on the stone causeways as the clumsy, puzzled animals were run along them at a gallop by sweating, panting stablemen. Adelaide would stop dead every now and then and become absorbed in the contemplation of melancholy stallions with straw-plaited tails which stood, their shiny black hocks turned outwards, all adown the smooth bits of stone flagging that intersected the rough cobbles. Ensor punctuated his protests at intervals with "My dear Mrs.—" but she took no notice and, if she heard, did not care to supply the name. Now and again Phyllis would turn and smile a sweet, irresponsible smile at him, and sketch an inviting gesture. Ensor liked all children, and especially girls of that age and, after one of these demonstrations, followed her mother and her with less travail of spirit and fewer protests. He rather wanted to see this "Mary-be-damned!" who was said to be waiting, cold, tired and neglected in the car. Another of Adelaide's children? Perhaps an ugly one? How Adelaide would detest her in that case!

They reached the outer fringe of booths and the raucous voices of the salesmen and the heartrending moos of cows faded out of hearing, and the old Antelope Inn, where he lay last night, came in sight. Many conveyances and a small Rover car stood in front of it. He was faced with the immediate problem of acceptance or refusal of Adelaide's invitation. There was a child in the motor, hunched up and cowering under the lee of the rolling swathes of the hood. She seemed about ten years old, and obviously cold and tired of waiting. As they approached she fixed her eyes on him with a kind of timid, animal interest—the way animals always begin by thinking you are going to be unkind to them. She did not take her eyes off Ensor as he approached, and her wide, flat face did not light up in the least at sight of Adelaide, who answered Ensor's tacit inquiry:

"No, not mine. The cook's." She raised her voice—almost shouted. "You remember Gertrude? The cook who couldn't cook?

Ha, ha! Didn't you all worry me about it. It kept you away from me for months, Wald. Her name's Mary. I have her here for her health, and I leave her in the car because she is afraid of bulls. Now, Phyllis, be quick! Run and get the things at Storr's, and come back. We're not on time, and it's a fairly long run home."

She began busying herself with some rugs, to talk to him on intimate matters. He hardly heard. Phyllis saying to Ensor in a child's flirtatious way, "Now, mind you come!" obeyed her mother's orders, and Ensor, slavishly obeying those of Adelaide—it seemed the easiest thing to do—went into the hotel, paid his bill and collected his belongings.

He had no idea why he had accepted the invitation, unless it was that the other child, looking up once, had seemed to him to have seconded it in a dreamy, spiritless way that touched him. He already pitied her. She seemed so lonely with these two strong, healthy, forceful people. He fancied that he might perhaps make her cheer up a bit if he could get her to take to him. Children did as a rule, and Adelaide would probably be grateful to him, for she seemed, in her own hard way, to be anxious to befriend her servant's child, taking her out in the car and letting her own girl play with her. The two children seemed fond of each other for, when he came out of the hotel again, they were both stowed in the car under one rug, and had snuggled up against each other to keep warm for the long ride across the Plain of York.

Adelaide took him in front beside her, and they started. She drove in a careless way which suggested the hand of little practice. She took risks and showed ignorance on some very fundamental rules. This did not disconcert Ensor; he had physical courage and considered himself capable of taking on any risks that a woman at all events could take. Full tilt they ran along dull roads, blackish under foot, and hedge-bordered with a sullen, craven green. The Plain of York, in all its mediocre dreariness, quickly unrolled itself before them. Adelaide's lips were pursed and dry; she moistened them now and then. She made no attempt to point out landmarks or objects of interest. There were no features to point out. Dull, dusty, briony shoots and tendrils of clematis were spread over the hedges like a netted coverlid on a lodging-house bed, neutral tinted nettles carpeted them at the base, and at due and distant intervals clean, neatly made gates shut off the entry into fields each one like the other. The same kind of stupid, spiritless bird rose up now and again and flew stilly into the bordering fields to alight on some tedious brown furrow that hid the one behind it. Mean clumps of trees that sheltered no possible lover's walk or trysting-place punctuated the road or looked over it here and there.

Every now and then Ensor heard the little girls behind him whispering and chuckling in the floor of the car, where they were squatting in avoidance of the cold wind that blew steadily over the Plain. At least he heard Phyllis's voice, and took Mary's for granted. The two seemed to be very good friends...

And then Adelaide suddenly broke her self-imposed fast, and began to talk to him in those wire-drawn tones of hers which had always suggested to Ensor the idea of a rope lashing the water, or trailing along a gravel walk, and which he longed to bid her lift, try to get taut again. The passion that smouldered in her eyes seemed only to lend an edge to her voice. Ensor, searching for the minutiæ of change in her, could think of no feature that had altered much in twelve years except her mouth. It had always been rather vixenishly straight, and had now lost all suggestion of curve. Opening raspishly, it seemed to close again in a helpless sourness. Her face altogether reminded him of the matronly, yet sometimes old-maidish, faces of those mentally starved, materially satisfied women of the Renaissance that he had seen in pictures and reproductions. It was the same drawing about the cheeks, the same anxious slope of the flesh away from the consumptive hollows of the bones. Her small, nervous hands, claw-like, handled the wheel with ill-regulated vigour—an obstinate determination to excel. Her vanity, pathetic and obvious, amused Ensor and, since it made in the long-run for efficiency and pluck, commended itself to him. He liked women to show grit and did not, on the whole, object or ever had objected to be managed by the hand of competency.

As he reckoned, she was not very proficient, and had to give most of her attention to driving the car. Pride probably incited her to carry on a conversation in which she attempted to amuse her guest with a trickle of ideas long since formulated by herself or by others.

"Isn't it a grim country?" She spoke cheerfully. "They say there are more heirs and heiresses of solitary habit and tottering reason to the square inch here than in any other country in England. You see"—she knitted her brows—"these old, feudal people—they are mostly Catholics—have all along gone as they pleased and paid no attention to eugenics. They've neglected every known psychological rule; for one thing, they have intermarried so fearfully—"

"Your old preoccupation, eh?" said Ensor, smiling.

"Don't sneer, Wald, I beg of you. Why, we met and took to each other on that ground—if you remember our discussions—and I am keener on it than ever. I hate anything of a misbegotten or deformed nature like death or sin, as indeed it is." She looked at him steadfastly, indicating by her manner that she was about to say something startling. "Do you know that, if I was not a Christian woman, I should find myself beating Mary here—that hideous child behind us that I am so far indulgent to—within an inch of her life."

Ensor made a sound indicative of his wish and his conviction that she should lower her voice. Adelaide accepted the criticism and, to some extent, heeded his remonstrance. She continued, laughing:

"But as she is poor faithful old Gertrude's unique *rejeton*, I stay my hand and, instead of the lash, give her Parish's Food."

"It's very good of you," Ensor murmured, much oppressed. He remembered the awful tale of Gertrude's first baby hidden in the chest of drawers and, moreover, he was afraid Mary had heard—he felt those big, helpless, opaque-seeming eyes of hers plumb in the middle of his back...

"—Dead against my own theories, too," Adelaide went on. "That sort of distinct evidence of at least one parent's physiological ineptitude ought jolly well to be stamped out at birth."

"Perhaps," said Ensor slowly and strainedly, "perhaps Mary is going to be a poet. I fancy John Keats had those beautiful, suffering eyes she has... I only got a glimpse of her before we got in..."

"Eyes of a sick monkey—pah!" ejaculated Adelaide brutally and quite loudly. "Let us not think of her. Tell me all about yourself."

Wald Ensor obeyed her, as he was henceforth to do, more or less, and began to render her a full account of his doings during the last twelve years, without asking for any reciprocal confidence on her part. As he talked on in the even, rather tame style which in him was aggravated, not diminished, by deep feeling, he was painfully conscious of a duel waged within him by two opposing and violent moods.

One side of him longed to lay his hand on Adelaide's and get her to stop the car and allow her prey to step out, go away beyond the range of her terrible, puissant personality which alarmed while it interested him. The other side—the explorer, the adventurer—turning away in thought from her image, desired to stay and see it through and have another look at the two young creatures for whom this living mass of barren theory was making herself responsible, more especially the cook's ailing child. A long, attenuated but distinct tendon of passionate feeling seemed to connect him with her... something like the knotted cord-like sinews that the cook extracts from the material she is manipulating. As if he were the mother of a child that has never been divided from her?... He remembered feeling as he felt now towards a monkey caught on a tropical island that the captain of his ship was bringing home to colder and more unsuitable climes, and which resented it in sadness and melancholy.

With regard to the adventurous side of the business he could not help wondering if, when they reached the place called High Walls—a name Adelaide had tossed to him—a fond husband would come to the portal and welcome his wife and the stranger she had chosen to bring home? For Adelaide had volunteered no information about herself, and he had been too shy to ask for any. He had gathered that she was well off and had bought High Walls with her own money, for Dr. Favarger had died some years ago and left his only daughter everything.

He expected her house was some handsome old ancestral place, purchased of a decadent heir with this money, that the car presently would stop at some pillared gates with stone balls on top, opened by a curtsying lodgekeeper, and turn in at some handsome, leisurely drive bordered by fine old trees. Although he knew the name of the place he was surprised when, after going for half a mile or so along a bit of road bordered by hedges on the one side and a high buttressed, red brick wall on the other, overhung by heavy elm trees, Adelaide, without any warning, stopped the car opposite a small, half-sunk door in this very wall.

"I live here. Wald, will you ring?"

Rooks cawed in their nests in the sad clumps of the trees that seemed to fill the enclosure, and a dog barked shrilly. Ensor, as he stood in the roadway after having rung, had the sense of being at the postern gate of some embattled fortress standing tall and grimly self contained on the gloomy level of the Plain.

Time passed. No one came to the door. The dog inside continued to bark, and Adelaide's voice sounded unreal in the silence and the great spaces. Yet she was talking as people talk in towns:

"Nice old place!" she was saying jauntily. "I bought it because it agreed so well with my own peculiar mentality. It belonged to one of the crocky-minded noblemen I told you of. He killed his man-servant, I believe. He came to need only one room—somewhere else—and padded—so I got this cheap, freehold and all. It needs delightfully few servants to keep it up. That's what I like. I hate servants about; they always spy on you... Hullo!"

She stood up in the car and called out. Her voice was not good. It irritated. At last a blue-gowned, golden-haired, well-nourished maid appeared, and stood holding the door but not attempting to make herself useful in any way. It was Ensor who helped Adelaide out, took her rugs and picked up her bag. Then he turned to the two children... Phyllis had already leaped out. Ensor looked at the other child, sitting or rather crouching alone on the wide seat. Their eyes met for a moment—Adelaide seemed to intercept them purposely...

"Mary, stop in the car! No, you may as well come in with us..." she said fussily.

A lad appeared and tooled the vehicle off somewhere. Piled with motor-rugs, Ensor stumbled along a narrow, stone-flagged path that led a very short way to the squat house which appeared. They walked Indian file. On the stone perron an ugly puppy rushed at them from the side of the house and covered Phyllis with paw marks. The child tried in vain to abash and quieten it. Adelaide from behind, in her unnatural, would-be forcible tones, called it off and bade it come to her. The dog obeyed but, in Ensor's opinion, without enthusiasm.

Adelaide seemed to think differently. "You see," she said, "he loves the hand that chastens him. I have to keep him up to the mark; all these people"—a glance at the pretty, silly maidservant—"are so tender-hearted, all except Gertrude, she has good strong hands."

"I do hate to hear Kraft howling," remarked Phyllis.

"All young things, including Kraft-Ebing," said her mother gravely, "need to go through a period of correction before they are fitted for social purposes. And this is a good dog, or you bet I shouldn't keep him or trouble to whip him. I hate mongrels, human and otherwise, don't you, Wald?"

Her eyes hardened as she laid them on the puny child, holding an immense rug that trailed on the ground. Like a new servant, she seemed too shy and helpless to put it down or act at all until some order was given. Ensor took the rug from her; she did not look up. He began to think this evidence of Adelaide's philanthropic kindness was half-witted...

"Go in at once, Mary! Don't stand fiddling there. Go to Gertrude—both of you!"

Her remarks were directed at Mary, who stood hesitating; for Phyllis had already gone towards the heavy baize door at the back of the hall before she spoke.

Someone did thrash the puppy next day, for Ensor heard it howling beneath his bedroom window. It was very young; its crying was for all the world like the whimpering of a child that was being beaten. He could not lie comfortably resting in bed through the noise, though he knew that dogs must be trained. He rose and employed the hour or so thus gained on the day to examine carefully the position of the room he was in, studying its means of exit and approaches in the style of all well-seasoned travellers. He then put on his hat and went out by the back entrance, half stumbling over and apologising to a maid who was scrubbing the steps of it. He examined the house, noted its shape and the extent of the garden, and counted the number of tall elm trees that surrounded it and were, in their turn, circumscribed by the high, dull, red walls that gave Adelaide's house its name.

High Walls was a composite building finished in the late Georgian period, but including portions dating from almost every period after Elizabeth. The actual Elizabethan part had been more or less built up and formed the kernel of the interior. Some enterprising architect, employed by the half-witted nobleman, had carefully enclosed and hidden its merit away, then applied a frontage that offended every canon of art and taste and depressed every eye. The walls, Ensor fancied, represented a recent addition of this fantastical personage, and answered to his need for seclusion, for the hideous, expensive portal and the colonnade of the facade had been designed to impress from a distance those approaching it from the road. It was now dwarfed and crushed out of all proportion by the encroaching pale which cut off air and space and gave the house the air of an asylum or a prison.

His voyage of discovery ended, he went quietly in from the garden by the front door in the middle of the colonnade which was open. The perron was still wet from scrubbing. He found himself in a shiny-floored hall, carpeted here and there with wild beast skins. There were two sofas, and he recognised, spread honourably on one of them, his own particular present to the whilom Miss Favarger. This corner of the hall, rendered dark in daylight by the pillars of the colonnade, was palisadoed off with old German screens and arm-chairs with high backs that successfully fended off draughts from the front door and permitted it to be used as a lounge and smoking-room. The walls were panelled and moulded in dark browns and yellows. Heavy antlered heads of deer hung in one or two places; their sad and glassy eyes leered down pensively. He noticed, as he went round with his pince-nez raised, that there were some very good engravings; all pictured the usual gloating cruelties of the sportsman. There was the print of the two fighting stags of Landseer, their antlers interlocked in death; another of the rabbit in the trap, and one of the deer pulled down by its yelping enemies. Beyond, in the dining-room, there were some prize-fights and coaching accidents. All these works of art were repugnant to Ensor, for he was, if he thought about it, inclined to be anti-vivisectionist.

He returned to the morning-room, because, on the broad hearth, although it was July, charred logs rested on the iron dogs and fell slowly away into a bed of soft grey ash, forming a glowing heap of detritus that was never cleared away in this old Yorkshire house. The roaring flame lurked somewhere at the heart of the pile, but gave no warmth, and the man used to Californian summers felt chilly and longed to stir the logs up into wintry activity. He knew how to behave, however, and, taking up an out-of-date local paper which was all he could find, sat down on a sofa with a patient eye fixed on the main staircase, which he presently expected his hostess to descend.

The paper was dull to one uninitiated in local gossip, and he dropped it and began to go over again in his mind those last words Adelaide had said to him as she ascended that very staircase last night. One small, finely shaped foot was on the step. With her small housekeeping bag in one hand—the bag he had not seen her without since they came to High Walls—she had held up the other hand, saying gravely, with no suspicion of archness: "Good-night! Sleep well. I shan't."

Disconcerted, he had said nothing, but had let her go. He was outraged, not so much by her words as by the look with which she had punctuated them. It made him remember, with an intense, shy, conscious memory, that last time he had really seen her, looked at her independently—into the eyes she had turned to him on the doorstep of her home—the "eyes of a sick monkey"—she had given him the phrase herself. After that moment all was maze and flurry. He remembered the wide room in Portland Place, and the yellow sofa behind the door. And then when, shamefacedly, they had stood together again on the wide, gleaming doorstep, and his Adelaide, placated, reproachless, seeking not to bind him, leaving their next meeting to chance, had let him out into the dawn...

He had admired her for her bold and fine, her sturdy, a-moral attitude, her reliance on the support and efficiency of her own standards and principles. And now, as then, he was sure that she denied nothing, deprecated nothing, dropped nothing. Even the yellow sofa of his dreams was there in the hall; he had recognised it overnight, a handsome piece of Empire furniture on which she had spread his gift, a great golden spatulate beast, lazily sprawling... wearied and satiate...

He brooded over the ways of women, of which he proudly imagined himself to know nothing, when a servant came through the outer hall bearing to-day's paper, which she roughly laid down beside him. Before he could question her as to her mistress's morning procedure, she passed again through the red baize door which led, he imagined, to the kitchen regions. She had left the door open. A waft of sounds came to him—voices—one he fancied was that of the famous and omnipotent Gertrude on whom, so far, he had never set eyes. The other voice he knew to be that of Adelaide. She was already down and afoot then; she had become a good housekeeper and set her house in order betimes!...

She was there; she was coming to him. She held the handle of the door, finishing a sentence which he could not hear. But he did notice the way in which Gertrude permitted herself to answer her mistress, and it set him against the cook at once. Her tones were raucous, coarsely good humoured, and her language grossly familiar...

"With me? You've told Phyllis? Well, that's quick work, I must say."

"It's got to be done," Adelaide told her sturdily, over her shoulder, "and the sooner the better. From now."

"The other one'll miss her!"

"That can't be helped. *You* needn't mind—yours will profit. This very day, mind!"

There was a pause; the handle of the door shifted backwards and forwards in Adelaide's hand. The cook had got back into the kitchen some little way before she replied, and the vicious emphasis with which she spoke was accentuated by the clang of a dish roughly set down on some pantry shelf or other:

"I don't mind, but it seems a queer sort of way to go and treat one's own flesh and blood!"

Adelaide let the door go sharply and came forward to greet her guest. She was surprised to see him already down and said so. She looked excessively handsome, if a trifle pale. She pushed both hands through the cloudy swathes of hair that lay right across her forehead. She always arranged her hair across, not over or back from her forehead. It became her.

She stood chatting to her guest, telling him that breakfast was not ready yet, because that lazy little Phyllis, whose business it was to make the tea, had had a fit of temper this morning early and was not even dressed... While she was speaking, Phyllis herself looked over the banisters and addressed her mother in the fashion that Ensor disliked, calling her by her Christian name. He fancied that perhaps the child was allowed, nay enjoined to do so in order to minimise the effect of her size and precocious development on the age-estimation of her mother, a natural weakness to which Adelaide, like other ladies, was probably prone.

"Oh, Addie!" the child said appealingly, "*is* it true what Gertrude says? Mayn't I really have Mary to sleep with me any more?"

"No!" her mother replied; "it's high time Gertrude began her training. Now don't make a fuss... it would be no kindness to keep Mary any longer with you, spoiling her for a good servant and unfitting her for her station. Go in and make the tea and call us when it's drawn."

Phyllis obeyed, sulkily. Ensor was glad to see her put up some sort of a fight for her little playmate and companion. Adelaide perched, with a sudden childish movement, on the arm of the sofa, showing a pretty ankle in its openwork stocking. She looked like a capable gipsy as she sat there dangling her everlasting bag...

"I've been asking Gertrude," she said carelessly, "if she remembers you, and she says she does. You must look her up after breakfast."

"But I never saw her," he said, and would have liked to add, "and don't want to now," remembering her voice so lately heard. "You mean the cook you had in Portland Place?"

"Yes. Not much of a cook, was she? But so faithful. I needed it. And she needed me. She had a lover who was a prize-fighter, and he deserted her and left her with that wretched child you saw to bring up. Mary is a bad case of atavism, I am afraid, for *he* was a fine fellow!"

"I don't want to see Gertrude, anyway," Ensor said decidedly. "Wasn't that she beating the dog this morning?"

"Yes. She's got good strong hands, and no compunction like I'd have!"

An exultant gleam... an instantaneous flicker of intelligence as though by some new, unexpected mode of presentment he had been afforded the sight of the fork tongue, suddenly protruded, of a viper, crossed Ensor's excited, feverish vision. The viper stood for Adelaide during the space of half a second. He shuddered, and Adelaide suddenly, but with an air of intense premeditation, slipped off the arm of the sofa and kissed him.

Impelled by some sudden eclosion of all that was morbid in his nature, Wald Ensor, towards the end of the year, married Mary Adelaide Frances, the widow of J. Dibben, Esq., of Brighton. It is a fact that, until he bestirred himself to apply for the licence, he had not known the name of the father of Phyllis. Adelaide never refused, but seemed to prefer not to speak of him. Ensor could understand how this Dibben, some healthy, ordinary man of no preponderating degree of intellect, should have managed, soon after marriage, to alienate a capricious, easily bored creature like Adelaide. He was too modest to imagine that he himself had the power to amuse or interest her much, but judging from her behaviour he felt justified in believing that he himself suited her, since, in his company, she attained the nearest approach, for her, to a state of repose...

And for him, his new wife took possession of him body and soul, quietly and utterly. He hardly realised it, for she appeared, on her part, to be making some slight sacrifice of individuality, with a view, perhaps, of enslaving him completely. Though to everyone else her manner was curt, unpleasant and at times unbearably arrogant, she stayed her tongue and curbed her temper whenever her opinion happened to clash with that of her husband. And had she allowed her natural acerbity full play, the fact that she was now about to become a mother for the second time called up all Wald Ensor's chivalry and tenderness. Indeed, he rejoiced at his approaching paternity. The want that had formed deep in his heart, created by the premature death of his child out in California, was about to be satisfied; the void that, for want of a better, he had filled with Adelaide's child, whom he played with, gave presents and was kind to. Yet he remembered how at first the little Mary, Phyllis's foster-sister as he once called her—he would never forget Adelaide's look!—had seemed at first to be going to be his favourite. Phyllis Dibben was unsympathetic to him; he did not think hers was altogether a nice nature; she was just a beautiful savage. Still, she was a child and a pretty one, and Ensor's love of children was a real and true sentiment that carried him safely over an absurd, unexplained prejudice.

Though Adelaide and he had met for the first time on the common ground of their love of children, Ensor had come to suspect that his own was the truer development of that particular instinct. Adelaide admired presentable specimens of childhood only, and the beauty of Phyllis, as an undeniable guarantee of her own eugenical perfection, afforded that toll to her vanity, that satisfaction of her pride that was needed seemingly to evoke the motherly in her. Why else did she so neglect the wretched child she had begun by petting and more or less treating as her own? He had seen Mary, now a drudge, on the day he had come across them in Beverley, sitting side by side in the car with Phyllis's own child—dressed alike, even. The turn of affairs, justifiable possibly—Mary might have grown overweening—had been so sudden as to outrage his sense of decency. His large heart was capable, where children were concerned, of embracing the halt, the maimed and the eugenically incorrect, and he would have liked his Adelaide to have been equally tolerant. He could hardly endure to let the question stand over till Adelaide was more fit to deal with it.

Meanwhile he spoke kindly to the little girl whenever he met her about the house. She did not walk; she crawled—something like a limp. He had an idea that she was slightly deformed—but then, it wasn't always the same leg! He now realised that it was Mary he had stumbled over that first morning kneeling by a side door scouring some steps. Her translation from the padded seat of the car to the hard stones of the yard had been so sudden that he could not conceive it to be she.

There was the other servant, Auretta, but she generally seemed to work out of doors and in the laundry. She seemed a hefty girl, strong enough to have taken on Mary's job as well as her own. But why not employ a third female servant?

One day, when Adelaide seemed fairly well, he had spoken about these domesticities to her, and made it an opportunity to mention Mary. Adelaide had made no mystery about her cruel régime, she loudly justified it. The girl was to be brought up as a servant, and her play-days were over. Yes, Phyllis had taken a fancy to her, a fancy she had indulged on the understanding that it was temporary. Mary had shared Phyllis's room and her meals and walks and games to please Phyllis. But it would not do to sacrifice the whole future of someone else's child just to please Phyllis, and she had to stop it.

Ensor was furious at her fiendish rationalism and want of consistency in suddenly setting one child, brought up in obedience to the caprice of another, in comparative ease and idleness, to do the rough work of the house, eat inferior food and, worst of all, the cutting her completely off from such softening, educating influences to which she had been accustomed. But he listened; he said nothing, only thought it over as he stood there. If possibly the child could hold on a bit, it would be as well not to worry Adelaide until she was safely over her forthcoming experience, always a rather severe trial to women of her temperament. Then surely milder councils would—must—prevail; he would get Mary reinstated in her place as foster-sister to Phyllis—that was what he would like best. Oh, very much best, for he found he was developing the deepest, the queerest feeling of tenderness for the ugly, sad, unchildish child! But, if that were impossible, if Adelaide still refused to allow it, he would get hold of the mother and work on her, pay her to insist that Mary might be taken out of this and sent to some bright, well-managed school or home of her own class to be brought up and trained. Not that he liked the notion of her being trained for a servant; she did not look as if she would ever be strong enough... But there were other professions... he would see...

So he dreamed of a possible, moderately happy future for a little human being who interested him quite absurdly and, meantime, he did what he could for her, and that was very little. She now never appeared in the better part of the house, shut off by the red baize door, and he sometimes fancied that Adelaide very much disliked to see her cross the threshold of it into the other. Yet the oldest and most architecturally interesting part of High Walls lay beyond that door, and Ensor was something of an antiquary and had been articled at one time to an architect. Not to annoy his wife, he was careful to conduct his investigations of the historical portion of the house from the back of it. There Mary's work chiefly lay, and he sometimes spied her at her task of ablution of stone steps and flagged paths, armed with her heavy pail and piece of hearthstone, scouring, swirling a wet rag about ineffectually, spreading long spider-like arms in a radius of their length all about her, and producing a wet surface to be succeeded by a bright brown sanded one where before all was dull, unvisited dust and dirt. She had such terribly long arms for a child of her size and age; she was, moreover, left-handed, like himself. He would stand for quite a long time looking down at her rusty red ribbon top-knot, knowing that the child was fully aware of him, but was too well drilled and too timorous of the gentry to look up and seek his notice. How had they managed to transmogrify her so quickly from playmate to Phyllis, sleeping with Phyllis, driving about in the motor with Phyllis and her mother to the submissive drudge who never looked up till he spoke to her, and then with a sad, cowed expression that went to his heart. If she were actually carrying a pail too heavy for her, or trailing a broom long enough for one twice her height, he felt justified in taking pail or broom away from her at once and learning from her the place where she wished it put. It was difficult to get her to speak at all, and she got shyer as the days went on. He felt that conventionality forbade the master of the house to go down on his knees and scrub the stone floor in her stead, yet he realised that it was hardly a child's work, and imagined vaguely that the School Board, if they were aware that a girl of ten, one of their potential scholars, was living deprived of every form of training, might have something to say about it. He rather dreaded some sort of fuss, trouble for poor Adelaide. Mary was given no tuition of any kind; he was sure of it. Though High Walls was five miles distant from Market Weighton, there was a school about half a mile off in the nearest hamlet consisting of a few cottages. But Mary, he was sure, never went beyond the garden.

High Walls, or High Red Walls, as Adelaide had attempted to style it, was curiously self-contained in its girdle of red brick. Tradesmen never penetrated within their circumference. Adelaide used the motor, and did her own marketing. He remembered that it used to be said of the house in Portland Place that anything might go on there. The same might be said of High Walls! Adelaide had chosen to live here, maybe because she traced some affectionate analogy with the home of her birth, the house where her mother, a north-country woman, had died. She had bought High Walls outright he learned; she made her own gas; she kept her own fowls and her own cows, and ordered her clothes from Paris, constantly fetching large wooden cases, that had crossed the seas, from Beverley Station in the ever useful motor. About everything she did, in her brusquerie, her jerkiness, there was a suggestion of eccentricity...

but she was clever enough—everything she said or did went, as it were, on all fours...

There was no doubt, however, that for one reason or another, because of her shyness, love of solitude, or lack of social instinct, that his wife had succeeded in creating a vacuum all round her, an area sterilised of amenities, of talk or even gossip. Gossip, Ensor felt, would be a godsend. But, since their marriage before the registrar three months ago, Mrs. Ensor had had no visitors. He went to Beverley now and then on business, and knew of three inhabitants of that town who maintained that they had driven or motored out to High Walls to pay their respects to the lady he had married. Even had they done so, they would have been told, "Not at home." These problematical visitors were the wives of men with whom Ensor now and then came in chance contact, and who had enjoined it on their womenfolk to call on the queer, uncivilised woman whom this nice, civilised man they rather took to had married.

Ensor was perfectly aware that Adelaide was not popular. For, if people had, even before he came, realised her existence in the neighbourhood, they forbore to mention it; the calls were only a tribute to his own charm and obvious, pleasant, gentle manliness. Ensor was a man's man, the kind of man whom women find dull, and, as Mrs. Ensor never returned a call, never seemed to expect to be asked to anything, it was easy enough to enjoy the husband's company and make him free of what there was of society in these two sleepy little market towns. Before he had been there long, Wald Ensor was a member of the Conservative Club of Beverley, and had been put on the Library Committee of that busy little place, while in Weighton he played golf and adjudged prizes. Drawing-rooms knew him not, or hardly at all; he could not very well go about among the women without Adelaide, and he did not care to do so.

He constrained himself to take part in whatever was going, to attempt to fulfil his trivial duties as a citizen when they came his way, partly from a sense of duty, partly—he was conscious of it—because the monotony of his existence in that lonely country house was sapping his vitality, jagging his fine equable temper, and dulling his sense of good fellowship. The desire to travel again came over him sometimes in a great wave. If it had not been for Phyllis and Adelaide, he said to himself—if it had not been for Mary, he did not say or even think to himself—he would certainly have proposed to his wife to leave her for a time; he knew that it would have shaken him up a bit and made him nicer to her when he came back.

He could not somehow talk to Adelaide now; he thought it was because of her condition. He had come to think that everything, the plans, questions and so on, must be deferred until Adelaide, in her own phrase, was "through." She thought and talked of nothing else. It was an event of extraordinary importance to her. When it had taken place he would ask her about the social ostracism he deprecated. He would find out if it was self-incurred, a voluntary effort on her part? Or was it a case of sour grapes, and had she been clever enough to make a virtue out of necessity? Or had she from pique, temper or caprice, so obstinately refused herself at the beginning when she first had come to settle in Yorkshire, that people had grown tired of making overtures; overtures ever repulsed by the sour chatelaine of the lonely house encircled with its belt of trees and walls, like the Palace of a Sleeping Beauty.

He could not ask her this now, he could not ask her anything. He literally knew nothing about the woman he had married and taken to his breast, together with the child that a man unknown had given her, and whom he had superseded so easily. He did not know how long she had lived in Yorkshire, why she lived in Yorkshire, and why she had taken a mansion that was little better than a prison in which they two lived immured.

She did not seek to prison him there with her, she made no objection to his leaving her for hours at a time; he did not think she would have minded his leaving her for days, only he never did. He was strongly held by her picturesque indifference, shot with the attractive bursts of passion he remembered in the days when she was not as now, concentrating all the force of her being on the bearing of a healthy child, a wonderful child, a child that should be even more eugenically perfect than Phyllis. Though he did not know that he was weak, he knew full well that she was strong, and that when he was not loving her he was afraid of her. Yes, he, Wald Ensor, the man that had shot tigers and braved artillery, and dug for gold in circumstances of incredible fortitude and endurance, was afraid of this thin, hawk-nosed, bow-lipped woman with the bony wrists, the small feet and the vanishing waist.

She was ruining him, she was breaking his spirit, making him a craven as, in another department of life, Gertrude, the cook, with her "good, strong hands," that he shuddered to look at, was making of Mary, the piteous human being over whom she had power even as Adelaide, his wife, had power over him. He was sure of it. With her cruel, if necessary, training, Gertrude was weakening and killing her child by inches. In obedience to the mistress's savage theory of economics the body of the maid's child was being maimed, her mind dwarfed and annulled, her moral and physical growth both contravened. For the strong will of Adelaide was behind the enslaved Gertrude, and Adelaide spurred by a system which drove her to do what she considered right by the child of humble birth domiciled under her roof. Adelaide *was* right, economically right; it were indeed useless and unpractical to bring up the cook's child in luxury; the wrench of unpreparedness for the degradation to her true station in life would be all the more severe later on. But only a criminal want of imagination in Adelaide could inure her to the thought of such a situation. Ensor smiled bitterly under his drooping moustache, and forced himself to remember that his wife had the defects of her qualities, and that philoprogenitiveness was not one of them. He had gauged her aright in the old days at Portland Place, or was it that sly, all-seeking old father of hers who had first sown the doubt in his mind...?

"*Adelaide, fond of children! She only thinks she is. Cruelty masked by philanthropy!*"

And, what was that he had said about mother's vanity and its importance as a factor in unkindness? He remembered the old man's pawky sneer as he said it:

"If a neutral woman kills or ill-treats the child of another, no natural feeling except cruelty, the most natural of all, can possibly come into play, not even vanity..."

Not even vanity! The beautiful Phyllis, her own, petted, cherished! Mary, almost deformed, disgraced by nature's hand, an injury to someone's vanity, but not to Adelaide's, at any rate...

He would hide his head in his hands as he considered the terrible antithesis.

Get Mary away... to a Home... out of his sight... out of his life! O God! But he must do something as soon as Adelaide had given birth to the wonderful child that was to be theirs. That was settled. Meanwhile he suffered strange, unreasonable torments, agonies.

He grew shy in presenting himself in the back of the house, but, loafing about as near as he dared in that direction, sometimes would see the hem of Mary's frock or the reach of her thin long arm as she scrubbed and lathered and polished. Then, with a groan, he would prevent himself from turning the corner of the yard or outhouse lest he actually came in full view of the child at some one of her debilitating tasks. One morning, going to a cubby-hole in the back part of the hall to look at a photograph he was developing, he came upon Mary standing by the window-sill eating something out of a tin plate that rattled under the spoon in her shaking hand. The thermometer was below freezing-point. She had a darning-needle in the other hand, and a heap of stockings lay on a chair from which she had evidently risen. He pitied but dared not speak to her. He clenched his hands, anything to keep him from lifting her up and, boldly facing Gertrude, carrying her off with him to America or the Antipodes...

Just before Christmas, feeling he could bear it no longer, he got on to his bicycle and rode out to Weighton on purpose to buy something, he did not know what, for Mary. Too handsome a present might be taken away from her as unsuitable to her station; he had better get her something to eat, something nourishing, something that would "disappear." He was about to invest in chocolate *fondants*, the best, in a neat box with a smart ribbon round it, far smarter than the wretched bow she wore on her hair, when he suddenly realised that the cook's child, having fallen from grace full three months ago, would no longer appreciate the kind of sweetmeat that would appeal to Phyllis, who was an exceedingly greedy child. He asked for and procured plain, wholesome candy, and rode home, tired and depressed. The impulse which had sent him out was a little spent. Poor Mary was the cook's child, after all, bred to servitude, doing only what her mother had done before her. He was a meddling busybody and would probably only succeed in getting the poor child a beating...

He was thinking of Adelaide and Phyllis now—of the rich sensuous beauty of Adelaide's child, and the uncanny handsomeness of Adelaide. Her devilish attraction swayed him, always more especially when he was tired and overwrought. It was her eyes...

He got the candy, a fat packet that would rejoice any normal child's heart, and went boldly through the red baize door and asked for Mary.

Gertrude, the cook, coarse, stout, homely but possessing a fine pink complexion, was standing at the chopping-board in the cheerful, brass-bound kitchen. She suspended her operations and, raising her chin, regarded him quizzically. With a kind of good-humoured smile, so it appeared to him, she slightly deferred her reply... then she said calmly:

"Mary's in the scullery." Raising her voice she called, "Mary! Here! You're wanted."

Quickly, obediently, a drooping, crestfallen figure of infancy appeared and stood stock-still in the sunlight that poured through the doorway flung from the window open wide far back in the stone scullery she came from. It framed her in light and lit up the filmy mass of cobwebs that hung over her head; but it could not irradiate her any more than the bogey in the fields which flaps, lank and dull, in the full glare of noontide. And this was a living child rendered, by what means he knew not, unsusceptible, like the scarecrow, of light and joy! The depressed red bow on the top of her head looked as if it had not been untied for weeks. The hem of her skirt was partially torn off; it was, anyhow, far too long for her, and she or someone else had fastened it up clumsily with a piece, two pieces, of string. It was short enough now to show a dirty pair of white cotton drawers. She stood now waiting patiently, blinking a little; ugly, shapeless, piteous... Gertrude said nothing, but looked from one to the other, comparing them, quietly enjoying herself like a rough in the front row of the pit...

After a while, as if the play had lasted long enough, she said, "Come here! I must put a pin in for you."

Mary came shuffling up with no appearance of unwillingness. She did not seem to dislike her mother; that was all that could be said, and Ensor was glad to be able to think it possible that the cook was not *always* unkind to her child. But, to keep a child in such a shocking state of neglect, even if there had been no excessive corporeal punishment, was distinctly culpable. Oh, these north-country women! He stood dubiously handling the packet of sweets, while the mother proceeded, with many a shake or pull, to modify her child's disorder, which she had the sense to see injured her in the opinion of her master, if master he could be called who had no authority. At last, summoning his courage, he pulled out the packet and put it into Mary's hands as she stood there, pending the adjustment of clothes that could hardly be called such, so ragged and insufficient were they.

The packet fell to the ground, dropped with strange, unchildish negligence from a nerveless hand, and the child did not even look up. A spasm of pure agony transfixed the heart of Ensor. Gertrude noticed the violent contraction of his features. She picked up the packet of candy and actually put a bit into Mary's mouth. Ensor did not see if the child retained it, for he was groping on the ground for the pieces which had fallen out of the bursten packet.

"Say 'Thank you,' silly!" Gertrude adjured. The child stood astonished, bewildered, entirely upset, it seemed, by such attentions as are usually awarded to the protected, cherished young of any class. She was passive through fright; it was easy to see that her one idea was to hide, and that her eyes were looking for a corner to run into. But her mother had hold of her, ordering her attire, shaking her as if she had been a small, frail nut tree. It made her cough...

"That's rather an unsuitable length for a child's dress, surely?" Ensor remarked, when Mary stood erect and disengaged at last. The peccant under-garments had been shoved into their proper place, hidden, and her long, loose frock draped into panniers all round her.

"She's thin, that's what it is," conceded Gertrude. "Nothing won't stay up round her. The dress too long, sir? No wonder! It's one of Phyllis's Miss Adelaide threw away because it wasn't good enough for her beauty to wear. So it had to do for my Mary, hadn't it? *We* can't afford to have our clothes made on purpose for us, can we? Now, run away, child, run away and play!"

She grinned. Mary did not move.

"You're intended to grow into your clothes, I see," Ensor said helplessly. "Well, make haste and grow, there's a good girl."

Mary smiled, at last. Even if the gentleman's words were absurd and irrelevant she could not be deceived as to the kindness of his intentions. Then the poor smile, spiritless and without brilliance, faded off her face like sunlight on a dull grey wall on a rainy day. Gertrude took up his speech and answered it.

"Grow! Her! Never fear. Mary's one of those stunted-from-birth ones Miss Adelaide's always talking about. Just look at them thundering long arms!"

She caught up and extended to its full length the bat-like, skinny limb to which she alluded. The owner suffered this liberty; her stupid, glazed eyes were fixed on Ensor, and seemed to him to be saying, "*Save me!*"

He stammered out: "Couldn't she be sent to the sea for a month or so? I would arrange it... that is, if you could spare her, Gertrude?"

Agonisedly he waited on the cook's answer, for she was the child's legal guardian, with absolute power over it for life and death...

"Spare her? Lord, yes," Gertrude answered calmly. "The work she does isn't worth speaking about. You're nobbut a poor hand with the broom, aren't you, Mary?" To Ensor, without troubling to drop her voice: "'Twould be no good, sir. I'm thinking Miss Adelaide's begun her grand training too late."

"What do you mean?" he asked fearfully.

"She'll be training her into her grave, that's what she's doing."

It was too much. "Sh-h! for God's sake, woman!" he muttered, and sought his wife. Something must be done.

He had no authority except where Phyllis was concerned. And though Phyllis's physical upbringing left nothing to be desired, he considered her mental education to be defective, and said so often. Adelaide placed no obstacle whatever to his realisation of certain views he had formulated and insisted on to the verge of tediousness with regard to the moral standards to be inculcated in a young, growing girl, but listened patiently while he talked about it, and her thin lips wore something nearly approaching to a smile while her husband thus took a practical interest in the future of his stepdaughter. He had to reason broadly and generally; he could not lay his whole mind before the wife of Phyllis's father. For that father counted, and not, in Ensor's idea, favourably. Phyllis had certain tendencies which he deplored, and which he conceived her to derive from the parent he did not know. She had undoubtedly a strain of the coarse and the callous; her father had probably had these characteristics very strongly developed. She had also some of the tiresome tricks that he distinguished in Adelaide, and which careful training might cross and deny and finally eradicate. She was sly, she was morbid, she was headstrong and reckless of the claims of others...

So, acting with Adelaide's authority delegated to him unquestioningly, he kept a strict watch on the books Phyllis read, and the conversations she heard or took part in. He did not countenance her frequent visits to the kitchen and her odd and odious familiarity with Gertrude, the cook. He had asked Adelaide if he might not prohibit the child from entering the servants' quarters altogether, and seal the red baize door that led to them against her use. He would like to forbid all entrance and egress by it, and force Phyllis to give her word of honour that she would observe the prohibition.

"She may give it, but she won't keep it," said Adelaide lazily. "You can't wonder. She's fond of Gertrude because she gives her titbits, and Phyllis is greedy, poor darling! And then"—she looked up in his face—"there's your beloved Mary! She's about—the kitchen is her domain—and you must remember the two were brought up together. They were like foster-sisters before you came. You altered everything. And now, I am going to have *your* child!"

He stooped and kissed her, full of premature paternal emotion. Adelaide was supposed to be not quite so well to-day. She was lying on the famous tiger skin that he had given her, spread over a low, wide couch in the hall. She lay on it always so that the brute's savage head was close to her own. Loving and akin, the live Adelaide and the dead beast he had given her, both reeked of each other. There was all the hot suggestion of the jungle, of careless natural savagery in the juxtaposition of the tiger's snarling teeth, Adelaide's dusky eyes and the bars, spots and splashes of black that showed on each side of her spare form, like caked, dried blood upon the gold. It was his wife's constant boast that her beautiful figure was hardly altered by her present condition. The cruelty to the unborn implied in the attainment of this unnatural shapeliness was lost on the simple fellow.

"Our child," he said, kissing her again passionately, "is the thing that matters."

Then the thought of that other child went through, pierced his heart like an arrow. He rose from his knees. All the blood in his body came into his face. He stood looking down on Adelaide, who had returned the passion of his caress with all the force of which she was at present capable. A bar on the tiger skin, a zebra mark bitten in, zigzagging across the yellow fur, focused his eyes...

"Adelaide," he said softly, "could we not take Mary back into this part of the house again?"

"No," Adelaide said. She spoke quite quietly too, but Ensor knew her; a storm was coming...

"Then," he said pleadingly, "could she not be sent away for a bit"—his immense struggle betrayed itself in his voice—"or for good?"

"You cannot interfere with what is Gertrude's business," came plumb and sharp from Adelaide. "If Gertrude likes to leave me, she can of course take her child with her, but I cannot do without Gertrude, and Gertrude will *never* leave me. Ask her."

She turned away and laid her hot cheek against the flat head of the tiger.

"And I was so proud and happy!" she wailed.

He knelt down again. Her breath was coming quick and uneven. He feared for her and caressed her—it was what she wanted. But he embraced her for the first time without zest, and she knew it.

"It's no use," she said; "you have spoilt it all. And all for the sake of a dirty, misbegotten little wretch whose own mother can't stand her, and beats and neglects her. I don't blame Gertrude. Don't you understand, Wald, Mary is one of the wrecklings, one of Nature's faults that ought to have been smothered at birth. I wish I had. I wish somebody had. My father would have had her put away fast enough, if I had asked him, only, like a fool, I was kind to Gertrude, and kept her counsel and saw her through with it. But now, through you chiefly, I have come to hate the very sight of the child! You—*you* to come snivelling to me about her! You!"

She laughed horribly. He hated her. Her passion was spent. She raised herself and looked her husband up and down contemptuously.

He murmured perfunctorily, rising to his feet: "Don't, don't excite yourself!"

"I won't excite myself," she said squarely, turning her face round to the wall. "No fear! I'm better now. I *won't* let you hurt me. I'll even discuss the unwholesome brat if you like, that'll show you I don't care. Get on—now! Talk quietly and tell me what's wrong about Mary's upbringing."

"Thanks! You are very good," Ensor murmured. "Are you sure it won't upset you?"

"No, I tell you." She sat up and faced him. She pulled a basket of needlework towards her and busied herself with it. Her hands did not shake. Ensor admired her. After all, if she had no nerves, if she didn't care, he might as well say his say about the child, get better terms of existence for her, and be done with the subject once for all. He made up his mind that he would not say much; would not descend to particulars of Mary's ill-treatment unless she asked for them. He began gently:

"I do think, don't you, that when all's said and done, Mary's young; and even a servant's child ought to have some joy of its life. It oughtn't to be made to slave like a grown-up. Hang it all, a 'simple child should lightly draw its breath' not to the tune of housework and floor-scrubbing! The sight of that poor kid carrying those heavy pails about makes me quite sick. I should like to tell you what I saw yesterday. Gertrude must be a fearfully unnatural parent..."

"Well, speak out! What did you see?" Adelaide asked sharply.

"You were out driving. Mary was standing by one of the high windows in the old hall—"

"She'd no business to be there at all. Suppose a caller came?"

"No callers do come. Why don't they, by the way?"

"I've snubbed them all. They daren't show their noses here. I hate people. Go on. What was your paragon doing in the old hall?"

"She was eating something out of a tin platter, such as you feed dogs in, laid on the sill. The platter was not over clean, and I don't know what the mess was, but it looked most unappetising, and she seemed to be—yes, actually picking something—something disgusting—something alive out of it!"

"Pah, you sicken me!" Adelaide screamed.

Ensor went on relentlessly, now he was wound up:

"I put my hand on to her little scrubby head with that faded knot of ribbon on the crown—"

"I wonder you can touch it. Don't touch *me.*"

"—and I told her not to eat the nasty stuff, and what was it? She said it was bits Gertrude cut off the toast before it went into the dining-room, the same as the dog had. It looked days old—quite mouldy. I shouldn't like to give such a mess to my dog. I can only account for her being willing to eat it as a morbid taste of the young, growing child, and I bade her throw it away and not eat between meals. It shows the shocking state she's in; and she must be inventing, for then she said—"

"What did she say?"

"That it was her breakfast. 'Nonsense!' I said. But she stuck to it. She seemed afraid to speak, yet she stuck to it. I say, Adelaide, I know you aren't very fit just now, but oughtn't you really to make some inquiries? Does Gertrude beat her or ill-treat her? I hear sounds, of a morning sometimes—not so much lately since you've been seedy. They freeze my blood until I realise that it's the dog getting a licking, which I've no doubt it deserves... though, in my opinion, women ain't to be trusted to beat dogs, let alone children. Oh, Adelaide, reassure me! Don't you see, a man can't stand even the suspicion of such a thing going on in his house? A helpless child, not even our own..."

The drops of sweat stood on his forehead. Adelaide spoke as it were a prepared speech which it was now in order for her to make.

"*Your* house!" she said. It was hers, and the man winced. She continued, raising herself a little in her chair:

"Look here! Mary's a liar as well as a pig. You've owned it, you've shown her up. *You* may call her morbid, but that's not all! Just a filthy, dirty, beastly liar, I say! And, Wald, I am now going to bear *your* child and, if you want me to produce you a healthy one, born alive—you haven't had much luck with children, they say—you had better not worry me, the vessel into which the spirit has been poured"—her voice grew solemn—"for God has given me another chance. Let me take it, for I warn you, I'll never, never try again. I shall kill myself if this one does not come off all right."

She glanced at the watch that lay on her breast and made a suggestion:

"Suppose you be wise in time and leave off meddling in domestic concerns and go and attend to the things that are in your own province. You've a meeting of the Library Committee in Beverley at three—it's full time."

She lay down again on the sofa with the air of one performing a sacred duty. Ensor obeyed her and went about his business.

An important meeting of the Library Committee was on for to-day at which he had announced his intention of speaking, for the subject interested him personally. It was a question of morals as applied to the feast of contemporary literature spread before the youth of Beverley and Weighton. Ensor's contention was that as young girls formed the main contingent of novel-readers in all provincial towns, it behoved far-seeing and right-minded city councillors to see that no works pernicious in quality or deleterious in tone should be delivered over to their private consumption. Their elders, with a taste for life, spiced and otherwise, should purchase outright the literature their souls loved, and leave the shelves of chance to works of limpid purity and unimpeachable if dreary moral tone.

The Library Committee was composed of enlightened men and women, for it had been founded by an exceedingly busy and fussy Mrs. Marrable, "a bit of a Socialist," as she called herself. She was at any rate a person professedly open to all the new ideas. The

Committee were a little afraid of her, and had come to look to Ensor, the shy, silent embodiment of Conservative, almost retrograde, feeling in their midst, to oppose her. He generally began his sentences with: "I know I am a bit old-fashioned." This was a capital counterblast to Mrs. Marrable and her "bit" of Socialism. They found him invaluable, a sort of slipper on the wheels of frenzied progress, for Mrs. Marrable was not easily gainsaid. She was a relation of the Bishop's cousin, and had lived in Beverley for years in a big red house, where she entertained Saturday-to-Monday parties from London. She had no daughters.

Another influential member, Canon St. Leger, unmarried, and living in the best house in the Close, was a friend of Ensor's, though he had not asked him to come in so much lately...

Indeed, looking round the green baize-covered table where all the Committee found themselves at last seated, it occurred to Ensor that he had not shaken hands with a single one of the members since the last meeting, and that was a month ago. For that reason, he supposed, they seemed strange to him, although they were all, or nearly all, people with whom he had been invited to take pot-luck on any occasion, lunch or dinner, when he had ridden in from High Walls on his bicycle and found he had put it too late to get back. All except Mrs. Marrable, with whom, for political and temperamental reasons, he had always cared to have very little to do.

While the Committee dealt with some purely financial and business matters, which called for no more attention from the members of the Committee than was implied in passing a vote of confidence or holding up hands for a resolution, Ensor wrought himself up into a strange state of nervous apprehension. It might have been mere perverse fancy, but as a matter of fact not one of these people had spoken to him since they sat down, or recognised his presence except by a nod of salutation such as the barest courtesy demanded. The attitude of each several person could be accounted for separately. So-and-so had come in late, such a one had too many irons in the fire to be able to spare a word till the meeting was over; but still, there it was, the indefinable uneasiness, the disagreeable doubt that perhaps morbid imagining had established. No one had actually addressed a word to him!

He brooded over this as he sat stiffly on his bentwood chair. He was tired, overwrought and annoyed, for the child Phyllis had shown a sad racial cloven foot to-day. He was afraid she was not going to turn out so well as he could have wished. And, by and by, other business being disposed of, the Committee were invited to deal with the question of detailed selection of books for the Library. It was a subject on which Ensor was keenly interested, and here he had so much to say that he forgot his preoccupation, and did not allow his natural shyness to interfere with the expression of his opinion. He was strongly against the determination of Mrs. Marrable to permit, nay to encourage, the introduction of a certain novel, the work of one of her literary confrères, into the list of the Library. Ensor had had the book sent him from London so as to acquaint himself with its supposed nature. He had carefully kept it out of the way of his women-kind, until, having thoroughly digested it, he threw it into the fire. Yet this book was to be placed on the shelves of the Library to which Adelaide subscribed, and a copy of it would be sure to find its way to High Walls!

He could not bear the idea of such a girl as Phyllis, eager, sensuous, full of strong, exuberant, readily-awakened sex instincts, sucking in the unhealthy, unnecessary knowledge presented so cleverly by this book, and it seemed to his hypochondriacal imaginings that the tendency of the rest of the Committee was to override his objections *per se*. He grew tremendously excited, and the Committee wondered to see the usually still and discreet man, who had married the lady they called the terrible Mrs. Dibben, make such a violent exhibition of himself.

"I have a nearly grown-up daughter, as you all know," so he ended his speech, and for the moment felt every inch a father. "Well, let me tell you, that I had rather see her lying dead at my feet than realise that she was taking into her pure mind anything so poisonous, so pernicious, so destructive of all moral health as the work in question. I would rather see her physically starved, neglected, maimed even, than ruined mentally by such murderous nourishment..."

He stopped, he felt that the sense of the meeting was not with him. The silence that swallowed up the last word was hard and disapproving. The Chairman, Canon St. Leger, drummed on his desk with a pencil... Mrs. Marrable, divesting herself of her feather boa with the air of one throwing down the gauntlet, and tilting forward her chair, rose.

"Do I understand," she said, speaking with privileged indistinctness, but Ensor heard her for all that—"do I understand from Mr. Ensor's eloquent speech, that he cares to throw his perfect moral shield merely over a member of his own or immediate family? What about the stranger within his gates? And I have yet to learn that spiritual injury and moral oppression are the *only* enemies worth combating! Talk of mental starvation, indeed!... Mental!... There are worse things than mental starvation. There are blows!..."

She appeared to become hysterical and quite incoherent.

"Such hypocrisy... such disgusting hypocrisy I never heard of. Let Mr. Ensor look nearer home, I say—let him be wise in time and set his own house in order—before we are forced to put the Society on to him!"

"Mrs. Marrable, I must beg you to observe... this language is quite impermissible here," Canon St. Leger said, avoiding Ensor's eye and the deprecating gestures he automatically made. "Indeed... I must really call upon you to apologise!"

"To me," Ensor said, white to his lips.

"Yes, I'll apologise—not to you, sir—to the Committee," said the lady, "and they'll accept my apology. They all know what I mean. In the interest of Humanity, it is time some steps were taken, and I'll take them..."

She folded her boa tightly round her neck and passed out. Canon St. Leger swiftly put the retention or refusal of the book in question to the vote and closed the meeting.

Ensor, dazed, his eyes blurred with unaccustomed passion, walked away like a condemned man—condemned for a crime of which he was unwitting.

He rode studiously home, meditating on these things to the point of falling off his bicycle. He was stunned with the impact of the undeserved disagreeable, and knew not what to think or whom to ask for an explanation. And when he got home he found real trouble awaiting him. Phyllis, who had been ailing rather unaccountably for some time past, had shown definite symptoms of illness during his absence. The little local country doctor (but quite "good"), had been sent for, and had been and gone. He had pronounced the child's uneasiness to be due to a milk attack of typhoid fever, so Adelaide, afoot, her eyes alight with excitement, told the sluggish, depressed man who dismounted from his bicycle at the door, where she came to meet him...

"Have something, Wald. You look pale... That meddling brute of a doctor has gone and ordered a nurse all off his own bat!" she fretfully informed him, leading the way into the drawing-room and closing the door. "I was *so* angry with him when I heard what he had done. Of course I should have nursed her myself. I shall sit up as it is. The woman is here now, so we must make the best of it."

Ensor was secretly of opinion that Dr. Hodgson was right, and that the state of Adelaide's nerves would have made her but an indifferent nurse; he, however, contented himself with remarking that neither he himself nor Dr. Hodgson would approve of her sitting up at night.

"But I shall have to. No nurse can do both. Oh, Wald, I do so detest strangers coming into the house! They go prying about, making up all sorts of absurd conclusions and telling the ass of a doctor everything..."

An expression of indefinable apprehension crossed her peevish face, and her husband was touched, taking it, as he did, as indicating the state of nervous tension she was in. Phyllis's illness... her own condition...

He took her limp hand and kissed it.

"My poor Adelaide, what have you to fear? There's nothing really wrong for him to find out. I don't quite approve of the status of Mary in the house, but, after all, that's the cook's affair, not ours... By the way..."

He was going to tell her of Mrs. Marrable's insinuations, but concluded he had better not mention the matter at this juncture... He merely asked abruptly, "Where is Mary? I haven't seen her about for the last few days."

"Gertrude has sent her away to some friends at Cullercoats, I believe. She asked me if I could spare her."

"And of course you did, kind girl!" said Ensor.

"Oh yes. The work she does isn't worth thinking about. I told Gertrude we should never make a servant of her... Good-bye. I must go to Phyllis. I want to keep an eye on that Nurse Ferrier. I didn't like her face. A mischief-maker if ever there was one!"

Adelaide was gone, and Ensor fell a-thinking on the painful scene of to-day. He was obsessed, now that it was over, by the recollection of a fluid and retreating Committee. He saw black coats and the grey mantelets of the country ladies melting away from him, fleeing from his contact. He could not account for the social ban under which he appeared to lie. This was the culminating incident; he remembered now other slighter acts of neglect and inattention in the past which he had been too little self-conscious to observe or to piece together in a pattern of general avoidance and cold-shouldering. The arraignment of the woman Marrable did not disturb him so much as the nervous acceptance of it by the Canon. Mrs. Marrable was a shrew, a local terror, a person of advanced views, and the author of the book in question was a friend of hers, probably.

But Canon St. Leger, a decent, sober-minded man, a man of his own stamp!... He saw his thin hand toying with the suspended pencil, he heard again his meek, milk-and-water reproval of Mrs. Marrable's unparliamentary language... He could not away with that...

He wandered about the garden half the night with the puppy, now fully trained to be a perfect house-dog and companion. It followed him in an orderly manner from covert to covert under the high beetling wall with the thick beds of nettles growing luxuriantly at the base. Once, however, there was a skirmish; the dog grew quite excited at what must surely have been a not unusual sight for him, the yellow knob of a small boy's head peering over the wall, supported presumably from behind by a human Japanese ladder of other small boys. It was a favourite game in this neighbourhood.

"He! He!" they crowed and chuckled. "Who lives 'ere? Old Mother Brownrigg and her girls! He! He! No one ever comes out here alive...!"

The dog barked and sprang. Fear of his ultimately reaching them at last dislodged the grotesque cohort. Ensor, his nerves a little shaken by this drift of words, only half heard, turned and made his way back to the house. It was absurd to mind. Children were always climbing up the other side of that wall; it was nice to climb, it had jutting courses of bricks half-way up, and the village curiosity was provoked and stimulated by the air of quasi-mystery which Adelaide chose to foster about High Walls, and that her witch-like appearance abroad, always heavily, mediævally cloaked and motor-veiled, abetted. She dressed like a toadstool in the day, and in the evening like a panther. Striding along, her step confident, her eyes abstracted, her whole manner carelessly insulting, no wonder the children were afraid of her, gave her nicknames and made up stories about her.

He met the doctor coming out and questioned him about Phyllis. His anxiety was easily allayed. The big girl was strong enough to resist a whole army of adverse microbes. He also saw the new nurse, a tall, thin sprig of a woman with some indication of character. She was very cold and civil, especially when she spoke to Adelaide. He thought he saw plainly that she disliked the mistress of the house already. Another! Poor Adelaide!

He knew he was right, as the days went on. The two women detested each other, skirmished every time they met, issued cross orders and confused Gertrude and Auretta. But the professional defeated the amateur. Dr. Hodgson, meek, little insignificant man, resisted all Mrs. Ensor's hints and manœuvres and, finally, her most palpable efforts to get rid of Nurse Ferrier, who was, on her side, careful to give no positive offence or commit any crime which might lead to her dismissal on other grounds than medical ones. She was a capital nurse, even Adelaide admitted that, only Phyllis no longer wanted one. But Dr. Hodgson said she did, and further implied that a nurse would stand between Mrs. Ensor and all fatigue or anxiety undesirable to a woman in her state. This was the only argument Adelaide dared not, or did not care to, gainsay.

The distracted woman vented her annoyance at the doctor's tactics on her husband and, to punish him, would not let him see Phyllis. As she spent most of her time in the girl's room, which opened out of her own, Ensor saw very little of her. He found himself not very much cast down by this arrangement; he was much out of sympathy with his wife, fretted by her irritability, and was glad to defer their meeting until that need for the nurse's presence which so enraged her should pass away.

He wondered, sometimes, when that would be, and thought he would like to ask the nurse. But she rather sternly, and with a sort of frigidity put on over and above her statutory nurse's manner, passed him in the hall or on the stairs. He began to fancy that Adelaide, moved by her strange taste for regulating the movements and gestures of others, had bidden her enter as little as possible into conversation with the master of the house. Well! Well!...

He missed Mary, to whom, in the present upheaval, he could have paid a little more attention. Still, presumably she was well. Adelaide had apparently carried out his expressed wishes for once, and had insisted on Gertrude's sending her child away for sea air. He missed the daily appeal of the dark eyes set in paleness, the weak gestures with her hands which Mary often used in lieu of speaking, as if mere movement made less stir and drew down less attention on her from the cruel powers above. Though her face was pale it was always clean, he remembered. And a queer thing—he never remembered her sitting down! Did she ever sit down? He had seen her squat, he had seen her stand, but he had never seen her sit except that first day in the motor-car when, the dark fur cap on her head, and the dark fur up to her chin had made her look almost a lady. She was dressed exactly like Phyllis, then, he remembered. Strange monitory caprice of Adelaide's—an instance of her sheer love of power—to raise, and then to degrade! No man could do such a thing except, perhaps, some savage Asiatic potentate, one in whom caprice remained the only lust left to satisfy.

He did not care to affront such scenes as he had gone through at Beverley any more, and he took his name off the Committee. He stayed at home and spent this dreary, uneventful time mostly in wandering about the house, followed by the dog who had grown attached to him. It generally lay at his feet in the hall while he sat reading papers endlessly, smoking far more than was good for him. Thus he caught the doctor on his way through the outer hall to see Phyllis; she was going on well, and Adelaide did not expect to be confined for a couple of months or so. The nurse flitted by, soft on her screw soles, going up and downstairs and taking no notice of the solitary man. He never saw Gertrude at all.

He was thinking seriously of going away from High Walls until Phyllis was quite well and Mary had come back, and he had got as far as the handling of *Bradshaw* and the turning down of the page marked "Continental Trains" when, one day, the nurse chose suddenly to leave the orbit in which she generally travelled, between the door of ingress into the servants' quarters and the staircase that led up into Phyllis's sick-room, and came straight up to Wald Ensor. The deflection of the moon from her course could not have surprised him more. She spoke.

"I beg your pardon, sir, but have I your permission to take Dr. Hodgson to see Mary?"

Her eyes drooped, and seemed to look down both sides of her nose. With her white cap like a frontlet, her brown hair fluffed out in ascetic waves over her forehead, she was not altogether an unprepossessing woman. She was looking down at him, her lips were coldly pursed, and Ensor felt just as he had felt in the Beverley Committee Room...

"Certainly, Nurse," he stammered. "But Mary—is she at home?"

"She is at home, sir, and in my opinion very unwell."

"What is the matter with her? I want to know. Mary is a special pet of mine."

The lame, absurd words came from his broken lips that he had that moment bitten till they bled... He was not thinking of what he was saying. He was overwhelmed by an avalanche of doubts. Adelaide had lied to him!... "Hasn't Mary been away at all?" he stammered.

The nurse raised her eyes and gave him one straight, winged glance. She had strong black eyebrows that met across her nose, and a pout that was determined...

"She may have been. Not that I know of." Her nose was in the air. "Well, will you see her, sir?" she ended more kindly. "Perhaps you would like to see how she is for yourself."

"Yes," he replied, "I should, indeed. But I understood she had been sent away to the sea for her health! Let us go. I don't know where she sleeps when she is at home."

"You shall see, sir, if you will come with me."

Her calmness was only a mask, Ensor felt; the quiet words covered an indignation that nearly broke through her professional reserve. She was boiling over with rage. She walked through the red baize door with an assured step, never turning or looking round at the shamefaced man who followed her with humble, downcast head, his morning paper still crumpled up in his hand.

The door marked the transition between the oldest and most modern parts of the house. Ensor had never been up the second and original staircase which led to the attics, and it was up these that Nurse Ferrier now proceeded to induct him. It was rather dark everywhere, for a heavy shower was impending. The first few drops fell before they left the part of the house where the windows were large; as they went on into the older part they would have seen their way better with a candle. The stairs, uncarpeted, low and uneven, led up through low doorways which caught your head into wide, emaciated corridors whose panelled walls were worm-eaten, pale with age and desuetude. Doors set plumb in the wall opened into many rooms, at each of which in turn Ensor expected his guide to stop and enter...

Another flight of stairs leading to just such another corridor! The air was faint, it seemed to have been sealed for centuries. Ensor, sickening a little as he followed Ferrier, Indian file, in the dark, permitted himself to ask some sort of question in order to know if she was still there. Where were they going?...

Her white hand, framed in the white cuff, was extended back to him in the dark.

"Up to the top attic, where Mary sleeps alone," she answered. Her tones, though grave, were kindly and protective. He was only a man! With a thorough beast of a wife!

"A child, to sleep all this way from everybody!" he murmured.

She grunted. They had reached a flight of five steps built in by walls on each side. She pushed open a door at the head of it, and they came out into the semi-twilight of a large bare room. When his eyes became a little accustomed to the light, he realised that it was the famous attic, left untouched since mediæval times, which was said to occupy the whole of the top of the house.

"Take my hand, sir," she said quite gently. "It's rather bad going—for those that don't know it—the floor's so uneven, and—you may get a shock. Mary's here—or was, yesterday. We will search..."

The attic was long, like the aisle of a church, with plenty of side chapels, embrasures formed, shut off by a partition of jagged beams and whitewashed lath and plaster. Each had a small dormer window. The boards of the floor seemed to meet in a pattern of interwoven flanges—it was very much perished towards the middle, and they walked along it carefully. Ensor saw out of each little window as he passed, the wide stretch of green, rolling, innocent country...

The nurse, who had been peering carefully into each embrasure, seemed puzzled... "It was this one," she said, at last. "It's so dark with the rain that I can hardly see, but I was up here yesterday and I got scolded for it! Ah! Here she is." They stopped in front of one of the chapels—

The child was lying under the window on a large but depleted mattress, just at Ensor's feet. A shawl with ragged fringes was thrown over her, and the dull, stained grey tick of the mattress showed beyond it. There seemed to be no bed-linen, and the child's night-dress, which might have been originally of pink flannel, was of a curious, ingrained, dull colour... Ensor started and felt sick... some sort of smell...

"Ah, sir, you see!" the nurse said, and, bending down, called, "Mary! Mary!"

She had soft tones, he noticed in his pain, as well as harsh ones. The child, who seemed to be half dozing, opened her eyes and turned them up at her visitors. She still had on her ridiculous top-knot, straining the hair from her forehead. The back hair had come forward and was matted on her face. One hand lay open on the shawl and the other was under her cheek. Slowly her eyes closed again and she lay quite still, a grey patch on the darker ground of the pallet...

"Mary!" the nurse said again. "Mary, here's Mr. Ensor to see you..."

The child's eyes did not open, her mouth did. The nurse bade him, in a tone of command:

"Take her up, sir!"

Wald Ensor knelt down and lifted the upper part of the wretched, filthy little body half on to one knee. As he handled her he had the sensation of her dry, harsh skin which reminded him of parchment. She coughed as he unavoidably jerked her in lifting, and he felt like an executioner.

He had rehabilitated himself in Nurse Ferrier's good opinion. She now spoke familiarly, as if he and she were accomplices in a good deed.

"Did you ever see such a disreputable nightdress? Not been washed for weeks, I should think. And what a place to let a child sleep in by itself night after night! Some people ought to be shot!"

Adelaide's husband realised that the nurse was abusing Adelaide, yet it seemed to him impossible to take her up for incivility—or answer at all. For her cheap blame was so incommensurate with the horror aroused in him by the sight of the child's condition that he had no words.

Nurse Ferrier saw that he was feeling as a man should feel—and more. She respected his wretchedness and asked him gently:

"Will you stay with her, sir, while I fetch the doctor to her; it's just on his time for coming. I may have the luck to catch him before—before Mrs. Ensor sees him."

She crept away. Ensor heard her close the attic door and there was silence. He was left alone with the dying child across his knee. For another second or two Nurse Ferrier's heels tapped on the stairs... retreating, as Mary must have heard them before she lapsed into her mortal stupor. She had heard no step for days but that of a servant, neither mother nor father... Her father was dead, her mother was busy, but still...

The man tried frantically to collect his thoughts in the terrible silence. Beyond a little dry, patient cough, composed as it were of ashes and dust, Mary lay quite still across his knee. He had changed his position and now he sat on the floor beside the mattress with most of her body on his. His eyes had grown accustomed to the lighting of the place, and he saw that the small windows in the embrasure opposite had, some of them, panes. The one over Mary's bed had none. The glass had evidently cracked and, falling out, had left jagged pieces in the corners of the frame. From one of these there depended the fragments of a check duster such as Mary habitually carried twisted through her leather waistband. She had reached up and stuffed it in there to ward off the cold. His mind, now grown futile in horror, exulted in hypotheses: she had probably shielded herself thus from the weather at the cost of a beating for a lost duster.

The shower was over and the sun had come out and sent warm rays across the worm-eaten floor, the floor whereon, in the old days, the feudal servants of the manor-house had slept, weary feet to weary feet, fastened in, lest they rose and slew him, all night by their lord, with no egress save by the little locked door at the foot of the staircase. He dared not leave them free to murder their taskmaster in his sleep. There might have been at that time about a hundred healthy farm hands keeping each other warm and their spirits up through the long night with jests and story-telling; now, this enormous garret held but one sickly, fearful, solitary child...

Oh! Who had done this?... His head swam with dreadful certainties.

A great blue-bottle flew in at the window and buzzed in and out of the rafters over Mary's head. She was past noticing it, though it irritated Ensor and he wanted to get up and chase it away. But he could not bear to deposit the child on the filthy pallet again. The same with a cockroach that made blundering rushes from one joist to another of the decayed ribs of the flooring. He let it alone. There were probably vermin in that bed, and on the child, even, but he was past caring... He could not beat his breast, *Mea culpa! Mea culpa! Mea maxima culpa!*—or tear his hair, for his hands were tied, occupied with the task they should have set themselves months ago—the work to which his downpressed heart had all along instigated him. But in this moment he expiated fully what he described to himself as his rotten carelessness, his wicked, easy-going acceptance of Adelaide's excuses, his shameful apathy in the face of the awful crime that was being enacted in his house—in Adelaide's house indeed, but the shame was his. Here was a helpless child dying under his roof of neglect, or worse, and three days ago he had the face to stand before the Beverley Committee, composed of decent people, and had been puzzled by their unfriendly behaviour. They were naturally outraged by *his* conduct, of which they probably had an inkling, or more than an inkling! Those boys looking over the wall! He had expostulated with the Committee for admitting an unpleasant work of fiction into their list—a mere solecism at worst. He was thinking of Phyllis's morals whilst Mary starved! He knew now what Mrs. Marrable had meant. That harridan was in the right! He was little better than a murderer. Mary, dying of neglect and worse! His hand stole towards the open front of the child's nightgown. With sudden resolve he turned her body right round on his knee and pushed the garment down to her middle...

Yes, the scars that play such an important part in evidence when these sort of cases come before the court were all there, fresh and old scars; deep and superficial; healed, ill-healed and still suppurating. He turned the body round again and felt Mary's pulse. It seemed to him to be almost non-existent. He knew nothing about the meaning of its scattered beats, and he wished the doctor would come...

Another long ten minutes—agonising, interminable! She might be dying?... The nurse had probably not been able to catch the doctor before he saw Phyllis and, in order to evade Adelaide, was waiting to waylay him until his official visit was over.

And, as the child lay across his knee, to all appearances comatose, something grey and loathsome did crawl out from the screwed knob of black hair on to the white bone-like forehead... He pulled out his handkerchief from his breast coat pocket—no sense of disgust weakened his efficiency. Such things are! It was all part of the horror which had surely now culminated, leaving him seared and stunned and shamed to the death.

The child sighed, and with a pathetic reverting to the childish ways that had been scorched and made to perish out of her, crept closer into his embrace. Her sigh might have been one of relief, at pleasure in finding a breast to lean on? Ensor fondly hoped it.

The blue-bottle buzzed, the black beetle looked out again from the crinkled folds of the *Daily Telegraph* which Ensor had flung down... He did not move, he hardly thought, he was conscious only of the child nestling in his arms as if he were its new-found father, and a peace was his, a peace he had never known, as if his soul had at last found its billet...

When Nurse Ferrier came up at last with the doctor, he smiled, as might a man undergoing a righteous punishment on the cross.

"Do what you can for her, Doctor," he said pleadingly.

"Why wasn't I called before?" Hodgson began angrily...

Nurse Ferrier touched his arm. Ensor saw the kindly, womanly action. Yes, he was down—no need to rub it in...

The doctor pulled the duster out of the window hole to make more light for himself and, returning, took the child up from Ensor and, laying her squarely down, examined her. When he had found out what he needed to know, he gently pulled the shawl into position so as to cover her, and rose from his knees.

"Mr. Ensor, I must see Mrs. Ensor about this," he said gravely.

"I'll take you to her," Ensor said wearily. "Nurse, stay with Mary, please."

He was pleased to give an order and see it obeyed. On the way downstairs he summoned breath to ask a question:

"Is she dying?"

"Probably," was Hodgson's curt reply; it was all he would vouchsafe, and all Ensor felt that he deserved.

*

Adelaide was in the hall and came swimming up to meet them.

"Where have you been, Doctor?" she asked. Her eyes fell and rested scornfully on her husband... "Wald, you look bad. Go and get yourself a whisky and soda."

"Yes, do, Mr. Ensor," said Hodgson. "But first"—he turned to Adelaide—"Mrs. Ensor, it is my duty to tell you both that, if that child upstairs dies, I shall refuse a certificate and order an inquest."

Wald almost admired Adelaide now for her pluck. A spasm of cheap annoyance, such as a servant's misdemeanour might arouse, no more, crossed her face and, turning, she led the way into her morning-room. He heard her say over her shoulder:

"Nonsense, Doctor, she's only shamming. It seems to me you want a drink too. That was thunder we heard just now. It's upset you both. Wald, be good enough to send Nurse Ferrier straight to me here. I'm going to sack her."

She went into the portion of the hall that was screened off and, seeing that both the men disregarded her gesture of invitation and stayed in the main hall, she shrugged her shoulders and flung herself on to her tiger skin, turning her back... motionless...

The doctor looked at Ensor and spoke meditatively.

"In Mrs. Ensor's present state..." he murmured, "perhaps I had better speak to you alone, Mr. Ensor?"

"Certainly," Ensor said, leading the way into the dining-room. "I may say, before you speak, that I knew nothing of this. But that's no matter," he went on, "the blame is mine."

He rang the bell. "Ask Gertrude to come here," he said to Auretta, who appeared at the service door at the end. The girl hesitated. She had something in her hand.

"What is it? What is it?" her master asked testily.

"I was going to show the doctor, sir, what Mary had to eat." She eagerly held out a plate for the inspection of the two men. It was a tin with some toast rinds and the remains of dripping fat adhering to the sides. In her other hand she held a mug, into which Dr. Hodgson peered.

"H'm, a concoction of tea leaves!"

"She was fed, sir, worse than the dog," the girl began volubly. "Biscuits was bought for him, while poor Mary, she had only the scrapings from the plates, and times they was all maggoty! She never complained, not she, too frightened for that, for if she did she got the stick—"

"Who beat her?" Ensor asked furiously.

"Mrs. Ensor, till she got ill. She used to take the poker to her. There's all the marks on her back now—you've seen 'em, Doctor?"

"Yes, yes. Hold your tongue now," Hodgson said.

He turned to Ensor, who stood quietly beside him, receiving the unbearable douche of Auretta's revelations with such fortitude as he was able to muster.

"If the child dies there will have to be an inquest. I must give the nurse some directions—where is she? Be off, back to your work!" he bade the grinning girl. "And ask Nurse to come to me."

Nurse Ferrier, severe, quiet, composed, appeared in place of the hysterical Auretta, and Ensor scrutinised her face for news as if he had not possessed the gift of speech.

"Is she dead?" at last he breathed.

"No, sir, no," the nurse answered kindly, recalled as it were from other thoughts. Ensor did not catch the almost imperceptible shake of the doctor's head that came hard upon her words. She continued softly, prettily almost, appealing to her chief: "We won't let her die, will we, Doctor?"

"Not if we can help it," he replied gruffly. "Get yourself a drink, Mr. Ensor, and buck up now! There will be a lot to do presently."

Ensor slowly walked away and the doctor turned to the nurse.

"I wouldn't give a farthing for that child's life, you know," he said. "Have you brought her down?"

"Yes, Auretta and me; she's in the spare bedroom. Mr. Ensor would wish her to have the best of everything, I think?"

Her long, drooping eyes were raised to the doctor's for a moment. She wanted to talk to him and he knew it. But he did not, however, at this juncture, care to throw any deductions he might have made from facts patent to both of them into the common fund, and he interposed the chill of professional etiquette between himself and her possible confidences.

He walked quickly, passed, meditating the while, down the narrow flagged way that led from the house door to the gate in the wall where his horse was being held for him by the half-idiotic lad Jimmy; the only male creature, except her husband, whom Adelaide would tolerate about the place. To-day, however, expecting as usual to have the whole of the path to himself, the doctor almost hustled a person of quite a different type from Jimmy's; a smart, slight, efficient young fellow slipping briskly up to the house. Hodgson apologised. The stranger, who was dressed in some sort of uniform, looked curiously at him as if about to speak, but thought better of it and passed on.

After some little time Gertrude came to her master in the dining-room, where he had summoned her. She had the air of one anxious to get back to her work, primed with insolence, bolstered with the indifference of the very fat. Her apron was spotted here and there with gravy, or blood—she had been drawing chickens, or killing them—but Ensor felt faint...

Her face was round, pink and full fed. The bib of her apron was pinned up at the corners over her wide breast—she had no right to have a breast at all—no right to be even made like a woman—the agent of Adelaide's hellish system who, with her "strong hands," directed by personal lust of cruelty, had cordially carried out his poor, mad wife's orders...

Yet, all the while he was talking to her the consciousness was his that his contempt for the maid was equalled by the maid's scorn for the master. This execrable creature looked down on him; in her small eyes lurked the conception of him, Wald Ensor, as something mean and pitiful—and yet likeable. Yes, Gertrude appeared to award him a certain amount of good-humoured commiseration as the hen-pecked husband, the niddering who let his wife "ride" him and get him into trouble. For trouble there was going to be; the reputed master of the house would surely be held responsible...

"I couldn't come before," she said defiantly. "I've had to be up with Phyllis. The child was left all alone because of this business. Be done as soon as you can, sir, for I must get back to her."

"Right! You will tell me before you go, please, how long this has been going on? How long have you been neglecting and ill-treating your own child?"

"Mary, d'ye mean? Well, you see, Mary was all along only allowed to be here, as you may say, through the kindness of Miss Adelaide, as being her cook's child." She continued, as if repeating a lesson learned by heart:

"Miss Adelaide—I beg pardon, Mrs. Ensor—has always been very good to me, and I've been very good to her. But it stands to reason Mrs. Ensor wasn't going to bring up my bastard like a lady. Mary Adelaide, that's her name, just had to be trained to be a servant and work for her bread as her mother's always done, and when she was a lazybones and didn't work, she had to be beat."

"And what was the work you set a child of ten to do?" Ensor asked, striving at calmness.

"Child of ten? She's fifteen, same as Phyllis! Never growed, that's what it was. Well, let me see! She cleaned the silver every day, sitting down to it, and swept a room or, maybe, two—there's a mort of them in this house—and did down the steps and her own darning and mending of her pretty little costumes..."

"Psha! What did she have to eat?"

"What the girl showed you!" Gertrude said, throwing up her chin in sullen pride of evil doing. "Scraps what was left over from the day before—that is, if I remembered to give it her, and blest if she ever reminded me when I forgot her! Liked to go hungry! No spirit; shameful lazy she was, too, and one had to take a stick or the poker to her to make her get on. Whoap, go along! was all the kind words she got, and a neat cut across her back! Plenty hidings! She was that lazy they never had time to heal before there was a new stripe laid over the last one."

"My God! A young child!" he covered his face with his hands and sat down heavily.

Gertrude regarded him. Some shifting of values took place in her heavy brain. She came a step nearer, and her voice lost some of its accent of coarse bravado.

"You must know, sir, I had my orders."

"Your orders, woman! Your orders to play the murderess! You, the unnatural mother—"

"Don't you be in such a hurry to say hard things of me, sir. Look a little nearer home for the unnaturalness if you will have it. Some folks is very blind and deaf too."

"What do you mean?"

The cook said, opposing her sinister patience to his simple violence, and raising her apron to her face: "I'll say no more, sir. I must be going."

"Stop!" cried Ensor furiously. "You brute!"

"Call me a brute, sir?" She spoke almost modestly. Then her temper rose. She flushed all over her fairness.

"I told you wrong, sir. It is not Phyllis I'm a-going back to. Quite another sort of person. Do you know who's waiting to talk to me in my back kitchen, where I told him to stop till I'd done with you? 'No one won't go away from here, mister,' I said, 'so long as I give you my word. But I've something I'd like to say to Mr. Ensor first, before you see him.' I said it would be best for all parties if I could get it said and done with. I haven't, that's the worst! You don't help me. I never saw such a numskull of a man! But anygate, this man's not going back without a word or two with you. This is him." She took a card from the bosom of her dress and, holding it delicately and ironically between her finger and thumb, handed it to her master.

The nurse met the doctor on the doorstep when he came back half an hour later. Her manner was profoundly instructive as she came forward, her finger on her lip, and he knew what she would tell him.

"Mary's gone, Doctor. Twenty minutes ago. And Mrs. Ensor has bolted herself into her bedroom and won't answer to anyone. I'm afraid she is bad. And"—she dropped her voice—"there's a gentleman shut in the library with Mr. Ensor. Here's what he brought. I found it on the floor of the dining-room just now."

She produced the card, stained with blood where Gertrude's fingers had grasped it.

"Only fowls'," she said apologetically.

The doctor took it. "'*Society for the Prevention of Cruelty to Children. Inspector G. W. Kelson*'!" he exclaimed. "That's Mrs. Marrable. She said she was determined to put the Society on to them."

"She is a bit late!" the nurse said.

"By half an hour," he replied, as they went upstairs together.

"You never heard anything like it!" she whispered. "The girl here they call Auretta has been telling me, and who she is and all. What they've made the poor thing suffer! Doctor, they made her get up at five every morning to bath—Mrs. Ensor was very particular about it—in cold water, even in winter, then she used to sit up on that landing near the east window darning her own stockings and Phyllis's till nine, and then they'd give her a crust or two saved from the day before. She ate it out of the dog's pannikin on the window-sill, not even a table, and when I first came they made her keep out of my way—hid her—for fear I heard that cough she had. Doctor, they've just killed her by inches, that's what they've done."

"Not by inches, by yards!" corrected Dr. Hodgson. "Why, the child's back was covered with unhealed sores—suppurating! She didn't weigh more than forty-eight pounds—sixty-two, she should have. Systematic neglect and worse! They'll have to answer for it."

"But Mr. Ensor knew nothing of it, I'll swear," the nurse said quickly.

"I dare say not, he's a decent sort enough," Hodgson replied, "a little weak, perhaps; lets his wife lead him by the nose..."

"She's a caution!" the nurse proclaimed with fervour. "Not nearly good enough for him!"

"Ay! But she'll get off—her condition! They always admit that."

"Get off, Doctor, when it's her own child she had murdered? Of course you know it's her own child?"

"I suspected it," he said quietly.

They had come into the wide, lightly-papered spare bedroom with its three tall windows looking out over the gravel sweep in front of the house. They were open wide. Jimmy could be heard sharpening his old-fashioned tool ready for cutting the scrap of lawn beyond the gravel. And, standing by the bedside with her apron held up to her face was Gertrude. She took her hands down and stood stockishly, revealing a tearless, sullen, swelled face with the remains of some beauty. Her cap was pushed up on her hair, disarranged, uncovering her high-boned forehead. She said to them:

"Leave me be a minute, sir. This is a bad job, that it is!... but I don't blame myself, for I've only done my duty by Miss Adelaide, who was good to me when I got into trouble with my first—"

The nurse was responsible for the slight interrogative lift of the eyebrows which encouraged the woman to proceed:

"It—died. Miss Adelaide's father, that was a doctor, he gave me the certificate of death. In that big house you could do things and no one any the wiser. He used to do things himself... Gosh! What I've seen in them London basements!... just like prisons! Miss Adelaide had Mary nine months before her father died, and I helped her to keep it from the old fox so that he left her all, loving her the same, thanks to me..."

Nurse Ferrier, returning the doctor's shy glance with a full effect of partnership, ceded with him to natural curiosity. They had done their duty... and now, by a strange stroke of good fortune, these subordinates had the principal witness to themselves—it would not be for long.

"How old actually was this child?" the doctor said.

"Mary's fifteen, the same as my Phyllis. Born the same year. There looks to be a bit more than six months' difference between the two, doesn't there?"

She sat down and, spreading her fat, capable hands on her knees, smiled proudly; a moment after she restored her features to the pomp and circumstance of the death-chamber.

"How was the exchange arranged?" Dr. Hodgson said.

"Well, you must know that the two was brought up together. Brighton. They both got the same food and all. Miss Adelaide hated hers, and liked mine. Then... she brought *him*—Mr. Ensor—along in the car from Beverley. She tore round to me in the kitchen, long or ever she'd got her things off, and said we was to change the two children round from that moment. Can't say I objected—'twas mine would come off best. That night Miss Adelaide said to me in her room that I might keep Mary as low as I could, and she'd have the sense to die and get herself out of the way—laughing like. But He began to interfere... Terrible fond of her, he was. Used to come round to the back part with sweets and buns. I got the sweets and the dog got the buns—I've no faith in other folks' baking. He hadn't an idea why he took such an interest in her, nor hasn't now... but he'll be having his eyes opened for him!"

Her two listeners showed a disposition to turn her out unless she contrived to keep more strictly to what she could tell them...

"Mary was that tough, however! I couldn't treat her unkind enough for Miss Adelaide. She would take and beat Mary herself. Said I was too soft-hearted. Mr. Ensor must have heard Mary being corrected many a time. He thought it was the dog! I used to wonder what he was made of that the cry of his own flesh and blood didn't reach him and tell him what was what. But I don't believe he ever saw what she was getting to eat, by Miss Adelaide's orders—part of her plan to stop Mary growing up. She led me such a life about the food that I said I'd wash my hands of it, and she said she would see to her food herself, and Mary got so thin that all her ribs showed. What she'd got was more like a cave than a stomach—and her hands—ough!"

The voices downstairs had ceased, and the cook rose to leave the room. Nurse Ferrier followed her to procure some hot water and one of Phyllis's sponges for what she had to do. The doctor, at the window overlooking the gate where a little car was standing, stood slashing his leggings with his riding-whip and deciding what he would say. He liked Ensor, and wanted to make it easier for him. That was why he had listened so unprofessionally to the maunderings of the cook, which seemed to make the case not look quite so black for Mr. Ensor after all. But, as for Mrs. Ensor... the mother expectant?... Need that fact come out?...

Nurse Ferrier, dabbling her sponges in hot water, going backwards and forwards with towels, talked—she had not talked so much for weeks.

"The likeness!" she said. "Doesn't one see it strong now she's dead? I must say I noticed it from the very first moment he came up into the garret where they put the poor thing to sleep. Nobody'd been near her for days. Gertrude thought Mrs. Ensor had, and Mrs. Ensor thought—God knows what *she* thought! There wasn't so much as a jug of water there, and her temperature over a hundred and five!

"Gertrude says that, after Mr. Favarger's death, they went to Brighton first and then came up here to Gertrude's country, and Mrs.

Ensor bought High Walls because it was so private and she didn't care to be seen about much. I expect she was ashamed of her baby being such a wretched specimen. She never expected Mr. Ensor to come back and marry her, Gertrude says; she doesn't really hold with marriage, though she called herself Mrs. Dibben. Took the name of Gertrude's man—he was a prize-fighter—the kind she admires, Gertrude says. He was in prison at the time or *she'd* have had him too. But he never came near to trouble them, and they were all four going on quietly behind their High Walls and the two children being brought up like sisters. Mrs. Ensor, Gertrude says, had almost come to believe it that it was the other way about, and that the beautiful child was hers and the ugly one the cook's. Of course Gertrude didn't care. But the day she picked up Mr. Ensor again at Beverley Fair, Mrs. Ensor came rushing into the back kitchen like a mad thing, and Gertrude with her arms all over suds, and said she had told Mr. Ensor in the car that Phyllis was hers and Mary Gertrude's, and that was the way it was to be from now on. Doctor, what do you think of that?"

"I'm not quite sure that I believe it."

"I do!" said Nurse Ferrier stoutly. "That woman—Mrs. Ensor—is bad enough for anything... rotten all through, mind and body. She simply couldn't have a nice, clean, well-coloured child like Phyllis."

Dr. Hodgson said, "There! The Inspector's gone!" Leaving his post at the window he came to the bedside, whence the nurse proudly stood away to let him survey the child's body, now straightly and fairly disposed, lying softer and warmer than it had ever had the luck to do in life...

"She looks nice now, doesn't she, Doctor, now I've put on her one of Phyllis's smart nightgowns. I sent Gertrude round to Mrs. Ensor's room to get it."

"How is Mrs. Ensor? Did you gather?"

"Quite calm, Gertrude says, though she knows everything."

"She is determined not to let herself have a miscarriage, that's about it," said Hodgson, buttoning his coat. "She's got plenty of courage of a kind."

"Courage to be cruel," the nurse exclaimed, glancing at the bed; "and I should say, if she thinks it necessary to starve her children to death if they happen to be born weaklings she'll have to kill the next, too, even if she does have a good confinement, and I've my doubts about that. She is far too keen about it..."

"What's that?" Hodgson interrupted her, cocking his ear for the sound.

"Mrs. Ensor's door."

"He's gone straight to her, then."

They looked at each other.

Ensor, speaking urgently to his wife at the closed door of her room, could get no answer. He did not give it up, but continued to call her gently now and again by her name. She had a pet name chosen by herself for him to call her by. That might have brought her out, but he could not bring himself to use it now.

Half an hour seemed to elapse. He heard a groan, and then another. Though he hated her it frightened him, for there was no one with her. He changed the tenour of his appeals, made them severer, more urgent...

"Adelaide, even if you are ill, you must not shut yourself up like this. You may do harm to yourself and to—the child. If you won't see me, at least let me send Gertrude to you."

Then she spoke:

"Wald, I'm not very ill—not more ill than I expect to be; for I am going to have a child—it will not be quite yet. As soon as it is born I shall kill myself, but not till then, so you need not be afraid."

Her voice came fainter, she had turned away from the door—he was astonished at her self-control—"*not more ill than I expect to be.*" He felt that he ought to see for himself. Bitterly, dispassionately, he again made the attempt...

"Let *me* see you then," he said gently, "just for one moment."

"Is it to scold me?" Her thin voice sounded, gentle, close to the door.

The key was turned in the lock and he went in. His wife stood in the middle of the carpet square, half defiant, half apologetic. Her attitude, deprecating his anger, was a great concession from her. Her beautiful, mournful eyes sought his. They held no such cruel gleams as had lurked there lately when they had talked—talked of Mary. Her dull black velvet peignoir was gathered round her; she held it looped in one thin hand. A moving sight, yet he was not moved! He only thought of her health, pathologically, as a doctor may. It was his duty. He had neglected his other duties lately.

She put up her sharp chin. Her hand let slip the heavy folds of black and they fell round her, trailing...

"Kiss me, Wald!" she said.

"No. I cannot!"

"Cannot?"

She turned and moved towards the sofa newly placed across the foot of her bed. Her stumble over the long, embarrassing folds of the garment she wore may have been meant to act as a mute reproach, but it could in no wise affect him or induce him to comply with her request. She breathed heavily and sat down on the sofa.

"Ask Gertrude, then, she will tell you all you want to know."

"Ask your cook? Adelaide, tell me yourself. Oh, why—"

She answered him passionately, rocking herself backwards and forwards: "I could not bear the sight of her, I tell you! She was a degenerate. She disgraced me. She wasn't fit to live. She ought never to have been born—never even have been conceived! Ah, but it is her father she shames, not me."

Unwarrantable insult! But what matter?

She sat up very straight. "I am a normal, healthy woman, and all disease is repugnant to me. It's a law—a law that was infringed... she pays the penalty. Just to see her going about day by day, the living testimony of someone's unfitness—of beastliness! Why, the sight of her peaked, suffering face, old and yellow—she looked like that even in her cradle—from the very first moment that Gertrude showed her to me—that finished me! Dried up the milk and the feelings of a mother I *had*. For I insisted on seeing her at once; *I* was fit enough. I was up and about in a week... Then, when I came to look closer, her awful hand—did you know that she had a finger less on her right hand?... Still, I nursed her myself. I—faugh!"

She put her handkerchief to her bitten lips. There was blood on it when she took it away.

"Then, when *you* came...! I saw you look at her in the car, and again when we got out, and you carried the rugs for her as we walked up the drive—a reproach to me—that was enough! I made up my mind then, that very minute, and I have never repented it. Never! Never! I tell you. For you would never have married me if you had known, and I meant to marry you. I loved you. Yes, you have the same ideas as me, more or less, Wald; that's what I liked—what I chose in you. Only, Wald, what I didn't know was this—you were a coward, yes, a mean, canting, respectable, conventional coward. What they used to call, when knights were bold, 'lily-livered'—or is it 'pigeon-livered'?"

"Sneer at me, Adelaide, if you like, but explain. Damn you! Explain," he cried.

His forehead was wet with sweat; his hands curled and uncurled with a furious desire to choke the terrible words, that must come, in her throat before she spoke them.

"What is there to explain?" she said. "I hated the child and I beat her. I beat her to death!"

He groaned in helplessness, overcome by her fierce self-sufficiency.

"But had you no sort of human feeling, no woman's tenderness? You've been a mother—there's surely such a thing as a mother's heart?"

Adelaide looked at him wearily, shuddering...

"Been a mother—yes. And you—what about *your* tenderness—*your* heart? We used to wonder that *your* heart didn't tell you when you heard her calling out—screaming—yelling! I beat her, I tell you, I beat her within an inch of her life. Filthy, hateful object that I'd brought into the world—through you! Pah!"

She flung herself down. Her tone was so piercing, so foreign, so unknown to him who had learned to expect every variation in Adelaide, that he cried out, in panic fear merely:

"For God's sake, keep your head, Adelaide! Don't go mad now, on top of it all!"

"Oh, I'm not mad, not a bit of it, can't you see, you fool? But no, you can't see, you can't see anything, unless it's under your nose. It *was* under your nose, and you worried and worried, and yet you didn't see it! Here you are! Mary's your child—and mine! Mine and yours! Don't you remember that night—that night after *Tristan*?"

"No, I remember nothing. Be quiet, now!" He held up his hand as if to ward off a blow. "Where is she?"

"My God, *I* don't know," Adelaide said. "What does it matter now?"

She had squatted on the sofa, making a hideous grimace. Her pains had begun, but he took no notice.

"I'm going to Mary," he murmured.

She rose, rushed forward and bolted the door behind him.

The doctor and the nurse were still waiting by the body of Mary. The nurse, enjoying herself thoroughly, continued to develop her physiological views, leaving the room only for a moment to get some white flowers to lay on the child's breast. Hodgson, on the other hand, found himself plunged still deeper in his quandary. He wanted to be of use to Ensor, and do what he could in allocating the blame, which her husband was so generously anxious to take on his own shoulders, to the quarter where it properly belonged—to Mrs. Ensor, who, being by temperament hardier, stonier, less nervous on the whole than her husband, would be able to stand prison—to put it crudely—better than he. Moreover, the law would be merciful to her in her then condition.

Hodgson could not fathom her. Such a complicated, abnormal case as hers seldom, if ever, came his way. He was merely an overworked, overdriven country doctor, riding about daily from one case to another. That the maladies of the hardy, normal if worn-out wives of the labouring classes were of a painful, dreary similarity, and relieved him of the necessity of keeping himself up to date with new departures in medicine, was perhaps the reason he did not break down from overwork. His old mare, who carried her sleeping master on her back along the same old roads to the same old cottages to attend to Hodge's wife's seventh baby, was older though less well preserved than he.

The nurse had left the room. He was alone when, suddenly, he heard the click of a latch and a step in the corridor that was not that of the nurse. The door of the room was opened with deliberation, and the pale object of his surmises and his sympathy walked into the room. He did not seem to see Hodgson, although the doctor thought that he moved his head slightly as he went by and gave what might pass as a grunt of recognition. Wald Ensor's well-known politeness survived in the overthrow of all his standards and ambitions. Little Hodgson was devoted to him from that moment; he stood humbly aside. It was the man's hour of Calvary. For no one, so far as he knew, had told him that Mary was dead, and he must know it as soon as his eyes rested on what lay on the bed.

He slipped out of the room so as to intercept Nurse Ferrier on her return. She had an armful of ragged white chrysanthemums, staining her white bib with the dank moisture of their leaves. The two stood together, glancing nervously, now at the door of the room where the body lay—now at that of Mrs. Ensor, whence came no sound of stirring...

Five minutes later Wald Ensor came out of the bedroom carrying the body of the child in his arms, very carefully. As, with his burden, he passed his wife's door, it was opened sharply, and, as suddenly, closed again. Mrs. Ensor had looked out.

Hodgson and Ferrier timidly followed the master of the house downstairs, wondering what he was going to do, afraid that he had gone suddenly mad and that they would have to interfere. But, so far, he was perfectly quiet, restrained and measured in his movements. He walked steadily, balancing what he carried on both arms outspread as a nurse does a baby, down into the hall where the autumn fire leapt on the hearth and the charred logs tinkled as they fell. He went through into the portion railed off with screens and arm-chairs and, stooping, deposited the body of his child on the great tiger skin which lay spread over the sofa—the old, wide, yellow one from Portland Place. The creases were in the skin that his wife had made lying on it only yesterday. Her favourite place—O God! Her bag—one of her bags—lay on it. And, with a violent but appropriately gauged gesture of one arm, Ensor swept it off. He again maintained his so light burden with both hands and laid it slowly down on the couch. Then, kneeling down deliberately, as though he were in church, beside the little white-robed form, he smoothed the folds of the nightgown his hands had disarrayed and, half raising her, half taking her in his arms, covered her face with kisses long and deep.

The nurse and the doctor had approached and now stood quite near to help him if by any chance he should faint. He took no notice of them, nor did he lift his head when Gertrude, her apron cast aside, a puzzling figure with unaccustomed black surfaces thus displayed, pushed open the door that led into the kitchen and stood there on the threshold, her strong uncovered arms resting on her hips...

"Go back!" the doctor said in a loud whisper, but she took no notice of him. Her dull, faithful eyes were fixed on something she saw at the head of the staircase—her mistress, who was even now descending. She was not fit... The nurse, professionally anxious to prevent her coming any farther, darted towards her, and her dress caught in a nail in one of the newspaper screens, which fell and lay half over the end of the couch where Mary lay, shadowing the face...

Wald Ensor looked up then—saw that it made no matter; he kept hold of the child's hand while, behind his back, Adelaide continued to descend the stairs. Gertrude had gone a step to meet her, but her mistress waved her away. She had nearly reached the bottom when Ensor, seeming at last to be aware of her, rose; she was coming to him—and Mary! No! No!

Adelaide tottered when she reached the last step—she had expected another—but came on bravely. Not until her husband lifted his finger and pointed it did she cease to advance. She stood there without taking hold of the banister, a black, formless shape, her white, sharp chin stuck up in a way she had and maintained while Gertrude held her shoulder and Ensor spoke.

"Listen, all of you," he was saying, in the same gloomy, intent voice he had used all day. "Forgive me, all, and you, Padre—" He seemed to take Hodgson, who had gone close to him, for a priest, for he spoke as one rehearsing an office of the Church:

"I pray to Almighty God this woman may not live to bear another child!"

Ensor stayed for the inquiry into the death of Mary Adelaide Ensor, aged fifteen years and three months. He buried her; he bore himself like a man in every way for the first time. Then he left England, and his wife never saw him again. She survived the birth of his son, stillborn.

THE END.

ALSO AVAILABLE

On a moonlit night, a wearied traveller dressed as the Devil calls at the mossy gates of Holcot Grange. Fleeing some bloody misadventure in London, the stranger claims to be heir to the manor which for generations has remained lordless. But among its benighted tenants the enthralling beauty Julia Roseingrave has been waiting—and now her means of escape has arrived. As whispers of witchcraft echo through the grounds and the boundaries between lord and servant fray, a cursed romance begins to smoulder—and the spectre of death draws near.

First published in 1933, this historical novella of Gothic love returns to print alongside six deliciously dark short tales from the British Library vaults, bubbling with wickedness and the occult.

ALSO AVAILABLE

The fabric of Dorothy K. Haynes's weird fiction is truly the stuff of nightmares, where horrors cruel and mundane are interwoven with threads of dark fairy folklore, orphanage miseries, twisted witchcraft and uncanny timeslips to deliver heady supernatural thrills.

In this new collection, Haynes expert Craig Lamont presents the essential classics of her strange storytelling alongside rarities from obscure anthologies and magazines—and five stories exhumed from the family archive which have never been published before.

With appendices featuring an illustrated letter by Mervyn Peake and typescript images, this volume knits the irresistible pull of Haynes's unique brand of the uncanny with a rare opportunity to discover new material from one of the great weavers of Scottish horror.

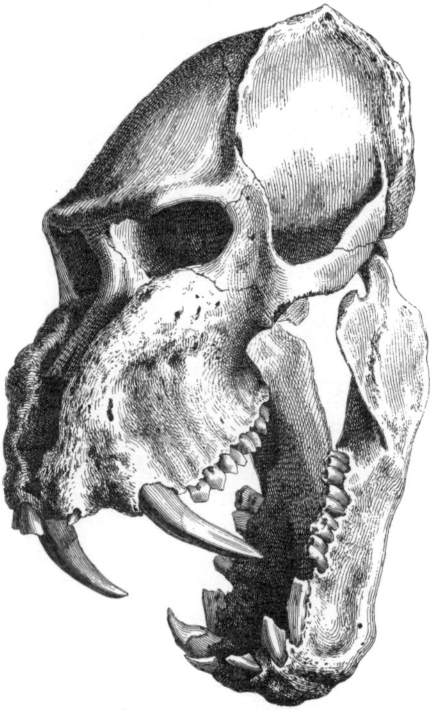

For more Tales of the Weird titles
visit the British Library Shop (shop.bl.uk)

We welcome any suggestions, corrections or feedback you may have, and will aim to respond to all items addressed to the following:

The Editor (Tales of the Weird), British Library Publishing,
The British Library, 96 Euston Road, London NW1 2DB

We also welcome enquiries through our social media accounts, @BL_Publishing.